Shattering Time

by

KJ Waters

Available at most fine book retailers.

Visit *www.kjwaters.com* for more information.

Other works by KJ Waters

Stealing Time -- Book 1 in the Stealing Time series -- **http://geni.us/StealingTimeLink**

Blow – A Short Story -- http://geni.us/Blowlink

Subscribe to my newsletter on the website to receive special offers and sneak peeks.

Shattering Time

Published by Blondie Books

Cover art by Blondie's Custom Book Covers and Jody Smyers Photography.

Created in the United States of America
    www.kjwaters.com
    www.blondiebooks.com
    www.jodysmyersphotography.com

This book is dedicated to

three of the best people in the world – my kids.

Thank you for your love and support!

Prologue

Stealing Time

Ronnie fell for what seemed like an eternity as a sensation of moving a million miles an hour downward disoriented and terrified her. Smells changed, air pressure changed. She reached out and tried to reconnect with Mathias. Her heart broke knowing she would never see him again. Light sped past, wind blew against her face, and cold wet air pressed against her skin. Everything spun and twisted like she was drunk and out of control.

Then it stopped.

Ronnie gasped and gulped greedily filling her lungs and then expelling as quickly as possible. Her hands touched something cool and hard. Stones? Was she on the ground? Acrid smoke assaulted her nostrils. Oh my God they're going to burn me. "No! Please no!" Ronnie screamed, shocked at the strength of her voice.

Someone helped her up. She took a breath and expected excruciating pain. Instead her vision cleared and she was surrounded by white tiles, a white sink, and a toilet.

"Ronnie, are you okay?" a male voice said, but it wasn't deep enough to be Mathias's. Her hands went to her throat and her arms were no longer tied.

"Where am I?" She was standing up now and looked down waiting for the noose that should have been restricting movement. Instead she could see bare tan feet and naked legs. The man turned her around and she expected the tired, stubbled face of Mathias.

"Ronnie, where is the watch?" It was Jeffrey. He sounded angry.

She stared in disbelief. "What are you doing here?" She wasn't sure if she could trust her vision. Like E.T. she reached out and touched his face. Her knees buckled and he pulled her in tight hugging her close, kissing the top of her head, keeping her from falling to the floor.

"Ronnie, are you okay?" Jeffrey repeated.

It was merely a death vision, one experienced as a body fades away into the light. She had seen a movie in eighth grade from the perspective of a man about to be hung. The entire show focused on his dream about the rope breaking, him swimming downstream and escaping. In the second it took him to fall on the rope, the vision played out in a long stream of hopeful thoughts with his life being saved. That's all

1

this was. It was a wonderful vision of her back in Florida in Jeffrey's arms. It made sense as it was where she had been so desperate to return.

He grabbed her hand and looked at her wrist. "The watch! Where is the watch, Ronnie?" The room was filling with smoke and she started to cough. She reached for her sleeve to cover her mouth and realized she was wearing Jeffrey's shirt, just as she had when she left. The black dress was gone. Her eyes watered and the smoke was making her choke.

Jeffrey shook her. "Ronnie, focus. Where did you put the watch?"

"Mathias has it. He held it in my hand ..." This was her dream, he should be hugging her. Why the hell wasn't he happy to see her again? Why was he asking about the watch?

A sharp pain pierced through the vision. She reached down to her leg hoping the surgeon wasn't cutting it off. Ronnie crumpled to the ground. Everything faded to black.

Chapter 1 - Stolen Time

Saturday, August 14, 2004, north of Orlando, Florida.
The scent of death lingered. The horrors were still fresh, still raw, and her own grisly destruction forever burned into memory. In this moment, Ronnie Andrews straddled time, caught somewhere between the eighteenth century and the sudden and unexpected return to her normal life.

She took a deep breath hoping it would calm her rapid heartbeat. Greedily she took another breath as her throat threatened to close off her air supply ... again. She was really home. The constant struggle was over.

Ronnie stood in her apartment face-to-face with her best friend Stephanie McKay trying to make sense of what had happened. She had no idea how she had returned so suddenly from London in 1752. The modern furnishings and comforts struck her as overwhelmingly luxurious adding to the turmoil boiling inside her chest.

Fluffy, her white Persian cat, rubbed against her leg and purred loudly wanting attention. Ronnie picked her up and closed her eyes burying her face in the warm soft fur, needing an escape. It was surreal, but reality was knocking and she would have to share her experience with Steph.

Her friend narrowed piercing blue eyes. "You okay, Ronnie?" Her familiar Scottish brogue was comforting. Though Steph was only five foot two, she was as fierce as any Amazon warrior.

Ronnie pulled herself together and hoped her voice wouldn't shake too much. "You must have been so worried about me the last few days."

"Last few days?" Steph shook her short blonde curls. "I saw you last night, Ronnie. What the hell?"

"Last night? What do you mean?" Ronnie asked.

"Luv, you are sounding rather batshit crazy right now. Here sit down, let's sort this out." Steph took her elbow and led her to the overstuffed chair in the tiny living room and sat across from her on the loveseat. "It's Saturday. Ronnie, you're scaring me. What did that jackass do to you?"

Steph's angry expression surprised her. "What jackass is that? Surely you're not talking about Jeffrey." Steph had never been shy about expressing dislike of Ronnie's boyfriend. They had been together for a year and a half when he was offered a position at the Central Florida Cloud Physics Laboratory last spring.

3

Steph's deep-rooted anger toward Jeffrey was making her nauseous. She pressed against her stomach willing it to settle down. From the beginning, Steph had not trusted him but could never express exactly why. She said it was just a gut feeling. That had never been enough to satisfy Ronnie. If Steph had something more tangible she might have given it a second thought, even if it was coming from one of her most trusted friends.

A knock at the door startled them. Steph welcomed Nick Sharer, who had just popped out to the car to retrieve something. They both returned to the couch. Though Ronnie had heard a lot about Nick, this was the first time they had met.

Ronnie sank further into the chair and studied his handsome face. His short light brown hair shone in the low light of the room. His high cheekbones framed kind blue eyes hinting at a wisdom his early thirty-something features belied. She never imagined meeting him under such strange circumstances.

Ronnie felt Fluffy's low rumble of happiness that was in stark contrast to her own emotional state. "Nick, what happened to your arm?"

"Oh, this?" He held the fiberglass cast protectively. "I knew Hurricane Charley broke my finger but it turns out he broke my arm and collarbone too." He touched his shoulder on the same side as the cast. "You should have seen Steph when she saw the damage to my finger." He laughed and Steph looked at him like he had completely lost his mind. "Well Steph, you threw up."

"Come on, let's not change the subject." Steph crossed her arms. "What the hell happened last night, Ronnie? You went to Jeffrey's weather lab, didn't you? I'd love to know what the hell he did that got you so upset. For God's sake Ronnie, you don't even know what day it is!"

"Ladies," Nick looked from Steph to Ronnie, "let's not get all out of sorts here. Ronnie, why don't you start at the beginning and maybe we can sort this out." He ignored the glare from Steph. "You left your apartment and then what?"

A wave of nausea engulfed Ronnie. "I've not eaten in almost twenty-four hours." She hoped that was the cause, but the emotional weight of what she'd been through sat in her gut like a lead bullet. She stood and walked to the kitchen with Fluffy following close behind. "You guys want anything?"

"No," Steph said.

"What do you have?" Nick said. She could hear Steph scolding him, and peeked over the breakfast bar to see them across the tiny apartment living room.

The room was encased in shadows with the low light creeping in from the only window in the living room barely making it to the kitchen. Everything in the fridge was likely ruined since the storm had knocked out the power last night. She opened the cupboards to see if there was something worth offering but the food choices were limited.

"Whatever you're having, Ronnie." He smiled.

Ronnie grabbed a box of Triscuits, three almost-cold Diet Cokes, a plate, and the peanut butter. She leaned against the countertop feeling overwhelmed and absently shoved a handful of crackers in her mouth. A purring Fluffy rubbed against her leg.

Ronnie opened the silverware drawer only to remember all of it was still packed from her move from Virginia Beach four days ago. She'd been so busy preparing for the storm she hadn't gotten to it yet. The box of plastic knives was on the counter and she grabbed two and made her way back to her friends now regretting the mouthful of food. She set the snacks down on the coffee table and lost a Diet Coke in the process.

Steph picked it up off the floor and said, "Thanks, Luv, now get back to it."

Ronnie handed Nick the other Coke and wanted to apologize for the lack of exciting snacks but instead chewed the dry crackers, took a swallow of the Coke, and sat down. Her legs were shaky. Crap, she was getting low blood sugar and would have to get some protein or she'd feel horrible soon. Ravenous now she opened the peanut butter, spread it on a cracker, and handed it to Nick.

"Thanks."

"Oh my God, Ronnie, start at the beginning," Steph said. "Enough with the stalling."

Sadness overcame Ronnie and she fought to gain her composure, thinking of Mathias. The compassion reflected in his dark eyes forced into her mind and a flush crept up her neck. She could almost feel the solidness of his arms around her and taste his kiss. Would she ever see him again?

Ronnie composed herself. "The beginning is as good of a place as any." She told her friends the events that took place yesterday before *it* had happened, gathering her overnight things, driving to Jeffrey's weather lab, and eating dinner. Her friends listened intently.

"That is the crux of the entire thing." Another wave of sadness washed over Ronnie. Mathias was the only good thing that had happened to her. She wiped away the tears.

Steph took Ronnie's hand. "Luv, what entire thing? Please tell me. Tell us." She glanced at Nick.

Ronnie squeezed her hand and looked at Nick. How could she tell them what happened? It was too strange. She didn't even know Nick he would think she'd lost her freaking mind. So would Steph but they'd been friends forever and she would know she wasn't making it up. She leaned back feeling lightheaded.

"He served me dinner and we … I …" She shook her head. "I went back in time, Steph. I swear to God, I have no idea how."

"You bloody what?" Steph said. Nick's mouth dangled open. He looked away, likely uncomfortable with this new information.

"I went back in time and I have no freaking clue how that happened, but I went to eighteenth-century London." Her lips trembled. Sitting in her own apartment surrounded by friends made it all seem impossible but the feelings, the smells, the sights were still fresh in her mind. It was not a dream. It had been her reality for what … the last three days?

Steph stood up. "How the bloody hell did you get there, Ronnie?" She was yelling now.

Nick went to her side. "Steph, come on let her tell us without you getting angry. She's a mess, look at her."

Ronnie sunk lower into the chair. "Steph, have you ever in your entire life seen me like this? Have I ever made shit up?" Steph's reaction surprised her. She had not expected anger from her dearest friend. Not when she needed her the most.

"Ronnie, you know why I'm yelling. It was that fanny-boy of yours. He drugged you or something. Why else would you be like this?" Steph's face was red.

"Do I need to gag you Miss Angry-Pants?" Nick shook his head. "How can you yell at her like this?"

"Nick, you don't know the history. Jeffrey is a ..." Steph shook her head. "You're right. Ronnie, I'm sorry. I'll keep my gob shut. Tell us what happened and we'll get this sorted I swear."

Steph sat back down and Nick turned his attention to Ronnie. "It's only been a day. Why do you think it was longer?"

Ronnie took a deep breath. "Nick. I was gone for days and days. I don't know how else to explain it."

Steph shook her head and appeared to swallow an angry remark. Her expression softened, "Ronnie, just tell us what happened."

She'd already dipped her toe into the pool of awful memories. Might as well dive in. "After dinner, I felt sick and went into the bathroom. Steph, it was the weirdest thing. I was sucked into space, pulled a million miles away into the sky. I could see my body on the floor of the bathroom as I sped off and then I bashed my head on the ground in 1752 London." She told them about the people she'd met and how she ended up in Newgate Prison. Nick and Steph sat motionless as she gave them the short version of what had taken place with her attempts to escape and return to Florida. The anger had left Steph's expression to be replaced with wide-eyed shock. Nick looked more flabbergasted as each layer of the story unfolded.

"Steph. I died ... it was horrible." She wiped her eyes, "I really died. Then, I was in Jeffrey's lab again."

"What the hell?" Steph's face turned red and she sat with her mouth dangling open.

"Steph, Jeffrey gave me a present for my birthday and ..." Ronnie touched her wrist but it wasn't there. "Oh my God, it's gone." She wiped away a tear, remembering the last time she held it in her hand in another time and place.

"What was the gift?" Steph asked sounding like the fight had left her words for the time being.

Ronnie's hands were sweaty, and she'd have to lay down soon if her blood sugar didn't even out. "Oh Steph, remember the watch we saw at the little shop in London? The rose gold one?" Steph nodded. "Well, Jeffrey had it replicated for me. But this one was waterproof."

"Well, where is it?" Steph asked, "I'd love to see this amazing gift." She was trying to sound calm but undertones of anger lingered.

"I don't know." Ronnie flushed again. She knew Jeffrey would be mad. "I think it's back in time."

"Are you sure you don't have it anymore? You had it on after dinner, right?" Steph's voice was shaking.

"Yes, I did."

"It was on your wrist when you went back in time?" Steph grabbed Ronnie's wrist to check for herself. "Was it there when you came back?"

"I had it on when I left and ... well, no, that was the weird thing." Ronnie looked away trying to remember through the fog. She had first thought seeing Jeffrey was just a dream after being so desperate to be back in Florida, but now she knew it was real. What had Jeffrey said to her?

"Ronnie," Steph prodded.

6

"Jeffrey was there holding me when I came back. He wanted to know where the watch was. He was mad."

"I'd be mad too, that thing must have cost a fortune," Nick said but was met with a smack from Steph.

"Really?" Steph asked. "He was mad because whatever he did to you had something to do with the watch."

"Steph, come on," Nick said. "That's crazy, why are you so sure Jeffrey did something to her?"

"Jeffrey is up to something, I can smell it," Steph crossed her arms. Ronnie put her head in her hands. Was her friend right? Was Jeffrey behind it? She hadn't had time to process any of this yet. She looked at her friend. "Steph, if you're going to help me you have to stop doing that!"

"Doing what?"

Nick answered for Ronnie, "Blaming Jeffrey. Let's keep an open mind so Ronnie can tell us what happened." He got close to Steph and whispered, "We don't want her shutting down."

Ronnie shook her head. "Nick, grab the duct tape, we'll shut her up so I can get this out of me and into the light of day."

"Okay, I'll stop blaming Jeffrey." Steph held up her hands. "But Luv, you have to admit this is a crazy story."

"It is not a story. This is me telling you what I've been through." Her eyes stung as more tears fell down her face.

Nick grabbed Steph by the neck pushing her for effect. "Hush."

"Yes, yes, I'm sorry. It is just so strange," Steph said. "Tell me everything that happened when you came back. What did Jeffrey say and do?"

Ronnie took a deep breath. A massive craving hit her. "Bread."

"Bread?" Steph looked at Nick.

Ronnie stood up and went to the kitchen, grabbed the bag of wheat bread and crammed a piece in her mouth as she made her way back to her chair. Her friends stared at her in disbelief. She crammed another piece in and chewed.

"Um Ronnie, is there something you want to tell us?" Steph asked.

Ronnie responded by shoving yet another piece in her already full mouth. Such desperation must be what crack addicts experienced. It was way more than low blood sugar. She'd never felt like this before.

Chapter 2 – One Slice of Bread in a Big Cosmic Loaf

"Ronnie, are you okay?" Frown lines showed between Steph's eyes.

"No, Steph, there is nothing okay about how I feel right now." She wanted to lay down but Steph and Nick were on the couch.

Overwhelming grief hit her hard. She had lost Mathias, maybe forever. Would he survive his wounds? Would Jack hunt him down and finish the job? Ronnie sobbed uncontrollably—she had to let out all the panic, fear, loss, and horror from the awful things she'd witnessed before continuing.

It had been so real, so intricate, so horrible, and nothing like any dream before. She'd always been a bit of a psycho with her night terrors, especially when she was stressed, but after she'd woken up she always recognized it as a dream. This time, it had lasted for days and everything was all so real, so painful, and so dreadful. Did Jeffrey have something to do with it?

Steph knelt and put her arm around her shoulders. "Let it out, sweetie. It will all be okay. We'll figure this out."

Ronnie blew her nose and tried to tamp down the wretched feelings. She held another piece of bread and rolled it into a ball like her mother showed her for those Saturday mornings when she wanted more sleep but Ronnie was up early and hungry. "Oh my God, I need to call my mom!"

"I'll find your phone." Steph walked into the bedroom and yelled back, "Where is the bag you took with you to Jeffrey's? Wait, never mind."

Nick stood up. "Ronnie, why don't you lie down, you're looking a bit droopy." He motioned for her to move to the couch.

She clutched the bread bag like it was her childhood blanket and moved to stretch out on the couch. Steph carried Ronnie's overnight satchel into the room and set it on the coffee table. "Find your phone, Luv. Maybe you can get a signal to call your mom."

Ronnie dug around in the bag found her cell phone and opened it. It was one of the new flip phones that reminded her of the *Star Trek* communicators. There were no bars and therefore no cell service but it had nearly a full battery and read *4:52 p.m. Saturday, August 14, 2004.* Saturday? It was hard to believe it had been less than a day since she'd left. Her life had been turned upside down. She dialed her mom's number just to be sure, but the screen turned blank. She set the phone down on the table then grabbed the decorative pillow to support her head.

"How the hell did Jeffrey get me here with all the storm damage?" Ronnie asked.

Steph shook her head. "What I want to know is how the hell did he get you home without you remembering?" She pointed to the satchel. "See if the watch is in there."

Ronnie sat up and dug around in the bag. Not finding it she emptied the contents onto the table and the bottle of K-Y Jelly rolled toward Nick. She snapped it up and hid it back in the bag.

Nick looked away turning a shade redder. "Uh, Ronnie, can I use your bathroom?"

"Yes, over there." She pointed to the guest room past the kitchen.

"No watch?" Steph said rummaging through her clothes and toiletries.

"Nope." Ronnie patted her shorts pockets and dug through her purse.

"Did you bring anything else?" Steph looked around near the front door.

"No, I don't remember getting dressed or driving here. Why would that be?" Ronnie felt her sternum. Her bra was on. Why would Jeffrey bother to put her bra on if she were passed out? "Um, don't answer that."

Steph mimicked putting tape over her mouth.

Nick returned. "Steph? You're behaving, aren't you?"

"Of course I am." Steph got up and pulled a barstool over to complete the circle of the couch and overstuffed chair. Nick sat down.

"Did you find the watch?" he asked.

Both women shook their heads.

"Ronnie, why are you eating like a starved homeless guy?" Nick nodded toward the half-empty bag.

"I'm feeling really weird like I'm desperate for food." Her jaw was aching because she'd been shoving bread in her mouth so fast. Fluffy jumped up on the couch and rubbed against Ronne's leg. She absently smoothed down her fur.

"Your body is probably trying to catch up after all you've been through. Just rest and let's see if that helps," Steph said. "Plus, you didn't eat breakfast or lunch, so you're probably just having one of those spells of yours."

"Yeah, I hope that's all it is. What if this has damaged me somehow? What if the cravings are from a reaction to the time travel or whatever this was?"

Nick and Steph looked at each other with worried expressions. "Do you want to go to the hospital? We were just there for Nick's arm. They've cleared the roads on I-4 and it's just down the street from here. That's why we stopped by because we were close and I was worried about you."

"I don't know, Steph. I mean something really, really weird happened to me but if I tell them what really happened to me I'll be thrown in the loony bin."

"You could just tell them your symptoms and let them check you over," Nick said. "They don't have to get inside your head."

"Let me see if I can calm down. It should end soon if it's low blood sugar. I've certainly had enough calories." Ronnie lifted the bag for emphasis.

"We really need to figure out what happened. Is there a way we can look up something from your experience?" Steph and Nick were holding hands now. They were just friends, right? Ronnie wondered if they had crossed that line last night. She hoped so as Steph had always spoken highly of him.

"That's a good idea, Steph. Have either of you ever heard of the Gregorian time shift?"

Nick looked at Steph and shrugged. "Nope." They sure were acting like a couple.

"In seventeen fifty-two, England lost eleven days in the month of September," Ronnie said hoping it was a real event that had happened. Or was it something that just didn't get much historical play? She'd have to do a search and see what would turn up.

"You're kidding, right? Nick said. "How do you lose time like that?"

Ronnie stood up and walked with shaky legs to her laptop. She opened it and turned it on. It booted but she couldn't get an internet connection. "No, I'm not. They had to catch up to the rest of Europe who had made the change to the Gregorian calendar from the Julian calendar in the fifteen hundreds. I didn't know that either, but if it's true that would help support going back in time. I could also look up the people I met back then to see if they were real."

"That's a great idea, Ron, but we'll probably have to wait for the power to come on," Steph said.

"Yeah you should write everything down and you can look it up later." Nick stood and turned to Steph. "I really want to go check on my parents. I've not been able to reach them with cell service down and they're probably worried about me. Do you mind?"

Steph stood and put her arm around his waist. "You go check on your mom. Do you want me to come too?"

"No, I'm good. What are you going to do about getting home, though? You'll be stuck here," Nick said. "Ronnie, we didn't see your car in the parking lot."

"It's probably still at Jeffrey's lab."

"Is it okay if I hang out here for a while, Ron? He can come back later and we can get your car or whatever we need to do," Steph said and Nick nodded in agreement.

"Yeah that would be good, I'm not sure I want to be alone right now." Ronnie watched Steph and Nick hug.

"Bye Nick, great to meet you." Ronnie stood up.

Nick hugged her and turned to Steph, "I'll try to come back around ten in case I can't reach you on the phone. I can take you back home then if you want. See you, Ronnie, hope you feel better."

"Okay, sweetie, see you in a bit." Steph walked Nick to the door and then shut it behind him.

Ronnie crossed the living room and dug through a partially unpacked box with the hope of finding a notebook. Her legs were shaky but felt a bit more in control. "So, are you two a thing now?"

"Oh, Ronnie I never told you about our night. It's just horrible what we went through. You can see what happened to Nick." Steph pointed to her arm.

"Sit down and tell me everything," Ronnie said, lying back down on the couch with the notebook clutched to her chest.

"Well, I guess we did get closer. He ..." She visibly blushed. "Um ... well, he came over when you went to Jeffrey's and we got dirty pulling in my potted plants." She smiled, pink-cheeked.

"Oh, you got dirty?" Ronnie asked.

"Yes, we didn't actually do anything." She looked away and rubbed her upper lip.

Ronnie knew there was more to it. "He's a really nice guy. Plus, he's much better looking than you ever let on. Damn girl. He is hot."

She smiled obviously smitten. "But Ronnie when we were about to ...um well... mess around we were interrupted by Hamish. He'd gotten out in the hurricane when we put the plants in the garage." Steph continued to tell her about their misadventures as Ronnie pictured her friend's orange tabby cat.

By the end of the telling, they were both crying and hugging each other. "God, Steph you've been through hell. It's no wonder you and Nick are close after that crap!"

"I know. Nick handled everything so well, Ronnie. He's such a good guy and finally dumped that stupid chick from the gym. For once we're both single at the same time. He's always been there for me but only as a friend, so it's exciting to have a man in my life and to see how it all goes. For now, we have to figure out what happened to you."

"He's a keeper, Steph."

"What is that book you're hugging?"

"Oh, I liked your idea of writing everything down. I think it might be the key to figuring this thing out. Help me." She handed Steph the notebook. "We can go through what I remember and search Google later."

"Okay, let's start with all the names you remember." Steph sat across from Ronnie and wrote everything down. An hour later they had gathered a few pages of information.

The doorbell sounded. Ronnie got up and peeked through the peephole.

"Who is it?" Steph asked, setting aside the papers they had been working on.

A distorted view of Jeffrey showed through the glass and she was hit by a momentary panic. Was she ready to deal with him right now?

Chapter 3 - Bird on a Wire

"Ronnie, it's Jeffrey." He tapped on the door.

Crap he'd seen her in the peephole glass. Ronnie opened the door.

"Babe. Hi." He kissed her cheek and stepped into the apartment. "Are you all right?"

"Yeah." She hid the empty bread bag behind her back. "What are you doing here?" It was the first time he'd been in her apartment since she moved from Virginia Beach four days ago, that she remembered anyway.

"I had to check on you." He was holding a bag from Jason's Deli. "Babe, I'm really sorry I had to get you out of there before I called my boss. Did you have any trouble with the smoke?"

"Smoke?" Ronnie had a vague recollection of smoke. "I …"

"Hello, Jeffrey," Steph said sounding a bit like Seinfeld addressing Newman.

"Stephanie." Jeffrey looked up and took a step backward. "Good to see you."

"Right," Steph said not buying it. No one called her Stephanie except her family in Scotland. Jeffrey was either being obtuse or just clueless. Steph plopped down on the couch and crossed her arms.

"I brought you dinner." He handed Ronnie the bag. "I wasn't sure if you had any food in your fridge and figured I was on my way anyway." He eyed Steph smiling. "I didn't know you'd be here."

"It's okay, I just ate." Steph wasn't trying to be friendly.

"Why can't I remember leaving the lab?" She watched his face closely but it only showed surprise. "How did I get dressed? How did I end up here asleep in my bed?"

"Babe, I'm not sure why you don't remember. You were talking to me and seemed normal." He tapped his fingers on his thigh. "It's probably just the stress of the storm and all. Again, I'm sorry I had to bring you home and leave you."

"Yeah. I'm okay, it's okay …"

Steph rolled her eyes. "He might want to know about the bread."

Ronnie showed him the bag.

"What is that?" Jeffrey asked showing irritation about Steph's presence.

"She ate the whole loaf." Steph shook her head.

Jeffrey waved his hand as if to make Steph disappear and took Ronnie's elbow. "Can we go for a walk or something?"

Ronnie could almost hear him will her friend out of the room.

"I'll let you two talk," Steph made a hasty exit to the guest room. "I'll be here if you need me. Fluffy, come here." She waited for the cat to run in before she shut the door. The bedsprings squeaked.

Ronnie sat down at the breakfast bar, opened the deli bag, and pulled out a sub wrapped in paper. "Thanks for bringing me food." She unwrapped a roast beef sub. He should know after a year and a half together she liked turkey.

"It's the least I could do." He sat on the barstool next to her and put his hand on her knee. "Ron, it about killed me to leave you here alone, but my God it was horrible. The fire damaged some of my equipment and ..." He looked up at the ceiling. "Well, it's a friggin' nightmare. I'm not sure if I'll get the grant now."

She reached into the bag and pulled out two Diet Cokes, at least he got that right. "I'm sorry, I hope you get the grant, I know you need the money to keep your experiment going." She handed him a can vaguely remembering the smell of smoke. Why didn't she remember more?

"Yeah, you and me both. How are you feeling? You seemed a little out of sorts when I left you last night." He tapped the Coke and cracked it open.

"Jeff, I feel really weird. I've eaten the entire loaf of bread and half a box of crackers. At first I thought it was blood sugar, but it feels different."

"Shit, really?" He turned the barstool to face her. "When did this start?"

"About an hour ago. Why don't I remember getting here? It's completely blank. Did something happen to me at the lab?"

Surprise showed on his handsome face. "Happen? Like what?"

Ronnie cleared her throat. "I don't know. Jeffrey. I ..." she struggled for a way to start such a weird conversation.

He took her hand.

She picked up the Diet Coke and took a swig. "I ..." She shook her head and pulled her hand out of his. Would he yell like Steph did? "I need to understand what happened during the storm." Steph had been so certain he was behind this.

"During the storm, you were with me. What the hell Ronnie?" He cradled his Coke.

Ronnie stood and paced across the room. It had been a long week and her brain was too tired to be subtle. She walked back to him. "I went back in time."

"What?" His eyebrows knitted together.

"There is no other way to explain it."

He stood up. "You're wasting my time, Ronnie. I have a lot to do at the lab."

She grabbed his arm. "Jeff! Sit down. You have to listen to me. I am not joking around or wasting your time. It is the most disturbing thing that has ever happened to me and I need your help figuring it out."

"I'm supposed to believe you went back in time? What does that even mean?" He tapped his fingers on his leg again.

Ronnie took a deep breath. He was going to be difficult. Damn it. "Yes, I somehow went back in time to the eighteenth century, Jeffrey. Do you know anything about this?"

"How could I know anything? You're only just telling me now." He was angry.

"Well, I was thinking maybe your experiment had something to do with it," Ronnie said.

"My weather experiment? The anemometer somehow sent you back in time? Seriously, Ronnie, you've lost your mind."

"It has me completely freaked out, Jeff. Let me tell you what happened and maybe you can shed some light on it."

"Okay, I'm eager to hear this. Go on." His lips pressed together.

Was he bullshitting? It made a lot more sense that he was behind this, or at least his experiment was. "You've had nothing to do with what happened to me?"

He stood up and towered over her, hands on his hips. "What happened to you? You're not making any sense, Ronnie." He was outright yelling now.

The bedroom door opened and Steph stepped out. "Why are you two shouting?"

"I am not," he bellowed.

Ronnie stood and took a step away from Jeffrey.

"Steph, she's talking nonsense. I can't get her to explain why she is upset." He waved his hands around in frustration.

"Yelling isn't going to help," Steph said. "Trust me, I already tried that."

"Jeffrey, just sit down and let me explain." Ronnie pointed at the couch. "It has to do with the watch, too."

He turned toward her and narrowed his eyes but seemed cowed when her expression registered. He sat down crossing his arms. "Go ahead."

"It started after …" Ronnie glanced at Steph. "Well, after we were on the bed." Steph rolled her eyes. "I felt sick so I got up and went into the bathroom."

Jeffrey nodded.

"I almost threw up but then I had this weird feeling … it was like all the air was sucked out of the bathroom and I was pushed to the floor."

Jeffrey shook his head. "I remember you getting up and you were in there for a while, but I can assure you the air was fine. The lab has a high-efficiency particulate air filtration system. What was so upsetting?"

Ronnie fought back tears. She knew this would be difficult but hadn't expected him to be such a jerk. She closed her eyes and relived the moments when she first arrived, sharing with Jeffrey what she remembered. The smell of the horses and clink of metal still clear in her mind. It seemed so strange then, as it probably did to Jeffrey now. His face showed a scowl but softened as she went on.

She described the abuse by Jack, the man who found her, and her encounter with Catherine, his pregnant wife. Steph reminded her about Mathias, which Ronnie hadn't really wanted to get into, given her feelings for him, but then felt obliged since he did everything he could to try to save her.

Finally, he inserted, "You have such a great imagination, Ronnie. I love how you've made it like one of those historical dramas."

Steph shot Jeffrey an angry look.

"Jeffrey," Ronnie's voice shook, "I didn't make this up. This is what happened!"

"You actually believe that? Ronnie, seriously, this is like a bad movie."

"Bloody hell, Jeffrey, you're such a pompous ass." Steph shook her head. "You can't even listen to what she has to say?"

Jeffrey smiled. "I am listening. I'm just not buying it really happened. Steph, of all people you know her best, her dreams are weird as shit."

"This is different, Jeffrey." Ronnie wiped at a stray tear. "It was over several days. I ate, I slept, and I felt pain. It was not like a dream at all."

"Several days? You were only in my lab for a few hours." He shook his head.

"I was there for three days." Ronnie wiped her eyes.

"What the hell?" He cocked his head to the side. "Did you ever find the watch?"

"Well, no. I just looked through my bag."

"Jesus Ronnie, do you know what that cost? That was pretty special."

Heat warmed her cheeks. "I'm really sorry. It is one of the things I don't get about last night."

He glanced at Steph. "What does this have to do with the watch?"

"I know it sounds really weird, Jeffrey. The first few hours I was there, Jack, a guy that …" How could she explain who he was? "The guy who picked me up off the street claimed to be my brother …" Sheesh, that was convoluted. "He took the watch. I was sure it had something to do with me being sent back in time."

Steph nodded. "Right."

"Ronnie, let me get this straight. You're saying the watch I gave you is in the eighteenth century?"

"Yes."

"Ron, you were in the lab, you were definitely not somewhere else. Seriously, I don't know what to make of this. It's got to be the suckiest excuse for losing an expensive gift I've ever heard."

"Excuse? This is not some story she made up to cover losing the watch," Steph said. Ronnie could see the telltale signs of jaw clenching as her friend tried not to lose her temper.

"Steph, you sat through this whole diatribe and didn't question it?" He laughed. "As opinionated as you are you probably tore her a new one."

Ronnie gripped her temples and pulled at her hair. "God, you're impossible. What is the fucking point of telling you if you can't even take the leap of faith that it happened?" Ronnie said, holding back tears.

"Whoa, Steph did you hear that?" He pointed at Ronnie, "She cursed. I don't think I've heard her curse more than three times in my life. Please, babe, go on. I'm sorry, but it's just hard to believe." He took a deep breath and dramatically let it out. "How did you get back?"

Ronnie slumped deeper into the loveseat. She couldn't decide if he was somehow involved or didn't believe a word she was saying. Neither choice was okay. "I don't know where I was. Steph?"

"Just after Jack took the watch, tell him how Mathias helped you run away and visit the fortune-teller," Steph said.

Finally, through tears, Ronnie told him how she had returned.

"You're telling me death returned you?" He shrugged and looked from one to the other. "Like a good book the plot thickens." He threw an arm across the back of the loveseat and crossed his ankle over his thigh.

Ronnie stood up. "Could you be any more condescending?"

"I really could. You've seen me, Ron." He showed straight white teeth in almost a smile.

"Fuck you, Jeffrey." Steph stood. "I think you caused this and you're just acting cool to cover it up."

"Well fuck you too, Steph. You've both lost your minds. Time travel? The only thing I caused last night was multiple orgasms. No reason to drag me into the world of *Looney Toons* with you both." He stood and swigged down the rest of his Diet Coke and then slammed it on the coffee table. "I don't have time for this shit. I have a grant to rescue." He dug in his cargo pants pocket and pulled out Ronnie's keys. "Damn it. I drove your car here."

"You're leaving?" Ronnie asked, tears welling again.

"Well so are you if you want your car back. I need you to drop me off at the lab."

Ronnie turned around unable to keep her emotions in check. Too many days of fear and terror had worn down her usual toughness.

Steph squeezed her hand. "I'll go with you guys. Come on let's get this over with."

Ronnie excused herself and ran to the bedroom slamming the door. Deep heart-wrenching sobs wracked her body. There was no other option but to let it out. Frustration, anger, and hurt flowed into the Kleenex. It had been real. How could she convince him?

"Come on Ronnie, I need to get back to the lab," Jeffrey yelled from the other side of the door. She could hear Steph lay into him. She'd have to let it go for now. Numbly she stood up and blew her nose, looked in the mirror, and realized nothing could improve her looks but a dark room. "Doesn't matter," she told herself.

She walked past Jeffrey and Steph who were still yelling at each other. Ronnie opened the front door and walked to her car, ignoring both reasons she had moved to this hellhole called Florida. There were so many things she wanted to tell Jeffrey, to make him understand what she had been through but he had chosen to mock her instead. She wanted him to be there for her like a good boyfriend should. But he wasn't going to be the man she needed.

Steph and Jeffrey followed her to her '95 Thunderbird and Steph got in the backseat. Ronnie tossed the keys to Jeffrey. "You drive, I've no clue where anything is."

It was a short uncomfortable ride with no one willing to break the silence. Ronnie looked out the window and tried to let the hurricane damage distract her from dark thoughts. There were endless trees down, the power was out at all the traffic lights, and it was slow going. Finally, they reached Jeffrey's work and he pulled over just before the security gate.

"I'll stop by tomorrow to check on you. I really hope you feel better, Ron. I'm sorry this ended badly." Jeffrey opened the door.

"Don't bother," Steph said.

He got out of the car and stooped to peer into the backseat. "Why don't you just shut the hell up, Steph?"

Ronnie held her hands up as if that would catch the angry words and protect her from their damage. "I've had enough tonight, Jeff. Please just stop." She got out of the car and walked around to the driver's side. "Just go back to work already."

He went to hug her and she ducked into the car. "Bye." She was surprised Jeffrey had already turned and walked away.

Chapter 4 - Pulse

Jeffrey slammed the lobby door of the Central Florida Cloud Physics Laboratory but it didn't close as dramatically as he wanted. What he really wanted was to slam it so hard it broke off its hinges. That damn Stephanie McKay was going to jeopardize the trust he'd worked so hard to create with Ronnie. Something would have to be done about her. Ronnie's loyalty was stronger to Steph and that would have to be remedied.

He swallowed his anger as he approached the security desk. "JT, what's up my friend? Some hurricane, eh?"

"Hello, Dr. Brennan, it was a nightmare. I found a hot mess when I got home. I was cooped up with my whole family—my mother and her boyfriend, the kids, my neighbors. I think we had someone sitting on every surface of the house."

"Everyone okay?" Jeffrey leaned on the desk.

"Yes, sir, just a small tree down in the backyard. No biggie. Glad they were there though, my mom's house was flooded and a huge tree is sitting in her bedroom." JT reclined in his chair and stretched showing off thick brown forearms.

"Oh no, sorry about her house, but glad your gang is all fine." Jeffrey leaned in toward the security guard. "We still good about last night, right?"

JT leaned forward, looked side to side, and then whispered, "Yup, yup. The tape is erased."

"Even the end when I left with her?"

"Yes, and I've reset the counters like you showed me so it doesn't have any gaps," JT said.

"Great, may need that, you just never know." Jeffrey was relieved. JT had been on duty when Ronnie was at the lab during Hurricane Charley. It was unlikely anything would come of it, but he had covered his bases. "It was her birthday, you know. How could I leave her in the storm alone? I mean ..." He wagged his eyebrows.

JT laughed. "I feel you, man, you need to take care of your woman."

Jeffrey smiled. "Exactly. Just cover for me if it ever comes up. I'd hate to take heat over a little private birthday party." He looked both ways to make sure no one was around. "You got the envelope, right?"

"Yes." JT smiled brightly.

"Was that a sweet little bonus I threw in there?" Jeffrey wanted to make sure the man would stay silent.

JT nodded his head, "Very generous of you, Dr. Brennan."

"Appreciate you, JT. I really do." Jeffrey nodded. "Hey, at least here you have no one in your hair." He brushed the side of his head to emphasize the point.

JT laughed and shook his shaved head. "Good one Dr. Brennan."

"Have a great day." Jeffrey briskly walked to the belly of the building as he replayed Ronnie's version of events. He should have felt guilty for sending her back into such a lion's den of problems, but he had given up guilt a long time ago and replaced it with ambition.

He was relieved that JT hadn't mentioned the small fire he had quickly extinguished right as Ronnie returned. Hopefully, it hadn't registered anywhere in the system of smoke sensors. He still had no explanation for the excessive power drain. It had been so intense it caught one of the circuits to the power capture unit on fire, melting some of his equipment. Nothing else seemed to be affected but he would have to research what caused the surge and make changes to prevent its reoccurrence.

Excitement burst forth and he did his best to act normal, but a chuckle escaped. The enormity of what he'd done hit him squarely in the jaw. He had successfully transported a human subject to another place and time. All the years of work, the dangerous experiments, and the risks with his job, health, and future had all come to fruition in one glorious moment. Finally, the mystery of time travel was his! He would be the most famous inventor in history. Move over Einstein and Edison, look out da Vinci, Jeffrey Brennan had arrived! He pressed the elevator button and waited, nearly jumping out of his skin with adrenaline. If he'd been alone, he would have yelled at the top of his lungs. The elevator opened and he stepped on. As soon as the door shut he did a happy dance. Fuck Stephanie McKay. In a year, she would be a distant memory and he would be talking movie rights with Hollywood directors, up for the Nobel Prize, driving through ticker tape parades in his honor.

For now, he basked in the moment of victory. Never mind that it opened a Pandora's Box about the morality of sending someone back in time if the inhabited body had to die in order to return its guest to the present. He indulged that train of thought for just a moment but quickly wrapped it up to not ruin his celebration. Did Ronnie die because of a glitch with the small size of Hurricane Charley and the ensuing complications from removing the watch?

This technology had so much potential. He realized he had forgotten to push the button to the basement, Jeffrey laughed at another of his absentminded professor moments.

Ronnie's revelation that she'd ended up in another body had been an absolutely spectacular twist. He had never anticipated such a method for transport. It raised so many questions about the experiment. Ronnie had said the girl Regina had been hit by a carriage just before she arrived. Did the time travel force Ronnie into a body that had recently died, or was it a link between Regina and Ronnie on some level that had caused the placement? Was the carriage accident a coincidence? Or trigger? Did Regina die as a result of sending Ronnie back? What happened to Regina once Ronnie left that body?

His previous research had been wholly inadequate to make such conjectures. He needed to find the videos of the cat experiments he'd done years ago in Virginia Beach. Could they have been placed in other cat bodies as well? He had reviewed the footage but hadn't been looking for those clues.

He was so glad he'd used the amnesiac injection after Ronnie's return. It was quite useful for lessening the dramatic emotional and physical impacts of the experiment. It had been incorporated into standard procedure after the first cat came back and died in his arms. Its heart rate was off the charts and he had theorized the cat had literally been scared to death.

The elevator door opened and a waft of Channel No. 5 hit him. It was such a classy scent on such a dirty girl. His mind instantly went to Hannah's naked flesh spread for his pleasure.

"Hey Hannah," Jeffrey said as he turned the corner.

"Oh my gosh!" Hannah Volpe took a step back. She was the scientist in the lab next door. "You scared me. Hi, Jeffrey."

"Hello there, Dr. Vasu. Good to see you." Jeffrey inwardly cringed at the sight of the lab director, who was leaning against the wall behind Hannah, his dark skin a stark contrast to her creamy coloring.

Dr. Vasu pushed away from the wall and straightened his tie. "Good morning Jeffrey. I was just telling Hannah about the phone call I received earlier."

Jeffrey nodded to Hannah who gave him a nervous look. "Please tell me it wasn't Neil Armstrong asking to visit the two new moons we just discovered on Saturn?"

Hannah shook her head. "What two new moons?"

"Come on, you don't read the paper?" Jeffrey asked, but could tell something was up. She wouldn't even crack a smile.

"Ha ha, well no," Dr. Vasu said. "It wasn't from Neil. I got a call from the Special Response Team out of the Tampa office."

"Okay." Jeffrey glanced at Hannah who looked away. Was this about the fire in his lab last night?

"They are part of Homeland Security." Dr. Vasu cleared his throat. "They were inquiring about potential unusual activity on our campus Friday night during the hurricane."

"Interesting, why?" Jeffrey hid the fear rising in the pit of his stomach.

"I was just discussing this with Hannah. You two were here, is that correct?"

Hannah barely shook her head and widened her eyes.

"Well, yes, I was testing my power gathering device during the storm with fantastic results."

"Great to hear, Jeffrey. Please let us go to my office to discuss the call." Dr. Vasu nodded his head in the direction of his upstairs office.

"Yes Dr. Vasu, I need to attend to something quickly. I'll be up in a few minutes, is that okay?" Hannah said.

"Yes, we can discuss this further in private." Dr. Vasu lowered his glasses to look Jeffrey in the eyes. "Please without delay, this is a very important matter."

"Absolutely, let me just set my things down and I'll be right up." Jeffrey reached for the lanyard around his neck and used the keycard to unlock the door to his lab.

He set his briefcase on the desk and quickly gathered the notebooks related to his time travel, shoving them in his briefcase. He glanced around the room for any remnants of Ronnie's visit. The blow-up bed and traces of their dinner were gone. No sign of the fire. A faint lingering air freshener scent masked the mild smoky odor, he hoped. A soft knock on the lab door interrupted him.

Hannah stood nearby wringing her hands. "So, what is this about, Jeffrey?"

He ushered her in looking to be sure no one was in the hallway. "I don't know, it's the first I heard about it. What did he say to you before I showed up?"

"He mostly just said what he told you. Shame he couldn't manage to look me in the eyes while he did." She glanced down at her button-up blouse. His gaze lingered not blaming Dr. Vasu one iota—it was a nice view.

"So why would Homeland Security call here?" Hannah's delicate eyebrows were almost touching.

Jeffrey sat on the corner of his desk and crossed his arms. "I've no idea. What were you working on last night?" He examined her face. She did walk in on him during the most panicked moment while trying to return Ronnie from eighteenth-century London. Did she suspect anything?

"Jeffery, you know what I was working on. And you paid me handsomely. Did this have anything to do with steering Hurricane Charley for you?"

"No," he shook his head. "This is random. I think it probably has something to do with Cape Canaveral and its damage. It's not fared too well through the storm."

"This could really put a damper on my research if I have to waste time talking to the Feds during a really busy hurricane season." She bit her full pink lips.

"It will blow over. Let's figure out what the good doctor knows and just stick to the truth about last night. Not that I paid you anything, of course, but that you monitored the storm for your research."

"Jeffrey, I didn't get permission from the lab to steer the storm. I'll lose my job if they know I used it to cause so much damage in Florida. I could have easily steered it toward the gulf." Hannah stood and walked toward the door to the hallway. "We should get going, Dr. Vasu is waiting."

"No one will know that you steered it. Besides, if you sent it to the gulf you'd have destroyed New Orleans or Mobile." Jeffrey shut and locked his briefcase, leaving it on the desk. "They can't trace anything, can they? Would anything show up on a satellite or other equipment?"

"No, there are no visible traces of my storm steering. Just all of my notes and recordings of the radar and whatnot."

"You'll need to remove any evidence about the steering but keep everything that shows a legitimate reason for being there to study the storm. Bury the rest for a while."

"I know. I will." She opened the door.

Jeffrey followed and closed the door behind him. The nuance of her being vulnerable with this situation was a twist. She was usually in charge and dominant. A twinge in his pants reminded him of how good she was in the sack. How would she be as a submissive participant? He imagined pinning her to the bed as he had Ronnie and the twinge bulged a bit more. It was entertaining how stressful situations got him going. In the elevator, he tried to catch her eye.

"Relax Hannah. Just keep your cool, this is going to pass. It was a powerful storm and they're just making sure there is no security threat."

Hannah grunted in response.

"You're not going to fall apart on me, are you?" Jeffrey asked not sure if she were near tears or just stressing out.

"Me? Never. I'm just worried something will screw this up. I've made the biggest discovery of my career and I can't even publish it. I am regretting taking the money and putting myself in this situation."

Her expression was determined, not close to tears. That was a relief. He liked strong women, not teary-eyed wallflowers. "That's the irony, Hannah. Without the money you wouldn't have made the giant leap in your research to make this discovery. You will be an international hero when you share what your storm seeding and steering can do. Think of the possibilities. You can save nations from natural disasters. Will you use these powers for making millions or for saving humanity?"

"Both, I hope. But Jeffrey, if the government finds this they are likely to take it from me."

"Don't think like that. You need to protect it, sure, but that is only after you have something to protect. You have to redo the experiment and this time record what you can do."

"I know. I plan on doing that. If I find funding to get out to the Caribbean I can see if my storm seeding skills will work. That's what worries me, if any federal investigation keeps me from pursuing this, the hurricane season will end and there will be no more research until the sea temperatures rise again."

"You're forgetting the southern hemisphere. You could research down there all winter if you get the resources." He patted his pocket. "Just keep your shit together through this. If they suspect something you will have them up your ass."

"Up my ass? That's a good one, Jeffrey. That's just where you'd like to be."

He smiled and walked out of the elevator, holding the door open as she followed. "Keep it cool now and maybe I can take care of that for you later."

She smiled. "What about your Victoria's Secret friend?" She was referring to Ronnie's underwear she had found on the floor of his lab during the storm.

"I can invite her if you like." He raised his eyebrows knowing she wasn't into threesomes.

"I'll pass." Hannah opened the door to the administration corridor and they made their way to Dr. Vasu's office.

The last time he had been there was for his interview in December. The only change was the small Indian flag had been moved to the bookshelf. Dr. Vasu was on the phone and motioned for them to sit. Hannah took the chair farthest from the door and adjusted her white sweater to cover what had captured Dr. Vasu's attention earlier. Jeffrey stuck out his lower lip. She looked away.

Dr. Vasu sat on the edge of his desk, still talking on the phone about the roof tiles on his house. "I don't care, just fix the damn roof." He slammed the phone down. "Bloody hell, my house is leaking and I cannot get a contractor to fix it! Did either of you sustain any damage from the storm?" he asked.

"I still don't have clean water," Jeffrey said, remembering the shower at the gym this morning.

"No, I'm in an apartment," Hannah said.

"My roof was damaged by a small tree skidding down and pulling off some tiles. I just need a man to replace a few tiles and there is no one available. They're all booked and meanwhile these daily thunderstorms are going to kill me. The tarp can only do so much."

"I'm so sorry, Dr. Vasu," Hannah said flicking open her sweater. His eyes darted immediately to the desired location.

"Bummer." Jeffrey wished the old man would get to the point. He was eager to get back to the data on the cats.

"Okay, so the call I got this morning," he pulled his eyes away from Hannah's cleavage to look at Jeffrey, "from the Special Response Team. Do either of you know what that is?"

"I haven't heard of it before," Jeffrey said.

"They are part of Homeland Security and this is serious. They claim there was an unusual pulse that came from somewhere near Orlando. They're still narrowing down the precise location as we speak but the agent wanted to know who was on-site during the storm and if there were any unusual experiments running. There were several scientists here and I've spoken to them as well. I need to know what you were working on that night. Jeffrey, were you working on that side project you asked me about when I hired you?"

"No, I'm not able to work on that until I have the power situation settled. I made great strides during Charley though."

"What were you working on during the hours of," he reached backward and grabbed a paper from his desk, "Ten twenty-seven p.m. and again at eleven forty-five?"

Those were the times Ronnie left and the small fire started upon her return. He maintained a neutral expression. "The power capture device was working at its peak around that time. It may have spiked the power where I was capturing it all, but it wouldn't have made any unusual signals or pulses. It's the same thing I've been working on since I got here." He glanced at Hannah who narrowed her eyes. "Except I was able to test it during natural conditions."

"I agree, that shouldn't create anything unusual." Dr. Vasu rubbed his nose. "Hannah, what were you working on at that time?"

"Uhm." She glanced at Jeffrey. "I was monitoring wind speeds and making some tweaks to my steering mechanism. But really everything was the same ol' same ol', Dr. Vasu."

"You two weren't … ah …" He cocked his head to the side. "Because that is against company policy. Fraternizing with your coworkers will get both of you sent to another lab."

"Ha, right, Dr. Vasu. You know I have a longtime girlfriend. I'd definitely not stray." Jeffrey pulled out his phone as Hannah's expression grew from worried to angry. "Have you seen her?" Jeffrey opened his phone and flicked through the pictures, found the one he took of Ronnie wearing his dress shirt and nothing else with only one button done up. "See."

Dr. Vasu took Jeffrey's phone to get a better look. "This is your girlfriend?" He looked up and quickly returned his eyes to Ronnie's picture. "What long legs she has." He handed the phone back to Jeffrey who held it up for Hannah to see.

She made a noise and crossed her arms, looking away. "A keeper."

"Hannah, don't fret you're beautiful, too. Just in a different way," Dr. Vasu said, glancing down her blouse again. She was more sensual than beautiful, her face a bit long and her legs not the lean tanned look of a model like Ronnie.

"I don't need your approval on my looks." Hannah moved her attention to Jeffrey. "Either of you."

"Easy now." Jeffrey reached out to pat her hand.

She jerked away. "What did the Homeland Security agent say? Are they coming here to look around?"

"They're still making general inquiries. If they have a reason to suspect something is coming from this lab will they pursue it." His expression turned serious. "There is nothing I need to know, is there?"

"Nope. Not from my body of work, Dr. Vasu." Jeffrey tamped down the panic. It had never occurred to him the time travel might have created a detectable pulse of some kind.

"I was only monitoring the storm for my research," Hannah's brown eyes were wide, "so nothing from my end to raise any alarms."

"In the event they discover anything further be prepared to let them into your lab to inspect." Dr. Vasu moved to sit behind his desk again.

"Sure thing, Dr. Vasu." Hannah's cheeks were turning pink, such a pretty color.

"Don't worry, Ms. Volpe. They won't touch your sensitive equipment but merely have access to your machines and to review the backup systems. You know the one we use for situations such as this."

"Interesting, you never mentioned that you were spying on us, Dr. Vasu." Jeffrey leaned forward in his chair. "Seems that's the type of thing that should be disclosed in our contracts."

"Dear boy, you do not remember signing the employment contract? It is clearly stated in there on the last page." Dr. Vasu opened a file drawer and thumbed through. "Do you want to see the language?"

"No, I'm sure it is in there. I just don't recall reading it," Jeffrey noticed his colleague's panicked look. "Not a big deal. Just wasn't aware there was another system. It's good to know if I lose my data or something."

"Yes, that is precisely why we do it. There have been outages, especially with the research you're working on. It should be of some help to you if anything should go wrong." Dr. Vasu nodded and closed the drawer.

"Can I ask what type of system you use? Is it an off-site router, or is it in-house?"

"Oh, I'm not sure. That's all the IT guys' territory. I just tell them what I want and they take care of everything." Dr. Vasu smiled and stood up. "Thank you for coming up to discuss this matter."

"No problem, Dr. Vasu. Please let me know if there is anything else you need," Jeffrey said coolly, hiding the panic building inside. Dr. Vasu never mentioned the backup system. Admittedly, he hadn't read every single word of the ten-page beast, probably as they had expected. Did the lab already know about his experiment? Or was this just one of those backup systems that were never really accessed? Was there also a backup system to the video JT had erased? Shit, was this going to blow up in his face?

"Yes, just let me know, Dr. Vasu." Hannah's cheeks were nearly red, and with her pale skin it was hard for her to hide a blush.

They stood and walked out of the meeting. Jeffrey returned to his office with his mind in turmoil about the potential disaster that would occur if the feds poked their noses around too much. He quickly scrubbed his computer and gathered any lingering time travel notes and equipment to take home when he left for the day. Then he repaired the circuit that was damaged during the fire.

Chapter 5 - Worlds Collide

"Do you still think Jeffrey had something to do with this?" Ronnie turned to Steph who sat next to her in the Thunderbird.

"Are you kidding? Yes." Steph guided them on a short drive on I-4 and down a few side streets back to Ronnie's apartment parking lot.

"Steph, really? He certainly isn't acting guilty. He seems to be flabbergasted about the whole thing. He is so logical—he can't accept it." Ronnie put the T-bird in park.

"No, I think it's the fluster technique." Steph opened the car door. "He gets you flustered and upset so you don't pay attention to how he acts and he can gloss over it."

It had worked if that was his plan. But it just didn't ring true. Steph just didn't know how to read Jeffrey. As they walked toward her apartment she noticed a woman knocking on her door.

"Who is that?" Steph asked.

"No idea," Ronnie said walking toward her. "Can I help you?"

"Are you Ronnie Andrews?" She wore navy blue pants and a striped work shirt with a *First One Courier* patch sewn on the chest.

"Yes, I am."

"This is from Mike Walsh, at Managed Healthcare Synchronicity." The woman handed her a small envelope. "Sign here." She held a clipboard with a pen attached. "I will wait for your response."

"Oh, okay." Ronnie's heart leapt at the mention of Mike's name, surprising her. His bright smile flashed in her mind and she scolded herself for being so excited. Ronnie opened the door and they all walked in. She tore open the envelope and eyed the girl who waited in the foyer.

Steph stood next to her. "Who is Mike Walsh?"

"My boss." Ronnie unfolded the letter to find very neat cursive writing.

"Oh right, the hot dude you interviewed." Steph elbowed her.

"I don't think I mentioned his looks."

"I've seen him. He's posh." Steph leaned in to read over her shoulder.

Dear Ronnie,

I apologize for Hurricane Charley's rudeness that has rained on your parade. He has stormed out of town and won't bother you anymore.

I hope you have fared well through the hurricane. I apologize for this odd way of contacting you, but since the internet and phones are down I didn't know how else to let you know what is going on. I would like to meet with you either today or tomorrow to give you some background materials to read through. I think they will give you a leg up for when we start. We have a trip to Puerto Rico in the next few weeks and I think it will be a good opportunity for you to meet Carlos Munoz, our biggest customer on the island.

Please respond to the courier as to a convenient day and time to meet. I was thinking the Barnes & Noble café at Altamont Springs Mall either tonight at 8:00 or tomorrow morning. I was there earlier today so I know they have power and coffee, thank God.

Our offices will be closed through Wednesday, August 18 due to the storm damage and power outages. It may extend beyond that depending upon when the power returns.

In case you need to reach me and the cell service is back on my number is (407) 555-5555. If for some reason you need to reach me and the cell isn't working my address is 2405 Maitland Avenue in Winter Park. Feel free to stop by or leave me a note.

Mike Walsh, Senior Vice President, MHS

The courier stood patiently. When Ronnie finished, she handed her a clipboard with a pen attached, this time with a blank piece of paper.

Ronnie took it and turned to Steph. "Should I see him today or tomorrow morning?"

"If it were me I'd go now. You're gonna sleep like the dead tonight ... Oh, sorry, Ronnie. I didn't mean ..."

Ronnie's stomach did a flip and she pushed the horrible memories of the time travelling out of her mind. "Maybe I should tell him tomorrow night is better."

"It's your new boss. Give him what he wants." Steph wagged her eyebrows. "Plus, it will help you forget about you know who." She mouthed Jeffrey's name.

"I've seen him. You should definitely meet him tonight. I mean ..." The courier smiled. "Seriously."

"That settles it." Steph grabbed the clipboard and pretended to write, "Miss Andrews will be happy to meet you at eight p.m. tonight at the Barnes & Noble Café. Please arrive shirtless and bring the K-Y."

Ronnie burst out laughing. "Steph! You're so bad!" The courier girl laughed too. Steph held the clipboard out for Ronnie, who scrawled a short note accepting the invitation for that night and handed the clipboard back to the courier. "Thank you."

"My pleasure. And now I get to see him again." The courier waved and walked out of the door. "Sa-weet!"

Ronnie shut and locked the door. "God, Steph, how am I going to meet with Mike? I feel so discombobulated from my ..." she sat down on the couch, "misadventures."

Steph took the note from Ronnie. "Oh, you have his cell and address now. 'Feel free to stop by' how very interesting."

"Steph he's my boss, don't do that."

"Yes, but I know who he is. Half the women at the company have the hots for him," Steph said.

"Really, I didn't know that." Ronnie pictured Mike's perfect face. Steph had handed Ronnie's resume into MHS a few months ago, where she worked. "So, is he a womanizer? He is certainly good-looking enough."

"That's what's so weird. As far as I know he's not gone out with anyone since he's been with the company. Five whole years, Ronnie. Not even a little flirting. He's not married but he must have a girlfriend or something because despite all the attention he has not taken anyone up on their offer."

"Hmm, a mystery. But good for him, at least he's not one of those playboys. I cannot stand that type." Ronnie had been taken with Mike right away. She instantly felt a connection with him like she had known him forever, which was weird because she only met him the one time during the interview. He was very genuine, with a great sense of humor with clear blue eyes framed by black lashes that she could get lost in. It hadn't escaped her notice that he was tall and muscular, as well.

"Tell me about it. My brother is the worst hound dog you've ever seen," Steph laughed. "Makes me want to boak. He probably has every disease known to man. A proper manslut, Ronnie."

"Ha ha! Is that Ian?" Ronnie had met him in June when they had visited Glasgow.

"Yes, little bastard is coming here. Mum has had it with his constant drinking and carrying on." Steph waved her hand in the air. "His slacker friends have driven him into a life of crime so mum has it arranged for me to straighten him up."

"Get out? The famous Ian McKay is coming here? When?"

"Wednesday." Steph shook head, making her blonde curls bounce. "I've spent my childhood babysitting the lad, now I have the pleasure as an adult. Yay."

"Oh man, I'm sorry Steph." Ronnie shook her head. "That's going to put a damper on all of the wild sex you're going to have with Nick!"

"Offffft! I can't even think about that. It's been so long, Ron."

"Yes, but he is a hottie and you're gonna jump his bones, you said so yourself you were close to it in the shower before all hell broke loose with the storm."

"Ummm hmmm." Steph's complexion pinked and she looked away.

"Ha! I know that look! So where will Ian sleep? How long will the l'il horndog be staying?"

"In the guest room. Maybe until he is rehabilitated. Got any holy water handy?"

"Nope. All I have is Sam Adams lager and that's not going to help poor Ian. He is going to have a field day with the American women here in Florida. What the heck are you going to do to help him?"

"Who knows, he can't get into too much trouble. He won't have a car and his loser pals from Glasgow won't be here to corrupt him. Hopefully, a few Sundays at church and a bored life under my wing will help him snap out of it. Heck, maybe I'll enroll him in the community college."

Ronnie gave her a look. "Right, is he the college type?"

Steph's smile faded. "Och, no, he's the Bar L type."

"Bar L?" Ronnie hadn't heard that phrase before, but Steph was full of quirky Scottishisms.

"Barlinne, it's the jail in Glasgow."

"Lovely. You're going to have a fun few weeks, Steph!" Ronnie patted her back.

"Yup! The wee scrawny hellion is going to give me my first gray hairs."

The clock on the dining room wall read 7:10. "Damn, I need to get in the shower." Ronnie grabbed the flashlight off the top of the fridge and carried it into the dark windowless bathroom. The cold and very fast shower was well worth it. She chose a knee-length flowery silk skirt and a white tank top, simple earrings, and flip-flops. It was a good compromise between work and casual.

***

Ronnie parked the T-bird at the Altamonte Springs Mall in front of the bookstore. Her stomach was in knots. She took a deep breath and let it out. Her new boss needed to see her as competent and in control, not a basket of nerves and stress. A flash of her final moments in death's arms in London gripped her. She squeezed the steering wheel. It was 7:56. He was probably here already.

"Ron, it's going to be fine. He's a nice man." Steph patted her arm. "You're just having coffee for Christ's sake. He's already hired you. Just keep it together."

"I know. I'm just a bit frazzled, Steph, I need a good night's sleep and …"

"Right, chin up, shoulders back! Let's go," she said opening the car door and closing the conversation.

"Okay, do you want to meet him?"

Steph smiled confidently. "Yes, but I think I met him once before. It would be good to eyeball him again though."

"Ha! Eyeball him. Is that your way of saying 'grope him with your eyes'?"

Steph laughed. "Noooooo! That's your job since I have my own man to grope."

They walked across the hot pavement into the bookstore.

"Okay love, you come find me when you're done. I'll be upstairs reading." Steph pointed up the escalator.

Ronnie grabbed her elbow and dragged her toward the café. "Come with me to say hi, just help me break the ice." They walked in and looked around for Mike. A dark-haired man, a head taller than anyone was in line, wearing a white polo shirt. He turned around and smiled. His piercing blue eyes bore into her soul. She stopped in her tracks unsettled by the intensity of feelings. He waved her over. "Hi, Ronnie. Great to see you, tell me what you want."

God, what if she acted like a spaz or something.

Steph squeezed her elbow as they walked toward him and whispered in her ear, "We want you to take your shirt off."

"Decaf, please." Ronnie ignored Steph's cheeky comment. "With room. Mike this is my friend Stephanie McKay. She works at MHS too." They shook hands. "Steph, this is my boss, Mike Walsh."

"I think we met awhile back at the vision conference," Steph said.

"Oh yes, I remember you. You had the suggestion to meet in Scotland next time so we can learn to golf properly." Mike smiled. God, he was handsome.

They made small talk for a few minutes and Steph excused herself by hugging Ronnie and then disappeared up the escalator.

"I'll save a table," Ronnie said and looked for an empty one.

"Good luck, it's pretty crowded in here." Mike reached for his wallet to pay the barista.

Ronnie walked the length of the café looking for a place to sit. She made her way back to him and he handed her a coffee. "Decaf." He was a lot taller than she remembered, over six feet.

"Great thanks."

"Let's look outside there might be a free table." He smiled down at her.

They opened the door and were hit with the humidity of a Florida summer evening. It must have still been in the nineties. To the left was an empty table with a dark green umbrella and Ronnie set her coffee on it as he pulled the chair out for her. A man with manners. How nice.

Mike sat opposite and handed her a green folder. "Here you go. I've put together a summary of the project we're working on. But before we get to that tell me how you are doing?"

"I'm good," she said unconvincingly.

"How did you fare the storm?" Mike leaned toward her. She was distracted by the bunching of his shirt sleeves around tan well-developed biceps. "And sorry about the weird note, I didn't know what to do. I knew you'd have a few extra days and if it were me I'd want to put them to good use."

"Yes, I appreciate you reaching out." She looked away wishing he wasn't so visually stimulating. Her nerves were already frazzled.

"Were you in town when Charley hit? I thought you said you'd be here on the tenth." His eyes sparkled, and he had shy smile playing at the corners of his mouth. His demeanor was anything but shy, though. He was definitely in control.

"Yeah, I was lucky enough to be here three days and what a storm, right?" She could feel the panic rising. She silently begged, *please don't talk about the storm.*

"I fared well, luckily just a huge mess to clean up in the yard. I hope you weren't alone for the storm. I kept thinking about you hunkered down without a friend in the world." His eyes crinkled at the edges, adding to his handsomeness.

"Well, I was lucky. I have friends in town so I had people to stay with." Why didn't she just tell him she'd spent it with Jeffrey? Maybe she didn't want to get too personal?

"Well, that's good. Is that why you moved from Virginia Beach, to be near them?" He scooted his chair forward letting a man pass behind.

"Yes, it was definitely a factor. I was really glad to get the job, though." Ronnie tried to make her hands stop shaking. It was hopeless so she hid them under the table.

"I'm glad to have you on our team." He turned and bent low to dig in his leather computer bag. Ronnie couldn't help noticing the line where his lats ended along his rib cage showing off his efforts at the gym. He pulled out a white three-ring notebook. "I have a few more things for you. I put together some background information on Carlos Munoz. He's our connection in Puerto Rico, we hope to get into his good graces and then expand on the island." He wiped his forehead.

She took the notebook and set it on the table between them. "Tell me about Carlos, what is he like?" Mike was so close to her at the table she wanted to look him in the eye, but it was too intimate. He had such presence and command. The only thing that gave her an edge was the shy smile that gave away something. She wasn't sure what. Was he a bit nervous too?

He sat back in his chair and shrugged his shoulders and cocked his head to the side. A slightly uncomfortable expression flashed across his face. "He is your typical macho big shot."

Ronnie laughed. With that short sentence Mike had said volumes about Carlos. Was it a lack of respect? An argument? There was something there but Ronnie wouldn't be so rude as to ask outright. She didn't know Mike well enough yet. "Ha! That sounded like a polite avoidance."

"Oh, you are good. Was I that obvious? I mean what did I say?" He ran his fingers through is hair and let the mask of being in control drop, just for a second, but Ronnie picked up on it and it made her relax more.

"It wasn't really what you said, Mike. It was all of the body language that went with it." She laughed and leaned in toward him. It was refreshing to see a crack in his armor.

He looked toward the parking lot, probably carefully crafting his answer. "Let me put it this way. Carlos is Puerto Rican. Do you know many Puerto Rican men?"

"No, please enlighten me." He was adorable when he squirmed a little.

"Well, macho is an understatement. He will really enjoy meeting you and I'll have to warn you he will be quite charming and do his best to get on your good side. I'm confident you'll move us forward on this deal." Mike leaned one arm against the back of the chair and the fabric of his white polo shirt was taut against his meaty chest. She tried to not look but it was impossible. He looked away giving the appearance of allowing her the space to enjoy the view without penalty of his eyes on her. He was probably used to being checked out.

"So, he's a charmer. Okay, I'm up for the challenge. As long as he doesn't actually try to seduce me, I'll be fine." She laughed and wished now sitting in the heat that she'd gotten an iced coffee, or at least added her usual cream.

"Oh, he will try to seduce you. But it will be a disaster if you let him. I'm sure you deal with that all of the time, don't you?" His smile showed one slightly unruly incisor that added to his appeal.

"American businessmen just flirt, they don't actually try to seduce me, or at least no one has yet." She leaned back and could feel the electricity between them. He showed the shy smile again and wiped it off his face with a tan hand. "Why would it be a disaster?"

"Well … you would just be another notch on his bedpost. It's all about the chase." He shook his head looking serious for a moment. "It has nothing to do with the capture."

"There is nothing to worry about here. First, I'm not interested in men like that, no matter how charming they are. Secondly, I'm with Jeffrey." She looked away, not wanting to dwell on that point, "And I'm a professional. I don't mix business with pleasure."

"I'm glad to hear that. I wasn't questioning your morals. I'm just letting you know what to expect. Carlos is Carlos. We're just there to sell him the system and then we'll get back to the states and give him what he bought." Mike watched her closely. Was he worried she was insulted?

"Sounds like a plan." Although an awkward plan since the first thing Mike had to tell her about Carlos was his womanizing.

"Who did you leave behind in Virginia Beach?" he asked, suavely changing the subject.

"My mom. She's sad I'm gone, but she feels better that Steph is here." Ronnie nodded toward the door. "She's my best friend and Mom knows she'll take care of me."

"And Jeffrey, does he take care of you too?" He watched her closely.

Ronnie pushed hair behind her ear and looked at the neutral ground of the parking lot. "Mostly." She thought about Steph's accusations and Jeffrey's yelling and wanted to talk about anything else.

"That's good. I'm glad you were looked after during the storm. I assure you we don't have hurricanes hit often. I've been here five years and nothing even came close to shore. Even if they do they usually hit the coast and move out to sea. I've never seen one like this."

"I know, didn't they say on the news that it has been forty years since a major hurricane hit central Florida?" She sipped the coffee and tried to remove the permanent smile she seemed to have around Mike. Her cheeks were beginning to hurt.

"They also said there are several other tropical depressions brewing. It's supposed to be a really active hurricane season." He wiped the sweat off his forehead again. "We really need to get out to Puerto Rico in the next few weeks and I'd hate to be waylaid by bad weather."

Ronnie caught her breath. A moment of panic passed over and she bit her lip to make it stop, to anchor her to this moment. She wasn't ready to travel anywhere after just returning from the horrible days she'd spent in the eighteenth century.

He leaned forward and touched her hand. "It'll be okay, I promise." Did he sense her mood change?

She pulled her hand away, surprised at the affectionate gesture. His face showed tenderness, and it made her tear up. Ronnie wiped her eyes as heat rose in her cheeks.

He leaned back against the chair and pushed his hand through his hair. A familiar mannerism that reminded her of Mathias. He used to do that when he was stressed. She studied his face but didn't see any resemblance except for that tender expression, broad shoulders, and dark hair. An eerie feeling crept over her like she was straddling two worlds. Mathias was merged into Mike and they were both sitting there in front of her. It was too much, Ronnie broke down and sobbed. She stood up and covered her face. "I'll be right back."

"Wait. Ronnie, please." He took two steps toward her but she turned and ran into the bookstore.

Ronnie pushed through the doors into the cool air conditioning and saw Steph coming down the escalator.

"What in the bloody hell, Ronnie." When Steph stepped off the escalator she hugged her and spoke into her hair. "What happened?"

"Nothing. I need to get home. Could you go sit with him for a minute while I pull myself together? I don't want him to leave."

"Sure luv." Steph turned to look at the café. "Where is he?"

"Outside to the left." Ronnie wiped her eyes. "I'll be right back I just need to calm down."

"Okay, I'll meet you out there. The loo is upstairs just at the top of the escalator."

Ronnie took the escalator up and went into a bathroom stall. She leaned against the cool tiles and took a few deep breaths. How embarrassing to lose it like that in front of her boss. She wanted to come across as confident and in control.

The image of a merged Mike and Mathias hit her again. It must have been that compassionate look that did her in. What had happened to Mathias? Was he still alive? Had he survived all his injuries after she … left? She remembered the last words he'd said… "I love you." Her heart broke into a million pieces and fell down her cheeks onto the floor.

Mathias was two and a half centuries away and there was nothing she could do to reconnect with him. She didn't even know if he had lived through that day. There was so much more to cry about, she hadn't even had a chance to deal with the raw emotions of pain, loss, and betrayal by Jack, and it was hard to stuff it all back inside until she could sort through it and decide how to feel. Finally, she attempted to pull herself together.

What was it about Mike that caused her to lose it? It felt like much more than a look. It was as if in that one silly little moment he knew her loss, felt her pain, and was put in her life to help her deal with it. Her logical side scoffed at the stupidity of that concept. "That's a bunch of emotional hooey!" She blew her nose and wiped her eyes. "Get it together Andrews," and locked those feelings inside to deal with later. Now was not the time or place to try to understand Mike or the nightmare of what she'd lived through. All she knew was that he added a small bit of comfort to an otherwise emotional disaster that awaited her untangling, most likely with Steph in the wee hours.

Chapter 6 - Shadows of Darkness

Ronnie tidied her makeup in the mirror and brushed her hair before taking a deep breath to go find Mike. She hoped she'd not fall apart again. Steph would help keep her strong. She made her way down the escalator and kept her thoughts on simple calm things. The colorful Vera Bradley bags made her think of her sister-in-law and that did a lot to steady her nerves. She opened the door to the outside café. Steph and Mike were talking in the corner. He had pushed his chair away from the table and crossed one leg over the other, showing off a meaty calf. He looked much more relaxed. They both laughed and Steph followed Mike's gaze toward her.

"Hi," Ronnie said shyly, putting her hand on Steph's chair back. "Sorry about that. Just haven't slept much and the storm has completely stressed me out."

"It's okay." Mike stood and took a chair from an empty table and put it next to him, closer than she had been across the table. "Steph was just telling me about Mr. Strong's secretary." He smiled.

Ronnie sat down and her knee almost touched his.

He said quietly, "I'm sorry if I upset you. I didn't mean to."

"No, it wasn't anything you did. Let's just say it has been a really, really long few days."

Steph rolled her eyes. "You could say that. Hey Ronnie, Mike just invited us out to dinner. There is a café down the street that's open. The fridge is full of rotten food by now and we have to eat something. What do you say?"

Her stomach lurched and she shook her head.

"Come on it will be a good way to let off some steam. Let's get a few margaritas and let Mike buy us dinner." Steph leaned in close. "Ronnie, Mike is a super nice guy. Plus, you've got no power at home, so we'll just sit in a dark room and stress out."

Before Ronnie could answer Steph said, "It's a great idea, Mike. Shall we follow you?"

"No, wait." Ronnie held up her hands

Mike stood and pulled out his car keys. "Just for a quick bite to eat, Ronnie. I won't keep you out late. I promise." He flashed a winning smile and she noticed he had very small dimples on either side of his mouth. Could he be any more attractive?

Ronne cut her eyes to Steph and mouthed, "You're evil."

Steph smiled and took Ronnie's arm. "We'll meet you there at Mimi's Café, right?"

"Yes, see you in a few," he said and walked into the parking lot.

They made their way toward the Thunderbird where heat leftover from the sunny day rose in waves off the dark pavement. "Steph, have you lost your friggin' mind? I just broke down in front of him and now we're going out to dinner?"

"Trust me, Ronnie, I'm helping you over this awkward moment. Think how weird it would be to walk into to work after that. Now we can go out and have a few laughs, eat an actual dinner, and you two can get past this."

There was a certain amount of logic to it, but Ronnie thought of Jeffrey's reaction. "Fine. But we leave when I say, okay?"

Steph opened the car door and sat down. "Okay. I wish I could get Nick on the phone so he could join us." Steph pointed to the left using her cell phone. "Go out this way."

They made their way about a half mile down the road to Mimi's Café. Ronnie debated about telling Steph about the weird merge of Mike and Mathias but didn't want to get emotional again. It could wait till she could bawl her head off in the privacy of her own home.

Mike was waiting near the hostess stand and lit up when he saw them. The hostess led them to a table in the back of the restaurant. Ronnie and Steph sat on one side of the booth and Mike sat on the other. Everyone studied the menu while the waitress took drink orders.

"We have a limited menu because of the storm," the waitress said while chewing a wad of gum, red lipstick faded around the edge of her mouth. "Our trucks didn't come in so we're cooking what food we have. Here are our specials, if you can call them that. It's more like eat this or," she waved her hand toward the door, "go somewhere else." She laughed, showing white mishmash teeth. "Hamburgers, cheeseburgers, bacon burgers or …" She looked at the palm of her hand, "cobb salad."

"Salad," Steph and Ronnie said in unison.

"What are you the Bobbsey Twins?" Mike laughed and ordered a hamburger. "Well, this is fun. Thanks for breaking up the monotony of this *post hurricane zero TV or power what can you do by flashlight* type of night."

"Oh, I know it's hot and boring. When are they saying they'll have power on again?" Steph asked.

"Who knows? Depends on where you live I guess. Hey, have you found any gas stations open? It seems they all have plastic bags tied to the pumps." He said leaning back with his arm across the back of the booth. His legs were so long they were nearly tangling with hers under the table.

"I filled up before the storm," Steph said.

"Not sure," Ronnie said, now shy. He looked at her and smiled, making eye contact for a tad longer than necessary agitating the butterflies in her stomach.

The waitress brought two iced teas and a bourbon on the rocks for Mike. Ronnie stirred in some sugar and played with the straw paper while trying to think of something to say. Mostly, she just wanted to stare at Mike and piece together this feeling that he was somehow connected to Mathias.

Luckily Steph was there to pick up where she couldn't. "Do you think we'll have power before the next storm hits? I heard there are several in queue." Steph stirred her tea.

"I hope so because I'm tired of sweating all night." Mike shook his bourbon to make the ice cubes clink against the glass. "At least here I have some ice, right?"

Ronnie laughed a bit too hard. His squinty smile made her a bit giddy. Steph was on to her, though. She had created this situation by taking Mike up on his offer. How did she know Ronnie was attracted to Mike … other than that stupid laugh?

"I was telling Ronnie," Mike said, "We need to get out to Puerto Rico soon. I hope there aren't any storm delays." He stole a glance at her.

Ronne forced a smile. This is where she had broken down before. A moment of panic hit her and she took a deep breath. "How soon Mike?" Her voice rose unnaturally at the end of his name, making it sound awkward.

"As soon as we get you up to speed. I've got us scheduled for next week but who knows with the storms."

"Okay." Ronnie swallowed the panic and looked at Steph for support. "I'll do my best to be ready." There were too many things to deal with—she had no idea how she would handle a business trip so soon. Best not to dwell on it now or she would lose it again.

"Ronnie, we'll be fine, no one expects you to know the job yet," Mike said leaning toward her.

Steph deftly changed the subject, "So how much damage did you get, Mike? Was your house okay over there on Maitland Avenue?" She glanced at Ronnie to be sure she caught it.

He set his drink down and leaned forward. "What's that? How did you know I lived over there?" His eyes were doing that squinty thing again.

"She was there when I opened the letter." Ronnie shook her head. "She's a nosy busybody."

"Nope, I'm merely a good reader. Shame Ronnie didn't use the letter I penned for her as a response," Steph said laughing.

Ronnie smacked her arm. "Steph!" Mike looked confused, "She was just trying to make the courier laugh."

Mike shook his head and that shy smile returned for a flash before he could disguise it again. "Not really much damage except for my shed is a pancake. It's a damn nuisance to clean everything up. What about you Steph?"

"It was an utter nightmare. There was a fire in my neighborhood. But other than that, …" Ronnie patted Steph's arm.

"Wow, that is crazy. I bet it was scary night, though." Mike pressed his lips together and squinted.

The waitress appeared with their food and they were quiet for a few minutes while they ate.

A tall curly haired man approached the table and punched Mike on the shoulder. "Hey man, there you are."

Mike looked surprised, but then his face lit up. He stood and shook the man's hand and hugged him. "Billy, what are you doing here?"

Billy was tall and very good-looking with broad shoulders, trim waist, and dark eyes. "Couldn't raise you on the phone so I figured you'd be here, Mike. Aren't you going to introduce me to these lovely ladies?"

Mike's body language said he didn't really want to but the hug and warm welcome indicated he was clearly good friends with this guy. "Well, sure, but you're going to have to ..."

Billy reached across the table to take Ronnie's hand and shook it firmly. "Billy Nemish, it's great to meet you."

Mike laughed nervously, "Billy this is Ronnie Andrews, my newest employee, and her friend Steph."

"Stephanie McKay, but you can call me Steph."

He shook Steph's hand. "Hi, Steph."

"Billy, we're having a meeting about work. Can I catch up with you another time?" Mike said.

In response, Billy sat down and scooched all the way in the booth to sit across from Ronnie.

"No man." Billy patted the seat next to him. "Come on, I'll leave in a bit, you've not told me about hiring anyone new especially not anyone as hot as this." He nodded at Ronnie.

Mike pressed his lips together and shook his head. He grabbed Billy under the armpit and hauled him up. Billy stood a few inches taller than Mike. "Nope, we've done this once Billy, remember how that turned out?"

"Come on Mike, just one drink, I'll leave when I'm finished." Billy's voice raised in protest.

"Billy, no..." Mike ran his fingers through his hair.

Steph smiled. "Oh, come on Mike it won't hurt anything. Let the poor man stay. We need to get going soon anyway."

"What a nice thing to do, Steph," Billy laughed. "You rescued me from the utter embarrassment of my best friend not wanting me around."

After a few minutes of small talk Steph asked, "Billy, the entire office is wondering why Mike doesn't date anyone."

Ronnie sat back against the booth and looked away, shocked at the audacity of her friend. It was not that she didn't want to know the answer but they hardly knew Mike.

Billy laughed. "This geezer," he shoved Mike's chest, "is afraid to ask anyone out!"

Mike looked pissed but covered it well. "I've never been afraid of anything in my life, Billy, except for that time we swam across the Niagara River."

"Dude, we were lucky to survive!" Billy laughed again, another booming sound that made Ronnie want to join in. He waved to the waitress and ordered a beer. Steph asked a myriad of questions about their adventures. It was no wonder Mike didn't want him here. He probably knew all his deep dark secrets.

Mike mouthed *sorry* to her and shook his head. Steph and Billy carried on with the stories.

"This guy right here is fearless." Billy clapped Mike on the back. "Dude really is not afraid of anything, but now that he's all grown up and a boss and responsible for his life."

"Billy we're thirty-five. We do need to grow up eventually," Mike said.

"I know, but I've not been through what you have." Billy leaned toward Steph and Ronnie conspiratorially. "He was all fun and games until about five years ago."

"Billy." Mike grabbed his shoulder and pulled him back. "Don't." Mike's expression turned dark.

Billy leaned back against the booth and appeared to be deciding if he should say more.

"Let's just say everything changed. And to answer your question Steph, he's a stud. I have no idea why he doesn't just take advantage of what God gave him and find the babes before he is old and decrepit and no one wants him." He laughed. "Believe me, I've tried every time we're out."

"Enough!" Mike slammed his hand on the table. "This is why I didn't want you to join us. You've got no boundaries. You've got to respect I'm here with my subordinate."

Ronnie flinched at the choice of words.

Billy's smile fell. "I know, but dude, eventually you'll move on and we can have some fun."

Ronnie decided to make a break for it. "Steph, we need to get going. Sorry guys, we gotta run. Steph is meeting a friend at my house in a bit. Mike, can I pay for our salads?"

"No, no it's all good. I'll put it down as a business expense. We did talk about work a bit." Shadows lingered behind his eyes as if something dark was lurking. That would explain why he'd taken a break from dating, but five years? Surely a bad breakup wouldn't take that long to get over.

"Thank you, Mike. That's very kind of you," Steph said.

Mike's relief was palpable, but his words betrayed it. "Are you sure you have to go?"

Ronnie nodded. "It's been a really long day. I'll see you Wednesday. Let me know if we're closed after that. I might have some questions for you with all the materials you gave me earlier. Maybe we can meet if the offices don't open up before then."

His expression softened and he said quietly, "I would like that."

Ronnie couldn't help a goofy smile. She'd like that too.

"Right, well we're off." Steph stood and Ronnie followed. "Nice to meet you, Billy. Thanks for dinner, Mike."

"Great to see you again, Steph." Mike stood and let Billy out of the booth.

"The pleasure was all mine," Billy said to Steph as he bent down to kiss her hand. "Beautiful lady, it was a delight to meet you." Then he took Ronnie's hand and looked into her eyes. "Your beauty makes me breathless."

Mike interceded. "Nemish, you're laying it on pretty thick. Let go of her hand already."

Billy promptly let go and held his hands up as if in surrender. "Hey man, I was only being friendly with your new employee." Then he turned to her. "No harm meant."

"It's fine." Ronnie smiled. "It was great to meet you and learn so much about how wild Mike used to be. It may come in handy later."

"Anytime. In fact, I could tell you a lot more if you gave me your number. We could go out for drinks later," Billy said.

The look on Mike's face said it all, he was irked. He seemed protective, and she liked it. "Ha ha, no thanks Billy. I have a boyfriend. I'm sure we'll see you around. Night."

"Goodnight, ladies," Mike said. "See you on Wednesday, hopefully."

Steph waved, "Bye. Billy, nice to meet you."

Ronnie locked arms with Steph as they walked out of Mimi's. Ronnie stole a glance back to see Mike grabbing Billy by the back of the neck.

They made their way to the car and Steph said, "Well that was interesting. I'm wondering what happened five years ago, aren't you?"

"Yes, did you see his expression change?" Ronnie was sure there was something sad and terrible in his past.

"Yup. Definitely something there, Ron. I hope you don't mind me being so bold by asking. It never quite seemed right. I mean look at the man. He has such presence, such good looks, why doesn't he mingle a little?"

"I'm curious too, but I know there was a nerve struck." They made their way to Ronnie's car. "Steph, I really hope I don't have to travel soon. I'm not sure I'm up for the stress."

"Well, if you're lucky," Steph opened the passenger door and sat down, "maybe we'll have another storm and you'll be off the hook."

"Oh God. Don't say that." Ronnie's heart leapt into her throat.

Ten minutes later they were back at Ronnie's apartment and walking up the pathway to her door. "Steph, I have to tell you what got me so upset at the bookstore."

"Okay, hit me with it."

"Mike mentioned the Puerto Rico trip and that he hoped it wouldn't be waylaid with another storm." Ronnie inserted the key and opened the door, instinctively hitting the light switch to no effect. "I panicked. Steph, he put his hand on mine and looked at me with such compassion."

"Did he now?"

"Hey, leave the door open while I find the damn flashlight."

Steph obliged. "You're doing it again, Ronnie. You bring up a heavy topic and then stall."

"I'm not stalling, I'm searching for the light." She shuffled toward the kitchen and found the small flashlight on the counter. Luckily, she'd added fresh batteries yesterday in preparation for the storm before she knew about going to Jeffrey's lab. Yesterday was a lifetime ago. She would never be the same. Nothing would ever be the same. A small part of her shattered.

She clicked on the flashlight and made her way back to Steph allowing the tears to gather amongst her eyelashes. "Steph, it was his look and how he touched my hand. It was so familiar, so much like ..."

She lit the candle on the coffee table using the matches nearby.

"Like what?" Steph had already shut the front door.

Ronnie sat down on the loveseat and Steph sat in the overstuffed chair mulling it over, trying to feel it again. "It reminded me of …"

"You mean the bloke from the past? The Austrian guy Matthew or whatever?"

"Mathias. *Mah t'eye us.*" Ronnie said it slowly.

"What was the feeling?"

"I'm not sure. It was so weird. I had this feeling that Mike…I don't know." Ronnie bit her lip it sounded so crazy, sadness was welling in the pit of her stomach. "Just for a split-second Mike and Mathias were the same person." Ronnie studied Steph's face. It was a crazy thought.

"Wow, that is really weird. It has to mean something, though." Steph tucked one leg under the other.

Ronnie shook her head. "How can that make any sense? Probably just emotional right now with all I've been through and the fight with Jeffrey."

"Could be, but Ronnie, I'm Catholic and we believe in fate. Maybe that feeling is meant to guide you."

"Guide me to what, Steph?"

"I'm not sure, but I feel it's important." She handed Ronnie a tissue.

Ronnie wiped a tear. "I want to dismiss it, just like I want to dismiss everything about my experience, but I can't shake the feeling it's a key to something."

"Do you remember what you told me about the fortune-teller?" Steph asked.

"What part?"

Steph continued, "She told Mathias you two would meet again in another life."

"Oh my God. I didn't put those two things together. You don't think …" Ronnie fell back on the couch as the hairs on the back of her neck rose.

Chapter 7 - Sink or Swim

Sunday, August 16, 2016

Ronnie slept fitfully with demons haunting her usual blissful slumber in a blur of hate, horror, and desperate chases. She woke at 7:15 a.m. wishing she had shut the blinds before going to sleep. It had been so dark and the candle was in the living room for Steph and Nick. He had come by at 10:00 as promised and Ronnie went to bed shortly after. Her body and mind were exhausted and she wanted to give the two lovebirds some time alone. Their voices were comforting as she dozed off to sleep and knowing Steph would be there if needed.

Ronnie rolled to her stomach and pulled the pillow over her head and woke with a start a few hours later not having moved a muscle. Her neck was stiff and she stretched. What a huge relief to be in her own bed, albeit unrested and stressed. Exercise usually did the trick at unbundling the wired feeling and allowing her mind to clear. Ronnie slipped on her bathing suit and then brushed her teeth. Looking around for a ponytail holder, she gave up when she found her goggles on the dresser. It would be a battle to fight the tangles afterwards but she didn't have the patience to look for a hair thing among her half-unpacked bags.

She went into the kitchen and grabbed a protein bar. Steph must have been asleep, the door to the guest room was closed. Was Nick in there with her? A twang of envy hit but quickly faded. Jeffrey could have spent the night but given how he was acting that would have gone badly. Better to be a little stressed than completely a mess from a big fight.

She shut the front door and made her way toward the pool area along a narrow winding path past the other apartments. Wonderful morning smells hit her, wet grass, the flowers blooming just outside of her apartment. She breathed deeply taking it in and feeling the sun on her shoulders. Halfway down the path, she wished she'd worn a cover up. Her turquoise bikini didn't cover much, not ideal for a morning stroll.

She made her way to the small gate that kept loose toddlers from drowning themselves. A handwritten sign covered the usual *Caution No Lifeguard* sign. This one read *Pool Closed Until Power Returns.*

"Crap." Ronnie debated going in anyway but thought of the cesspool of germs that would be growing without the filtration system and chlorine working.

"Ronnie." A male voice cried out.

Jeffrey's golden brown hair was shining in the sunlight. In his hand was a grocery bag and flowers.

"What are you doing here?" she said.

He walked toward her hiding the flowers behind his back playfully. "Just bringing you breakfast. Look I'm sorry about how I acted yesterday."

She wanted to lash out at him but decided not to spoil the good mood. "Hi, I didn't expect to see you."

"Damn babe, you're looking hot today." He kissed her cheek and gave her a side hug and presented the lavender roses. "I got these for you as a *sorry, I'm an ass* gift."

"Wow, they're beautiful." She buried her nose in them. Lavender roses were her favorite, they had the most fragrance. "Thanks."

His hand slid down her back and grabbed her ass. "You had to be in the blue bikini, didn't you? How am I supposed to keep my hands off you?"

"Jeffrey stop. Someone might see." She pulled away looking around to see if anyone noticed his blatant groping. They retraced her steps back to her apartment.

"Are you out to meet your new neighbors? You're definitely going to make a good impression." He laughed and glanced down the front of her body lingering on her breasts, stomach, and lower bits.

She crossed her arms. "I was trying to get a swim in but the pool is closed. No power."

"Shame, you'd look even hotter wet." He flashed a sexy smile.

"What did you bring for breakfast?" She wasn't ready to forgive him despite the flowers and compliments, but to her disgust her body was more than ready to bend to his will.

"Your favorite—scones." He smiled and waved the bag.

"Oh yum." An image of him licking crumbs off her tan stomach assaulted her as she used the key to open her front door. Nick and Steph were at the breakfast bar holding hands and laughing. They separated and Steph stood up. Nick stood too and took a few steps toward them.

"There you are. And look you brought trouble with you." Steph said nodding at Jeffrey.

"Trouble with flowers." He said in a neutral tone. "Hi, I'm Jeffrey Brennan." He held his hand out to Nick.

"Hey Jeffrey, good to meet you. I'm Nick." Nick awkwardly held out his left hand. "Sorry, man just getting used to this." He nodded at the cast.

"What the hell did you do? Steph's not breaking your bones already is she?" Jeffrey said laughing.

"No." Nick laughed good-naturedly. "It was Charley beating me up. Much bigger attacker than this wee lassie," Nick said hugging Steph.

"Damn, that's a shame. Seems we all had a strange night," Jeffrey said. "Brought breakfast for my lady." He nodded at the bag and set it on the dining room table. "You mind if we eat? You can join us if you like. I brought half a dozen."

"Steph is a scone snob, Jeff," Ronnie said. "She's probably not going to approve of our American version. Be right back." Ronnie could hear them discussing the virtues of proper scones while she stepped into her bedroom and slipped on an oversized T-shirt, then returned.

"They're not scones they're fancy muffins. No resemblance to the real thing," Steph was saying. "Did you bring any coffee?"

"No, I had some already. Didn't think Ronnie was a morning coffee gal." He was right, she wasn't.

"Right. We were going to head out for Denny's or something that's open. You want to join us?" Nick asked.

"No, I think we'll stay here," Jeff answered. "Ron, what do you want to do with the flowers?" She'd set them down on the table to greet Steph and Nick.

Ronnie took the flowers into the kitchen slightly irked at his bossiness. Curious at what the furnished apartment held, she opened the cupboards to search for a vase. She had rented this apartment unit until the closing on her new house next month.

Steph followed her into the kitchen. "I can't go back home, Ronnie. It's too empty without Hamish. Do you mind me staying here a bit?"

"God no. I really don't want to be alone, especially at night. And I'm so sorry about your wee kitty." Ronnie removed the paper and shoved the flowers in the glass.

"Good, we can hold each other up now," Steph said, the corners of her mouth turning down.

Nick walked into the kitchen. "Steph, we should go. Breakfast will be over soon."

"It's Denny's, breakfast is never over." Steph put her hand on his chest. "Had enough of Jeffrey?" Nick smiled and raised his eyebrows. They walked toward the door. "Bye Ronnie."

She grabbed the flowers and two paper plates and brought them to the table. "Bye guys. Have fun."

"Bye Jeffrey, nice to meet you," Nick said.

"Yeah, see ya, Nick." Jeffrey waved. "Enjoy Denny's."

Jeffrey opened the bag and pulled out the scones.

"I wasn't sure what kind you liked so I got a few different ones."

"Great." Ronnie felt a bit queasy, knowing what she was about to tell him would likely create a fight but she had to tell him everything. Hopefully, he'd let her speak this time and maybe she'd figure out if he was involved.

He pushed aside the mail to make room for his plate and lifted one sheet of paper. "What's this?"

She glanced at it. "My new boss wanted to give me some things to look over. The office will be closed until Wednesday and I can get started over the next few days."

"But why is he sending you notes, Ron? His address too? 'Feel free to stop by…'" His lips were in a thin line.

Ronnie's face went hot. "Yes, what is he supposed to do? Phones are down and he can't e-mail me. He had to tell me the offices are closed."

"Right." He tossed the letter on the table. "A bit personal don't you think? Did he come over here to deliver this?"

"No, a courier came by. What is the big deal?" She took the paper out of his hand, folded and put it back in the envelope.

"Something about the guy bugs me. Why is he so interested in you?" His eyebrows knit together.

"I'm his new employee is all. He was worried about me being here and the storm hitting." She knew this would bug him but Steph was right, it had been worth it to smooth over the awkwardness.

"So, did you meet up?"

"Yeah, Steph and I met him for coffee last night and then Steph rudely invited us to dinner with him." She looked away.

"You went out with him last night?" He sat back in his seat looking at her coldly.

"We met to talk about work stuff. Then while I was in the bathroom Steph accepted his invite out to dinner. It was innocent Jeffrey. Steph was there and we just talked about work."

He tapped his finger on his leg. "You wouldn't mind a bit if I went out to dinner with Hannah Volpe?"

"Who the hell is Hannah Volpe?" She stared at him in disbelief. "No, never mind it doesn't matter. If you had to meet for work I'd not make an issue out of it no matter who it was."

"She's the hot chick in the lab next to me," he said coolly.

Ronnie shook her head. Why did he have to escalate this? "This is a stupid conversation. Mike knows I'm with you and really, he is just my boss, Jeff. I moved here to be closer to you."

"You also moved here for that job, Ron." He tapped his finger on the envelope. "But let it go."

"Let it go? You talk about the hot chick in the ... never mind." Ronnie stood up and went into the kitchen and grabbed a bottle of water. "I think you just like to fight with me," she said through the breakfast bar.

He followed her and leaned against the wall. "Why would I do that? I came over here to make up for yesterday."

She cracked the bottle and offered it to him.

"Thanks." He took a sip. "Let's get to that. I know you wanted to tell me what happened, and I am sorry I lost it yesterday. Please, Ronnie, let's not start up again. I want to calmly listen to you." He took her elbow trying to lead her back to the table.

She pulled away and grabbed a water. He stopped and watched her closely, probably not sure if she was going to snap. Taking a deep breath, she calmed herself. "I do need to tell you this. It is important."

"I'm here for you, Ronnie. I'll do my best to listen," he said softly.

"Right. I see that's gonna be a challenge." She took a swig of the water, hiding the aggression behind the bottle.

Ronne plopped down on the couch and he brought over the plate with the scones, offering one. "Thanks."

"I promise to listen this time while you tell me what you think happened yesterday, okay?" He said the last bit tenderly and it did a lot to soften her mood.

"Okay." She still hesitated about getting into it with him. Both times when she explained what had happened, first to Steph then to him, it had been met with anger and accusations. Steph's words still echoed around in her mind that Jeffrey was involved. She examined his face looking for falseness, for lies. Was he keeping the sheep's clothing on a bit longer? Ronnie rubbed her eyes. It had been such a long night and she could feel the weariness creeping back into her bones. *Sink or swim.*

Ronnie started at the beginning, despite having already done that yesterday but it was important for her to get it all out, and not forget anything. He sipped his water and asked minor clarification questions. When she got to the point where she and Mathias escaped from the priest's examination he stopped her.

"Ronnie, look at your arm there." He pointed to a small mole on her forearm. "Is that where the wax landed on you?"

She rubbed the tiny spot trying to remove it. "Yes. Oh man, I didn't even realize that was there." A momentary panic hit her. Had this mole always been there, or did it appear after?

"Do you think that your mind chose that location for the wax drip because you already had a mole there?" he asked.

"I don't remember it being there. But Jeff, my mind didn't create this."

"I remember it being there." He lifted her arm and kissed the spot in question.

She pulled away surprised at his tenderness. "It was there? You're sure?"

"Yeah, I remember seeing it before. Did you think it magically appeared?" The condescending laugh was gone, replaced by a more playful attempt to keep the peace.

"No." She didn't know what to think, all of it was too unbelievable.

"How did this end? When I found you in the bathroom you were mumbling something and the watch was gone."

Ronnie pressed into her temples and then rubbed her eyes. "Jeff."

He took her hand. "Yes."

"This part is where it gets really weird."

"Ronnie, since you opened your mouth about this whole thing has been weird, how can it get any worse?" He shook his head but the mocking tone was gone.

"Believe me it was horrific." Tears fell from her eyes unexpectedly. She wiped them away.

"Please tell me, babe." He squeezed her hand.

She spent the next fifteen minutes describing how she managed to get back to 2004 while deftly leaving out details about Mathias, hoping he didn't deduce her feelings. He was jealous enough already about Mike.

His face turned beet red and the pen fell from his hand. "Babe, seriously? Are you saying you dreamed you died?"

"It wasn't a dream. This whole thing was something entirely different. Jeffrey, I felt pain, I slept, I ate." She took a deep breath and slowly let it out allowing the horror splash over her like the blood flowing out of the bodies. It would never leave her. It was burned into her memory, the disgusting smells, the haunting sounds. She told him quietly about the crowd and their rabid, desperate scavenging of the newly dead and dying. She told him of the last few seconds in 1752 and how she had returned to the bathroom in his lab.

He stared openmouthed and finally managed to say, "What the hell Ronnie?"

She sobbed and let out some of the fear and raw emotion. The loss of Mathias hit her hard and she couldn't look at Jeffrey. Would she ever see him again? What had happened to him? Jeffrey wiped at her tears and then held her close as heart wrenching sobs tore through her. Finally, she reached for a Kleenex and wiped her eyes and nose.

"Ron, you've got me really worried." The corners of his mouth were turned down, an emotion she'd not seen on him before.

She studied his face.

"I've never heard of someone dying in a dream before. Usually your mind doesn't let you die. It ends it just before that happens."

"Have you heard anything I've said? This was not a dream, Jeff." She wanted to rant at him but she was too exhausted.

"I know what you've said. I just don't know what to make of this. Do you think... I mean is there any possibility of ..." He wiped his eyes. Was he crying?

"Possibility of what?" She sat back and watched him.

He shook his head and turned away. She pulled on his hand. "What?"

"I just think maybe you should see a doctor? I mean this sounds like..." He wiped his eyes again. Yes, he was definitely crying. "Your mind slipping or something."

"My mind?" Her cheeks burned.

He turned toward her. "Ronnie, do you have any mental illness in your family?"

"What?" Tears stung her eyes. "Jeff, no. Don't say that. I'm not slipping. This was my reality for days."

"Do you hear what you're saying though?" He said it tenderly, with pity, and that was harder to swallow than the anger. "You even said it yourself, that it had been your *reality* for days. Reality does not take you to the eighteenth century where you are tried for being a witch. It just doesn't. What if it is a chemical imbalance that made you imagine these things? Or something else?"

She couldn't stand the way he was looking at her. He didn't believe it had actually happened. He thought she was losing her mind. "I'm not crazy Jeff. It wasn't ..." She ran into her room and flopped down on the bed. She pulled the pillow over her head to block it out. Could she be losing her mind?

He followed right behind her. "Ronnie, really? Please don't be mad at me but I've never heard anything like this in my life." He sat on the bed and put his hand on her back. "Let's just have you seen by a doctor. Maybe they can find something to help. Or maybe it was just a reaction to something that made you hallucinate." He slid his hand under her cover up and rubbed her back, leaving her bikini-clad butt exposed. She rolled over and he moved toward her. "Babe, please. You can see my doctor, it would make me feel better. Just to have you looked over, you know."

She sat up. "Jeff, I'm not crazy! I'm not. I have no explanation for what caused this, but it was real. I lived through this."

"No Ronnie, you died through this. That is so, so disturbing." He kissed her forehead.

"It was horrible." She wiped her eyes. "Please don't make it worse by making me feel like I'm a lunatic. I'm not."

"Babe, I know you're not. You're the most together woman I know. I guess that's why it's so disturbing. You aren't delusional now. It maybe was just an altered state or something."

"Jeff," Ronnie wanted to scream she wasn't crazy. After all, it was something he did that made it happen. She didn't know how he'd react and his anger wouldn't help.

"Babe please just see Dr. Esposito, he's a nice guy. You won't have to tell him what happened exactly. Just have him look you over."

"Jeff ... Steph thinks you caused this."

He visibly retreated, moving backward as he sat on the bed. "What the hell does that mean?"

"I was at your lab when it happened. The watch you gave me was back in time too. Maybe it was an aftereffect of the power thing you're working on? Maybe another lab was doing something strange and it affected me?"

"But babe that's not something a weather experiment would do to someone. Plus, I didn't have any weird experiences. How could it affect you and not me?" He spoke rapidly.

"Something sent me back in time. I know it did. I want to find people and places that will prove that I went back. It can't be that I'm crazy." She took the end of her long T-shirt and wiped the tears.

Jeffrey's eyes moved to her hips, thighs, and blue bikini bottoms. He laid down next to her and wrapped his arms around her. "Babe, we'll figure it out."

She buried her face in the nook of his shoulder and felt his solid warmth along her body. "Just promise me you'll see my doctor, okay?"

"I'll think about it." Her mind was a jumble of anger, fear, and sadness.

He kissed the top of her head and rubbed her back again, pushing the cover up to her shoulders. She melted into him and let her tired mind loose. At least she'd told him what happened and now was determined to prove she'd traveled back in time, somehow. Jeffrey pulled off her cover-up and threw it on the floor. He then continued lightly rubbing her back, inching his way down toward the bikini bottoms.

"I'm glad you were able to tell me the whole thing, Ron. I'm sure it seemed real to you, but babe, either way it will be okay, I promise." Jeffrey slid his hand along the top band of the bottoms and followed it across the top of her butt and back up to her shoulders. He stopped briefly to untie the top around her neck and then her back and pulled it off flinging it onto the floor.

His skin was warm and she melted further as his hands slowly caressed her newly exposed flesh. He grabbed both her wrists and pinned her to the bed as his tongue flicked sensitive flesh. Ronnie's mind asked him to stop but her body overruled this time, keeping the words from emerging. He let go of her wrists and removed his shirt, adding to her excitement. His caramel-bronze muscles flexed delightfully as he arranged himself between her legs, his stomach against hers. He kissed her softly at first and slid his tongue between her lips, increasing pressure and intensity as he pressed into her soft and ready flesh grinding against her.

His skin was hot and she could feel his arousal. Ronnie grabbed his shoulders and ran her hands down his muscular back, gripping his lats and then sliding inside his khaki shorts, pressing him harder into her with only the fabric of her bikini bottoms and his shorts separating them.

His lips grazed her neck creating goosebumps across her flesh. Jeffrey sat up and went to lock the bedroom door, returning with shorts sliding down his thighs as a smile played on his lips.

Kneeling on the bed he put one hand on each knee and watched her face as he opened her legs. Both hands slid down her inner thighs until he reached the blue bottoms, caressing the soft fabric and what was beneath with both thumbs. She lifted her hips and he removed the last bit of clothing. He opened her legs again and dragged his tongue over her inner thighs, slowly making his way to where her legs met. Ronnie melted under his touch, her excitement growing, the need for his flesh overpowering her anger.

Jeffrey nibbled lightly all around making her squirm. His hands slid up her tanned stomach and caressed her breasts, pinching and squeezing as his mouth explored her wetness.

He knew how to tease deliciously bringing her to the brink of release and backing off, shifting positions and trying another angle. The anger, the fear, the horror of what she'd told him slipped away and all her mind could focus on was his wet mouth exploring her most delicate flesh until under his command he brought her to an intense orgasm.

Ronnie tried to be quiet but it was impossible. A sidewalk heading to the pool was just outside the window. It made no difference. Jeffrey knew exactly how to manipulate her into losing her mind, leaving the argument behind. Ronnie decided in that moment she didn't care even the slightest bit about the fight. Whatever it had been.

Finally, she returned to her senses. Jeffrey kissed his way to her mouth while slowly, sensually sliding against her body until he entered her, carefully, kissing her deeply as he stretched her to accommodate his need. He grabbed her legs, pinning them to her chest and slid all the way in, making her gasp, goosebumps covering her entire body.

"Ronnie, you are mine. Every inch of you is mine." He accentuated *mine* with a thrust. It was better than any drug known to man. Her already worked up need was met again and again as he proved how well he knew her body.

Chapter 8 - Hot Boss

Wednesday, August 18, 2004

Mike Walsh's bright eyes smiled before his face did. "Ronnie, great to see you, again."

It was Ronnie's first day of work on the job at Computer Technology Services Incorporated and she was duly nervous. "Hello, Mike." Her intention was to say something witty, but that just wasn't doable. Mike's eyes were the color of a clear summer sky and made her think of the beach. His black lashes seemed oblivious to the effect they had on the deep blue they framed.

"Let me show you your office. I'll introduce you to the team and get you up to speed."

"Great. Thanks." She chastised herself for pure lack of anything intelligent to say.

"You're just down this hall. This is my office." He pointed to the big cushy corner office with dark wood and a 180-degree view of the small pond on the back of the campus. It hadn't changed since she interviewed there a month ago.

A few offices down and on the opposite side he stopped. "Here, you are. No window but it's as close as I could get you to my office."

Ronnie walked in and set her bag down on the desk. It was a simple set up with a glass front wall and blinds. If she looked through the office across the hall she could see outside as long as they didn't close the blinds. "Thanks, this is great."

Ronnie sat in the chair and looked around feeling the room's vibes. It was going to be a good place to work. Mike was good-natured not to mention easy on the eyes. She'd never had a hot boss before and time would tell if that was a good thing or not.

"I'll let you set up. Someone from the help desk will arrive soon to help you get onto the computer. We can meet later for lunch if you like."

"Yes, that will be great."

Twenty minutes later a slight man with a black moustache knocked on the frame of the open door.

"Hi, I'm from the help desk."

"Ronnie Andrews." She shook his hand and made small talk as he arranged her desktop and showed her how to log into the group shared location.

He stopped and looked up from the keyboard. "You're lucky to get this job, there were a lot of people vying for it."

"Oh really, I'm very grateful."

"You can imagine every female with aspirations sent their resume in. At least the ones in-house that know Mike." He shook his head smiling. "Even his secretary interviewed for the position."

"Ceil did? Oh, wow, I bet she was disappointed to not get the job. What happened when it was announced?"

"She was crushed. The e-mail system nearly crashed because of the inquiries alone." He squinted as he smiled. "Girls gone wild and whatnot."

"Ha ha. What is up with that?" She was shocked that out of all the talent in the company she was offered the job.

"So many people want to work for him. He is mysterious, you know?" he said, lowering his voice and glancing past Ronnie through the glass window into the hall. "He's a powerful man, definitely a chick magnet."

"Mysterious?" Ronnie parroted. The way he said it almost in a whisper sounded like a murder mystery.

"Well, they call him ole Ironsides. No one ever penetrates the barrier." He laughed and shrugged his shoulders. "He isn't married but doesn't hook up. He doesn't even hang out with any of the dudes that work here."

Ronnie was amused by descriptive slang. "Why Ironsides and what is he like to work with?"

"He is a former marine. Tough as nails." He paused in typing and turned his head, "Iron. Nails." He shook his head. "Never mind. He is a great guy and treats people with respect."

"That's good to hear." That matched Ronnie's first impressions of Mike.

He continued, "He has a great team and the drama stays out of his department because he doesn't put up with any nonsense."

They made small talk as Ronnie opened her bag and pulled out a few personal items. She arranged the desk to her liking as he set up the account. This young guy's comments about Mike were amusing. It seemed everyone was curious about him, men and women alike. When he was finished, he showed her around the computer and left.

At 9:00 she met with the team and sat briefly at each of their cubicles learning about their role in the company. By noon a mixture of excitement and panic about the job gripped her. Would she get up to speed in time for the trip to Puerto Rico? It loomed on the horizon like a giant iceberg aiming for the Titanic. Ronnie returned to her office, deciding it was time for a cup of coffee. In the hallway, she ran into Mike and for a split second, she was lost in the blue clarity of his eyes.

"Are you ready for lunch?" he asked, lighting up as she walked toward him.

"Yes, I am starving." She'd forgotten how tall he was.

They walked to the end of the hall and turned right into the cafeteria.

"So how did it go with my team?" He spoke above the din in the room. It was lunchtime and busy.

"It went great." She watched his lips as he talked. They were full and looked like they'd be soft to the touch. Bad train of thought. He had enough women after him and surely he'd not want another. Ronnie straightened out her mind and they chatted until they called Mike's name. He carried the tray holding their food back to his office.

"It's so nice to be out of the dark apartment. Man, am I sick of that place," Ronnie said. "It was starting to change my personality." She followed him into his office. "All the gloom and doom and sweaty humidity. How can anyone have lived here before electricity?"

"I know, right? It's unfathomable. I'm sick of the noisy night critters making a racket outside of my bedroom window all night." He motioned to the small table in the corner. "Please, sit."

He set the tray down and then opened the blinds on both sides of the great expanse. "This is a great view, isn't it?"

She noticed his broad sculpted shoulders and deep V to his waist. "Mmmhummm." She hid a smirk and took a sip of the Diet Coke.

Thunder rumbled in the distance. The six-story building towered over the trees and other obstructions nearby leaving a perfect view of the bubbling clouds.

"Looks like a storm is brewing." He turned and closed the office door and sat back down. "God, I love a good rumble." Lightning forked off to the left. "One, two, three, four, five." The thunder interrupted him and shook the windows. His face lit up. "One mile away! It's definitely coming fast." He smiled winningly at her, his white straight teeth almost glowing in the low light. "Oh, hey I forgot you had some trouble with the hurricane. Does this bother you?" He asked, smile fading making him look older and wiser.

"No, really I'm okay. I usually like storms. Just had a bad go of it during Charley, but it isn't the thunder that bothers me." Nope, it was pretty much just the time travel and brutal death that she was having trouble with.

"Good, I'd hate to upset you." He sat next to her facing the windows and another lightning strike lit up the sky.

His excitement rivaled her father's love of storms. The scientist part of him would totally geek out when a storm hit and Ronnie would get an exuberant lesson on cloud dynamics and weather predictions.

The delightful aroma of her lunch forced her eyes away from the storm— mozzarella, tomato and basil sandwich on focaccia bread drizzled with balsamic vinegar. One fatal flaw was it would be embarrassing to get her mouth around that thing and get balsamic vinegar all over her face. She reached for the knife and fork and took a small bite.

"What's your impression of the team so far?" His eyes smiled.

She wiped her mouth. "Great bunch of smart people. You did a good job assembling the group."

He held her gaze for a bit longer than was professional. Losing her nerve, she looked away, not sure what she saw. It made her nervous. She'd never been attracted to a coworker before, especially not a boss.

"Well, thanks, I like to think of myself as the engineer. I choose the workers and plan the projects but they're the builders. They do all of the heavy lifting, I just organize it all."

He tackled the sandwich with gusto and it fell apart in his hand and splashed on the plate, and a fleck or two got onto his shirt. "Oh damn, look at that." He wiped at it with the napkin to no avail. "Crap."

She smiled glad for the distraction. Her dirty mind told him to just take the shirt off but she quickly told that whore to shut up.

Thunder crackled and vibrated the windows. "Oh, that scared me." She laughed as adrenaline kicked in and made her heart speed up. His excitement was infectious.

He stood again to close the blinds out to the hallway. He turned off the lights in the office so they sat in the semi-dark. "Nice ambiance. Now you can't see the mess I make with this sandwich." He held the unwieldy but delicious item up.

Another boom startled her, but he just beamed and took a sip of his drink. She thought this was going to be a lot of questions and answers but instead it was more like two friends just hanging out. It was a welcome relief after the busy morning being *on* to meet everyone.

"How long have you been with the company, Mike?" She interrupted the silence. At Mimi's he had said a little but she was curious about his past. Ronnie wanted to hear more without Billy there driving him into defensive mode.

"Five years. Just after I moved here from Rochester." He said, sandwich in hand. She watched him attack it and he looked up at her a bit embarrassed.

"What brought you here to Florida?"

He smiled. "I feel like I'm being interviewed now." He sat back in his chair and gripped the napkin. "I like you probing me for a change. I've certainly asked you enough questions."

She imagined probing his ribs to make him squirm. Was he as firm there as his upper body? Her cheeks went hot and she scolded herself for having such inappropriate thoughts. "Sorry, just curious."

He paused mid-bite and set the food down. "I moved here five years ago to get out of Rochester. Have you ever been in upstate New York in the winter? Horrible snowstorms, bitter cold for ever and ever. Here in sunny Florida we have hundreds of days of sunshine in a row."

"No, I've not been to Rochester. I'm excited to be snow free this winter."

"Yeah, it's really gorgeous. So why did you move down, other than this irresistible job?"

The rain pelted the window now. "I wanted to move here to be near my best friend. Steph moved down here a few years ago, and then my boyfriend did last spring. It seemed like a good sign to move here too." She rubbed her nose and looked back at him. "The irresistible job was the final straw that made me dump Virginia Beach."

"Well, I'm really glad you did. You are a great fit for this company and my department." He held her gaze a bit too long again and this time she was braver and didn't look away.

They sat like that for what seemed like forever with sparks flying between them until a knock at the door cut the tension. Mike smiled and rolled his eyes. "Duty calls. Come in."

Ronnie tried to hide her excitement by stuffing the sandwich into her mouth and acted busy wiping her hands and face.

"Mike," his secretary, Ceil, poked her nose into the office and looked in wide-eyed. "You have a one o'clock. Just wanted to remind you." She opened the door wider to look at Ronnie. "What's going on in here, why are the lights off?"

Mike stood and flicked them on. "Just a little lunch and a show." He held the door handle and said, "Bye Ceil," and nudged her out as he shut the door. "Damn, is it almost one?"

Ronnie stood and took the tray, holding her drink so it wouldn't spill. "No problem, I'll see you later."

Mike spoke quietly, "Thanks for sharing your time, Ronnie."

His serious look added sincerity and it caught her off guard. "Thank you, Mike." She walked past Ceil who cut her eyes at her over angry eyebrows.

Ronnie spent the rest of her day learning the systems' deep dark secrets from the team. Her mind was exhausted by the time she was finished and there was no more room for new information. She'd have to start on the marketing plan tomorrow when she was fresh.

She checked her phone. Jeffrey texted he was going to take her out to dinner and would be there soon. They had decided last night to order the same food as the night she went back in time to see if that triggered anything. It probably wouldn't, but she wasn't going to turn down another lobster feast.

"Hey, you getting ready to leave?" Mike stood in the doorway.

She wondered how long he'd been standing there. "Soon. Is there anything else I need to do before I go?"

"Just wanted to see if you'd made a decision about the Puerto Rico trip. I need Ceil to make the flight arrangements tomorrow. We're watching the weather carefully with such an active hurricane pattern. I'd hate to be stuck on the island during a storm. As long as it all looks clear we'll be leaving next week before something else comes up."

"Yeah, about that," she said setting her purse on the desk.

He sat on the edge of the desk near her and she scooted the chair back to put a little space between them. Mike was so close she could smell his cologne, it was making her dizzy.

"Um … I'm really not feeling ready to go to Puerto Rico, Mike." God that sounded lame.

"Why not? No one expects you to be an expert on the project yet. You're just there to meet Carlos and get more inside on the scope of the project for the island." He looked worried.

"I know you said that. It isn't my readiness for *that* I'm concerned about." She bit her lip. She hated to disappoint him.

He patiently waited for her to get to the point, a neutral expression on his face.

She shook her head and let out a sigh. "Mike, believe me, I want to rock this job, I'm still a bit of a mess from the storm and not feeling ready to travel." Yeah, that sounded even more lame. "Just something that happened during the storm has me feeling fragile." She could hear her mom's voice in her head scolding her for sharing feelings at work. She should have phrased it differently.

"Sometimes a good hard shove out of your comfort zone cures that." He smiled and crossed his arms over his chest making the fabric at his biceps stretch to outline what was beneath.

Ronnie turned her head, it was too distracting. "I know." She lifted the hair off her neck and leaned back in the chair making a ponytail with her fingers.

"I'll upgrade your flight to first class." His smile grew. "Champagne toast over the Caribbean Sea?"

"Hey," a male voice behind Mike interrupted the nice thought.

Mike stood up and took a step back. "Hello."

Ronnie stood too. "Jeffrey, hey how are you?" If her cheeks weren't already pink they were bright red now. The chair hit the back of the desk awkwardly.

"What's this about champagne toast over the Caribbean?" Jeffrey said an edge of anger in his voice.

"Jeffrey, this is my boss, Mike Walsh. Mike this is Jeffrey Brennan."

Mike held out his hand, "Hello."

Jeffrey shook Mike's hand, pulling him in closer, "I'm her boyfriend."

"Great to meet you, Jeffrey. I've heard a lot about you." Mike stepped toward the door as Jeffrey moved next to Ronnie.

"Right." Jeffrey ignored Mike's pleasantries. "So, what was this intimate moment I interrupted? Champagne being served?"

Mike laughed. "I was trying to entice Ronnie into going on our first business trip by offering to upgrade her to first class. We really need her to help seal the deal in Puerto Rico."

"You have to entice her? Is this for work or pleasure, Mike?" Jeffrey narrowed his eyes.

Ronnie's cheeks grew hot and her anger rose.

"Mostly for work but there will be a little time for enjoying that gorgeous water, I hope. Look I'll let you go. Good first day Ronnie, I'll see you in the morning."

"See you, Mike," Ronnie waved.

Mike left and Ronnie grabbed her purse hoping to sidestep what she knew would be an angry outburst. "Let's go."

Jeffrey tapped his fingers against his leg. Damn, he wasn't happy.

They walked past Ceil's desk and she looked up from her papers with a scowl. But her eyes widened at seeing Jeffrey and her sourpuss softened a bit. "Night."

Ronnie nodded at her and Jeffrey said, "Good night."

Jeffrey leaned in to kiss her but she turned her head. "Not here."

He pulled his hand away. "Why, you afraid Mike will see it?"

"Jesus Jeffrey, he's my boss. Besides, we don't need to be kissing at work. Settle down." Ronnie walked in front of him hoping Ceil didn't hear their exchange.

They got on the elevator with a few other people. Jeffrey looked furious but she tried to calm her nerves. He would lay into her once they were alone.

They walked to the parking lot. "I'll follow you in my car. I'm parked over here." She said heading in that direction.

"I thought you were going to ride with me," he said motioning to his blue Mercedes.

"Nah, it will be easier this way." It would save her the wrath of an angry Jeffrey. She'd seen this before and the best place to receive it was in public, although not at her job.

"Fine." His lips pressed together making them colorless. "I'll pull around here and you can follow me to Del Frisco's."

She got in her car and smacked the steering wheel. "How friggin' dare he talk to Mike like that!" Jeffrey was so infuriating, and always in a new and unexpected way. Why did he always have to rub everyone the wrong way? She started the Thunderbird and the radio clicked on. "...an estimated cost of nearly one billion dollars in damage from Hurricane Charley. This fast and intense storm had peak wind gusts of one hundred and forty-five miles per hour, and reached one hundred and five miles per hour in Orlando, hitting a new record wind speed for our area. The Florida citrus industry is reporting massive losses from this storm and twenty-five out of sixty-seven counties in Florida were declared Federal disaster areas."

Jeffrey honked, waiting for her. She pulled out and followed him to the restaurant with storm fears, or rather time travel fears, swirling around her like the thunderstorm outside of Mike's window this afternoon mixing with her anger toward Jeffrey. She fought back tears. Was he behind her time travel? She had not had any luck at finding Mathias or Jack in any of her searches to help prove she had been back in time. A finger of doubt tapped on her shoulder but she brushed it aside. She wanted to believe Jeffrey, to trust he was as baffled as she was but Steph's resolved added to the equation.

The radio weatherman continued, "Twenty-two deaths were recorded in Florida as a result of Hurricane Charley. Its fourth landfall happened along Long Island as a tropical storm before it finally dissipated. It truly was the storm that wouldn't quit. The Atlantic is setting up nicely to provide more opportunities for future storms. Three tropical waves have formed off the coast of Africa and time will tell how they develop in the days and weeks ahead."

"Three more! Seriously this has to stop!" There was no way another storm would hit here, surely not. It had been sixty years since Hurricane Donna hit Central Florida. Why now? Why when she had just moved to Florida? Ronnie's growing panic caused her to shove aside the anger. Logic kicked down the door of panic and blurted, "It will not develop or steer into Florida again." She took a deep breath and blew it out, switching the station to anything but more horrible weather news. Smashmouth was on and she tried to get lost in the music.

Chapter 9 – Dinner with a Side of Jealously

Ronnie pulled into Del Frisco's parking lot and gripped the steering wheel. This would not be enjoyable. Jeffrey would tear into her about Mike. Hopefully, he would have calmed down a tad during the drive. She closed her eyes and tried to push away the anger. He could be so infuriating.

Tap, tap. Ronnie was startled out of a calming deep breath.

Jeffrey peeked in. "Hey, did you fall asleep at the wheel?"

"Hmmm," she answered, not wanting to leave the car's sanctuary. At least the meal would be nice.

They sat at a quiet table in the back and ordered drinks. Jeffrey's face took on a pinkish hue and he squinted at her. He was pissed.

As soon as the waiter left he picked up where they'd left off. "I'm really trying to wrap my head around this thing with Mike." His arms crossed and he leaned back in the chair.

"What thing with Mike?" She kept a neutral tone, despite the anger welling up inside.

He waved his hand around like he was swatting flies, "This whole romantic island getaway thing."

"Ha, you have a very active imagination, Jeffrey. I have to go to Puerto Rico for work. You really need to get a grip on this jealousy thing. It isn't becoming."

"Right, you can play it off as me being jealous, but the reality is that the two of you are attracted to each other."

"He was grilling me about my resistance about going to Puerto Rico. It was nothing more." She said it with confidence, but she knew he was right. Mike had shown his hand today, there was definitely something brewing between them.

Jeffrey shook his head. "No that is not what I saw. Look, just be careful around him. I don't like the way he looks at you."

"Maybe you don't need to come to my job anymore, Jeffrey. I don't appreciate you talking down to my boss and embarrassing me like that." Ronnie forced her face to stay neutral.

"Look I reacted like any guy would with some meathead cornering you like that. Why was he standing so close?"

Ronnie crossed her arms and looked away, hushing the Police song that popped into her head. "Just don't come to work anymore, Jeffrey. I'm on the job one day and you've already been rude to my boss. This isn't going to continue."

"I come in to find this guy all over you and I can't even say anything about it? Now you don't want me to come into your work?" He slammed his hand on the table. "Jesus Christ, Ronnie."

She flinched. "I don't want you at work because you're jeopardizing my job. You were so rude, Jeffrey. How is that okay?" Her stomach was doing flips now. Couldn't they just have a pleasant meal?

"You are not going to Puerto Rico with him." He leaned forward closing the distance between them. "Are you?"

"I will at some point. I'm not sure if I'm up for that yet. I don't even know the job well enough to present it." The swirl of anger duked it out with the panic welling up in her chest to make a turmoil of bad juju.

"Good." His angry expression dampened a bit.

"It completely stresses me out. He says it's just to meet the client but what if I screw it up? I mean I can't even speak in complete sentences about what they do yet. How can I present to a room full of strangers?" Another layer of stress choked out the panic, punched the fear in the face, and all three pulled her down to nearly crying.

"Tell him you can't go." Jeffrey leaned back in his chair.

Ronnie played with the straw in her iced tea until she was sure she could speak without revealing her emotions. "I already did, that is why he was offering first class tickets." She looked directly at him and felt a wave of strength again. "I've been through too much to deal with extra pressure right now. Can you back off a little? I need to decide based on what is best for me, not you. Not Mike."

"Just be careful around him. I don't trust his intentions." He shook his head and twisted his mouth.

"Why does that matter, Jeffrey. Don't you trust mine?" She had never given him reason to question her loyalty. Despite her attraction to Mike, it was not in her nature to cheat. They had too much to just throw it away for a quick fling.

"Look at him, Ronnie. He's built, he's your boss in a position of control, and he's probably a player. He has that *GQ get any girl you want* look about him."

"And that threatens you? That is not my issue then, it's yours." She crossed her arms.

"Ronnie, it's our issue. If he comes between us." His tone softened and he reached out to touch her fingers that clutched the iced tea. She did not yield.

"I'm loyal, Jeffrey. If you don't know that by now, then why am I even wasting my breath on this?" She pulled her hand away. "And by making such a big deal … it's you that is coming between us, not Mike. He has been nothing but a gentleman."

"A wolf in gentleman's clothing." Jeffrey crossed his arms and made his lips colorless again.

"He is not a wolf. Steph says he hasn't dated anyone in years, despite the ladies throwing themselves at him."

"How does she know?" He squinted skeptically.

"Steph works there too, remember. She's in a different building. I think you're making too much of this. Really." As if on cue her phone buzzed and she glanced at the text from her asking to join her at Mimi's with her brother Ian, a much more appealing dinner.

The rest of the meal Jeffery was cordial but Ronnie could tell his mind was still stuck on it. His mannerisms were the usual confidence erring on the side of arrogance. Ronnie relived the interactions with Mike during the day. He did look like a player, that had been her first thought too.

As Jeffrey talked about storms and weather, Ronnie wondered what it would be like with Mike. Would he be jealous of other men? Would he make her best friend overly suspicious? He hadn't so far. In fact, Steph really liked Mike.

"Babe." Jeffrey was waiting for a response.

She sat up and cleared her mind. "Sorry, I was spacing out. What did you say?"

He shook his head and twisted his mouth. "I said I'm sorry. I didn't mean to act like an ass earlier. I just love you and don't want anything to happen to us." He leaned forward and gently placed a gold foil wrapped box in front of her plate.

"What's this?" She lifted the box and shook it.

Jeffrey smiled brilliantly. "You'll see. It goes with the déjà vu meal."

The paper was the same as the night of her birthday and so was the box. "What have you done babe?" She tore through the wrapping and opened the container. It was the watch he'd given her on that fateful night. A rose gold replica of the one she and Steph had seen in London.

"What the hell?" Ronnie's jaw dropped. Mathias had the watch still. It had not come back to Florida with her. Or had it?

"I found it in the lab, babe. It was in the toilet trap. It must have slipped off your wrist and fallen in the toilet." His smile said it all. She was forgiven for losing likely the most expensive gift she'd ever gotten.

"In the toilet?" Ronnie imagined the sterile bathroom in Jeffrey's lab. There was nowhere else the watch could have hidden. All that was in there was the sink and toilet. The watch had been in her hand, it was possible she dropped it when she came back.

"Babe, I had it professionally cleaned, don't worry." He left his seat and helped her put it on her wrist, just like he had the first time. "I promise it's germ free."

Ronnie kissed him, her mind spinning with the joy of finding the watch mixing with the disconnected feeling it gave her. The last time she saw that watch was in Mathias' hands.

Chapter 10 - Scots and Tots

Wednesday, August 18

Stephanie McKay looked around the baggage claim area. Her brother was here somewhere. His plane had been delayed and he was probably not in a fine mood after jumping the pond to come see her.

"Ian!" She called out to her younger sibling. A lean man in a black T-shirt and blonde hair turned around and she realized it wasn't him. Another man with a buzz cut and tattoos was leaning over to grab his bag. Nope. Too muscular. She'd not seen him since she went home with Ronnie in June. Mum had packed him up and shipped him off to stay with her, to straighten him out.

Someone hugged her from behind. Scared near to death, she struggled for a second and realized it was Ian.

"Lass, I got ye and I'm no gonna let you go." It was the game they played as kids. She had to say the magic word and he'd let her free.

"Ian McKay, let me go!" Steph struggled against his grip that pinned her arms down to her sides. He knew it drove her to distraction.

"No until you gie me the werd," he said in his thick brogue.

"Keysies!" she said between her teeth. Did he have to start with this nonsense?

"There's a good lass," he said and turned her around. "Look at ye, your hair is straight as a pin!"

Steph touched her hair and smoothed it down. "Yes, my hairdresser insisted on something new." She usually wore it curly but had left it this way for the day.

"It suits ye. You're stunning Stephanie, really ye are." He said holding her hands and looking her up and down.

"Oh stop, ya wee charmer." Ian McKay was an expert in making a woman feel attractive.

"Nah, I mean it. You must be getting laid because you look all glowy and pinkish," he said touching her cheek.

"Gie me a hug, Ian. It's so good to see you. I've missed you" The irritation melted away. They'd been so close as kids and barely kept in touch now that she'd moved away and he was grown.

He smiled and obliged. "A right reunion here in the baggage claim. Let me get my bag and we'll go fetch some American food. I'm starving to death. They barely fed me on that flight."

"Ian, you've not changed a bit. You're always starving. I hope mum sent money for the market so I can feed you."

"I guess you're right. I do have a new tattoo though, did you notice?" He said holding up his right arm and pushing up the sleeve. It was covered from elbow to wrist with a naked woman, legs spread wide on a motorcycle, nothing left to the imagination.

"Jesus, Ian, did you give up on getting a proper job. That's a bit graphic don't you think?" she said, not wanting to scold him but it was shocking.

"Ooocchhh, no, you sound like mum. I'll just wear long sleeves if I need to fancy up." He pulled the sleeve down to cover the revulsion.

"Not in Florida you won't. It's hot here." Steph shook her head. Why was he such a huge man child?

"Well, it's no like I'm gonna be a banker or a schoolmarm." He stepped between two men and grabbed his duffle bag off the baggage wheel. "Plus, she comes in handy when I'm…" He made a rude gesture and laughed.

Steph smacked his arm. "Ian Brian McKay, that's enough out of you!"

He held out his carryon bag. She took it and slung it over her shoulder and they made their way through the crowd toward the elevator to the parking garage. They rode up to the third floor enjoying the view of trees and flowers. The back half of the elevator was glass and it looked out onto the drop off area in front of the airport.

"Brilliant. Ah, it's jest brilliant, look at all of the wee flowers." He followed her off the elevator and they walked down to the car. "Bloody hell it's like an oven. Hold this." He handed her the suitcase and peeled off his sweatshirt, revealing the Celtic football jersey's green and white stripes.

She handed the bag back to him. "Thanks, what are ye driving now, Stephanie?"

"A Jeep Liberty." She popped the trunk and he loaded the bags.

"So that American food I was requesting. You have any ideas about where we should go?"

Steph put the car in reverse but paused. "What are you in the mood for, we can go anywhere you like."

"Hamburgers and Guinness, that's what I've been craving since I found out I was coming here."

"I found this new place last week, I'll take you there. Let me see if Ronnie can meet us. You remember her?" She pulled out her phone and sent a quick text. They backed out of the parking spot.

"Oh God yes, she's such an American Dream. I'd love to get her in the sack."

"Ian, she has a boyfriend. Plus, she has taste, she'd never go for a guy with a porno on his arm." Steph laughed and tried to push the image of the tattoo out of her head.

"Harsh, Stephanie," he said good-naturedly. "I think every woman wants the bad boy at least once in her life. I'm just here to make her dreams come true."

"Right, keep telling yourself that, baby brother. Someday it'll get you a wife."

They both got caught up on all the family happenings and events going on in Scotland. It made her homesick but at least she had a piece of home with Ian in her car. They pulled up into Mimi's parking lot and Steph looked at her phone. Ronnie had answered she was out to dinner with Jeffrey, and not particularly enjoying it.

"Damn, Ronnie can't come."

"Why not, she's no afraid of me is she?" Ian asked.

"Out to dinner with her *boyfriend*." She said the last word mockingly.

"Oh, that sounds like a story there, Stephanie. You don't like her boyfriend, do you?" Ian said as they walked into the restaurant.

"No, I don't." She wasn't sure how much to tell him. Ronnie probably didn't want her sharing her strange story with Ian. The hostess showed them to a table and they sat down and gave the waitress their drink order.

"I don't trust Jeffrey." Steph took a sip of her Coke and eyed her baby brother. His cheekbones showed more distinct edges than he'd had this summer. Was he thinner? Or just growing out of that baby face he'd always had?

"Why do you say that?" Ian sipped the root beer Steph switched when he was in the rest room. "Have ye got any reason to doubt him?" Then he scowled. "This is nae Guinness?"

Steph smiled, "Ian, it's root beer."

"What crap. Why dinnae you at least order me an Irna Bru?"

"Because that pish is only in Scotland, wee man." Steph shook her head. Irna Bru was the Scottish soft drink and one of a kind. "According to Ronnie, no. According to my gut, he's a sneaky lying sack of ..." She shook her head. "I can't really put my finger on it. I know that when she was in Scotland in June a few of our co-workers saw him out on a date in town here with another woman."

"Oh, seriously? How do you know it was a date?" He leaned forward on his elbows, the true Scot eager for gossip.

"Well, that's what Ronnie said. Jeffrey is smart and always talks her out of every situation. He told her it was an interviewee for a job at the lab. Another man did meet them later but from what my friends said they were really chummy before the other guy showed up." She sat back in the chair and thought of the twenty other red flags she'd felt about Jeffrey, most of which she had mentioned to Ronnie, but all were met with resistance.

Steph's best friend never believed her though. Jeffrey was a master manipulator and was seamless in his lies. Truth be told she was too nice, too kindhearted to think anything bad about Jeffrey. The woman had always been too trusting, even when she made new friends, she'd give them her whole heart whether they deserved it or not. In some areas that wasn't such a bad quality. It was why they became such fast friends when they'd met years ago in Virginia Beach.

"Maybe that's all it was, Stephanie, you're a suspicious woman. I've known you to instantly dislike a few of my friends as well." He leaned forward but she realized he was looking around her.

Steph turned around to see a woman in a short skirt sitting at the bar. Her long legs made longer with four-inch red heels to match her lipstick. "Yes, and ole Mick ended up at Barlinnie, didn't he?"

"Well, as a matter of fact, he's still in the clink." Ian lifted his root beer and took a swig, leaving a moustache behind. He licked it and eyed the leggy gal behind her, making it look like he was licking his lips over her, which he very well might have been.

"I've got a sixth sense about people Ian, you know that. I'm always right," she said. "Despite Ronnie not listening. Sooner or later he'll show her enough for her to realize what he is. I think she's getting close to coming around. Something weird happened during the hurricane. I can't explain it now since I'm not sure Ronnie would want me to, but he's bamboozled her into thinking he's not involved and my hands are tied. I can't push it with her because she gets so mad at me and then won't listen at all."

"Och lass, I'm eager to meet this prick. Maybe I can help your cause. It has to be juicy for you to be so worked up."

The waitress took their order. They caught up on friends and family news until the entrees arrived. She snitched a few of his French fries and they talked about old times.

A man walked toward her and stopped and pointed. "Hey, I know you. You work with Mike Walsh, don't you?"

She recognized his handsome face. "Yeah, you're Billy, right? We met here with Mike. I'm Steph."

"Oh yeah, I remember now. Ronnie's friend," Billy said.

Ian cleared his throat.

"Oh, and this is my brother, Ian. Ian this is Billy."

Ian held out his hand, "My pleasure, Billy."

"Billy Nemish, great to meet you. Hey Steph, where's Ronnie?" Billy beamed.

"That's what I keep asking her," Ian said. "She needs to be here." He patted the seat next to him. "Having a beer with us."

"Billy, you want to join us?" Steph offered.

Billy looked from Steph to Ian. "You sure you don't mind? I'm just here for dinner and will head home soon."

"Not a bit. You alone?" Steph asked.

"Just stopped in after dinner to see my favorite waitresses. Mike is over there." He pointed to the bar. The high-heeled chick was talking to Mike, and he looked over at them uncomfortably. Billy waved him over. "They kind of keep asking me to come back."

"Must be a good tipper," Steph said.

"Something like that." He smiled and rubbed his chin. "Hey Mike, look who is here."

Mike approached the table holding a beer and smiled as he saw her. "Hello Steph, great to see you." He looked at Ian and held out his hand. "Hi, I'm Mike Walsh."

"This is my brother Ian, he just came in from Glasgow." Ian stood up and shook Mike's hand. "Aye, ye grow 'em big here in the states, don't ya?" He looked from Billy to Mike who both towered over him. "Lads, join us for a pint, we're just getting our supper now."

"Sure, that'd be great," Mike nodded toward the red heels. "Better than what Billy has planned for me." Steph scooted over and let Mike sit next to her.

"Buzzkill. That's what I'm going to call you." Billy said as he sat next to Ian. "So, you're here from Scotland? Just to see your sis, or are you moving here for good?"

"Oh, we'll see. I'm enjoying the American women for now. They may convince me to stay with the skimpy clothes they wear here. Hotties everywhere."

Steph shook her head. "Really? Well, you're not staying here unless you can find a job and with that disgrace on your arm it's going to be hard."

"It's going to be hard all right, eh boys?" Ian held out his arm to show off the tattoo.

"Whoa, dude, that is hot as hell." Billy took Ian's arm and turned it so he could get a better look.

Mike looked away. "Wow, that's a statement piece, eh?" He widened his eyes.

"Yeah, I'm sure mum about died when she saw that on her own flesh and blood." Billy laughed and Ian sat back. "Yeah. Well, I didn't get it for me mum, Steph."

"You got it for your own pleasure, eh?" Billy laughed getting another look at the tattoo. Should have put it on your left arm man. Unless you're left handed."

"Exactly. I'm a lefty. Hey look at this, the tattoo artist is brilliant." Ian wiggled his fingers and the muscles on his forearm moved making the naked lady's crotch and stomach twitch.

"Oh my God, Ian! Stop that!" Steph smacked his arm. "You're a disgusting man."

Billy laughed a booming laugh and wiped his eyes. "Holy shit man that's the best tat I've ever seen." He tapped Mike's arm. "Dude, did you see that?"

"Oh yeah. I saw," Mike said. "My condolences Steph. How long is your brother staying? And please tell me he's not staying with you?"

"Thank you, Mike, I'm glad you're the gentleman here. Unfortunately, the clothead is staying with me and we have no determined departure date. I'm thinking as soon as possible."

Mike's eyebrows rose and he shook his head. "Where's Ronnie tonight?"

"She's out with Jeffrey."

"Her *boyfriend*." Ian mimicked her tone from earlier in the car.

Billy took the bait. "What is that about?"

"Oh, ye know. The guy is a ..." Ian said but was cut short when Steph kicked him under the table.

Steph followed up the kick, "Did I mention Mike is Ronnie's boss? Let's just say Jeffrey's not my favorite person."

"Steph," Billy chimed in. "Please enlighten us on the ways of Ronnie's boyfriend."

"He's a piece of shiet," Ian chimed in, "A bloody cheater, and a fucking untrustworthy cunt."

"For God's sake Ian, can't you keep your mouth shut?" Steph's cheeks turned pink. She really needed to get her brother under control. People here didn't use the same filthy language as they did in Glasgow.

Billy and Mike exchanged glances.

"What's that look?" Steph asked Mike.

"No look. Just that I had the pleasure of meeting Jeffrey today," he said, hiding a smile behind the beer he tipped for a sip.

"Get out, you didn't tell me that. Where?" Billy leaned forward.

"At the office. He stopped by to pick her up." Mike's expression was neutral.

"And..." Steph said. "What did you think of him?"

"Oh, nice enough." He coughed. "Ummmhummm. So how about those Buffalo Bills?"

"No, no, no." Billy tapped his hand. "Don't you change the subject! Inquiring minds want to know about this Jeffrey guy."

Mike sat back and put his hands up in self-defense. "He's fine. Nothing to tell really. Only he was rather pissed at me for some reason. Barked on about how she was his girl and I was only her boss." He shook his head and a small smile crossed his mouth. "Kind of funny really, we were just talking about ..."

"About what?" Billy prodded when Mike paused.

"Champagne and first class flights to the islands." Mike laughed. Billy high-fived him.

Steph laughed. "Seriously?"

"It was completely innocent though, but he walked in on us and I believe that's what he overheard, so naturally he jumped to conclusions. I'm sure she got an earful when they left. The man was about to bust a gut."

Ian shook his head. "I love it. I need to meet this guy."

"No Ian, you're not sticking your big nose in the middle of this. You will stay out of Ronnie's business. I feel bad we're all talking about her and she's not here to defend herself."

The waitress stopped by interrupting them. "Billy." She smiled coyly. "Hi, you want the usual?"

"Yes, darling, please," he said.

"I'll take a bourbon on the rocks and the steak," Mike said.

Billy stared at the extra wiggle the waitress added to her walk as she headed toward the bar. Ian leaned way over to watch as well.

"She has the finest ass," Billy said. "Oh, I'm sorry Steph. I didn't mean to be rude."

"Ooch, you're not telling a lie though," Ian chirped. "She has a stellar ass." Ian then pretended to fill his hands with it and squeeze.

Steph rolled her eyes and got a look of sympathy from Mike.

"Billy, I think you've met your soulmate," Mike said.

Billy and Ian looked toward the bar where the waitress waved at them. "Not her you idiot, him." Mike nodded at Ian.

Steph laughed so hard tears streamed down her face. Ian and Billy high-fived.

"My soulmate man. My American stud," Ian said.

Billy grabbed Ian and leaned him back in the booth, pretending to kiss him. Ian shoved his elbow in Billy's face, blocking the attempt. Upon noticing the tattoo, Billy stuck out his tongue and pretended to lick it.

"Oh my God!" Steph wiped her eyes, "Mike I think you hit the nail on the head. They're peas and carrots."

Mike shook his head. "Damn, does the world really need two of them?"

The food arrived and Ian and Billy carried on, talking about their conquests and Steph and Mike endured the conversation while they ate.

"I didn't know they served tater tots." Steph nodded at Billy's plate.

"Oh yeah." He looked sheepish. "Sheila likes to give me a little something special to help me remember ..."

"There is a story there, come on big man, tell us," Ian said.

Billy looked at Steph. "I can't really with a lady present."

"She's no lady, she's my sister," Ian said. "Whisper in my ear."

Steph shook her head, "Go on, don't let him winge over it."

Billy cupped his hand over Ian's ear. Ian's eyes got wide and he laughed showing slightly crooked front teeth. "Her nipples?" Ian picked up a tater tot and held it between his fingers examining it and then put it up to his chest. "Holy mother of God, man!"

Mike leaned his head back and looked at the ceiling. "Billy come on, have some decency."

"A work of art Mike." Billy grinned and avoided eye contact with Steph.

Mike shook his head and turned to Steph, "Is Ronnie going to be okay ... with Jeffrey I mean? He won't ... do anything? Will he?"

Steph sat back against the booth. Mike *freaking* Walsh was into Ronnie. She let that soak in. A guy who had never dated anyone in years, at least at the office, was into Ronnie.

"Define *do anything*. He won't hurt her if that's what you mean unless you count dying a slow painful death in a relationship with that guy," Steph said as she matched Mike's pained expression.

"Just tell me she'll be okay. I can't stand the thought of ..." Mike looked away and shook his head.

"Of what, Mike?" Steph asked. Mike was revealing a lot about how he felt. What a shocker.

He looked away and rubbed his chin. "Nothing."

Steph marveled at this new information. How would Ronnie handle his attention? Was she so wrapped up in Jeffrey that she wouldn't take a chance on Mike?

"Yo Mike, we need to get going, man," Billy said tapping his arm but changed tact on seeing his expression, "Dude, what's wrong? You look like your dog died," Billy said, gripping Mike's muscular forearm.

"Don't bring up Sparky again. I'm gonna cry, Billy." Mike wiped away a fake tear and glanced at Steph.

Billy stretched, looking around the bar. "Where is that hot waitress when you need her?" Then he focused on Mike. "Dude ..."

"What?" Mike said, turning toward Billy.

"Oh my God. I know what's bugging you." Billy eyed Steph.

"What?" Ian said, butting in. "Tell us."

"No, Mike will get mad at me. It's personal. He thinks I have no boundaries."

"You don't man, zero boundaries." Mike leaned back in the booth and lifted his chin toward Billy. "This one here is an open book and has a bit of trouble realizing not everyone wants their private thoughts out in the world."

"Maybe. You'd love to find out more about Jeffrey, wouldn't you?"

Mike shook his head. "No Billy, don't."

Ian sat up and looked from Mike to Billy. "I want to as well, mates. It is my personal mission to get more dirt on that skeeving bastard."

Everyone looked at Ian. "Whoa, brother, check you out." Billy chimed in first. Mike smirked.

"Why do you feel so strongly, Ian?" Steph asked.

"Ronnie is one of the finest people I know. And by fine," he cupped his hands over his mouth, "I mean...have you seen her ass? She puts this waitress to shame."

Steph smacked his arm. "Stop that Ian. She's my best friend."

"I know, Steph. Why should she have to put up with cuntface Jeffrey?"

Steph shook her head. "Ian, people don't use that word here. You have to stop that."

"What? They don't call him Jeffrey?" He mocked ignorance. "Look, Ronnie is a sweet lass, she deserves better than a cheating conniving man. I'm going to make it my pet project to find a way to get Ronnie to see what he really is."

"Oh Lordy, help us all." Steph shook her head.

"Hey man, you have to let us know how that turns out. Okay? We want the best for Ronnie too. She seems like a nice chick." Billy picked up his beer and finished it and waved the waitress over. They paid the checks and all stood to leave and said their goodbyes.

"Goodnight soulmate," Ian said to Billy who gave him a side hug.

Billy laughed. "Be over later, we can spoon."

"Goodnight you two." Mike shook his head. "Later man, you can spoon the little Scotsman, I'm heading home to bed."

"Mike don't be jealous, I'll come to your house when we're done." Billy's infectious laugh boomed as the two men walked out of Mimi's. Steph and Ian followed them out.

"How exactly are you going to find out anything on Jeffrey?" Steph asked once back in the car, curious what the little devil had in mind.

"I dinna ken. But I'll find a wee crack in his armor and find a way inside to muck about."

It was nice to finally have someone, well several actually, on her side about Jeffrey. Mike had really surprised her by showing his hand about Ronnie. He saw something dangerous in Jeffrey too, and that was on first meeting, which spoke volumes of Mike's people reading skills.

"Well, you be careful with that plan, Ian. Jeffrey isn't someone to let you do anything to him that he doesn't allow. He is a formidable opponent." She started the engine.

"Formidable? Listen to you. What the hell does that mean, Stephanie? What are you a lawyer?"

"Ya dumbass, you should've stayed in school." She shoved his shoulder and he dramatically leaned away. "Let's get home I'm knackered."

Chapter 11 - Rabbit Ears

Over the next week, Ronnie settled into her new position. Her efforts to find more information on the people from the past were hampered by storm damage to the local library and a general lack of records from eighteenth-century England. As time passed the grip of the horrible experiences began to release and she was finally sleeping more soundly and Florida felt much more like home.

Friday, August 27

She spent most of the afternoon in conference with her realtor and finally after signing nearly a ream of papers, she was the official owner of a beautiful three-bedroom house in Winter Park, Florida, only minutes from work and Steph. Gripping the keys in her hand she texted Steph that she was heading to the house.

Ronnie pulled into the driveway with her heart beating a million miles an hour. She'd never owned a house before. Jeffrey had convinced her that with the way the Florida housing market was going it would be a great investment. She had a small inheritance from her father's life insurance when he had passed away in 1999 and it was the perfect use of the money. He would have been happy she was using it on something so important.

Steph was certain Jeffrey was pushing her into owning a home so she wouldn't just move back to Virginia, or move in with him. It didn't matter, she was just happy to have her own place. For once she could do whatever she wanted with it.

Ronnie walked into the house and carefully shut the door. "Wooo-hooooo!" She let lose all the pent-up excitement from the hours of boring paperwork. Slowly she walked through the house, making a mental note of what changes she'd like to make.

When she was in the master bathroom the doorbell rang. She opened the door to Steph's smiling face. "Welcome to my new home!"

"Oooh, it's lovely!" Steph walked in and looked around. "This room is bigger than I remembered!"

The front living room had hardwood floors and a large picture window with a brick fireplace. "Give me a tour," Steph said, looking around eagerly. "Oh, but first open my gifty." She handed Ronnie a gift bag with blue and green paper.

"How nice, thank you Steph." Ronnie hugged her friend. "What's it for?"

"Housewarming of course." Steph tapped on the bag. "Open it."

"How fun." Ronnie reached in and let the paper fall to the floor. She pulled out a TV antenna.

"I have the rest in the car!" Steph pointed to the driveway.

"Rabbit ears?"

"Sweetie I got you a TV that can be plugged into your car or it can run on batteries. It needs the rabbit ears in case you're not hooked up to cable."

"Wow, that is so awesome! Thank you!" She hugged Steph and set the rabbit ears on the window ledge.

"How did the closing go?" Steph asked.

"It was fine. You can see they didn't clean it like they said they would." Ronnie waved her hand around showing the piles of dirt as if someone had started to clean and left their swept piles together. "But other than that, it was easy enough."

"What a great gift. The cable company said it would take another two weeks before they could hook it up because of Hurricane Charley. They're working on current customer repairs first."

"That's what I was afraid of, and why I got this!" Steph said, setting her purse down.

Ronnie gave her a quick tour showing off the three bedrooms, two baths, and the overgrown back yard.

"I love the layout, it's so open and so much light in the back room," Steph beamed.

They set up the TV and messed with the rabbit ears to get the local news. Steph grabbed a broom, dustpan, and cleaning supplies out of her car that Ronnie had asked her to bring over. They made small talk and worked their way through the house wiping and sweeping as they chatted about everything. When they stopped to take a break, they turned up the small black and white TV to hear the news.

"So, how's it going with your brother?"

Steph shook her head. "He's a hot mess, Ronnie. You won't believe the new tattoo he got." They sat on the floor Indian style near the TV.

"What's the tattoo?"

"Oh God, Ronnie, this stupid pornographic tattoo pretty much defines Ian." Steph shook her head.

"So ..."

"It's a naked woman on a motorcycle." Steph spread her legs demonstrating the position of the figure on Ian's arm.

"No! You've got to be kidding. That's ..." She shook her head trying to picture it. "What an ass."

"I know, I can only imagine what my parents said. It's no wonder they've sent him here to me. God help us, Ronnie, he's going to be trouble. He's home alone now, but as soon as he finds a bar within walking distance he'll be boozing it up again."

"Steph, I'm sorry. We should get back to work, it's going to be a while before we can be done. Did you see the bathrooms?"

"Right, very gross." Steph scrunched up her nose.

They continued to clean until the weather segment came on the TV. Ronnie stopped and waited for the weatherman to get to the point.

Steph must have seen the panic in her expression. "Don't worry Ronnie. If a storm does hit you can just go back to your mom's. You don't have to stay here."

"True." Ronnie's heart lightened. "Maybe I should head to Puerto Rico with Mike. He's pushing it hard."

"How hard, Ronnie?" Steph wagged her eyebrows.

"Ha, no not like that. He just wants me to go on the trip to meet our biggest client."

"What do you think of Mike?" Steph asked.

Ronnie remembered the excitement when she first saw him this morning. "I like him."

Steph smiled. "I knew you would. He's a good guy Ronnie. Doesn't hurt a bit he's a strappin' lad, eh?" She put on a thick brogue for effect.

"Doesn't hurt at all. Plus, he's a good guy," Ronnie said, her cheeks blushing a bit.

"Good guy is short for great butt, right?" Steph said and gracefully took the smack from Ronnie. "It did not fail to impress, Ronnie, you have to give me that one thing."

"Nope, you can't put words in my mouth. I didn't even look at his butt." This was a lie, his butt was fantastic, but she didn't want Steph to think she had the hots for her new boss.

"Lies! You're just being a good girl for now. Just you wait. Monday morning you won't be able to keep your eyes off it, if only because I've mentioned it."

Ronnie shook her head. "Nope," she held up two fingers in the Girl Scout pledge, "I solemnly swear I will not look at Mike Walsh's butt."

Steph laughed. "It will be impossible to not take at least one peek."

The weatherman came back on the screen. Dramatic music played that went along with the severe weather segments. "Breaking news. The National Hurricane Center has just upgraded Hurricane Frances to a Category Three storm and it is expected to continue to strengthen over the next few days."

Ronnie's heart nearly stopped. "What, you're kidding me!"

Steph set the broom down and walked over to the TV.

Terry James continued, "It began as a tropical wave off the coast of Africa on August twenty-first, one of a stream of storms brewing in the Atlantic. On August twenty-fourth, the wave intensified to tropical storm status and got its name." A graphic on the screen showed the path of Frances in the Atlantic Ocean. "Within forty-eight hours it strengthened significantly to a hurricane and by today wind speeds reached one hundred and thirty-five miles per hour."

"Steph, I have a bad feeling about this storm." Ronnie's panic rose. "It looks like it's heading right here."

"I know they all look like they're heading here at this stage." Steph squeezed her arm. "There's a lot of real estate between us and the storm, a lot of winds to steer it away."

The news anchor's face was deadly serious now, the giddy storm reporter from Hurricane Charley was tempered with the amount of damage it had laid at their feet. "Two new storms have reached tropical storm strength—Gaston and Hermine." The map of the Atlantic was littered with swirling masses in every stage of development. "We will be watching them closely. Already so far, this active hurricane season we've seen the storms Alex, Bonnie, Charley, Earl, and Danielle. Reaching hurricane status were Alex, Charley, Danielle, and now Frances. Stay up-to-date with the latest on the tropics right here on Channel Thirteen News."

Ronnie sat down, her stomach in knots. "Steph, what the hell is going on? How can this …" tears welled in her eyes and an overwhelming feeling of panic spread through every last nerve. She could not be here for another storm.

"Ronnie, really just don't even think about it. We're fine here, there is just no way another hurricane is going to hit us again." Steph knelt down and put an arm around her. "Don't panic, you will be okay, I promise."

Chapter 12 - Waylaid

Thursday, September 2, 7:30 a.m.

Ronnie lifted the receiver of the phone. Steph's voice was higher than usual. "Did you watch the news?"

She turned on the TV Steph had given her and adjusted the rabbit ears. "What is going on, Steph?" It was very unusual for her friend to call this early.

"Two things. First, last night Jeb Bush declared a State of Emergency for Florida."

"Crap." Ronnie's heart ticked a few beats faster.

"Frances is now a Category Four storm. Ronnie, that means the winds are one hundred thirty in speed or higher and they're expecting it to be a Category Five tomorrow." The panic in Steph's voice was palpable and it transferred to Ronnie instantly.

"Steph, this is exactly what I was afraid of, how can this be happening again?" She knew Hurricane Andrew was the last storm to hit as a Category five and it had decimated the area.

"It's as big as Texas and it's going to hit all of Florida. It's just a matter of where it makes landfall and hits the hardest. You need to head to your mother's Ronnie. Can you leave today?"

Ronnie ticked through everything she had to do to leave. "I have to go to work, I need to back up all of my work files and ..."

"And what?" Steph asked.

"I'll have to get my house ready for the storm. I need to ..." She stopped to listen to the weatherman. They were showing the cone of uncertainty. "Steph, it covers all of Florida, you're right!"

"Ronnie. Get to work and you can prep your house tonight. You should still have time to leave if you go early tomorrow morning." Steph's voice held a tone she'd not heard before.

"I cannot be here!" Ronnie's legs shook as she stood up. "I'll get going now."

Ronnie rushed off to work and made all the storm preparations outlined in the company e-mail. Around four she knocked on Mike's door.

He looked up from the stack of papers on his desk. "Hey Ronnie, are you taking off?"

"Yes, I'm going to my mom's in Virginia. I'll be back after the storm." She was hoping he'd not be mad about leaving the state with no definite date of returning. Part of her thought she may not have the nerve to return to Florida if she settled into the safety of her childhood home and her mom's protection.

"I don't blame you. Have a safe drive and think about us stiffs down here." He smiled making that crinkle around his eyes that usually melted her. Now she was numb. She forced a smile. "I'll call you when I know more about when I'll be back."

"Sure, be safe and I'll see you when you return." He nodded and turned to his computer.

Ronnie rushed home fighting major traffic. Everyone was hurrying around getting gas, buying water and groceries. She passed the Home Depot. The parking lot was completely full and she wondered if Jeffrey was stuck in there. He said he would help secure the roof.

Rushing in the door to her house she dug around in the guest room closet for her suitcase and finding the biggest one she owned dragged it into the master bedroom, flinging it on the bed. She shoved three-day's worth of clothes, her bathing suit, and goggles, Fluffy's food, and other things she would need. Her mind was spinning. Did she have enough gas? Could she find a hotel that took pets on short notice? Would her house be okay during the storm? It was a twelve-hour drive. She'd make it home by tomorrow night if there wasn't too much traffic.

Her cell phone's text tone startled her. Jeffrey's message informed her that he was heading over with dinner. Ronnie busied herself with the packing and watching the doomsday weather reports until the doorbell rang. A mixture of dread and excitement hit her. He always did that to her. Jeffrey was exciting to be around but could be so volatile. She didn't know if he'd be mad about her decision to leave town in the morning.

Jeffrey burst into the foyer, kissed her cheek and then pushed past her setting several bags down on the couch. "Okay, I've got the roof clips. Where's the attic entrance?"

"In the garage. Did you bring dinner too?" she asked.

"Yes. Can I just park in the garage? It'll be easier than bringing everything in," he said. "Can you put these away?" He nodded to the grocery bags.

"Sure, no problem."

He buzzed toward the garage and opened the door to find Ronnie's car in its usual spot. "Why don't you move your car so I can back mine up here and you should get your window's taped and clear off anything on the back patio."

"You don't need my help out here?" she asked.

"No, I'd rather you get those things done so we can eat dinner and be ready for the storm." He jingled his keys as if that would speed her along.

"Okay." Ronnie backed her car out of the garage. Jeffrey was waiting in his car and backed his Mercedes into the garage after she pulled out. She parked in the driveway and made her way through the garage. His trunk was opened and a large object sat under a tarp.

"What's that?" She pointed at the cover.

He stood between her and the car. "It's something I have to take into work when I'm done here. Just some weather monitoring equipment." He glanced back. "Okay, you better get busy since we have a lot to do before dinner."

"I'll get right to it." She thought it was a bit strange he didn't want her to see, though he probably didn't want her asking a bunch of stupid questions.

Ronnie ticked off in her head what she needed to do and got busy, first moving the few plants she'd brought from Virginia, dragging the patio table and chairs into the small shed out back. She wanted to put them in the garage but with Jeffrey's car and the boxes along the wall, there wasn't much room. When she was finished, she packed up her toiletries.

At least she'd be with her mother and hopefully not have any severe weather in Virginia Beach. If safely in her mother's house the time travel couldn't happen, could it? No storm, no traveling. She peeled her clothes off and jumped into the shower. It hadn't happened since.

Ronnie tilted her head back and let the steamy water run down her body. It had been a stressful day. She reached for the shampoo and lathered her hair breathing in the sweet flowery scent. A noise startled her and she looked over the shower door. It was Jeffrey.

"Babe." The shower door opened and the cool air made her skin crawl with resistance. Jeffrey's eyes traveled down her body lingering first on breasts and then lower down. She half covered herself but a thrill of excitement bubbled in her chest.

Lust showed in his eyes. "Maybe I need to join you in there Ms. Andrews. Shall I assist you with the laborious work of cleaning that fine body of yours?"

"I'm in a bit of a hurry sweetie. I still need to pack and get ready to leave." She shut the door and ended the cool air interrupting the bliss of hot water on her skin.

"Mmmmmhum." She heard through the shower door. A second later it opened and a naked Jeffrey joined her. Ronnie stepped back to make room in the small shower stall. He was covered with spiderwebs and flecks of dirt down the golden skin of his arms.

Ronnie reached for the bodywash behind his head and he pulled her close. Their skin was almost electrically charged where they touched. "You're a filthy man."

"Damn right I am." His eyes sparkled and he leaned in to kiss her.

She poured the clear blue liquid on his chest and he released the grip on her and flexed his muscles under her fingers. He leaned back against the shower wall, letting her wash him.

"Strangely enough I got really dirty right *here*." He did a quick pelvic thrust.

"Oh, that attic is such a beast. Let me take care of that for you." Ronnie worked her way down his abs, washed his hips and then knelt in front of him as her hand lathered down one leg to his feet and back up the other leg, creating the desired effect. She stood and smiled evilly as he filled her hand with firm warm flesh.

He closed his eyes and moaned, "Yeah, that part needs a good scrub. Soooo dirty."

She kissed him and slowly stroked his tongue with her lips, mimicking her hand motion, making the handful grow appreciatively.

He pulled her closer and she let go, arranging the once dirty object firmly between her legs. "What about you. I do believe I've shirked my duties in cleansing your person, Miss Andrews. He turned to grab the bodywash and filled his hand with soap, then filled it with one breast then the other, his hips pinning her against the wall making her dizzy with the sensation he was creating in both places of contact.

"Arms up!" he commanded.

She obeyed, smiling at the militant tone. He washed her collarbones, shoulders, and upper chest.

"Higher, Miss Andrews," he barked.

She put her hands above her head and he pinned them with one hand while his other washed her stomach and then reached between her legs.

"Spread 'em, babycakes."

Feeling lightheaded now, she spread her legs with one foot firmly against each wall of the shower. "Yes, sir."

He firmly washed tender flesh making her knees weak and she let out a loud sigh. "Ooooooh, yeah, that's nice."

"Is it?" He stepped back letting the stream of water rinse important soapy features, releasing her hands. He kissed her hard and urgent, reflecting certain parts of his anatomy.

He sucked her upper lip and bit playfully. "Baby, I'm going to make it feel even nicer."

"Mmmmmm, yes please." Every nerve in her body was ready for more.

He kissed her neck with open mouth letting his tongue explore her steamy skin and worked his way down to her collarbone, hands cupping breasts. His mouth surrounded pert sensitive flesh and she closed her eyes as he flicked warm wet tongue around in a circle making her melt completely. The hot water meandered down to her open legs and made rivulets across ever growing sensitive skin—a precursor for what was to come. Jeffrey was exceptionally good at the slow burn, at teasing her flesh until she was ready to burst. He knew her body better than she did herself. And the things he could do with his mouth!

He pulled away and reached behind him to arrange the showerhead to continue where his mouth left off then he worked his way down her stomach, slowly tormenting her with anticipation. He knelt between her legs.

"You smell amazing baby." His eyes locked on hers as he lifted her leg and draped it over his broad tan shoulder, leaving her exposed to his whim.

"Let me make you scream, baby." His eyes shone in the low light of the shower as he pressed his tongue into her in a playful lick. His lips pressed to her flesh and he gripped her ass to push her hips forward, controlling her as he took long slow licks.

She watched every taste of her flesh, adding to the lightheadedness that took over, everything merging sight, sound, and touch into one electrifying sensation. Their eyes locked and Jeffrey exaggerated every motion for her visual pleasure, slowing it down until his tongue was out of sight and his upper lip dented her skin, his chin poised perfectly to taunt her the most.

His lips tightened and she arched her back. "Ooooooh damn baby, yessssss."

"Mmmmmmmmm," Jeffrey answered, sending waves of excitement through her. Ronnie ground into his face and rode wave after wave of pleasure, holding his head tight against her.

Chapter 13 - Stuck in Town

Ronnie woke calm and satiated. She stretched her legs and rolled onto her back. Most of the time she slept in a T-shirt so the caress of the sheets felt particularly sensual against her naked flesh. The sun peeked in around the window shade and she wondered what the day would bring. Then it hit her. The day would bring Hurricane Frances to her doorstep! There was no way she could be here for that. She should have left yesterday.

"Crap!" She sprang out of bed looking around for Jeffrey. He was already up— nice of him to let her sleep when he knew she was trying to leave. The clock showed 8:31 a.m. *You should have left by now*. It blinked to 8:32, *too late*.

Her skin crawled with gooseflesh, longing for the warmth between the sheets, but there was no time for luxuriating. In the passion of last night, she had forgotten to finish packing and did not set the alarm. She clicked the TV on before gathering her clothes and headed toward the shower, pausing to lean on the doorjamb when the weatherman came on.

Terry James was tamping down his all-out roaring excitement for the good of the community. "In sheer size, Frances is nearly twice as big as Charley with wind speeds peaking at one hundred and forty miles an hour."

Ronnie held her temples. "No!" This was not happening again. And for God's sake she wasn't going to be here for it. She shut the door and turned on the shower. Flashes of last night assaulted her as the hot water hit her body. A dizzying passion washed down the drain as she fought the urge to take her time under the steamy spray. Panic won out and she finished soaping up and rinsed, longing for more but this was not the time or place.

Ronnie quickly dressed and finished packing. She combed her long hair and put it in a high ponytail, no time to mess with it. Once all her things were ready to go and she clicked the TV off, picked up her duffle bag, and made her way to the kitchen, wondering if Jeffery had gone out for an errand or was lounging with coffee nearby.

The door to the garage was ajar. She pushed it opened and found the attic ladder down. "Babe?" she called.

"Oh, hey you're awake." His voice was muffled from above. "I'll be right down."

"I thought you finished last night with that?" She craned her neck to look up the stairs.

The ladder creaked and she saw his sneakered foot on the paint-stained wood of the step. His tanned muscular leg was within reach as he climbed down the ladder.

"I thought so too, but after I saw the weather report I wanted to double check it. The storm is going to last for days, Ronnie. It will be so much worse than Charley, I'm afraid."

Her guts did a backflip. "I'm ready to leave. You want to come with me?"

"Leave, Ronnie, the traffic is totally backed up on the interstate. I don't think you're going anywhere."

All the blood left her face and her hands tingled. "What do you mean?"

"Seriously, they've evacuated millions of people along the coast and low lying areas inland. They're all on Ninety-Five right now."

"But I'm not going to be here, Jeffrey. Damn it, I should have left last night like I wanted to."

He raised his eyebrows. "You don't regret last night, do you?" He reached out to grab her arm, but she stepped backward.

"Look, I am *not* going to be here when Frances hits." She held her hands out. "I'm taking my chances out there."

"Ron, it's the largest evacuation in history. How do you think you're going to get on the interstate and make it to Virginia before the storm hits?" She could hear the frustration in his voice. "It's just not feasible."

"Jeffrey if I leave now I'll get ahead of the crowd and it won't be too bad." Her mind raced with every reason she should not be here.

"Really? It is already too late Ronnie." He turned her around and shoved her toward the kitchen door, back into the house.

"Just wait, they show both interstates, Four and Ninety-Five, all the way to North Carolina are clogged with evacuees. You'd never make it home in time and hotels will be booked. What will you do in your car on the road when it hits?" His voice took an angry tone.

They went to the TV and she clicked it back on. Sure enough, Terry James was showing Skycam views of the road. Traffic was crawling.

"Now what do I do?" Her cheeks flushed. With Jeffrey so thoroughly distracting her the night before, she hadn't left as planned. There was supposed to be time today to get out of town.

"Babe, I'll stay with you." He wrapped his arms around her.

Ronnie broke free, claustrophobic. "No, no, no. I have to get out of here!"

"Babe." He took her hand pulling her toward him.

"Aren't you monitoring this storm like you did Charley? Don't you have to be in the lab?"

"I probably should but if you need me, Ronnie." He hugged her.

"No Jeffrey, I can't." She pushed against his chest and looked up at him.

"You can't? Why can't you?"

She shook her head not sure what to say but she didn't want to be with him during the storm. "Okay, okay. Damn, I really wanted to get out of town, Jeffrey."

He kissed her forehead, "I know, but look it will be fine. Your house made it through the last storm with just a few branches down."

"A hurricane the size of Texas?" Ronnie pushed away from him and swallowed her fear. Would she end up back in eighteenth-century London again, or somewhere worse? It had been so horrific last time.

The phone rang and she glared at it as if it was an alien invading. Who the hell could that be? "Hello."

"Hey, love, I just wanted to see if you were on the road yet. You didn't answer your cell." Steph's cheerful Scots greeted her.

"Oh, God Steph, I wish. I'm staying here." Ronnie eyed Jeffrey, who took her waist and pulled her toward him. Ronnie stiff-armed him and he turned toward the kitchen. "Have you seen the news? Traffic is a nightmare, I'll never get home in time."

"What will you do now?" She could hear Ian in the background trying to grab the phone. "Ian, stop."

"Jeffrey's here," Ronnie said.

"No, seriously? Ronnie, you have to be smarter than that. You can't be with him during this storm. You just cannae."

Ronnie heard more shuffling and then Ian's voice. "Hi, Ronnie. How are you? What color knickers you wearing?"

More shuffling and Steph got the phone back. "Ya wee eegit, stop playing around this is serious. Sorry love, he's acting as if he's twelve. What if me and the eegit came to stay with you? I swear he won't go through your underwear drawers."

She could hear Ian in the background begging, "Please, please, oh please."

Ronnie couldn't help but smile, he was a hound dog for sure but he did make her laugh. "Are you sure?"

Ian was back on the line, "If you're short on beds I'll be happy to share yours, Ronnie."

She laughed. "That won't be necessary Jeffrey will be in my bed."

Steph was back on the line, "Not if I have anything to say about it. Ronnie, you have to tell him to shove off."

Ronnie's cheeks grew hot. It was the usual battle between Jeffrey and Steph. Either way, she would make someone mad. "I don't think I have enough food though and they're saying the storm should last the entire weekend."

"Hey, run to the store and just grab what you can. I'll bring what I have and call Nick. Your tank is full, right?" Steph said.

"Yeah, it is." Ronnie walked to the kitchen and opened the cupboards, making note of what she had. Not much.

Steph continued. "Good, better go now, the shelves are emptying as we speak."

"Okay, come over soon okay?" Ronnie hung up the phone, grabbed her car keys and walked to the driveway. "Jeff. I'll be back. I'm going to the store. Anything you need?"

"Yeah, buy some of those Starbucks ready-made drinks, we're gonna need some coffee."

"Okay." She knew she should tell him Steph was coming over but he would be pissed. Would Steph and Jeffrey kill each other? It would be uncomfortable, but maybe, just maybe, they'd learn to get along.

Ronnie dashed through the store grabbing what was left of the essentials and fought the frantic masses to get to the register. It was daunting to think about the many meals they'd have to prepare with five people there over the duration of the storm with no power. Would it be enough? There would be no turning back, the roads would be impassable after the storm and stores would be closed. After Hurricane Isabel, it had been weeks before the power returned in some of the Virginia Beach neighborhoods.

Ronnie jumped back in her car and fought traffic back to the house. As she pulled into the driveway she eyed the huge trees in her new yard, the potential for horrible damage was looming directly over her roof. In the side yard a giant loblolly pine tree five times the height of her house waved a branch in the wind as if to say, "Hello, I'm here to make your day." In the front yard, a few hickories and smaller live oaks shimmied in the light breeze.

Behind the house were the camphor, grapefruit, and orange trees, but the neighbors all had large trees that could easily flatten her single-story ranch. Jeffrey was right the trees had made it through Charley with no issues, but it was possible that one had been damaged during that storm. Frances was going to be a lot worse. She grabbed the groceries and made her way through the open garage door through to the kitchen, setting them down on the countertop.

"Jeffrey!" She might as well just tell him so she could stop stressing about it.

She heard a muted, "Up here." And she walked to the open attic. "Give me about twenty minutes, I'm almost done."

"Okay." Crap, she'd have to wait. Steph would be here by then. Ronnie busied herself with putting away the groceries and finishing the laundry she'd started earlier. Counting on her fingers she calculated the number of pillows needed. She and Jeffrey would be in her bed, Steph and Nick in the guest room, Ian on the couch.

She called Steph, "Bring pillows for you and Ian. You're welcome to have Nick come too. The more the merrier." At this point, it didn't matter and maybe Nick could diffuse the heat between Jeffrey and Steph to make the situation civil.

"Okay, that would be lovely. We were just talking about it," she said. "Did you tell Jeffrey you've invited the entire neighborhood over?"

Ronnie squirmed. "I'm about to. Just waiting for him to leave the attic. He's shoring up the roof." They spoke for a few more minutes making arrangements and Ronnie hung up, eager to finish the final preparations before her friends came over. How would Ian and Jeffrey get along? Jeffrey would probably look down on him, who knows that might get Ian's ire up and then what? Would Ian fight with Jeffrey? This was a big mistake. They'd be stuck in this house for days with all of them on top of each other.

She called Steph back. "What is it love, we'll be there in a few minutes can't it wait?" Steph asked with a bit of edge in her voice.

"Steph, I'm sorry. Just got worrying about Ian and Jeffrey going at it. Could you talk to him and maybe …"?

"Ooch, why don't you tell him to ride it out at his house alone? Woman, he is the only one of us that won't be easy." Steph didn't try to hide her anger.

"Maybe I should." She knew Jeffrey would not leave.

"Look we'll be there soon, I'll speak to Ian and let him know to be on his best behavior."

Jeffrey walked into the bedroom covered in cobwebs and dust. "Hey babe, I'm gonna hop in the shower."

"Jeffrey, Steph, and her brother are coming over. Maybe Nick too."

"Why the hell didn't you tell me before, Ronnie? I'm not sure I want to be stuck in the house with a gang of …" He looked away.

"A gang of what, Jeffrey?"

"I'm going to take a shower and decide if I can be here. Thanks a lot for this, Ronnie. I came over here to be with you, to make sure you're safe and you invite a mess of people too? Don't you want me here?"

"Jeff, I'm sorry." She forced her tone to be neutral, not angry. "I wasn't even planning on being here myself. I'm supposed to be in Virginia and away from this horror. I'm scared to death that *it* will happen again and when Steph called we decided she should be here too."

He looked at her, anger showing on his even features. "It won't happen again, Ronnie. You are safe here with me. Tell Steph to stay home, we really don't need more people here. It won't go over well I'll tell you that right now."

"No, I'm not doing that. I feel like I need both of you here. Can't you just help me out?"

In response, Jeffrey peeled off his shirt and wadded it into a ball and threw it on the floor. He walked to the bathroom and shut the door.

"Crap." Ronnie sat on the bed, feeling more stressed by the minute.

Chapter 14 - Scottish Mafia

The doorbell rang and Ronnie walked down the hall. Steph and Ian were holding pillows and a duffle bag, reminding her of sleepovers with her girlfriends from years gone. "Hey guys, come on in."

Steph hugged her, squishing the pillow between them and Ian joined in putting his hand around Ronnie's rib cage just under the underwire of her bra. She kissed Steph's cheek and deftly moved away from Ian's probing fingers.

"Where do you want me to put our gear, luv?" Steph shoved her pillow into the hug Ian was aiming at Ronnie.

"The guest room. Is Nick coming too?" Ronnie said.

"Yeah, he'll be here soon. His mom wanted to have his help with a few things." Steph looked toward the closed master bedroom door. "Is that gobshite here?"

"Yeah," Ronnie glanced at the door half expecting Jeffrey to storm out. "He's in the shower."

"Oh, so he's staying for the party?" Steph shot Ian a glance.

"Not sure. Just broke the news to him and …" Ronnie rolled her eyes. "Who knows?"

"Right, well he'll make the right choice I'm sure," Steph said. Ian started to say something but Steph put her fingers over his mouth. "Nope, you're going to keep that trap shut. I heard enough in the car."

Ian's expression softened and he nodded. "Aye Stephanie, I'll be yer man and behave." He looked at Ronnie and licked his lips and added, "For now."

Ronnie shook her head, the hound dog better calm down or he'd be in for a bloody nose. "Ian, you're on the couch tonight. Sorry, I don't have a lot of room, but it'll have to do.

"Ooch, nay bother, lass, eet'll be fine," Ian said good-naturedly.

"For now, put your things in Steph's room." Ronnie pointed past the master bedroom. Ian disappeared down the hall.

Jeffrey opened the bedroom door and stormed out, but he swallowed his words when he saw Steph. They eyed each other like nervous dogs. Ronnie knew them both well enough to predict one of two outcomes. A huge fight or one would retreat to make peace for her sake.

"Ronnie, can we speak in your room for a minute," Jeffrey added a cordial smile, but it came across as pained.

Steph gave her a sympathetic look, "I'll be gathering our things from the car."

Ian walked toward them and eyed Jeffrey. "Aye, mate, I'm Stephanie's wee brother, Ian. You must be Jeff."

"It's Jeffrey. Nice to meet you, Ian." He was the picture of politeness, but the tone was flat and it was clear he was sizing Ian up to be an extension of Steph.

"Right, man. Hope you don't mind us crashing here. Ronnie begged Steph to protect her from... uh... I really don't..." He stopped mid-sentence in response to the glare from Steph. "Oh, sorry."

Jeffrey motioned to the bedroom. "Ronnie."

Ronnie obliged. It gave her strength knowing Steph was nearby. Jeffrey shut the door and crossed his arms. His face said it all. Ronnie flopped on the bed adopting a casual pose.

"What in the hell are you doing? Why would you invite them over?" He pointed at the door.

Ronnie studied his face, wondering if he'd yell with Ian likely listening to every word. He pressed his lips together and tapped his fingers on his thigh. Yup. He was really pissed.

"Jeffrey, do you remember what I've been through during the last storm?" She said in a tone calmer than she felt.

He looked down at his feet and shook his head. "Don't you use that against me!"

"Against you? This isn't about you Jeffrey. The last time I was thrown back in time and couldn't get back. I'm freaking terrified that it will happen again. I should have gone home today!" Frustration burst out of her.

He sat and took her hand. "I know, Ronnie. I know, that was a mistake. You should have left yesterday but who knew the traffic would be so backed up?"

She pulled her hand away. "Geez, I don't know, you do happen to work at a weather lab." She said it with the proper amount of snark but instantly regretted the look it elicited.

He showed restraint, despite the rising flush that crept up his neck, and stood and paced to the window and back to face her. "Ronnie, that's why I want to be here. Me. Not them. I want to make sure you're okay."

"They do too, Jeff. I've brought the A team so I can make it through this storm and not completely lose my mind." The last words echoed in her head. That is what Jeffrey had accused her of the last time they'd discussed it. Was that her subconscious putting that out there?

"Good choice of words, Ron." He sat next to her again and took her hand. "You know how I feel about Steph and now that guy ..."

"Ian." She let her hand stay in his, this time as a peacekeeper.

"Yeah, what the hell am I supposed to do with them here for days on end? Seriously, I may fucking kill someone, all the digging comments from Steph backed up by her own flesh and blood. I can't think of a worse scenario for a miserable few days for me. Why didn't you just leave well enough alone?"

Ronnie shook her head, hoping to let loose the kill someone comment that flapped around like a kite caught in a tree on a windy day. "You know why." She looked away, not wanting to say the truth.

He dumped her hand in her lap and stood. "Well, you've chosen your side I guess. I'm not going to stay and be beat down by the Scottish Mafia."

Ronnie wanted to laugh at that expression, but she was afraid it would ignite more anger. She'd have to remember it for later use on Steph and Ian. It could be funny when delivered without the hatred. "Jeffrey, I want you here. Can't you do that for me?"

His lips were a thin line as he shook his head. "Babe. I'd do a lot for you but this isn't gonna happen. I refuse to be put down for an entire weekend. Is that guy Nick coming too?"

"Yeah." She looked away, knowing it would just add fuel to the fire.

"Jesus babe. Three of them against me? What the fuck are you thinking? You decided to stay for the storm and then what? While I was up working hard on something for you in the attic you invited all of Steph's compadres over to gang up on me?"

"Oh sure, my main goal in life is to ruin your day." She stood hands on her hips. "I love how you made this completely about you."

"Nice, baby. Really fucking nice." His face was fully red now and he clenched his fists by his side.

"I'm the one who has been through utter hell. You say you're here to protect me? Well so is Steph and she wasn't there when I went back the first time."

His expression went blank and he slowly shook his head. "You certainly don't need both of us." Storming across the room, Jeffrey snatched the wadded-up shirt from the floor and tossed it into his duffle bag, zipping it curtly.

"I'm not going to put up with this." He stood waiting for her to beg him to stay but knew now, given his anger he was right. It would not go well.

Jeffrey dramatically slung the bag over his shoulder. "This is about me, Ronnie, because I'm the one who is here for you. I am the one who will protect you and keep you safe, not Steph. Not fucking Evan."

Ronnie quipped. "His name is Ian."

"Who fucking cares what his goddammed name is? He is here and I will not be. You have to always ruin things, Ronnie. I wanted to comfort you, to care for you, to make you forget your worries." He half turned away and then turned back. "But you have ruined all of that. Why? Why would you do that to me?" He towered over her wagging a finger in her face.

Ronnie laid back on the bed to get away from the spewing anger.

The bedroom door cracked open. "Ronnie, you okay?" Steph's big blue eyes peeked in.

"No," Ronnie said in unison with Jeffrey saying, "Yes."

Steph stepped into the room, holding the door handle, and looked from Ronnie to Jeffrey.

Jeffrey stepped away and held his hands up. "I give up. Look, please just take care of her, okay?"

"You're leaving?" Steph smiled sweetly. "You will miss all of the fun, Jeffrey."

"This is not the fun I had in mind, Steph." Jeffrey shifted the bag on his shoulder. He turned on his heel, stormed into the bathroom, and came out a second later zipping his toiletry bag.

Steph sat on the bed next to Ronnie and gave her a sympathetic look. "Jeffrey, we promise to make it fun. Won't you give it shot?"

He shoved the toiletry case into is duffle bag and stopped mid zip and looked up. "Fun? How the hell would *you* do that?"

Steph shrugged her shoulders. "For Ronnie. No other reason really."

Jeffrey shook his head. "Ronnie, I hope you don't regret this. I want you both to know I was here for you." He pointed at Ronnie. "You're the one who fucked it up."

"You're the one who is leaving, Jeffrey," Ronnie said. "I was hoping you'd stay with me, but if you can't I understand." She felt renewed strength with Steph next to her making it easier to poke the bear.

The bear walked toward the bedroom door, "You've not exactly given me a choice, Ron." He jerked the door open to find Ian standing there looking sheepish. Jeffrey pushed him out of the way. "You nosy little fucker."

Ian held his hands up. "Well, ya cannae blame me, man. I just wanted to see if Ronnie would be sleeping alone tonight." He took a few steps back keeping his hands up.

Jeffrey lunged at Ian. Ronnie and Steph rushed to get between the two men. Ronnie pushed Jeffrey backward as he reached to wring Ian's neck.

Steph pushed Ian down the hallway toward the guest room, "Ya wee clothead, what are you thinking?" She shoved him into the room followed after him and shut the door to barrage her little brother with incomprehensible Scots.

"What the hell? Is he here to sleep with you, Ronnie? Is that why you invited them over?" Jeffrey barked.

"Seriously? You think I'd sleep with him?" Ronnie turned away, utterly disgusted at the accusation. "That I'd cheat at all? You sure don't know a thing about me if that is what you think." She crossed her arms and glared.

"Who the fuck knows, Ronnie. I certainly didn't expect you to invite those people here today." He reached into his pocket and pulled out his car keys. "This is utter nonsense. Why can't you just ask them to leave? That guy has made his intentions known, he wants to sleep with you. How can I leave you now?"

"Jeffrey, *that guy* wants to sleep with everyone. I'm no different than the chick at the bar last night. You can't seriously believe he's a threat to us?"

Jeffrey turned away and rubbed his face with both hands. "God, you infuriate me, Ronnie."

"Same," she said. Why wouldn't he just leave?

"So, send them home." He stepped toward her aggressively.

"Nope." She stood her ground willing him to open the door and walk out.

A loud clap of thunder made Ronnie jump nearly out of her skin. They both looked out the picture window. Ominous black clouds darkened the sky and the pavement was shiny with rain. Frances was on their doorstep.

"You will regret this Ronnie. I promise you that." He squeezed her elbow and turned to walk out of the house.

Ronnie watched the rain splash off her car. Crap, she'd have to move it so he could leave.

He turned on his heel and pushed past her to the garage. "Move your car."

Ronnie grabbed her keys and ran through the rain and was greeted by a wicked flash of lightning. Thunder shook the doorframe and she ducked in and slammed the door behind her, her heart beating a mile a minute.

Chapter 15 - Plan B

Jeffrey Brennan drove around the block while weighing his options. Damn Ronnie. Hurricane Frances flung a deluge of water from its outermost rain band onto the windshield. The wipers beat a steady percussion of *flick wack, flick wack* that created a song in his mind. "Fuck this!" He slammed his fist on the dashboard. He now had to either bail on the experiment or make an alternate plan. This storm was a chance to further the great strides he'd made during Hurricane Charley and send Ronnie back in time again.

The machine he fondly called TOTO was in place just above Ronnie's master bathroom where she'd end up when the nausea hit. It just so happened the location he chose perfectly aligned with the guest bathroom as well. The two rooms abutted sharing the wall with the sink and toilet. A perfect setup no matter which bathroom she'd end up in.

He thought of the Phase Two injection he had inserted in Ronnie last night while she was mid-orgasm. She squirmed a little as she lay face down bent over the side of the bed and he readied it for insertion while continuing to pound her. A slight tug of her hair as he injected the needle between the shoulders, coupled with aggressive … he had to adjust his cargo shorts as his body responded to the memory. A major jolt of excitement hit when he realized he was killing two birds with one hard fuck.

The placement was perfect—it was where she couldn't scratch it out and her bra or bikini top would likely cover the tiny lump. A trick he learned when dealing with the cats. The only place on their body they couldn't bite something out.

He had worked hard on converting the pellets he used on Ronnie last time, so thoughtfully stirred into her twice-baked potato, to a smaller bead. This innovation provided several advantages, one being the risk of Ronnie losing them into the toilet if the nausea exacerbated to that level. Phase Two could be inserted just under the skin almost painlessly and had the added benefit of staying for months if not years. Phase One, when ingested, was merely a matter of passing through her system and could only be expected to stay in a day or two at most.

Another violent gust of wind convinced him to get his precious car off the road. He had watched the neighbors leave yesterday while he was pulling into the garage. Would it be close enough to TOTO in her attic to have full control? Would the storm interfere with the connection?

He pulled into the neighbor's driveway and hoped they didn't have an alarm. The driveway wasn't visible from Ronnie's front or back windows. Glancing at his pristine track shoes, he gave up on the notion of them being his good pair and squished through the muddy side yard to the back of the house. Warm rain pelted him and ran into his eyes. He wiped them and lowered his head to keep the windblown droplets from blinding him. Luckily the gate wasn't locked and he made his way around the landscaping past the pool.

The lanai gave him coverage from the driving rain and he peeked in the sliding glass doors. It was pitch-black inside. He tried the door but could see a piece of wood barring it in the track. He tried the French door. The handle jiggled but remained locked.

Scrambling in the vast ocean of his cargo shorts pocket that was full of change, keys, and other paraphernalia, like flotsam from a tsunami. He finally grasped a pocketknife and used the box cutter tool to loosen the lower right pane of the French door, cutting around the edges, sawing into the wood. It lifted away and he reached inside to throw the dead bolt. He could just reinsert the pane with a little putty and no one would be the wiser. Jeffrey stepped inside and waited for an alarm to sound, holding his breath. Silence echoed back and his heart slowed just a tad.

Jeffrey pulled off the muddy shoes and set them by the door, and walked through the kitchen to the sink and washed his hands, then found the garage. He prayed there was room to slip his car in for the night. A dank musty smell assaulted his senses and he fumbled for the light switch. "Yes!" The sound echoed around the near empty garage and bounced off the pool floats hastily stored out of harm's way. A gleaming white Suburban took up one half of the garage, but there was ample space for his Mercedes.

Breaking and entering. Check. Now to get to the heart of the matter before the storm cranked up too much. He pulled out his laptop and set it up on the breakfast bar and plugged it into the wall. No sense wasting the battery while there was still power. In his bag were three backup batteries.

He drove his car into the garage and changed his clothes, leaving the wet ones hanging in the garage out of the way. Now to see if TOTO would oblige his wishes by connecting to his laptop. It should, given the parameters, but once the storm got going it was possible it would lose the remote connection. What would happen to Ronnie then? Would it reconnect to her once it regained the signal? He tried to remember if he had written the code to automatically reconnect. That would be a risk if she were lost in time, again. He relived a pang of fear from his troubles during Hurricane Charley but pushed it aside. That was not going to happen this time.

At least he wasn't at her house where he would have to deal with her friends and their suspicions. They couldn't accuse him of any wrongdoing when he wasn't even present. This might even shut Steph up about his involvement. The words of Steph's brother hit him again and his stomach did a flip imagining that little weenie's hands on his girl. He understood why the man would want Ronnie, but hopefully, he was just sleazy enough to spark Ronnie's decency and ire to keep him out of her bed.

Jeffrey looked at his watch. TOTO would be reaching peak capacity in the next few hours. First to test the connection and program her journey. Hopefully, it would be worth the cold hard cash he'd paid Hannah to steer this monster over Orlando.

He wasn't going to let a few bitchy friends get in the way of the work he put into preparing for this moment.

With the possible probe at the lab into the pulse during Charley, he had decided to remove the entire project from his lab and now it sat squarely in Ronnie's attic. All the paperwork and spare equipment was locked up in a storage unit under an alias, away from probing eyes, and hopefully away from water damage.

The work soothed him, allowing the anger from Ronnie's betrayal to fade into the background. Did Ronnie notice a tingle between her shoulder blades when he had activated the connection? He stretched and looked out the sliding glass door. Frances was having a field day dropping branches and palm fronds in the pool. Part of the fence had blown down and the neighbor's pool was visible.

If a tree didn't come through this damn house, it should be fine for the duration. "Shit." What if that happened after he sent Ronnie back? What if the equipment got wet or damaged? Or worse, what if he got hurt? Steph would find Ronnie unconscious on the floor, unresponsive. How long could her body survive like that? Most likely she would present as someone in a vegetative state. Either way, there would be no trace back to him. A MRI would show the pellet in her back but only if they were looking for it. Unless they did an autopsy and were specifically searching they were unlikely to find it. Well, he couldn't worry about every contingency until it presented itself.

Chapter 16 – Dazed and Confused

Ronnie sat on the couch with the swirling of activity around her feeling a bit shell-shocked from the encounter with Jeffrey. How the hell had she stayed in Florida? She was supposed to be at her mom's by now out of harm's way. She took a deep breath and let it out, hoping to release some of the stress. It was comforting to have Steph here and if she had been right about Jeffrey, there would be no time traveling. But Ronnie couldn't shake the horrible feeling she would die again tonight. The memories that had haunted her so thoroughly were still fresh in her mind, brought to the forefront with the storm overhead. The trees in the backyard were dancing and waving almost tauntingly.

"Ian, back up, now set it down here." Nick was giving instructions to Ian who was moving her captain's chair away from the widows in case one broke or leaked during the storm. "Perfect," Nick said, clutching his casted arm. "Ronnie, you okay with us moving the couch into the dining room?"

"Well …" Ronnie tried to shift gears and pay attention to what Nick meant. "Why?"

"We shouldn't be sitting near the windows and I think we'll be more comfortable on the couch." He nodded at Ian. "There are no windows in the dining room so we'd be safer in there."

"And plus, it's where I'll lay me head down. Nick says it'll be safer here." He pointed to the corner of the dining room that was protected by a half wall separating the dining and living rooms.

"Oh," Ronnie said numbly. "Okay, Nick, whatever you think is good. I'm not exactly in a …" She made finger quotes to accentuate her point, "smart place right now."

Ian walked toward her with open arms, "Here lemme gie yee a hug, lass."

Ronnie took a step backward, but let Ian wrap his arms around her.

"Relax for me, it'll be okay, I promise," Ian cooed sweetly.

It was comforting to feel his solidness. If he would just turn off hound-dog mode he might be fun. She rested her head on his shoulder and he patted her back. "Ian is here for you, you just let me know how I can help."

Steph walked in from the kitchen wiping her hands on her shorts. "Ian McKay, stop that!"

"It's okay Steph, I'm stressing out. He's being decent," Ronnie said, pulling away.

Ian released her and took a step back, dropping his gaze to her cleavage. "I know where my bread is buttered." He smiled "I'll be a good boy ... at least until we start the whisky. Then all bets are off."

Nick chimed in, "Steph, hide the whisky. He can fight me for it later if he wants."

"Oocccchhhhh noooo, the big man is nae getting between me and my Glenfeddich," Ian said laughing. Nick was four inches taller and outweighed him by at least twenty pounds. "I'll find a way. I always do."

"And that, little brother, is exactly why Mum sent you here." Steph boxed his ears making Ian step backward and hold up his hands.

Ronnie watched the exchange distractedly. The fear was mounting and her stomach was not enjoying the extra adrenaline. They made their final storm preps, deciding to sleep in the bedrooms but as a backup plan, move to the hallway if the storm picked up. They prepped all the flashlights with fresh batteries and Nick and Steph nailed blankets over the window next to the futon in the guest room that she would sleep in, just in case the window was broken by falling branches. She had given her room to Nick and Steph so they could have more privacy and the queen-sized bed. The third bedroom was full of boxes.

Nick looked exhausted, the dark circles under his eyes making him look much older.

"Nick, sit down, Steph and I can do the rest," Ronnie said. She and Steph pulled the rest of the furniture away from the windows and covered the computer with trash bags.

Nick sat for a few minutes watching them but it wasn't in his nature to observe others work. "No seriously it's okay."

"Dude you can rest, we've got it. Your arm must be killing you," Ronnie said. The lights flickered and the power went out. A blood curdling scream echoed from down the hall.

Nick clicked on his flashlight and then ran down the hall toward the guest bathroom.

"Are you okay?" Nick pounded on the door. Steph and Ronnie followed.

"Aye, just ... a bit startled by the blackout," Ian said through the door.

The women laughed. "Ian ya we'un, you afraid of the boogie man?" Steph said, elbowing Ronnie in the ribs. The door opened and Ian's face appeared, his eyebrows knit together.

"Dinna talk to me like a child, Stephanie. I'm grown."

"Grown scared in the dark." Steph pushed Ian's shoulder and he came at her putting her in a headlock playfully mussing up her hair.

"Ian, stop that!" Finally, he let her go.

"Why do ye always have to be such a clothead?" Steph stepped back and smoothed her blonde bob back down. "You have a flashlight in your pocket, don't you?"

Ian looked blankly at her. "Aye I do, why?"

"Why didn't you use it?" Steph asked.

"Ooch, Steph I had my tadger in my hand," Ian said, looking away embarrassed.

"You don't even wait until we're asleep for that, for God's sake Ian, have some decency!"

Ian looked confused and then laughed holding up his tattoo making it wiggle obscenely. "No, Steph. I wasn't wanking."

Ronnie turned away and shook her head, heading back to the living room.

"Good, you keep it in your pants, Mister." Steph turned on her heel and walked down the hallway. "Let's finish up. Shall we light candles and gather round the table?"

"Does everyone have a flashlight?" Nick asked. Ronnie reached into her pocket and pulled out the small mag. Ian had an orange camping flashlight from Nick's stash and Steph had a lantern that could convert into a flashlight.

Ronnie wondered what Jeffrey was doing right now? Did he go home? She was glad he wasn't here upsetting everyone. Why did he always have to cause problems? Just once she wanted to relax with Steph and Jeff getting along. It would be so normal, and so nice.

"Ronnie, where is Fluffy?" Steph stood and looked around the room.

Nick stood too. "Oh no. Not again. I'm not cat chasing this time."

Ronnie ran to her room and looked under her bed. It was Fluffy's usual hiding place. She shone the flashlight and could see the tail flicking back and forth. "Come here, sweetie."

A low meow escaped her precious kitty's mouth but she didn't budge. "Poor kitty." She coaxed the white Persian out from under the bed and picked her up carrying her down the hall to the living room. "She's fine, she is just freaking out from the storm." Ronnie sat next to Ian on the couch.

"May I pet your pu ..." he started but reversed it upon seeing Ronnie's face. "Cat?"

"Better not. She's agitated." Ronnie turned away from Ian, not in the mood.

Nick pulled Steph close and kissed the top of her head. "Nobody open the doors. My cast won't survive another mid-hurricane rescue."

"Stephanie told me about poor wee Hamish during Hurricane Charley." Ian pointed at Nick's arm. "Is that how you ..."

"Yeah, a transformer fell and took me with it." Nick lifted the cast. "But I'll be fine. Could have met the fate that Hamish did. So, I'm grateful to be alive."

"Aye, rough go, but as you say you're alive." Ian stood. "Hey Stephanie, where is that food we brought. I'm famished."

Nick looked at Steph, "Yeah, Stephanie."

Steph walked to the kitchen and brought the sandwiches they'd made earlier, setting them down on the coffee table with a handful of paper plates. Everyone grabbed one and started eating.

"Ian tell us why you're here in the states?" Nick put his arms around Steph as they stood near the couch.

Ian smiled at Steph, "I dinna think you even know the whole story."

Steph sat next to him and squeezed his knee. "Do I want to know? Does it involve Tony and the band of merry idiots?"

"Ah, Stephanie, you forget Tony is the smart one of us."

"Ooch, no, if that is how you're measuring intelligence ..."

"Stephanie, you know about Tony's family, right?" Ian asked.

"Aye, I do." She turned to Nick and Ronnie. "Tony, his best mate is in a gang of sorts."

"It's not a gang, Stephanie. It's just his family situation," Ian interrupted.

"As I was saying, he's in a gang and this wee clothead happens to have seduced the daughter of the gang boss."

"Let me tell it, you've put a little too much opinion in your version." Ian waved his hand as if to dismiss her. "It is not my fault that Tony's sister wanted to ..." He glanced at Ronnie, "jump my bones."

"Oh please, you were your usual woman chaser, I've no doubt," Steph said.

"No Stephanie," he placed his hand over his heart, "As God is my witness." A loud banging echoed around the room startling Ronnie. She turned around to look out the front window. Probably just a branch blown by the storm. The wind roared through the trees making everyone jump.

"I think God is throwing things at you, Ian," Nick laughed. "Maybe stick to the truth so we can make it through this storm in one piece, eh?"

Steph laughed. Ronnie tried to shake the uneasy feeling growing in her bones. She set Fluffy on the floor and walked to the window and cupped her hands to see out. "Frances is roaring out there." The lightning flashes showed the trees flailing around and the rain blowing sideways.

It reminded her of the last time she sat precariously on the edge of the exact situation just a few weeks ago as Hurricane Charley was ramping up. A moment permanently fixed in her mind for it was the last time she felt at peace. All the stress of the move from Virginia, and worry that Jeffrey had been ignoring her. Finally, he was giving her his full attention. She distinctly remembered the knot in her stomach releasing, feeling safe in his lab, despite the storm roaring outside, enjoying the marvelous dinner and attention he lavished on her. Just before the time travel, and all the fighting and awkwardness about her version of events and Mike.

Now he had stormed out of her house furiously. Living in Virginia Beach without Steph had been hard on her but when Jeffrey moved down here too, she felt that she was losing him. He pushed hard for her to move to Orlando too but seemed almost uninterested when she first arrived.

Maybe it was inconsiderate to invite Steph over but came from a place of such deep-seated fear. Terror of what had happened during the last storm, and equal terror of what this one could bring. She was no closer to any answers about what had sent her back in time to 1752 than the moment she had arrived. Steph was certain that Jeffrey was involved, but he seemed so adamant that her mind was slipping.

A jolt of electricity snaked its way down her spine making Ronnie stand up straight. *What the hell was that?* She looked around the room. No one else seemed to notice. A deep sharp panic started in her gut and quickly spread in every direction. Ronnie tried to slow down her breathing but it was running like a freight train puffing out smoke.

Steph interrupted her thoughts with loud angry Scots and several dramatic but harmless blows to Ian's head and torso. Ronnie watched this numbly, her mind not able to take it all in. Nick was laughing hysterically. Ian was defending himself and laughing. He was looking at Ronnie hoping for her reaction too, but she missed the story.

"Ronnie, you're not listening to my wee tale of debauchery. Is it too much for your delicate senses?" Ian said, his hands raised against Steph.

Ronnie wasn't sure if she wanted to hear. Her mind was too convoluted with possibilities of death and destruction. She sat back down.

"I need a drink. Who wants a glass of the good stuff?" Steph said. "Purely medicinal to help forget that this ..." she pointed at Ian, "shares my gene pool."

"I'll take my rations. I believe we get a pint a day, isn't that right Nick?" Ian stood and followed Steph into the master bedroom.

"Oh no, you're not going to find my stash," Steph said. She and Ian had a playful faux fight and disappeared into the room.

"Are you okay, Ronnie?" Nick scooted closer to her on the couch. "You look a little dazed and confused."

"Do I?" Ronnie's anxiety was ramping up. "I guess I'm wigging out a bit."

"I figured as much. I'm sure the storm is weighing heavily on your mind," Nick said, a look of sympathy crossed his handsome face.

"Yeah, and what it might mean for my night," she said.

Nick put his arm around her. "We're all here for you Ronnie. And *you know who* isn't, so I think this time you'll just have a fitful sleep and wake up here with us."

"I hope so." She relaxed against him. "If Jeffrey is even involved."

"Maybe you need to be drunk, that will help you forget anyway, maybe even sleep better."

Ian and Steph came out of the room laughing and talking. Steph clutched the Glenfeddich against her chest and Ian was trying to pry it lose. "Noooo, yer going to make me drop it. Get the ice you idget."

Ian obliged and Steph pulled out four glasses and set them on the coffee table. "The last bit of our storm prep is to raise our glasses."

Ian brought a cup of ice and indelicately put a few cubes in each glass. Steph poured a few inches in each.

"Ian, you first." Steph held her glass up and Nick and Ronnie copied.

"Hmm, okay. Let me see," he swirled the amber liquid. "May the roof above never fall in; may we below never fall out."

"Oh, very good, perfect for the storm." Steph raised her glass.

Everyone clinked glasses and raised it to the roof. Ronnie took a small sip that burned down to her stomach.

"I have to do this one, Ian, say it with me." Steph started and Ian joined in.

Dhé, beannaich an taigh,
Bho stéidh gu stàidh,
Bho chrann gu fraigh,
Bho cheann gu saidh,
Bho dhronn gu traigh,
Bho sgonn gu sgaith,
Eadar bhonn agus bhràighe,

Bhonn agus bhràighe.

"Whoa fancy," Nick said. "Is that the Gaelic?"

"Yes. It means, God, bless this house, from foundation to stairs, from beam to side wall, from roof to upright beam, from ridge to basement, from floor-joist to roof-truss, between foundation and attic."

They raised their glasses and took another swig.

It burned all the way down Ronnie's throat again, but she rather liked the tickle. Just taking the edge off a little. Ian held his glass up for more.

"Ya wee eegit." But Steph added more to his glass. "I've another one." Steph paused, a somber look replacing the good-natured smile. "To Hamish. The best cat in the whole world."

"To Hamish." They all raised their glasses.

Ian added, "Cha bhithidh a leithid ami riamh." And took another swig.

Steph wiped away a tear and Nick pulled her close. He kissed the top of her head and looked at Ronnie. His eyes were shiny in the low light of the candle. Ian took the opportunity with Steph's back turned to help himself to more Scotch.

Nick whispered something in her ear and she turned around and grabbed the bottle from him.

"Stephanie, I was going to make a toast and I needed a full glass," he said with mock innocence.

"Oh, right what is your toast, thank you for my sister's expensive Scotch Whisky?"

"Nay, lass, I merely want to say this to Ronnie." Ian got down on one knee and took Ronnie's hand. Steph rolled her eyes but let him continue. "Slàinte mhòr agus a h-uile beannachd duibh. Great health and every good blessing to you."

He took another swig. Everyone else did too. Ronnie faked it this time. Her stomach was nervous and not liking the little fire the whisky had started. Ian kept her hand.

Steph reached for his glass, "That's enough, Ian."

"I've another especially for you, Stephanie." He put his arm around her and moved the glass high out of her reach, "Alba gu brath!"

She held her glass and clinked his and repeated, then explained. "Ian toasted your health, Ronnie and we just toasted our country."

Ian raised his glass again hoping Steph would fill it but she held the bottle close. "No way, you'll be crawling into Ronnie's bed in no time."

He smiled and said, "If she'll have me."

Ronnie shook her head. "Um, no. Seriously, Ian, my boyfriend was just here."

"Yes, but the good news is he has departed. Look he'll never know. I'm no gonna tell him." He winked at Nick.

Ronnie made an uncomfortable face and Steph said, "Lock your door."

"Stephanie, you did hear about my mad lockpicking skills, did ye not?" Ian laughed.

"Just leave her alone or I will personally chop off yer wee bits," Stephanie said in her best older sister *do not mess with me* voice.

"You have always been the buzzkill. Always." He winked at Ronnie. "I'll no molest you, Ronnie, please dinna fash. I'm merely joking around. You know that, right?" For once the sly smile was gone and she almost believed it. "I do find you wildly attractive, but I know better than to take advantage of a lady in distress. If you need me, or just want to talk I'm here. I'm mostly messing about for fun. You know?"

The mask was off and she could see he meant every word. He was Steph's brother, after all, there had to be some good inside of him. "Thank you, Ian. I'm really stressing, I'd appreciate that. Maybe just tone it down a tad, you know?"

He followed Ronnie into the kitchen and helped her bring out the brownies Steph had brought. The booze was making her sleepy and that was a good thing.

They ate and carried on talking until Ronnie couldn't keep her eyes opened. "Night everyone, I'm going to head to sleep."

"Okay, luv." Steph stood and hugged her. "Come in if you need me. I'm hoping with the gobshite away from you this will be just a rough night with stormy sounds and nothing more."

"Thanks, me too." Ronnie squeezed her friend and Nick joined the hug.

"Sleep well, Ronnie, it's gonna be fine," Nick said.

"I hope so." The dread was dulled by her tiredness and she wanted to hold on tightly to the comfortable feeling.

Ronnie rolled the huge suitcase she'd packed for heading home into the guest room. Fluffy followed giving the bag a wide berth and curled up on the bed watching her get ready to sleep. Ronnie removed her earrings and looked in the mirror. The glint of the gold watch Jeffrey had returned to her glistened on her wrist. Something still did not seem right about how it went missing, and how Jeffrey had returned it to her during their uncomfortable dinner. Without a second thought, she unclasped it and set it in her makeup bag.

She quickly got ready for bed and lay down on the futon and was asleep in minutes.

Chapter 17 - A Window in Time

Jeffrey Brennan's stomach growled and he cursed the lack of forethought to take some of the food from Ronnie's when he had left. So many sacrifices he had to make because of her selfish behavior. At worst, he could snag some food from this house but he was trying to be like a good Boy Scout and leave no trace.

Annoyed at his body's weakness, he found his duffle bag and dug around for the can of almonds, shining the flashlight to enhance the glow of the laptop. Power was out now and he was eating up one of the batteries on the laptop.

Instead of food, he found one of his most prized possessions. Jeffrey ran his thumb over the smooth worn leather. It had been a bible of sorts from the beginning. He flipped to a random page and read the familiar words scrawled in neat blue ink from another era where handwriting was an expression of who you were. A fading art. Handwritten words carried more weight back then because each one was carefully considered and beautifully crafted on the page. Modern words now were scrawled on scraps of paper and thrown away once typed in a computer.

The words comforted him in this uncertain moment. He ran his index finger down the page and read what he had nearly memorized.

In this moment, my life changed forever. It was April 2, 1952, in a small hospital somewhere in central Florida. On this day, I woke slowly, quietly, with my mind racing. I did not know where I was, or how I had arrived. All memories erased, offering me an especially rare unencumbered mind, for it was clear of the usual ramblings of a doctorate student in the throes of writing a dissertation. In this distinctly immaculate space between fully awake and fully asleep, I saw my grandfather. He was not precisely angry but the underlying tone was evident in the timbre of his voice. I relished his distinct midwestern accent bringing forth memories of a happy childhood spent under his wing learning all the earth sciences.

"Ronald, you are heading down an erroneous path. Your research is floundering because of your obtuse thinking." He spoke as if I were a child again, and in this instant, that was an accepted thing. "It is as much

biology as it is chemistry. I want you to start fresh, move your studies to Mendelian genetics."

He faded into the fog of memory and I finally grasped his meaning. It was all there ripe for the picking and I merely needed to begin again with this new understanding. It was this instant that my focus shifted on my dissertation that later became what is now, A Window in Time.

I had just awoken from a coma due to a severe head injury and as luck would have it I had no lingering aftereffects other than occasional severe headaches. My family had traveled from Virginia to Florida for my aunt and uncle's funerals. A sad affair as they had an unfortunate boating accident.

On the return trip back to Virginia with my brother at the wheel and my parents in the backseat we were struck on the driver's side by a teen driver under the influence. The impact forced my body to eject from the automobile causing the head injury. Thankfully, my parents and brother only had minor injuries and I recovered without any damage to my intellect.

My hope with this journal is to capture my thoughts and experimental notes so that I may have a record of other pathways that may prove useful to revisit later. As this entry demonstrates, often a reevaluation of previous pathways may be the breakthrough that changes the history of the world.

Jeffrey closed the book and held it to his nose smelling the leather. *A Window in Time* had been the single most important discovery of his life. He opened the book to an earmarked page and ran his finger over the words.

London/August 1752

London/September 2, 1666

The third date Jeffrey had chosen was inspired by the funeral post from Dr. Andrews' journal. He had completely nailed it in the last experiment to 1752. It appeared that the doctor's hypothesis about the required host body's need to be genetically linked to that place and time, the soul, as he called it, would have a proper vessel to populate. Just on an intellectual level, what a brilliant time to send Ronnie to—so ripe with intrigue, danger, scholarly postulating. She had been in London during the Gregorian Time Shift in England.

He wished he'd been there brushing elbows with the intellectuals of that time and soaking in all the troubles and turmoil and could put to rest the uncertainty of the reactions to losing eleven days. Most of what he read was conflicting as some indicated there were riots, others claimed it was more sensationalized than in actual reality. Either way, it would be full of turmoil, conflict, and great social upheaval, unlike any other modern moment.

This time, the date and location was a leap of faith, since it hadn't been on Dr. Andrews list, but it met all the requirements. A blood relative was present, he knew the location and time, and it would be safe enough to send and retrieve Ronnie without too many complications.

A twinge of guilt about Dr. Andrews and the method Jeffrey had used to obtain the notebooks hit him, but he suppressed it. It had been a dark spot in his life and he had to bury it. He had no choice but to continue without the brilliant scientist on the course he had set. Perhaps carrying on his torch would make up for it in some small way.

When he started all of this, how could he have known the great scientist had a daughter, and for that matter that she'd be so beautiful and malleable. And flexible. He dove into that thought heartily remembering the variety of positions they'd tried last night. He never intended for it to go this far, for Ronnie to love him, to trust him with her life. But it fit so nicely into what Dr. Andrews had laid out in his notes. It was as if the stars had aligned to make all of this happen if he believed in such things. He preferred to make things align, with brute force and intelligence.

His computer beeped and he returned to the breakfast bar. The storm was at peak energy levels and a perfect time to start. Charley had been quick, with an unnerving *wham, bam, thank you ma'am* speed. Frances was a marathon session, needing lots of lube and breaks for food and water giving him room for playing around in time. Hannah had outdone herself although she didn't deserve all the credit. This storm was meant to be, it had formed on its own but Hannah's steering had brought it here and managed to slow it to almost a crawl.

At landfall, the wind speeds dropped significantly, as he had requested, but it was still not clear if that was naturally occurring. He would pay her as if it were true, but her skills were still developing. He wanted her to be happy and ride the wave of storms that were still seeding in the tropics. Who knows what else could get close enough for her to manipulate for his use?

Jeffrey grabbed a handful of almonds, shoved them in his mouth, and wiped his fingers on a paper towel next to the laptop. He despised fingerprints on the keyboard.

"Okay Ronnie-baby, batten down your hatches. Shit is about to get real." And he added for good measure, "Fo' shizzle."

The code was already set up, all he needed to do was press go. He paused thinking of how Ronnie looked as she slept. He imagined gently kissing her cheek and sliding a hand over her perfect ass. "Wake up baby, let's do this."

The code flashed on the screen showing it was under way. A surge of adrenaline forced him to his feet. "Please work, please work." Fingers tapped rapidly on his leg as he watched the code fly by filling the screen. Then it stopped on a single word: Launch.

"Yes! Cat Island here we come!" He pumped his fist in the air. "Fuck yeah."

He sat on the barstool and watched the progress. It took about ten minutes to confirm she was there. At least women were treated with respect in the 1950s. A gentler kinder location too as she loved the beach, so maybe a romp in the waves and then back home for a little rest while the second round was programmed. The details of this drop location were vague with only boating accident mentioned so hopefully it would be exciting but not too harrowing. It was going to be a long night. Damn, he wished he had those ready-made Starbucks drinks he'd left at Ronnie's. He was going to need some coffee.

Chapter 18 – Mangled Mast

Ronnie woke with a sharp pain in her stomach that forced her to curl into a ball. It was hot and sticky since the air conditioning had been off for hours. She felt around for the flashlight and held her stomach as she made her way to the guest bathroom, lifted the toilet seat, and knelt in front of it. Her stomach lurched.

"Oh God, not again." Frances was tearing it up outside and just like the ramping of Hurricane Charley, her stomach was in knots, but not only from stress. She focused on the flashlight shining off the blue tiles of the bathroom wall. She forced herself to take a deep breath and then let it out.

A dark mist oozed under the bathroom door. "No, no, please not again!" Ronnie gripped the toilet as if it would anchor her to this time, this place.

Her weight seemed unbearable and her elbows collapsed, splaying her on the bathroom floor, stomach doing a flip with the movement. Her mind reeled. "No, not again!" A spark of hope, would she see Mathias? Would she return to where she'd last been?

A loud noise made her flinch and she squeezed her eyes shut not wanting to know if it was the storm or something else. She used every ounce of her being to stay here in this time. But against her will, she was ripped apart, torn in two, as her body limply sprawled on the bathroom floor, her soul, her essence, hovered above. The flashlight rocked back and forth and Ronnie reached out for it, thinking it could make a good weapon wherever she was headed but her hand passed right through.

In an instant, she shot up as if pulled by an invisible force and in seconds was hurtling through the air at an ungodly speed, her hands and feet hanging below her making her feel like a string was attached to her spine.

It felt like the first hill on a rollercoaster when every ounce of your body is screaming madly and it's all you can do to let out the terror and excitement. Ronnie wanted to sob, to scream, to kick her feet, but none of these things were possible. Fear shot through her and made her fingers tingle. Like a strobe light, it was an odd mixture of high speed and slow motion at once. For just an instant she floated, but like a ride on a swing, the momentum was shifting, and she was falling, her speed increasing by the second. Her hair whipped behind her, the skin on her face stretched. Everything was dark but she could see small particles of light flying by.

Without warning it stopped, slamming her down into the darkness. It felt like she'd broken every bone in her body.

The only sound Ronnie heard was in sharp contrast to her emotions. The soothing *whoosh, whoosh* of waves lapping on the beach. She held her breath and listened. The distant seagull cawing added to the feeling of the sea. There was a distinct fishy smell bringing her back to her childhood summers in Sandbridge.

Ronnie forced her arms to lift, but without sight there was no way to confirm it. Her body was numb and disconnected. She squeezed her eyes shut and tried her best to calm down and let her mind react without fear clogging her thoughts. Slowly in tiny increments, her vision cleared leaving her with a very fuzzy brightness when she opened her eyes. An arm dangled above her and she put it back down. Then her mind caught up and it hit her right between the eyes. She had travelled in time. *Again.*

The rising fear made her ears ring. Could she will herself back? A voice broke the silence making Ronnie nearly jump out of her skin.

"Baby," sounded a kind, concerned man's voice. "Are you still with me?"

Ronnie tried to answer. She turned toward him.

"Oh, thank God. I thought you ..." He picked up her hand and kissed it. He sobbed. "I'm so glad you're still alive, baby." The sobbing continued. "I ..." His voice was shaking. "I should never have taken us out on that boat. I have no business..." He squeezed her hand. "If we survive this ... when we get back I will make it up to you." He pressed his lips against her hand and smoothed her hair. "I promise."

In small increments, his handsome face became clear. He had a crew cut, light hair, and even features. She tried to speak but only a croak came out.

"I've found a little water. Here, drink this." A strong hand held her head and he pressed a metal flask to her lips. The water was warm and metallic but it did wonders to sooth the sticky dry mouth she hadn't noticed before. "I've moved you out of the sun, you're already so burned."

"Where ..." Ronnie managed to croak.

"Oh, baby, you don't remember." He held his face in his hands and sobbed. When he looked up blue eyes shone back at her. It was too bright and she held her arm up to block the sun.

"We got caught in a storm, two maybe three days ago. I'm losing track. George assured me it was clear sailing. Why did I ever trust such a monster?"

"George, who..." Ronnie was glad he seemed friendly. Baby was a pretty good name after the welcome she got the last time around.

He shook his head and sat back on his heels. "George, you know the man you used to go steady with."

She shook her head hoping he would continue.

"Surely you remember George. He ..." His jaw dangled open. She noticed now he had small scabs on his nose, cheeks and the top of his brown shoulders. He was shirtless and the dark shorts he had on had a ridiculously high waist.

"Baby, George is the man you broke up with. I didn't know that until we were way out here." He waved a hand and Ronnie noticed the beach behind him. "He swore to me that it would be a glorious day and as much as you love the water ..."

"It's a nice day." Ronnie wished she could enjoy the beach.

"Baby, you don't remember the storm?"

She shook her head.

"I … the boat. It …" He sobbed again, wiping the tears away. "George sabotaged the mast. He loosened the bolts and sent us out into the storm. I …" He sniffed. "I didn't know it was the guy you had been seeing before. I'd never have listened to him."

Her heart went out to this man who felt responsible for the accident. "It's okay, we will just rest a bit and get back home."

The man shook his head. "No, don't you see? The storm took us out to sea. Rachel, our boat is in a million pieces." He stood and walked away, bent low and brought back a long board. "We smashed on the reef."

"Oh, no." His panic wormed into her mind. "How long ago was the storm?" The skies were clear and sunny.

"You really don't remember?" He stood and looked around. "If someone would come by and rescue us, but the water is so shallow here. Larger vessels won't come this close and I have no way to signal." He turned back to her. "I don't want to leave you but I need to see if I can find food. We've not eaten since …" He fought back tears.

"Go," Ronnie said. "See what you can find."

He helped her with more water. "Please… just hang on. Don't leave me, baby, please."

Ronnie smiled at him. "Get us food." It was all the energy she had left. She fought to keep her eyes open, to not worry the man.

A deep aching in her stomach kept her from sleeping and her head pounded. Her tongue felt like it was shriveling up in her mouth. Rachel? She must have been in someone else's body again. If she had any energy she would examine it further but she couldn't even open her eyes. Instead, she focused on the sounds of one of her most favorite places in the world, the beach.

A short time later she woke with someone yelling. Her first thought was that Steph was calling from the other room. She tried to sit up but her body argued intently at any movement. Peeling her eyes open she managed to turn her head and look out into the water. The man was swimming in the water and splashing around.

"Baby! I found some wreckage!" He treaded water. "I think I saw the forward cabin." He waved.

Ronnie did the only thing she could and that was exhale. In her mind, she screamed yes! Go for it. She closed her eyes and sent him, whoever he was, good vibes to find something of use. Even focusing positive energy proved to be too much and she must have fallen asleep again. When she heard the next noise, she woke up, almost jumping out of her skin. It was a bloodcurdling scream.

Chapter 19 – Red Sea in the Morning Sailors Warning

"Help!" The voice was more frantic now.

Ronnie strained to see where the sound was coming from. It had to be the man begging for help. No one else was around. Off about twenty yards, a frantic splashing caught her eye. Had he found the food and was bringing it to shore? How did he expect her to help him when she couldn't move?

He swam quickly toward her with fast even strokes. Then he stopped and was lifted out of the water. Was there a sandbar there? But then she realized something had him. "Oh no!" Ronnie lifted to her elbow her heart pounding in her chest.

He saw her and reached toward her screaming and waving his arms, punching the surface creating a dark splash zone in the water. Then he swam frantically again, this time unevenly, the right side without much power.

"Shark!" Ronnie whispered. She could see the fin above the water now, circling the man. "No, no, no!" Her heart sank, how could he get to shore, he was still ten yards away. She pulled herself up to a sitting position and her head spun, stars sparkling around her vision.

"Help, help!" He yelled.

Could she swim out there to save him? Would it be too late? She tried to stand but her legs were wobbly. Was there a weapon nearby to stab the shark? The man broke free and swam quickly toward her. She took a tentative step not sure if her legs would hold her.

"Go!" She tried to yell but it came out as a whisper, her throat too dry to manage much more. He swam unimpeded toward her but used an ineffective stroke. His legs weren't kicking and they dangled low in the water, dragging against his forward momentum. Ronnie rushed as much as she could and entered the warm water with gentle waves caressing her legs.

"Keep going!" She looked around for the shark but it wasn't visible. The man was close now. She smacked the water hoping to draw the shark in toward her and away from him. Just let him get to shore! A wave pushed against her torso and she lost her balance knocking her off her feet. Without thinking she swam instinctively toward him. Somehow it was easier for her to swim than it had been to walk—water had always been her element.

"Grab my hand!" He was so close she could almost touch him since his forward motion was nearly a crawl. With all her strength, she kicked toward him, her left hand grabbing his as if shaking it. Lifeguard instincts kicked in and with little effort, she pulled him toward her while twisting his arm, his body was limp now and it turned face up in the water, as the technique intended. Ronnie reached over with her right arm across his chest and gripped his armpit, nestling him along her hip and body. He didn't resist, but she glanced down to make sure his mouth was above the water.

Fear gripped and propelled her forward. The energy of the nearby shark communicated its hunger. Using the inverted sidestroke with the lower leg kicking and the upper leg stabilizing, she managed to slowly make progress toward shore, her head dipping underwater with each kick forward. Her foot touched the sand and she stood and walked backward holding him under the armpits. The water was dark red trailing behind him, fading from red to pink to turquoise leaving a trail of his life oozing out.

Ronnie pulled him through knee-deep water. He needed to be completely out of the water since sharks had no issues with moving in shallow water. With every ounce of her strength, she dragged him on the sandy beach until she collapsed and he fell on top of her, crushing her into the sand. Ronnie gasped for breath, unable to move from sheer exhaustion.

He was barely conscious but managed to roll slightly to his side freeing her left leg. Panting and drawing deep for strength, she shoved with all her might and finally broke free. Crawling out from under him, the first thing she saw was red sand. He was bleeding out fast. God, this was horrific. She was afraid to look at his legs, what if they were missing? She quelled the rising nausea and swallowed down the bile that had risen. She looked around. What could she use to stop the blood?

Ronnie pulled off the yellow blouse, catching buttons in her hair, but finally pulled it lose and braved a glance at him. Blood poured out of a seven-inch gash in his thick calf. It wasn't arterial blood and thank God his feet were still attached.

She bent his knee and wrapped the blouse just below and pulled tight, and knotted the tourniquet. Then examined the other leg. He had several deep cuts on his foot that were oozing blood and Ronnie covered them with her hands pressing hard and she glanced around for something else to use. His shorts were tattered near the tourniquet. She tore a piece and wadded it up, and used it as a dressing.

"Hey, you there?" Ronnie said, hoping he wasn't gone.

"Mmmmm," confirmed his consciousness, however fleeting.

Ronnie pressed into his foot and laid next to him on the sand, keeping the pressure. "You're lucky he didn't take off your leg. Just some cuts." It was mostly true. She didn't want him to panic, likely he was already going into shock from the loss of blood. If they could get some help he may be okay, but the longer the tourniquet was on the more likely he'd lose that leg. If he lived at all.

"My pocket," he said, weakly.

Ronnie sat up and felt his front pockets. There was a sizable lump in his left pocket, she dug in and pulled out an old-fashioned tin. She held it up in front of her face and read the label: Tuna Fish.

"Good for you!" she said. "Did you grab an opener?" She explored his pockets but they were empty. Chicken of the Sea would have to stay in the can for now. God, how frustrating. The one thing they needed most and it was right there out of reach.

Ronnie willed herself to a sitting position. Stars and spots fluttered around her head. She needed to get out of the sun. Motion in the water caught her eye. Several sharks were swimming just off shore.

"Get in the shade, baby," the man said, reaching his hand toward her. "Don't worry about me, I need to just rest a bit then I'll crawl there."

Ronnie crawled slowly, using every bit of energy she had left to get to the small flask where she had woken up. It would really help him. Eventually, she was there in the shade. Just a few minutes to rest and she would take the water to him. He had been so kind to her. The least she could do was give him a little water and hopefully he would have enough beans to get back to a shady spot with her. How much blood had he lost? She glanced toward him clutching the flask and was alarmed to see flies buzzing around his legs. The image of a fly laying an egg in his wound made her stomach churn but solidified her resolve to help. Every muscle ached.

Without warning, she had a flash of the cool tiles of her bathroom. Her eyes opened and she was back on misery beach. As bad as she wanted to return she needed to get to the man, to give him the water. Ronnie willed her body to crawl toward shore, toward the man who had risked his life for her. Flask in hand, she slowly, exhaustively moved one limb at a time trying to reach him. Halfway there her arms would no longer hold her weight and she collapsed. Another quick flash of the light on the wall of the bathroom and Ronnie lost consciousness. Blackness and a comforting lull soothed her ache. Her mind tried to will herself back to help the man, but there was no turning back.

Chapter 20 - Trust Your Gut

Ronnie fell down the pitch-black hole at a terrifying speed, small bits of light ripping past her. Her eyes closed in pure exhaustion. There was nothing left in her to fight it.

"Ronnie," a man's voice called out.

She recognized that voice. "Dad?" I couldn't be, he had been gone five years.

"Ronnie, I can't believe you're here. I've waited forever to find you," her father said, emotion choking his words.

"How are you here, Dad?" Tears streamed down her cheeks. She wanted to see his face, to feel his arms around her but all was blackness. Someone touched her arm.

"Ronnie, stay strong." His midwestern open vowels soothed her soul. "It is your strength that will get you through this. Don't give up on yourself. No matter what they say to you. Trust your gut."

"Okay, Dad," Ronnie sobbed. There was so much she wanted to say to him, to ask him. "I love you. Please tell me how I can hear your voice, now, after all these years."

A new sound interrupted her thoughts. The rush of air as she landed back into her body, making everything empty and black.

He gripped her arm. "Ronnie, are you okay, lass." Her body collapsed and he held her close. A flash of the hot sun and painful dehydration and exhaustion shook her to the core but was gone as soon as it registered.

Ronnie wrapped her arms around him. "Dad, oh thank God, you're here?"

Ian slid and arm under her shoulders, "Dad? I dinna ken about that name, it'll be hard to finish if you're calling me that."

Ronnie gasped, "Ian, what the hell?" She pushed him away, feeling utterly heartbroken.

"I found you on the floor, are you okay? You seem out of sorts." He said, sitting back on his heels.

She looked around. "Oh my God, I'm back!" She embraced Ian fiercely and let go, dashing down the hall to her bedroom. "Steph! Steph!"

Ronnie flung open the master bedroom door with Ian close behind, took two steps into the room and stopped dead in her tracks. Steph was on top of Nick in the bed, apparently in the middle of something important.

"Jesus, Mary, and Joseph," Ian said and did an about face. "Are ye shagging him, Stephanie? Oh, my eyes, I'll need to claw them oot."

Ronnie turned around abruptly but didn't leave. "Steph, it happened again."

Nick groaned. "Oh, you have the same impeccable timing as wee Hamish."

Steph made that distinctly Glaswegian noise, "Ooch. You're not serious, Ronnie!"

"Oh, don't mind me," Nick said. "I'll just be here holding my own." He laughed. "Wait I didn't mean that!"

Steph laughed, "Don't you dare! I'll be right back, babe." She turned to Ronnie, "Are you sure?"

"I am. One hundred percent. I'll be in my room ... um ... the guest room." Ronnie slowly made her way down the hallway.

Ian lurked behind her. "What is it, Ronnie. What happened again?"

She felt numb. It wasn't supposed to happen again. It wasn't supposed to kill her...again. "Steph didn't tell you?"

"I don't think so. She told me about Jeffrey ..." He said but he stopped when Steph walked into the room, pulling her robe tight around her.

"Leave, Ian. This doesn't concern you." Steph sat on the bed next to Ronnie clutching her flashlight in lantern form.

"Oh aye, it certainly does. I pulled her off the floor of the washroom. Something weird is happening and I want to know ..." Steph interrupted him by standing and staring him down.

"Okay, okay, I'm leaving." Ian held his hands up then walked out of the room, shoulders slumped.

"And I'll wring your little neck if you listen by the door. I swear I will Ian." Steph shut the door and sat back down next to her. "Sorry, he's a bit protective ... and nosy."

"It's okay. God, I was sure I'd not go back again, but Steph ..."

Steph took her hand. "Tell me everything."

"I'm so sorry I interrupted you guys." Ronnie nodded toward the door.

"It'll keep. Just tell me what happened already, Ron." Steph squeezed her shoulder.

"I was asleep and felt queasy, just like last time. Then I ended up on a beach." Ronnie relived the moment of impact.

"A beach? I was thinking it would be back in 1752. That doesn't sound too bad. When?"

"Well, you would think it would be pleasant. I tried to enjoy what I could of it but Steph," Ronnie wiped the tears that were escaping from her eyes. "There was a shark attack and I think I died of dehydration. I'm not sure."

"Bloody hell, you were attacked by a shark?"

"Well, not me. The man who was with me. He was trying his best to help me, we'd been shipwrecked for a few days." Ronnie told Steph everything that happened.

"Seriously, this is really weird, Ron. I thought with Jeffrey gone you'd be safe here, no chance of it. What do you think happened? Was it exactly like last time ... I mean the way you left and came back?"

Ronnie sighed. "Yes, almost exactly the same way. I've had this weird feeling all night that it would happen again. I really wish I'd left town like I wanted to. I don't think it would happen in Virginia."

Steph hugged her. "You want to sleep in our room with us?" Steph asked.

"Oh, God no Steph, let's not torment that poor man any more than we have already," Ronnie said nodding toward the master bedroom.

"Ha! He will recover, I'm sure," Steph said.

They talked a little more about the experience until finally, Ronnie's eyes were droopy. Steph hugged her, "You need some sleep. I'm sure whatever it was, has done its job for the night. Get some rest and pray the storm is over soon."

After Steph left Ronnie sat on her bed trying to digest everything that had taken place. It had happened again, A flash of the blood-soaked sand haunted her. Did that man die there on the beach? Who was he?

She took a few steps toward the dresser. Ronnie dug around and finally found the watch Jeffrey had given her for her birthday. It was an odd thought, but maybe, just maybe it would make the experience stop. She clasped it on her wrist and studied the rectangular rose gold face. It really was a stunning piece. Exhaustion overtook her mind and despite all the horror and worries rolling around in her head, she laid her head on the pillow and fell into a fitful sleep.

Chapter 21 - Lump in Her Throat

A loud crash startled Ronnie out of a fitful sleep. She pulled the window coverings aside and tried to see outside. It was pitch black and the window was fogged up. A sharp pain tore through her body and she stood up and stumbled toward the bathroom door, clicking on the small flashlight. Another intense pain and a wave of nausea washed over her. Ronnie pushed into the bathroom and leaned against the countertop, setting the flashlight on the sink.

"No!" Not again, this could not be happening. Her cheeks went hot and she knelt over the toilet. Her stomach lurched and she tried her best to keep her food down but it was no use. She flushed and felt the pressure crushing her to the floor. She tried to stand as if that would help prevent her from going but the force was too great and she collapsed on all fours. Mist oozed under the door and Ronnie squeezed her eyes shut. "Not again!"

She felt a tearing out of her very soul, painful and complete. She floated above her form on the floor then was pulled up away from the bathroom into the blackness, speeding faster upwards. Ronnie kept her eyes shut and willed herself to stay in Florida, in 2004. Failure was inevitable.

It seemed to take forever in between worlds almost lulling her into a comfortable place making her think of floating in the ocean, quietly rocking with the waves. But her most recent encounter in the water haunted her. She sat up and pulled her legs in close, in case the shark was lurking below her. Then she slammed to a complete stop.

An unfamiliar noise caused a momentary panic, making her freeze and listen intently. The air was chilly and smelled of wood smoke and body odor. Something moved next to her and Ronnie called out, "No stop!" Afraid something was about to attack her.

"Och, lassie, t'is another nightmare." A woman's voice made her jump. Someone grabbed her arm, and she jerked it away, fear rising in her throat. She swallowed a scream.

It was dark and she could only make out shadows. Or was her vision not working properly? A stabbing pain on the side of her neck made her cry out. "Ouch." Whatever she was laying on shifted.

"What is it Bessie, are ye tangled in your bedclothes again? Let me light a candle and I shall help ye."

"Have ye nay sense, t'is the devil's hour woman." A male voice off in the distance called out.

"She is nay havin' a good rest, husband," the woman said.

A terrible coughing echoed in the room. Horrible retching followed. Ronnie put her hand to her neck and recoiled from the pain. Her fingers tentatively touched again and an ungodly welt met her eager fingers. "What the hell?" Ronnie's voice was small and high.

"Let me see what is amiss," The woman said, pulling aside the blankets. Cold air shocked her flesh and Ronnie recoiled from the assault. "It's nay the bedclothes. What is it, lass? Angus, fetch me some water."

"I cannot, I fear I've no more will to move than a newborn lamb," the man said weakly.

Ronnie's pain was increasing. "Bessie, move your hair aside and let me see what you're picking at."

Her vision was clearing a bit, and she could make out a brighter light coming toward her. A hand reached to push the hair off her neck.

"No! Oh, blessed Jesus, no, this cannot be." The woman covered her mouth and made the sign of the cross.

"What is it wife, what ha'ye done to my we'un?" he bellowed.

The woman grabbed Ronnie's hand. "Nay, ye dinna want to touch it, it may burst, child." Ronnie pulled her hand out of the woman's grip and recoiled.

"What is it?" The man said and she could hear him closer now. She could make out two forms near her.

"Agnus set ye doon, you shoona be up." The woman pushed him away. Ronnie sat on the edge of the ... seemed like a bed as her feet dangled down but didn't touch the ground. She could make out a glow nearby and then felt dizzy. She laid back down and tried to tune out the intense pain in her neck. Her whole body, in fact, was in pain. Her bones ached and her body was wracked by shivering.

The man coughed again and it sounded like he was going to drop a lung right there on the floor. When he stood up, the front of his night shirt was covered by a dark stain.

"Oh Jesus, bless us." The woman dropped to her knees. The man wiped his mouth on his sleeve leaving a dark train across the white fabric.

"What are you carrying on about? Show me, wife." The man said, sitting on the edge of the bed near her.

The woman reached out and pushed aside her hair, revealing her neck. The man cried out and pressed his fingers into her neck, making her jerk away and nearly faint with the pain.

"What is it? Tell me!" The pain was so intense. What the hell was wrong with her neck?

"I feared coming to the city. I knew it was going to be too soon for us to return home." The woman sobbed and covered her face. Ronnie's vision sharpened and she looked at her surroundings. She was in a dark room, with a small fire to her left.

The woman held a candle up. "Show me again lass."

Ronnie moved the hair aside and he cried out. "It is black, oh bless me is it that far along?"

"What is it, please tell me." Ronnie's voice was surprisingly small and high.

"Plague, child. You are afflicted and it happened overnight I fear't this." With the light of the candle, she could see the man's white linen shirt was covered in blood.

The woman wailed again, "Nooo, it cannot be, you cannot be afflicted. My family is already reduced to just the three of us."

Chapter 22 – Nail in Your Coffin

Ronnie shivered and pulled the thick blankets back over her. The woman came to the other side of the bed and felt her forehead. "Child you're burning up."

"I'm so cold," Ronnie said through chattering teeth. It was hard to think because her brain was sluggish. The whole scenario scared her. Her hands were small but it was too dark without the candlelight to see much. Was she a child? She explored a bit and found no womanly features.

"Angus lay ye back doon." The woman helped the man over to a chair near the fire next to a small bundle of blankets just in front of the hearth. He must have been sleeping there before she woke up in this place. Where the hell was she?

"There is no fire and a bitter cold air is upon us. Please, wife. I've no means to do such business at this time."

The woman made a fire in the stone hearth. Shadows played around the room and Ronnie could see more details of the sparsely furnished room. On a table against the far wall sat a pitcher of water.

"Here Angus, let me help ye get to your pallet." The woman helped him position himself on the floor in front of the fireplace.

Ronnie tried to control the shivering, but it was no use. Her muscles were tiring from the constant barrage and her skin burned as if on fire.

"Lass, t'is the plague has crept up on us both." The man nodded to the blood down the front of his shirt.

Plague? Did he mean bubonic plague? "No, no!" She sat up again. The plague, she had the effing plague! All the symptoms fit.

"Lay ye doon, Bessie," the woman said. "I'll get ye warm again. Mayhap you can get some rest." She went to the fire and picked up a small pan with a long, stick-like handle. A minute later she lifted the blankets near Ronnie's feet and placed the end of the pan under the blankets near the foot of the bed. It was pure heaven. Ronnie pressed her feet next to the disk and closed her eyes letting the warmth sooth her. It was a great distraction from the pain, and she imagined the discomfort flowing out of her.

"Now, let us all rest." The woman blew out the candle and climbed back into the bed. The man coughed again and sounded horrible as he nearly threw up from the effort. Ronnie lay quietly trying to wrap her mind around the situation. They sounded Scottish, could she be in Scotland? It was becoming difficult to breathe. She couldn't tell if it was panic or disease, but the thought of dying of the bubonic plague was almost too much to fathom. Ronnie's mind sped through possibilities as she weighed her options. Would she be stuck here dying for days?

Eventually, Ronnie heard movement in the room. Ronnie opened her eyes, not realizing she had fallen asleep, and watched the old woman at the door.

"Oh sweet lass, how are ye now?" She approached the bed and sat down.

"Okay, I guess," Ronnie said, again surprised at her small voice.

"Eh, what's that?" The woman cocked her head.

Crap, she'd have to be careful, if this was witching times, she'd already been there and done that. "It hurts. A lot."

"Och, Bessie." She put a hand on Ronnie's cheek. "I'm heading out to the market to find some herbs for ye and your da. I will return as soon as able tae." She stood clutching a basket.

"Aye. I will look after Da while you are gone," Ronnie said, mimicking her Scots.

The woman opened the door, letting in a bitter cold gust of wind, leaving Ronnie alone with her thoughts and the dying man nearby. This was a good time to explore her surroundings for time period clues. She pushed the blanket aside and tried to get off the pallet in an attempt to stand, but she was so weak her legs wavered like noodles. Her feet were bare and instantly freezing cold on the wooden planks.

A knock struck fear into her heart. Was she supposed to answer? A fervent *tap, tap, tap* forced her hand and crossed the small room and opened the door.

A young woman wearing a white lace cap and holding a basket of kindling stared back. "Chambermaid, ma'am. May I enter?"

Ronnie stepped aside and the woman zipped past her and set the basket on the table.

The chambermaid pulled a bundle out of the basket and stepped toward the fireplace eyeing Ronnie. She stopped dead in her tracks when she saw Angus on the floor. "Pray my forgiveness, I dinnit know you …"

Angus rolled over, awake now, with the front of his shift covered in dried blood, browning from oxidation. "Mornin' lass." Fresh blood dripped and caught in his beard as he spoke.

The chambermaid screamed and dropped the wood in a dash out of the door.

"Ooch, lassie, ye shouldnae have let her in here. Now she will inform my cousin of our dire situation." He leaned on one elbow and shook his head.

"What will he do about it?" Ronnie said in her tiny voice.

Angus lay back down and sighed. "Isna going to be a good thing. This town has nearly been cleared of the plague, but it seems as though we have returned it." He waved his hand, beckoning. "Please warm yourself near the fire. You are shaking like a leaf."

Ronnie stumbled on new, shorter legs, toward the fire holding her hands out to soak in the warmth. She sat on the floor near him. It was deliciously warm, and her back was colder in contrast.

"What will your cousin do then?" she asked.

He squinted. "What a queer voice you have. I cannae understand your phraseology, lass."

Ronnie bit her lip. Not again, she'd not fool them with a fake Scots accent. Best she kept her trap shut and save herself from the witch discussion.

She needed to find something warmer than the thin linen shift she had on. Near the window was a trunk. Ronnie lifted the lid and dug around, finding a long black wool coat that must have been the man's. She held it to her chest and it reached her feet. She found a grey wool shawl and tried it on, but again it was too long and would cause her to trip. She felt like Goldilocks. Finally, she found a small brown roughly-made dress and slipped it over her linen shift.

"Your stockings are here." The man nodded to a few dingy grey garments near the fire. "Mum rinsed them out last night."

Ronnie crossed the room again, using up most of her remaining energy, and took the shortest pair of stockings. She then sat in the chair nearby and slipped the stiff wool fabric over her small white thighs. It was a strange feeling to be in another body, especially a child's. Her eyesight was improving and she could see more minute details in the room. A pair of small leather boots warmed near the fire. She bent to pull up the stockings that slipped down her skinny legs. Voices outside of the door made her stop and listen. The cousin must be returning.

The door burst open and a tall dark-haired man stomped dramatically into the room. His cheeks were flushed and his voice gave away his anger. "Cousin, pray tell is this? You bring the great dying to my inn, after all I have given you, and this is how you repay me?"

Angus sat up. "Aye, yee've been ever so kind to us. I swear on the Holy Bible I dinna know I was ill, I beg your forgiveness, Cousin James. Pray forgive my error."

"Ye know what I 'ave to do, ye have to know I must protect our inn and our city." Cousin James glanced at her. "Oh pray tell me the girl is not afflicted as well?"

Angus looked away. "I beg your forgiveness lass, it seems as if I am so cursed and have shared my misfortune."

"It is done. May God bless you cousin." James shook his head and turned on his heel slamming the door behind him.

"What will he do to us?" Ronnie asked, but before he could answer a loud noise pounded into her skull.

She followed the noise and realized it came from the door. The wood vibrated under her fingers.

Angus interrupted her puzzled thoughts. "It is for the better." His eyes were moist with emotion. The calm in his voice needled the panic inside her into a more desperate terror.

"He can't be sealing the door shut? How can you just sit there and let him!" She clenched her fists and stomped her feet, making the stocking bunch up over the one boot. Ronnie pulled them up yet again and found the other boot.

"We do not have long. It's best to lie in the arms of our Lord and wait for him to take us." He sniffed and wiped his nose on the filthy shirt.

110

Chapter 23 - Burn Baby Burn

"Oh no, that is not how this is going to go." Ronnie was not going to lie down and die, just as soon this obnoxious wardrobe was sorted. A pair of garter-like strings hung near the fireplace. Ronnie grabbed them and slid each one over her boots and up her small thighs, pulling the stockings up and folded the tops over the ribbon. Something outside the window caught her eye. A man was on the roof walking toward the window. He pulled a nail from a small box and started nailing the window to the frame.

She banged on the window, "No! Don't do that! Stop it!"

"Bessie, sit ye doon and let the man take care of this. It's for the best!"

"For the best? You'll just lie down and die here? We shouldn't be locked up here like animals. How can you just sit back and let them seal us in here?"

"We're on death's bed, the plague will take us in a matter of days. This method is to protect others from the ill humors we have brought upon ourselves." Angus lay back down near the fire.

"Nonsense! We might live! I'm not willing to just lie down and die!" She breathed raggedly, the stress sucking more energy out of her small sick body. "Some people survive the bubonic plague. Some do, we could?"

"Aye, we could but how many will become ill at our hands. This is …" Angus stopped mid-sentence and pointed to the window.

The man on the roof was leaning over to hear someone down below. "A fire?" He yelled back cupping his hands, then glanced at her and shook his head. He met her gaze, his mouth crumpling in a frown. "God bless you, miss." He said and snatched his box and climbed down the ladder.

"Fire?" She pressed her face to the window and could see black smoke rising in the distance.

A pounding on the front door pulled Ronnie away from the window. "Bessie, please open the door without delay. I beg of you!"

Ronnie ran to the door, "I can't they've nailed it shut!"

"Nay, please no! Why have they done such evil to their own kin?" The Scottish woman said. She had returned from the market already.

"Because we're sick. They nailed the window shut too!" She leaned against the door, yelling through the wood.

"Listen to me! The baker has set alight the bakery and now the whole city is ablaze. It will be here in a matter of minutes. You must get away, get out of there at once. Bessie, please."

"Oh my God, the baker?" Ronnie crumpled to the floor leaning against the door. Something deep in her subconscious nagged at her. "What day is it?" Ronnie screamed through the door, cheek pressed to hear.

"Day, why girl what day is it? I dinna ken what ye mean?" the woman answered.

"What is the year? The Year of Our Lord …" She looked at the man. "What year is it?" she yelled. "Where are we and what year is this?"

"Och, lassie what are ye going on aboot?" He said. "Tis the year of our lord sixteen hundred and sixty-six."

All her energy drained out of her body and she closed her eyes. The year 1666 marked the great fire of London. The bakery was clear in her mind. In June, she and Steph had stood right at the spot where it began on their London trip. It seemed more like a few lifetimes ago.

"Is this London?" Tears welled in her eyes.

"Why yes, lass. The city of London. You must remember we arrived just yesterday in the night. You were asleep in the back of the cart as we made our way to our cousin's inn."

The woman yelled through the door. "Bessie, get ye out of the inn, it will be alight in minutes. Grab your Da and I'll meet ye near the road that led us here."

Angus sat up and spoke as loud as his lungs would allow. "I will nae leave. It is God's will to take us this way. It will save me bleeding out my humors and the pain of the death rattle."

"Angus, ye cannae quit, we need you now to save the lass." The woman yelled through the door, pounding. "Angus!"

"I have made my peace woman. Go and make yours. This is a sign from heaven, I am being called to serve my Lord." Angus slowly knelt in front of the hearth and mumbled a prayer.

Ronnie grabbed a quilt from the bed and put it over the chest near the window. She looked around for something heavy to break the glass. Instead, she found a letter opener on the table and slid it into her hand. She'd fight her way out if the innkeeper tried to stop her.

Then she grabbed a log from the basket the maid had brought, wrapped the quilt around the log, and with all her might smashed the window. It took several tries but finally, she had enough glass broken to make her way out onto the roof. Adrenaline coursed through her veins and she stepped on the windowsill and climbed through the broken window. A hot smoky wind hit her face and made her eyes water. She walked to the edge of the roof and looked down three stories to the cobblestones below. "Crap!"

She noticed a boy in a window in the room next to theirs. He waved and opened the window. "Miss, miss, over here!" He looked to be about ten years old with dark hair and beautiful hauntingly blue eyes.

Ronnie quickly crossed the slanted roof tiles to the window. The boy took her hand to help her inside the small room.

"Thank you so much," Ronnie said.

"Hurry along now miss!" He grabbed a small chest in one arm and her hand in the other. They rushed down the hall and he steadied her down a flight of stairs and a hallway. It was impossible to catch her breath and she bent over panting.

"Come, miss, do not delay!" He stopped and pushed her from behind. They ran down the next flight of stairs and Ronnie struggled to keep up.

"Miss we're almost there, please." His face was pinched in worry. "Please come with me."

He took her hand and pulled her out of the building into a throng of people rushing down the road. Smoke was billowing just in the alley behind them. People screamed and shoved each other. Someone tried to take the boy's chest but he punched a man in the stomach and yelled for her to follow him.

Ronnie's lungs were screaming out in pain. The lesions on her neck echoed every beat of her heart. Then she stopped, too exhausted to go on. "Go ahead, go on!"

He stared at her, "Come, miss, please!"

"Matthew, there you are!" a woman yelled and grabbed the boy's arm.

"Mother, thank the Lord. Here." He handed her the chest and she shoved it under her apron, clutching it desperately.

"Come!" He yelled at her as his mother dragged him away. Ronnie stood there knowing she may have just given the boy bubonic plague from their contact. "Thank you!" she screamed. He pulled away from his mother and came to her side.

"Miss, please let me help you out of this place," he begged.

"No, you go with your mother! I'm sick, I can't get you sick too." She yelled over the noise of the crowd and crackling of the fire. Hot air encircled them and she pulled away from his grip. "Go!" His mother grabbed his hand and pulled him along.

"Miss!" He reached out, but the frantic crowd pushed them farther apart and soon he was swallowed up with the rushing of the panicked Londoners.

Ronnie ran to keep up with the throng surrounding her but grew weary, her legs hardly holding her up. Each breath excruciatingly painful. Deep soul-wracking coughs forced her to stop and the crowd shoved her forward. A spattering of blood on her hand made her panic and renewed her energy. She shoved her way to the edge of a brick building where she pressed against it panting. The door to the building was ajar and Ronnie slipped inside. The floor was packed dirt and the room sparse. By the fireplace was a simple wooden chair. She sat down and grasped her knees and tried to catch her breath.

The room was filling with smoke. Ronnie dropped on all fours searching for cleaner air and then rolled on her back, no longer able to hold herself up. In her hand, she still held the letter opener. The metal blade flashed in the low light.

A dangerous yet intriguing idea entered her mind. The times she had travelled death had returned her to present-day Florida. Would that be the way home this time too? Or would she die here in this time and not make it back?

Tears slid down her cheeks and her father's voice echoing in her mind, "Trust your gut."

Chapter 24 - Pink Cheeks

Panicked noises from the crowd running just outside the building were a stark contrast to the quite calmness in the little house. Ronnie could feel the heat on her cheeks, the fire was creeping closer, the roar of the flames and crashing of destroyed lives echoed around the small room. The air was heavy with smoke and her infirm lungs worked hard with the effort of breathing.

Her lifeblood screamed out to escape, to flee. Her mind stayed true to the course knowing running away would leave her fighting the plague and who knew what else. If she had learned anything from her last visit to London, it was that things could always be worse than ever imagined.

A small sound wormed its way into her heart urgently pleading. She shut her eyes and mind to it in hopes of a moment of peace to deal with her vile choice. It continued to nag at her and she focused on it. Then it hit her why her mind wouldn't let it go. It was a child's voice.

Ronnie sat up, listening more intently. Was the child in this building? She stood and her lungs filled with smoke, she pulled the top of the shift over her nose and listened intently to the cries. There was an opening in the ceiling on the far side of the room and nearby a ladder leaned against the wall. Ronnie wrestled to move it into place but managed to lean it against the opening. A deep bone shaking cough rattled her entire body, and she struggled to get clean air in her lungs. Bending low she breathed deeply and held it as she climbed the ladder.

"Anyone up here?" Ronnie called out as she neared the top.

A small pink face peeked out from under a blanket in the corner.

"What are you doing here?" Ronnie called out and in response, a little blonde head poked up from its hiding place.

"Ow, miss, me mum is at her work. I am to not move a muscle until she returns," the little girl said bravely.

"No, no, you have to leave. The fire will burn this building down in a matter of minutes. Don't you feel the heat?" Ronnie reached out, feet still on the ladder.

"No, me mum will punish me for moving. She needs to ..." The eyes grew bigger as if the fear of her mother's wrath was worse than the prospect of the fire.

"Your mum is waiting for you, I'm sure. She needs you to leave now so you don't get burned in the fire. You have to come now," Ronnie pleaded.

"How can you be so certain?" The girl crawled out of the small bundle of blankets on the floor closer to her now but still hesitating.

"You must come now. Do you see the smoke? It's near and we have to leave." Ronnie climbed one rung higher and reached out.

The little girl came closer but hesitated again. "She won't be cross with me?

"She will be delighted to see you're safe. Come here, climb down the ladder and let's go." Ronnie's legs were weak and the air was thickening. They were running out of time.

The girl came close enough for Ronnie to grab her skinny arm, "Climb down." Ronnie moved down the ladder making room for her on the top rung. Small dirty feet appeared above her and Ronnie continued down the ladder until she reached the bottom. The girl was maybe four or five years old and frightened, her eyes huge in the low light. Ronnie took her hand and led her out of the door.

Her entire world shifted, she needed to help this little girl but would she just give her the plague and make her suffer more? Ronnie let go of her little hand and pushed her from behind, toward the street. The crowd had thinned and the smoke was billowing around them. A mom and her two kids rushed nearby.

"Miss, miss!" Ronnie called out to the woman, not having the energy to chase after her. "Please help this child, she has been left behind by her family."

The woman stopped for just long enough to take pity on the girl. "Well, come along little turnip."

An older child ran over and took the little girl's hand and they all ran out of sight. Ronnie eyed the rapidly approaching blaze. It billowed as a wall of hot air, pressing her forward. The haven of the little house called her back making Ronnie hesitate. Her choice was grim. Death by burning, death by smoke inhalation, or death by her own hand. Would any of them return her to Florida? Would this be how her life ended? She thought of Steph. How would she handle her disappearing? What about her mother? It would crush her soul. Ronnie ran as fast as she could but the fever had taken most of her energy, and her lungs were ineffective in providing oxygen.

She stopped and leaned against a stone building, panting with her hands on her knees. She collapsed and leaned back against the cool stones. The crackling and roaring of the fire was catching up to her. Her choice was drawing near. Last on her list was being burned alive so that reduced her options. In a panic, she felt around for the small letter opener she had taken from the inn. Had she dropped it along the way? Would she even have time to use it?

A building collapsed nearby pushing her toward her decision. She found the small knife in a pocket in the dress she was wearing, not sure how it got there, but was relieved to feel the smooth warm metal. She turned it over in her hand and contemplated the best way to use it, then stood and tried the door to building, wanting a bit of privacy for the dirty deed, feeling this was something to do secreted away in a private place. That thought had her puzzled because any prying eyes had run away from the fire, but maybe there were a few souls willing to make the sacrifice at the temple of the fire God.

The door was open and the cool damp air hit her. It was dark and smelled of wood smoke from the large hearth. Ronnie shut the door. The fire hadn't come close enough to sully the air here yet. It would give her a little time to ready herself. She found a chair near the hearth and held the letter opener between her fingers, imagining it piercing her skin. This was unfamiliar territory. Suicidal thoughts were not her daily bread, but ironically to live she would need to commit such an act. Would it bring her back to Florida? Or would she just die?

Deep breath let it out. Ronnie closed her eyes looking for guidance. The distinct odor of smoke crept under the door frame and swirled around her. *Give me guidance.*

Ronnie did not want to die, but her choice now was grim. If she took her own life would it set her free? She thought of her last death experience in London. Her hand went to her neck and she was spurred on by this decision.

A searing pain nearly made her faint. She'd forgotten about the lump in her neck. Even if she survived the fire she would have to endure death by plague. Her stomach lurched. She took a deep breath and pulled smoke into her lungs to only set off a coughing fit. The smoke was creeping in, she had to choose now. When she caught her breath, she envisioned her mother's face and said goodbye. She imagined hugging her brother David. An image of Jeffrey's caramel eyes looking angry then softening. Was he causing this? How could he be involved since he was not nearby but Steph had been so sure?

Hot dry air encircled her and she pulled the linen fabric from the shift under her dress to cover her nose, trying to keep the smoke out. Flames licked around the door frame and between the cracks in the boards in the ceiling. Fear spurred her on. She coughed in an attempt to get fresh air into her lungs but there wasn't any. Without another thought, she pulled up the sleeve.

"What the hell?" The rose gold watch was there. It was loose on the small wrist of the child. It had gone back with her the last time she was in London as well, but not on the beach. Or had it been there too? She hadn't thought to look then, but surely she would have noticed.

A loud crash came from the house next door, likely from it collapsing from the fire. Ronnie didn't have much time. She imagined the small knife slicing through her flesh and without any further digesting of facts or consequences she boldly drove it into the faint blue veins at her wrist. She ignored the pain. Dark red blood flowed out of her small body and dripped on the table. Then a horrible though struck her. What if it took too long and she burned as well? It was too smoky to see much now. She tried to grip the knife to slit the other wrist but must have cut some tendons because her thumb wouldn't grip it hard enough to make it useful. Tears flowed down her face. Was it really committing suicide if she believed she would live again?

Gripping the knife in her left hand, she sliced through the stocking and then cut into her ankle where the pale green of a vein was evident. Pain made her eyes water but she hacked away, blood flowing freely. Weariness pulled her down to the floor and a calm peaceful warmth surrounded her and made her think of a lazy summer day floating in the lake with warm sunshine heating her skin.

A loud crash dragged her out of the stupor. Flames captured the sparse furnishing and the roof alight. In a matter of seconds, the stairwell collapsed. Fear tickled through the haze and she rolled away from a burning chair. A quick flash of fresh damp air filled her lungs. Her skin seared with the heat of the room as her worst fears were coming true. The acrid smell of hair burning brought tears. Loud noises assaulted her ears but she was unable to move or react. Another deep breath of fresh air and the sheer absence of pain washed over her. Then everything went black.

An alarming sound pulled her out of the comfort and warmth and she pushed herself off the cool tiles of her guest bathroom and wiped the drool from her mouth. There it was again—a roaring sound like a train.

Chapter 25 - Cheese Whiz

"Holy shit I'm back!" Ronnie grabbed the flashlight and leaned on the bathroom sink trying to catch her breath. Her hand felt her neck and she looked in the mirror. She was back in her own body again and free of the plague. The air was hot and sticky but didn't have the dry heat of the fire.

"Thank God." She made her way down the hallway to the master bedroom on wobbly legs. Ronnie pressed her forehead to the door where Nick and Steph were sleeping. Would she interrupt them again?

The same stormy sounds of fierce wind through tall trees made her step back. "Crap, the storm." She'd completely forgotten about Hurricane Frances battering them. Something large scraped along the roof and culminated in a loud crash. New noises of fear echoed around in her mind. The bedroom door opened startling her.

Steph ran into her. "What the ... Are you okay?" She grabbed Ronnie's shoulders.

Nick was right behind her with his flashlight beam flicking back and forth as he walked towards her. "What was that noise?"

Ronnie moved aside and let Nick out of the bedroom. He ran into the living room and she could hear Ian asking the same questions.

"Steph ... it happened again," Ronnie said, catching her arm as she rushed past her.

Steph turned, "No! Are you serious?"

"'Fraid so." Ronnie hugged her friend. "This time it was awful."

They walked toward the commotion Nick and Ian were making. Ronnie wiped her eyes. She held her hands out and sure enough, they were shaking.

"I don't understand it though. I was sure Jeffrey was behind this and now he's not here, and it's happened twice," Ronnie said absently. Her mind was rolling at lightspeed as it tried to process everything.

"Tell me what happened, Ronnie. Where did you go?" Steph attempted to flatten down her own wild hair and motioned for Ronnie to sit on the couch where Ian had been sleeping. She set the lantern down on the table adding a warm glow to all but the dark corners of the room.

Ronnie remained standing. "Oh Steph, it was so horrible, an absolute nightmare." She took another deep breath. God, it was so good to be back.

"Where and when this time?" Steph flung aside Ian's sheets that covered the couch and put her arm around Ronnie. "Sit and tell me everything." She sat down with her.

"I think it was the fire of London, you know sixteen sixty-six," Ronnie said, trying to calm her mind enough to make sense for Steph.

Steph's eyes widened. "What the bloody hell?"

"Ronnie, you're gonna wanna see this!" Ian ran toward her, shirtless and in a panic. His wiry muscles glistening. Was he wet?

"What is it, Ian?" Steph asked annoyed.

"The storm, lass, it's …"

Nick yelled from the kitchen, "Ian, Ronnie!"

Ronnie sprinted to the kitchen with Steph close behind. Nick was standing on the countertop, water pouring in around him. He was holding a tree limb, trying to push it back out the kitchen window. Water was pouring into the sink. Leaves and bark filled the counter and glass was all around.

Ian ran from the darkness and stopped behind them. He shone his flashlight on the ceiling. Light reflected off the stream of water pouring in. "Ronnie I'm so sorry."

She crumpled to the floor, head in her hands. A severe headache pounded in her temples. Ian helped her up and supported her to the living room with Steph on the other side. "Ronnie, are you okay?"

Ronnie nodded but her mind was spinning. Too many stresses all at once. Her body revolted and she slumped on the couch. "I need food or I'm going to crash … hard."

"Ian, stay with her. I'm going to get her something." Steph disappeared into the kitchen.

"Are you okay, darlin'?" Ian put an arm around her and Ronnie leaned against him.

Nick ran past. Ronnie could hear wet feet on hardwood fading away then he returned with shoes in his hand. "Do you have a tarp or plastic sheeting somewhere?"

"In the garage on the shelves near the door," Ronnie answered into Ian's shoulder.

Steph walked in from the kitchen holding a box of crackers and a spray cheese can. She stood in front of Nick. "Oh no, you're not going out there, not again. Nick remember last time?" She nodded to the cast on his arm. "Not again!"

"Steph don't do this, you know I'm going to take care of things. Plus, my cast is already soaked but it's fiberglass. For Christ's sake, my arm is almost healed." He continued on the warpath to the garage undeterred by Steph's anger. She followed on his heels.

The two of them argued out of sight, but Ronnie couldn't hear Steph's voice. She did hear Nick say, "Well get Ian then, he can help me."

Steph stormed past her and slammed a box of Tollhouse Crackers on the coffee table near her face. Ronnie jumped.

"Thanks," she managed. She opened the box and shoved three crackers in her mouth.

"Ian, I need your help. Now!" Steph barked.

"What the hell Stephanie, I'm not going out there in a hurricane!" Ian skootched away from her and stood.

"Do it for Ronnie. It's her house, you eegit," Steph yelled pointing at her, "Go help Nick and make sure he doesn't kill himself."

"Och for fuck's sake Stephanie, don't put on the dramatics. I'll help your man," Ian said, wiping the sleep from his eyes.

Steph held a can of Coke and plopped it down in front of Ronnie. "Here, love. I'll be right back. Ian, look at this."

Ronnie laid her head on the armrest of the couch and stretched out the full length as she tried unsuccessfully to tune out the chaos going on around her. Hurricane Frances was raging outside. How long would this storm last? She squirted bright orange cheese and wondered who made the unwise choice to buy canned cheese? Surprisingly it had a decent flavor. She closed her eyes and focused on the loud chewing that was temporarily drowning out the stormy sounds. Steph was making noise in the kitchen. Ronnie opened her eyes and instantly regretted it.

Her friend held a bucket under the stream of water pouring into her kitchen and towels were strewn about the floor. Ian was swirling the towels on the floor ineffectually and Nick was out of sight. Ronnie squeezed her eyes shut. She felt like crap. Her stomach was doing backflips as her head did a tap dance.

She thought back to the scene of the fire raging around her. Why was this happening? What was it about the storms that sent her back in time? She wasn't even at the weather lab. Then a strange thought crept into her brain. She had the watch on when she was in the fire. That had to be significant. Did she still have it on now? She vaguely remembered sliding it on her wrist before lying back down.

"Oh my God!" Ronnie sat up too shocked to feel queasy now. The watch was on her wrist and was covered by a red, sticky, goo. "Blood!" She was panting now and winced in pain as her head reminded her of the pulsing pressure within.

The last minute of her time in the fire of London flooded her vision and took over her thoughts. She had taken her own life. Correction, she had taken the little girl's life whose body she had taken over. Was it murder? Suicide? The watch ticked away oblivious to her plight as it clicked one minute into the future. Was it her blood? Or was it from the girl?

Ronnie stood up from the couch and screamed, "Steph!"

The watch was covered in bubonic plague infected blood. She stood up and ran to the kitchen yelling. "Steph, Steph!"

Steph was on her hands and knees sopping up the rain with some towels. "What is it?"

"Blood!" Ronnie held out her wrist.

"Oh, no, what did you do?" Steph said. "Are you okay? She stood and came to her side.

Ronnie's head spun and her knees felt weak. "No, Steph, this isn't my blood! This is from my time travel! It's proof Steph!"

"Let me see." Steph moved to grab her wrist and Ronnie stepped backward.

"No! Steph, don't touch it. It has bubonic plague on it!" Ronnie looked at the watch now and was shocked to see blood only the watch, still wet from her sudden return, but none of it was on her own skin. She could see no cuts around her wrist. Chills ran up her spine and she collapsed to her knees. Proof! But it came with a price. "Give me a baggie, Steph, I want to get this tested." She pulled on the clasp and carefully removed the watch, took the baggie from Steph and dropped it in, and quickly sealed it.

"You don't seem to have any cuts, Ronnie, are you bleeding anywhere else?" Steph asked wide-eyed.

"I don't think so. We can get this tested for bubonic plague and maybe get some DNA." Ronnie stood up and made her way, flashlight in hand, to her dresser and put the baggie in her top drawer. Spots grew around her vision and she bent over to make them stop. She had to lie down or she was going to be sick. Her body was crashing. This time traveling seemed to screw up her blood sugar or something. She eyed her bed and then remembered that's where Steph and Nick were sleeping. She ran to the master bathroom and promptly threw up.

Another wave assaulted her and she tried to tune out the storm raging just outside the bathroom window. She was not in a safe place, a branch could come through the window at any second, as it had in the kitchen. Her friends were all working hard to save her house and here she was completely useless.

Ronnie flushed the toilet and stood at the sink and scrubbed her hands and wrist. "Bad shape." If she didn't lay down this was going to be really, really, bad. Stressful things had to stop happening.

"Ronnie," Steph called from the hallway. "Where are you?"

"Here." Ronnie leaned on the sink.

"Wow, you look horrible are you okay?" Steph came to her side.

"Not exactly. I need to get this blood off me. Steph the body I was in was sick with the plague."

"You said that. What a nightmare."

Ronnie dried her hands on a towel and sat on the bed.

Steph stood staring at her. "Ian and Nick are on the roof, putting the tarp on. It's not so easy with the storm raging but they've got bricks holding it down for now. The water isn't pouring in your kitchen anymore."

"Oh damn." Ronnie held her head trying to squeeze out the pain. "Thank you so much for being here and for helping out so much. I'm sorry I'm not doing anything." She looked up. "I'm feeling really bad, Steph, can you get the food and bring it to the guest room?"

"I'm sorry you're feeling so sick. It's just like the last time you time traveled though, right?" Steph said, "Where you feel shaky and weird?"

"Yeah, you're right. It feels the same."

"You and Ian should hang out in the hallway, the guest bed is right next to the window, Ronnie. It isn't safe." I can grab your duvet to lay on."

"Sure. How is my kitchen?" Ronnie asked, not sure if she wanted to know.

"It's gonna need some work but if the guys were able to stop the leak it's fixable." Steph put her arm around Ronnie and walked her to the hallway. "Let me get your food and set up your bedding in the hall. Then you need to tell me everything that happened,"

They sat on the duvet and leaned against the wall in the hall. Ronnie told her everything that happened and ended with, "Then I cut my wrist and ankle to make it stop. I couldn't bear to burn to death, it was such an awful choice to make." She wiped away the tears, "You have no idea how relieved I was when it brought me back. I really wasn't sure if I'd return again, but look," She held up her hands palm out. "Here I am safe and sound."

"I don't blame you, Ronnie, I'd have done the same thing. Burning is a horrible way to go. I'd just have to deal with the mortal sin in this life from the suicide." Steph shook her head, "What a choice."

That feeling crept back, the low blood sugar, nausea, and panicky sensation. "I need to sleep. I'm crashing hard, Steph."

She handed her the pillow. "I'll stay with you, Ronnie. Get some rest."

"No, Steph. You go be with Nick. He is such a good guy to do all of this for me," Ronnie said.

"I want to be near you. What if something happens, what if you ..." Her huge blue eyes appeared gray in the low light.

"Go back again?" Ronnie said. "I really don't think I will. I have this deep hollowness inside, Steph. It feels like it's over for now. I don't know how to explain it."

"Okay, you look exhausted." Steph stood. "I'll send Ian here when he's cleaned up, in case you need something."

Ronnie rubbed her eyes as an overwhelming exhaustion spread through her bones. The Scottish Mafia would take care of her tonight. She laid her head on the pillow and pulled the sheet up over her legs.

Ronnie woke sometime later to find Ian a few feet away listening to a weather radio.

He smiled. "This isna how I imagined it, Ronnie."

"Imagined what?" Ronnie could barely lift her head.

"Our first time sleeping together." He winked.

He said it so sweetly Ronnie hadn't the heart to scold. "Thanks for being here Ian. I'm sorry it's not more glamorous." Her eyes refused to stay open and the pull of sleep dragged her down into the abyss.

Noises woke her some undetermined time later. Ronnie did not want to open her eyes hoping whatever it was would go away. It turned out to be a nearby meowing Fluffy out from her hiding place. Unable to move from pure exhaustion Ronnie clicked her tongue and Fluffy responded by lying near her head. The flick of her tail showed the poor kitty was agitated by the storm.

Oblivion overtook her and she rested comfortably until a nagging pain in her guts pulled her unwillingly from a deep restful sleep. She rolled over hoping it was just discomfort from the hard floor but it wasn't. It was time pulling her to another place. The bathroom door was only a few paces away and Ronnie crawled, disrupting the cat in the process.

Chapter 26 - Croatoan

Jeffrey stretched. Everything was going to plan. The only thing that wasn't going according to his strict procedures was a visual of the subject. He had no idea how Ronnie was handling this. She was the first person to ever go back in time … wait, he kept forgetting. She was the second person but that was not public information. Neither was Ronnie and her adventures, but perhaps he'd be able to share the research if he could get her to retroactively sign an agreement. No use worrying about that now.

First things first. Power was building up from the last expenditure, the storm was cooperating fully with his needs. He imagined toasting Hannah for supersizing Hurricane Frances, and a second toast for her steering skills. They were spot-on. What an absolute godsend to have her at the lab. He really had to pat himself on the back for making those arrangement and private donations to her research. She was proving to be a formidable scientist.

His computer barked at him, "Beep, beep, beep."

"Excellent." Now to add a variable to her travels. A visual of Ronnie's state of mind and physical heartiness would have been a reassurance but without that data, he would have to continue and add that information later. One of the things that made Ronnie a good subject was her extroverted nature. She always openly shared every detail of her life with him, at least if he played nice and didn't antagonize her too much. Another great asset.

He glanced over the notes in the experiment notebook. He had conducted trials on the same location but two different time periods by sending Ronnie to London in 1752 and then 1666. The small stop in the Bahamas in 1952 was the unknown drop time and he fervently hoped it had been a success. The computer tracking device implanted in Ronnie showed movement so she had survived the return trip. The first two trips were straight line shots to a parallel month and date in the past where the Bahamas trip went back to March of 1952. He was eager to find out if Ronnie had entered the host body in the right location. Damn Stephanie McKay for screwing up that portion of the feedback. He couldn't be sure everything was going well with Ronnie and the parameters of the experiment.

This next experiment would be a beautiful disaster and quite important to the very beginning of the nation. As long as everything cooperated nicely and he didn't end up stranding Ronnie. Would she hold up physically? He really didn't know the full effects on the human form, especially with multiple trips. It was a *once in a lifetime* opportunity, though, and he'd have to take the risk.

He keyed in the trajectory in the time and space coordinates, double-checked the code and details of travel and checked his watch. It had been an hour since the last trip. Everyone should be asleep and quiet in the house. Jeffrey checked the connection to TOTO and all was well. He took a deep breath and leaned back in his chair.

This was a spectacularly momentous day. A twinge of fear tickled at the confidence remembering the last time he felt this good about the experiment, and the near disastrous results that ensued. He was well aware one of his weaknesses was also a key element to his strength—overconfidence. He wasn't afraid of taking risks, in fact, he raced toward it with open arms. Occasionally it smacked him in the face but the beautiful fact it was responsible for his genius, his tenacity, and drive made it a surprisingly useful quality, even if it would someday result in his downfall.

A gust of wind crashed branches or other debris on the French door, but he was getting used to the stormy sounds. He hit enter to begin the sequence that would take her to the most fascinating location and time yet. He imagined her thin T-shirt bunched up around her waist as she slept. The white panties covering but just barely the outline of her beautiful ass, her small waist accentuating the fullness of her hips. One brown leg bent, the other out straight giving a delightful view between her legs. He wished she had not been such a selfish girl by insisting her friends stay overnight. She was missing out since he could have led her to such heights of ecstasy. Instead, she would have to take the trip of a lifetime while sexually unfulfilled.

Chapter 27 - New World

In very tiny pieces, Ronnie was aware of noises around her. It reminded her of a large group praying. It was comforting at first as she sorted through the possibilities. A hazy fog clouded her mind and she struggled to come up with anything plausible. Church? She'd not been to church in years, not since her father's funeral. Did she fall asleep at the pool with kids playing nearby? It was hot enough. It felt like home with the damp humidity heated by the sun, almost kissing her skin. Something about the scent of the place reminded her of the backyard in Virginia Beach where she'd grown up with a whiff of pine and briny waters nearby.

Then it hit her, she had traveled again. Full on panic burst from her chest shoving aside the sleepy sensation and replacing it with soul-clenching fear. What fresh hell would await her this time? The same yellowish disorientation engulfed her that always greeted her time travel.

Was Mathias here? A twinge of guilt tore through her. She had left him behind at the gallows. If she could just steal a little more time with him if only to find out what their connection meant. Just a few minutes to gaze into his soul and explore her feelings, to examine the disturbing vision she'd had of the merging Mike and Mathias at the bookstore.

Something landed on her cheek and startled her. It broke and crumbled down her chin, landing on her chest. Ronnie covered her face protectively and tried with every ounce of strength to force her eyes to see. Out of the yellow haze, the outline of a crowd appeared. More debris landed on her. She sat up, not realizing she had been laying down and forced through a dry hoarse voice. "Oh God, stop, please!"

A collective gasp from the onlookers and innumerable voices yelled out. One voice was clear through the rest, and struck fear into her heart, "It's unnatural! There's the devil to pay!" Another voice from the left spoke softly, but still tore through her violently, "She's in league with Lucifer!"

A cacophony of shouts and prayers rained down, timed perfectly with more physical assaults falling down on her. She curled into a ball protecting her head, crying out until she tasted dirt and was forced to keep her mouth shut.

A deep voice nearby startled her and she turned to him encouraged by his words. "Good people, stay your hands! We know naught from whose hand this is wrought? Shall we kindle God's wrath against us for eschewing his miracle, if indeed it be?"

A shadow on the dirt in front of her showed a man holding hands out wide. Was he protecting her from the crowd? Despite his efforts, a deluge of rocks and dirt pelted her arms and torso.

"Cease my friends! Are we not civilized Christians? Should we act as the savages do who dwell among us in the forests?" he bellowed causing Ronnie to draw inward curling into a tighter ball.

The onslaught slowed and she dared to open her eyes. The outline of a large figure looming above startled her. He was now close enough to touch. He must have had some power in the group because they listened.

He reached out to her. "Mistress, please allow me to assist you." He had an English accent.

As he helped her stand, she realized they were in a shallow hole in the earth about three feet deep. Murmurs of disapproval and a few gasps and screams added to the noise making it hard to decipher any single voice. Multiple hands grabbed and clutched at her arms. The man protected her by wrapping his arms around her. Ronnie held her breath and realized the loud gasping noise she had been hearing for a while now was coming from her own mouth.

The man whispered and Ronnie felt his breath on her cheek. "A truth, milady. I prayed for thy safe return. But I feared I would see it not. Forgive me."

His words were old and struck a pang of terror despite the kindness they relayed. Ronnie hid her face against his chest and waited while her eyesight was restored in small increments, then looked at the crowd. A mob of angry, old-fashioned faces looked like they'd been through hell and back and were dressed in black with the occasional white shirt beneath a doublet.

An older man grabbed her hand, "By God's blood, you live, Madam Coleman!"

Ronnie pulled her hand out of his grasp, not sure how to react. Tears streamed down his face, his hair combed but scraggly as if he'd not seen a pair of scissors in months. She stepped away from the man who rescued her.

A young woman stood on his left looking shell-shocked, her hair hidden under a white lace cap but a few dark strands were plastered against her face amongst the sweat beads that dappled her forehead. "What troubles you?" The woman recoiled and turned away. With lips trembling she spoke to the crying man. "By the saints, I speak no falsehood. Her eyes show hate. I beg of you, take me from her sight. I cannot abide her vicious glare."

Ronnie wanted to speak but knew that would further their suspicions. Their expressions said it all. She was supposed to recognize them.

The man held the woman's elbow and turned as they walked away, "Be warned my brother, Morris. We risk much. We risk our souls in this, for I fear the devil's work. And by God's mercy, it be not true. I fear she is lost to us."

Morris, her protector, turned to the man and said, "We are brothers in Christ, it is true. And upon that I ask thee, cease with it, Mr. Lucas."

Mr. Lucas's pockmarked face wrinkled in anger, "Do ye see it not plainly, sir? The woman was taken! She was gone up! We all saw it and taken to the bosom of the Lord. We did not wish it but it was so. We prayed, but still, it was so. And now she is back! It is unnatural I say!" His skinny finger pointed at her, "It is an ague upon you which clouds your judgment but the truth is there to see. Sarah Coleman once upon a time belonged to us, our sister in Christ. But her, I know naught. And I shall say it again sir, she is in league with Lucifer."

Morris turned away in disgust as if smelling the foul odor of the words. His voice now had a different edge, one of menace and danger, his anger palatable. "Hell's teeth man, must everything that giveth offence be the agency of Satan? Doth the fox that snatches the chicken sup at the devil's table? Doth the rain that falls upon thy sunny day? For the love of all the saints, that which we know naught but are no more unnatural than the trees, whose leaves blow by a wind we cannot see."

Ronnie's heart beat fast and her cheeks burned. In her world, she would have stood up for herself, but here, wherever this was, she was not willing to speak.

Another man yelled out, "Morris, watch yourself. Mark my words, she will be the end of you."

Morris shook his head and looked at the man with contempt. "Thou canst not paint this woman so bad. We sin against our own estate with such accusations." His voice now had a different edge, one of menace and danger, his anger palatable. "Entreat thee back to thine homes. This woman hath enjoyed a deep slumber, naught more."

Mr. Lucas turned to the crowd and raised his voice, breaking into a long speech that Ronnie couldn't completely understand. Either it was another language altogether or it was spoken with such a jumble of old-fashioned words it was difficult to translate. They understood him though for his words fired up the crowd. Slowly they closed in on her and Morris from all sides.

Morris held his hands up, "I beg of you be reasonable until we have seen to the matter with more thoroughness, and stay thy judgments until such day. Now, if you please, return to thy lodgings, or I shall see you to it myself."

"The devil resides within her flesh!" an older woman called out pointing at Ronnie. Her companion raised her fist and the people around her followed suit all yelling at the same time.

A trickle of sweat dripped down her back and Ronnie stepped closer to Morris, fear clouding her mind.

Morris stood between Ronnie and the woman and addressed the crowd. "We sin against our own estate with such accusations." Morris's voice now had a different edge, one of menace and danger, his anger palatable. "Entreat thee back to thine homes. This woman hath enjoyed a deep slumber, naught more."

Someone behind her yanked her hair making pain roar in her head. "Stop it! No!" Ronnie spun around and looked up at a man with long oily hair holding a white lace cap. It must have been pinned to her head because her hair fell loose around her shoulders now, where it hadn't before.

Morris grabbed the cap, returned it to her then addressed the man. "I cannot rightly say of this your purpose, but by all that is holy, you shall bide by my will or face my wrath!" He held up a knife and the man backed away. Morris waved it in a wide circle around them. The crowd backed away noisily protesting but giving him a wide berth. Morris's broad shoulders and thick muscles were enough to deter any man there, but the look in his eyes was infinitely more dangerous.

Morris continued, "And heed my warning well friends, and know this. Though there be many of you and but one of me, I shall not fall easily, nor shall I go with but one companion, I shall have as many as my blade may bite." He turned around to face the crowd behind him. "Return to the house of our Lord, pray for guidance, alas be fair warned this woman shall not be harmed or removed from my protection, not without this blade," he held up the knife, "sinking deep into their flesh."

Amidst grumbles and hateful glances, the crowd thinned and finally, only she and Morris stood in the dusty field. He turned to her, "My lady, forgive them their trespass, they are fearful folk, and in a place such as this I cannot always say I blame them."

She looked down at her outfit—a full-length black gown—and wondered why everyone, including her, wore such heavy clothes in this heat. A long sleeve shift under a dark overcoat covered her upper arms and chest. The light brown stains of fresh dry soil covered her in small clumps and she brushed them off her bodice and the front of the skirt. Why did they all look so beat up and disheveled? It reminded her of those dystopian movies where all modern society was lost and had nothing but true grit to keep them alive.

Morris's hands were shaking so violently he dropped the knife in the dry grass. He bent to pick it up and his dark blond hair shone in the sunlight, catching golds and reds. He stood and sheathed the knife wiping the tears from his eyes. His doublet was a tight fitting black material with small buttons up to the neck and formed a V at his waist. It spared no detail of thick arms and a broad muscular chest.

As he stood he averted his eyes, maybe embarrassed at crying in front of her. She tried not to stare but the pants he had on weren't pants at all. She wasn't completely sure what they were called, breeches maybe, but they told her a lot about the time period, for they showed his thick muscular calves and were ballooned out around is thighs. The pair he wore were deep burgundy and shone like silk in the sunlight.

"They see evil behind every bush and conjure a demon's name to every unknown thing. I stake no claim to such truths of this matter, but nor do I speak the evil one's name to hide my depth of ignorance." Morris held her upper arm and steadied her up a small hill.

Was this an English colony? Where and what time period could this be? She looked at her companion hoping he could shed some light without her giving away too much of her foreignness. She studied the nuance of his speech, his angular face, red cheeks flushed with anger and the heat of passion of his words.

"It pours hot coals upon my head to hear them take such grievous oaths and misuse the Lord's word so. I can call forth no portent as to what this all means, or the mystery of the hands which have wrought it, but of one thing I am certain. I see no evil in thine eyes. I see only beauty, and a thing that ought to be cherished." The dry grass crunched under their feet kicking up dust. She watched his full smooth lips as he spoke passionately, fervently, that were in direct contrast to the surrounding reddish-blond short beard.

Morris stopped and stared. "Pray, speak. Be free with it." For the first time since she laid eyes on him, he was still.

"Thank you for what you have done for me." She bowed her head not sure what the customs were, and not yet willing to speak much. "You have been so kind."

"We have lost so many, so quickly of late and to lose another so fair and pure was uncommonly cruel. I do not pursue the reasons why you were brought back to us, why God Almighty has spared the wrath he has brought upon so many here, now. I only sought to save …" His lips trembled and he dropped to one knee and took her hand, kissed it, and bowed his head, sobbing violently. A quiet prayer in another language escaped his hidden lips but she imagined their fullness as he spoke.

Morris stood and wiped his eyes. "I fear it unsafe for you to return to your own home. According to our good neighbors, you may find Beelzebub and Lucifer themselves playing at your hearth."

"I am grateful for your hospitality, Morris." She couldn't help notice a slight recoiling at her words. He covered it nicely with a smile, but it alarmed her. He was on her side for now, but that could change in an instant.

Chapter 28 - Out Cold

Steph woke with a start to her brother's stubbly bearded face inches from her own. "What is it?"

"It's Ronnie, come quick," he said almost panting.

Steph popped up out of bed and followed Ian down the hall to the guest bathroom, his flashlight shining off the polished cement terrazzo floor.

"She won't respond, Steph," he said, his voice higher than normal.

"What?" Steph walked into the bathroom and Fluffy was there, hovering over Ronnie's body, her tail twitching madly. Steph kneeled down and shook her shoulder. "Ronnie, wake up." The cat ran out of the bathroom and into the guest room.

Ian's worried eyes met hers. "I dinna ken why, she was sleeping soundly not too long ago."

Steph rolled Ronnie onto her back, exposing her stomach and white panties. She tugged the shirt down to give her some modesty and elbowed Ian, who was staring at the remaining exposed flesh. "Stop that, she's ill."

"I wasna ..." His mouth turned down. "Why won't she wake up?"

Steph put her cheek to Ronnie's mouth. She was breathing regularly. Steph shook her shoulders, "Ronnie, wake up." She slapped her cheek but Ronnie remained asleep.

"Ian, help me lift her." Ronnie grabbed her under her armpits and Ian took her legs. They moved her to the guest bedroom and set her down on the bed, Ian's flashlight tucked under his arm so they could see their way. "Go get Nick for me."

"Aye." Ian ran to the master bedroom and she could hear the two men talking. The storm was louder in this room with the window so close to the bed.

Nick walked sleepily into the room. "What is it?"

"She's not responding, Nick. I'm really worried." A pang of panic rose deep in her gut.

Nick sat next to Ronnie on the bed and lifted her wrist, feeling for a pulse, then felt her forehead. His eyebrows knit together. He lifted her eyelids and then sat back and shook his head. "Did she drink much tonight?"

"No, I was talking to her just before she went to sleep. She wasn't drunk." Steph looked at Ian, who nodded in agreement.

Nick grabbed her shoulders and shook her. "Ronnie, wake up!"

Steph felt a gut-wrenching fear. "Come on Ronnie!" She grabbed her hand and squeezed it. Still no response. Nick then reached for Ronnie's chest and Ian's hand grabbed it before Nick could touch her. "Aye, man, have some respect."

Nick jerked his hand away from Ian. "Stop it, I'm going to do a sternum rub. For God's sake, what did you think I was going to do?"

Ian scrunched his face up and shook his head. "No, I was 'jes keeping her safe, I dinna mean to imply …" He crossed his arms over his chest.

"We all know what you were thinking, Ian." Steph turned to Nick. "Go do what you need to do."

Nick pressed into Ronnie's sternum using two knuckles to grind into the bone. Ronnie was still, unresponsive. "God Steph, this is not good." He pressed his lips together in a frown.

"What do you think is wrong?" Steph asked, brushing Ronnie's hair off her face.

"Seriously, I don't know. If there wasn't a storm raging outside I'd say take her to the hospital and find out." He glanced toward the covered window. "That is not an option." He reached for her wrist and felt for a pulse again. "Slow even beats, that is a good sign, but why is she unresponsive?"

"I've got this horrible feeling she's done it again," Steph said, glancing at Ian.

"Done what, Steph?" Ian's blue eyes sparkled in the light of the lantern. "You've been keeping something from me since I set foot in Florida." He pronounced it Floor-id-a.

Steph shook her head and looked at Nick for support. She didn't want to tell Ian about the time travelling since he was such a loose cannon. Who knew who he'd repeat it to and that would not be good for Ronnie.

Nick tilted his head to the side. "Given the recent downward spiral, I think he may need to be privy."

Steph looked at Ian, wishing the man would grow up and be the guy she could trust, but that hadn't happened yet. "Ye scruffy wee lad, you're no allowed to repeat a word of this to a living soul."

"Not even Fluffy?" Ian glanced around for the cat, but she had been spooked by something, maybe even the same thing they were all spooked by, the sleeping beauty lying on the bed in front of them.

"No, not even …" Steph had a moment of weakness thinking of Fluffy, who would take care of her if Ronnie didn't come out of this? She could feel her face crumple and she fought back tears.

Nick sat next to her and hugged her. "It's going to be okay. She's healthy, we will figure this out." His solid warmth was reassuring. If he thought she'd be okay, then maybe she would be.

"Okay, nice wee breakdown Stephanie, but stop the waterworks and tell me what the fuck is going on, would you?" Ian was angry now.

"Calm your tits, little brother. Seriously, this is not about you and your needs. This is bigger than you, bigger than me, Christ it may be bigger than this world altogether."

"Oh, nice. That's cleared it up, thanks for the details," Ian said, crossing his arms. "Why don't you put a wee bit of faith in me for once? You and mum are always discounting me."

"Ian, you've not exactly been trustworthy." Steph shook her head. "Look, you will never say a word about this to anyone, except those of us in this room."

"Okay," Ian said eagerly.

"Swear to me, Ian." Steph studied his face. Was this going to blow up on her like everything always did with him?

"I swear on mum's life." He looked up at her and added, "I've never once said that to anyone, Steph, even when my life was at stake."

"Okay, I will trust you with this but you had better not disappoint me. Ronnie has…" How does one phrase such a stupendously difficult concept?

Nick rubbed her back and whispered into her ear. "Keep it simple, just tell him about …"

"Hey wait, this has something to do with the tadger boyfriend, doesn't it?" Ian blurted.

"The what?" Nick said.

"Tadger," Steph said, "It means penis."

Nick laughed. "Oh, perfect word for that guy, oh my God." Nick cradled his cast and shrugged one shoulder uncomfortably.

"We're not sure." Steph took a deep breath and looked at Ronnie. At least she looked peaceful. "Since the last hurricane, Ronnie has had a …"

Nick whispered in her ear, "Break in reality?"

Steph shook her head deciding that being direct and giving credence to Ronnie's experience was the best route to take. "She has gone back in time."

Ian's expression did not change. "Come again?"

"Look, Ian, it doesn't make any sense. She's the sanest person I know and yet the facts remain. During Charley, she went back to the eighteenth century and just earlier tonight it happened again."

"What the fucking fuck, Stephanie?" Ian jutted his head forward with his eyebrows making an angry V formation.

"Nick, tell him," Steph said, her emotions running high.

"You're taking the piss, Stephanie. Fuck you, seriously, fuck you. The boths of you." Ian turned away, shaking his head.

"Taking the piss?" Nick interjected. "You Scots are so delightfully disgusting. What does that mean?"

"It means you are making shit up so you don't have to reveal your big hairy secret. I get it, I'm a fuck up. I've wasted my life and no one will ever take me seriously. No need to rub it in, no need to torment me when your friend is in a bad way." He pointed at Ronnie and wiped his eyes. "Seriously, I've got feelings though. Let's all have a laugh at Ian's expense while your friend lies dying on the bed. Good plan, great idea." He shook his head. "And fuck the both of you twice."

"Ian, stop. I'm not kidding." Steph felt sorry for Ian, for once he was being raw, being honest with himself and the world.

He looked from Steph to Nick and back. "So, run this by me again. What the ..." He glanced at the chair in the corner of the room and sat down on the edge of it, his head in his hands. He looked up. "What the fuck, Stephanie. Nick, you're telling me …" He stood and flung his hands in the air to accentuate his point, "Ronnie traveled in time?"

"Yes," Nick said calmly and quite seriously. If Steph had not been so worried she'd be laughing right now. The entire conversation was preposterous. Except that it was true.

Ian started to speak but cut himself off. He stood and pressed his head to the wall mumbling a prayer in Scottish. Then he lifted his head and kicked the wall.

Nick jumped up and pulled Ian back, holding his arms from behind. "Hey, no need for that, man."

Ian pulled his arms loose. A new stream of Scots came out of his mouth and Steph tried to ignore the foul-mouthed rant. Finally, he calmed down and looked at Ronnie. "Wait, this means she may just be gone again? Maybe she is okay and this is just her being back in time?"

"You're a fair lot smarter than you look," Nick said clapping him on the back.

"We've never seen her when she's gone." Steph stood. "I just assumed she would be gone too, but it is possible, aye likely even, that is exactly what is happening." She hugged her brother. "God, I was thinking maybe she was sick from the time travelling. She's already gone back twice tonight. Maybe …" She released Ian and a wave of relief washed over her. "She is just gone. Like you said. God, I hope so."

"How can we bring her back Steph? What if I pinch her or something?" Ian said, then an evil look crossed his face. "Or I could," he made a vulgar movement with his hips, "revive her."

Nick punched his arm, solidly making a satisfying thwack sound. "Don't even joke about that, man. That will not be tolerated." Nick's lips completely disappeared into his face.

"Lighten up, mate. It was a joke." Ian rubbed his arm and looked like he was contemplating return fire, but instead plopped in the chair.

"Rape isn't a joke, Ian," Steph scolded. "And neither is Ronnie's safety. We all need to protect her right now. We thought it was Jeffrey causing this. She was in his lab and under his control the last time it happened. Now I don't know what to think."

"The fecking prick. You think he did it?" Ian yelled.

"We don't know. But he is a bit of a narcissist. It wouldn't surprise me if he'd use her for nefarious purposes," Steph said.

"But he's not here, how could he?" Ian said.

"Well, that's why we're not sure. I think if he were up to something he'd not have gone back home. He'd have stayed no matter what," Nick said.

"But what if he knew we'd be here and didn't want to get caught doing it?" Ian said.

"He couldn't have planned anything. You saw how he left unexpectedly," Nick sighed. "Look, we shouldn't jump to any conclusions. We have no evidence he's involved or if that's even why Ronnie is out. It's purely conjecture."

"I know, I know. But I happen to have seen the true Jeffrey and I'm sure he is behind this," Steph said.

A huge gust of wind and the scrape of branches landed on the roof, making Ian jump and Steph and Nick look upwards.

"Should we be in this room? Maybe we need to be in the hallway now," Nick said. "It's getting really dangerous out there."

"Fuck, what if the house is destroyed and Ronnie can't even run away?" Ian looked at the still form. "God, please keep us safe." He looked at the ceiling.

"Stop thinking that way. She'll come back to us soon." Steph reached out and hugged him.

Chapter 29 - Fear and Loathing

A trickle of sweat traveled down Ronnie's forehead. She mopped at it with the small white cap that she had forgotten until now was in her hand. Morris led her up a hill toward a copse of trees. The heat clung to her body, made worse by exercising. Morris must have been just as uncomfortable in a doublet and breeches with a lacy white shirt high on his neck. The doublet bore evidence of repair. At the top of the hill, they turned to the left past a thicket of brambles down a narrow dirt path past several houses and stopped just outside a small wooden structure.

Morris held the door open and his gentle smile with a hint of shyness were surprising after the fierceness he had displayed with the vicious crowd. She was first struck by how dark the tiny house was, despite it being full daylight. The floors were dirt and the rough-cut walls showed gaps in between the boards giving the impression of a hastily built structure. It must have been drafty in the winter.

Ronnie looked for clues to the time period. If the house was any indication, it was either in a remote location or way back in time. There was no glass for the one window, only a square hole with a swinging gate. On the table were a Bible and a beautiful egg shaped clock the size of a large orange that sat flat on the rough wood.

"I am remiss to have properly introduced myself." He bowed elegantly. "I laid eyes upon you since we arrived two years hence. We have spoken to one another on several occasions but we have not been properly acquainted. I am Morris Allen, son of John Allen. I believe you are Miss Coleman?"

The same fears that hit her every time she traveled pulled at her heart. The risks were high this time, probably higher than ever given the reaction of the onlookers. She nodded, wanting more information but afraid to speak and give away her modern Americanisms.

Curiosity overtook her, much like the cat, and she took the same steps with trepidation she always seemed to make and reached out for the table clock.

"A stunning piece to be sure." He stepped closer, "It was presented to my father as a nuptial gift from my mother. He offered it to me as a special relic upon my departure." He pressed the knob at the top and the glass sprung open. He closed it with his thumb. It was a gorgeous piece made of gold with a delicate design on the face. "I gaze upon it oft, as a memory to my parents, whom I will likely never lay eyes upon again."

Ronnie turned it over and ran her thumb over the cursive engraving, *To JA with affection RA, 1561, London.* "Fifteen sixty-one?"

His brows nearly touched and he shook his head. "Miss, please, I do not take your meaning."

She took a deep breath and exhaled, language always seemed to be her downfall. "Is this the year your parents were married? I can make a guess at your age with this information." She smiled hoping to smooth over the awkwardness of their language barrier.

He smiled back, and she made note of the slight crinkling around his mouth. "You are twenty-two years of age?"

His deep belly laugh filled her with joy. "It is not so, you flatter me, Miss Coleman, I am twenty plus five annum, and do not look a day younger."

Ronnie quickly calculated the date as 1586, if his parents gave birth shortly after their marriage. She turned away chewing on this information. The speech and clothing matched what she knew of that time period. Black dots flitted around her vision and she steadied herself by leaning on the small table near the hearth. Further back in time would only amplify her modernisms.

He took the small clock from her, as it sat delicately on her palm, dangerously close to falling on the dirt floor and placed it delicately back on the table. "Time has no real use here in the Colony, we will not be late nor early for any event. Most of us do not own timepieces, and there is no tower clock to remind us of the late hour. Never the less I enjoy its presence."

"Morris, can I ask you something?"

He nodded.

"Please tell me how did I end up in that hole?" Ronnie looked up into his kind brown eyes.

"Hole? I beg your pardon. That was no hole Mistress Coleman." He pulled a white handkerchief from his pocket and wiped his brow. "That was the blessed ground of your final resting place." The corners of his mouth turned down and he looked away blinking away tears.

"What are you saying? It was my grave?" Ronnie's face felt hot and she had a distinct urge to sit down, her legs nearly giving out.

"Mistress Coleman, please let me help you." Morris came to her side and grabbed her elbow, helping her into a nearby chair. "It is so, but blessed heavens you have returned to us."

Ronnie's head was spinning. She had arrived during her own funeral. That explained their reaction. No wonder they were talking about the devil.

He smoothed his hair down. "I believe you were also afflicted by the fever, as was my dearest friend with whom I shared this small dwelling. Imagine my utter torment when I was asked to dig both of your graves within a fortnight."

Nausea washed over and she leaned forward on the chair cupping her head in her hands willing her stomach to calm down. The pain in his words was palpable. "I am so sorry for your loss." Ronnie felt a twinge of sadness about her own father's passing, even though it had been years. The recent contact with him during her travels had unearthed the unhealed wounds in ways she'd never expected.

He sat near the fireplace. "My heart has shattered over the loss. He was nearly kin here and now I feel alone. I could not bear to see you gone as well. I was there by the gravesite pouring every ounce of my being into bringing you back." He blinked away the tears that had gathered among his lashes.

Chills ran up Ronnie's spine. "You honestly prayed for my return?" Tears flowed down her face as well and stung her eyes. "Why Morris?"

He cleared his throat and paused composing himself before speaking. "Mistress Coleman, I have always felt that something was meant to be between us. I have been far too busy this summer." He shook his head. "The fever has done much damage to our people and we are constantly having altercations with the native population. I did not pursue you as it did not feel the right time with so much turmoil."

"It's okay. I understand." A feeling of déjà vu overcame her. The memory of Mathias in London filed in around her like smoke filling a room. She studied Morris's face. Why did she have these feelings for Mike and now Morris? Their resemblance was similar only in their size, as their coloring differed with Morris as a blond. An overwhelming exhaustion halted the train of thought. She would need a quiet moment to sort through everything.

"You see, it is my duty to be the grave digger. Additionally, I repair the perimeter fence. My size makes me a good mark for these manual labor jobs." He lifted his arms to let her look at his long limbs and general girth of muscle. "My training back in England was of finer things, but as we must all do as we can to survive and flourish. We do what we can to support one another."

"We are not in England then?" Ronnie asked.

He looked up from his hands. "Not for a few years now. You do not remember our journey to the New World?"

"The New World?" Ronnie's mouth dangled open. Were they in America?

"Governor White brought us on this journey. You do not remember the treacherous voyage over the sea to this new world?"

Ronnie took a deep breath. Images from textbooks flooded her mind. Early settlers in America had left England for religious persecution or fortune. She closed her eyes and tried to control the sharp headache that tore through her forehead. This era would be immeasurably worse than the witch hunt she'd faced in the seventeen hundreds. "Morris, please, I know this will sound strange to you but what is the date?"

"I beg your pardon, Mistress Coleman. What is the date?" He shook his head. "Sometimes your phraseology is so unusual I do not take your meaning."

"It is the year of our Lord …" she looked at him.

"The year of our Lord fifteen eighty-eight. I am curious why this question has arisen as it is wholly out of the ordinary."

"Morris, I …" This was not something she could share and do him any favors. "It was a passing thought. I feel like since I woke up in that grave I know nothing of my life before." The year 1588. Could she be in the Lost Colony of Roanoke Island? The disappearance of an entire colony had baffled historians for centuries. Her father had been fascinated with the history of the people of this mysterious colony, as one of them was a distant relative.

"In time, you will recall everything. The fever has caused you to use your humors on healing, and it most certainly was well spent." He reached out to touch her arm.

"Perhaps." Ronnie knew she would never recall because it was not her life that had ended in that grave. There was no connection to Mistress Coleman other than the pure and simple baffling fact that she was currently in her body. It was a disturbing realization. She had bumped Mistress Coleman off, literally. It was so weird to be in this situation again. "I am sorry to have caused such a stir. I do not recall how I …" She couldn't find the words for her own death and burial, or at least that of the body she was now in. She cleared her throat, "passed."

"I believe you are cured of such ailments now miss. The happenings of this day have sent shivers down the entirety of the colony, as everyone will be speaking of this to their brethren for years to come." He poured water into a small ceramic bowl from a matching pitcher. "It would please me greatly for you to …" he wiped at his cheek. "I beg your forgiveness, it is impudent of me to tell a lady how to care for herself, but I have always been told I'm more frank than is good for me."

He held out a small grayish cloth. "You may find me out of doors while you recover." He bowed and walked out of the front door leaving Ronnie to stew in her own thoughts.

She absently lifted the cloth and caught a reflection of her face in the bowl of water, reminding her of the seer in London and the horrible future she foretold. Her stomach tightened at the thought of what she might have to go through to get out of this place. She ruined the image of a young woman's pale hair with dark smudges under her eyes, and dirt on her face. She wiped away the tears and tamped down the fear and horror of the death's she'd endured just tonight during Frances. Dehydration, burning, and suicide. Now to wake up in this place already buried once. Voices outside the window interrupted her thoughts.

Morris's deep booming voice full of anger drove into her soul. She stood on tiptoes to look out the roughhewn window. A man with a torch alight shook his fist and yelled something. He was accompanied by three other men holding gardening implements, one with a rake and the other with a pike. As she watched, Morris scuffled with the man holding the torch and deftly tumbled the man onto his back. He snatched the torch out of his hand and threw it on the ground, stomped on it putting the flame out. Two men came after him and he overpowered them.

They stood panting and talking heatedly. Ronnie had trouble understanding their old-fashioned words and wasn't completely sure if they were speaking another language altogether. Morris pointed back at the house. Clearly, they were discussing her. Fear gripped her. Were these men about to burn down Morris's house because he had helped her? She did not want to be responsible for anything untoward happening to him because of the kindness he had offered.

Ronnie set down the cloth and slipped out the back door making her way out of sight of the arguing men in the front.

Chapter 30 - Up on the Rooftop

A nightmarish noise outside woke Steph from a deep sleep. Nick, Ian, and Ronnie were all nearby sleeping in the hallway with blankets and pillows. A loud scraping noise across the roof made her cringe and fear rose in her throat. Nick's eyes opened and gave her a concerned look. The storm was blasting Ronnie's house and the wind howled through the trees outside. Nick reached for the weather radio and hit the power button.

"Severe damage along the central Florida coast from Hurricane Frances is causing millions of dollars, possibly even billions of dollars, in property damage, lost lives, and shattering hopes and dreams," the news lady said. "Tornados are likely in the northeastern portion of the storm."

"Wow, maudlin and dramatic today, eh?" Nick said, trying to eek a smile out of Steph.

She forced a grin. "What time is it?" She sat up on one elbow and glanced at Ronnie.

"It's seven thirty in the morning. I guess we can get up if we feel like it." Nick stretched and caught himself wincing in pain.

Steph crawled over to Ronnie and shook her. "Ron, wake up, wake up!"

She was lifeless as a ragdoll. Nick shook his head. Steph felt her neck to make sure there was still a pulse. There was.

Ian rolled over and moaned, "Get on wee ya, then."

Steph stretched and crooked her finger at Nick to follow her out into the living room. Nick obliged and wrapped her in his arms hugging her and kissing the top of her head "You okay, babe?"

"I'm just worried about her. When is she going to wake up?" Steph leaned her head against Nick's chest.

"I guess she'll wake up when she's ready. I don't know what else we can do." She felt and heard his words through his muscular chest. Steph pulled away from his embrace and walked to the front window. Leaves, branches, and debris were strewn about the yard. The storm was still raging on as strong as ever with the wind blowing the rain completely sideways. The trees were doing their best to hold on, branches flapping like exhausted dancers just phoning it in.

"Nick, when is this storm going to end? I just ..." She pressed her fingers into her eyes.

He wrapped his arms around her waist, the cast pressing into her hungry stomach. "I don't know. It's supposed to last until Monday. It's only Saturday, I can only imagine what the yard will look like by then."

"This is so frustrating." She turned around and hugged him, burying her face in his chest. "I don't know what to do, I can't help Ronnie, I can't make the storm stop." She fought back the tears. "I just want to take her to the hospital and find out what's wrong."

"I have a feeling she will be fine. The storm is going to do what it will do. Hopefully, the house will not have any more damage," he said into her hair.

Steph pushed away from Nick and ran toward the kitchen. "I completely forgot about the roof!" Water covered the floor and the roof was leaking madly.

"Shit, I thought that was taken care of last night!" Nick bellowed. "I bet that damn pine tree dropped another branch."

"Did you see loose branches last night when you were out there?" Steph asked.

"It was hard to tell, plus the storm has raged all night." He held the cast close to his body, almost protectively. "Can I get into the attic and maybe fix it from there instead of going out onto the roof?"

"I think so. Ronnie had mentioned the gobshite was up there last night. I don't know if it leads to here." She pointed up at the ceiling.

"How do I get into the attic?" he asked.

"Garage, I think." Steph pointed to the door leading to the garage.

"Be right back." Nick disappeared. Steph began the arduous task of cleaning up the glass off the floor for the second time in twelve hours.

Nick returned. "It's just at the top of the ladder there. Okay, I am just going to figure a couple things out, you get Ian. I just hope we can keep this kitchen roof from caving in."

Steph ran back to the hallway were Ian was sleeping. He was moving Ronnie.

"Ooch, will you no leave that poor wumman alone, ya eeegit," Steph said.

Ian turned around to look at her, eyes wide mouth open, "Stephanie I, it ... I was... she."

"Ian Brain McKay, what the devil are you doing?"

"Ooch, Stephanie, have some faith in my motives. I just got thinking what if she was in position for a long time I didn't want her body to be sore, you know. What do they call that? Bedsores?"

"Let me help you." Steph felt bad for chastising Ian but he was a giant flirt and womanizer. His motives seemed to be pure with Ronnie though. Still, a tiger couldn't change his stripes.

"Let's move her to the couch. I can keep an eye on her while I make breakfast. She'll be more comfortable than on the hard floor." They lifted Ronnie, Ian walking backward while Steph held her feet, and set her gently on the couch. Steph rearranged Ronnie with Ian's pillow under her head.

"We need your help in the garage," Steph said as she covered Ronnie's legs with a blanket.

Ian stood, glancing down at Ronnie. "When you say garage do you really mean go on the roof and mess around with a tarp in the middle of the fecking hurricane, because I'm nae going to do any of that nonsense again." He ended by lifting his chin and staring at her in defiance.

"No, we are trying to avoid that, the kitchen's flooded and there's another branch in the roof." Steph explained the situation while they walked toward the garage.

Ian stopped and glanced backward. "Will she be okay with no one around, Stephanie?"

"I can see her from the kitchen, Ian. I'll keep an eye on her."

"I suppose she'll be okay," he said following behind.

"Ian, will you come up with me into the attic." Nick held his casted arm. "I could use your help, man."

"There won't be any spiders up there?" Ian held up his hands. "I'm nae ready to admit I'm no feart, but I'll just say I may scream like a wee lassie if I see one."

"Scream away, it won't bother me. Only thing is spiders love it when you scream. It will bring the whole bunch around for a meal." Nick laughed and started up the ladder.

Ian gave Steph a look, "Yer man is nae funny, he is *nae funny*." He followed Nick and turned around. "Go check on Ronnie for me."

"I will." She had to chuckle. Ian was a softie. This was another layer she had not seen in her brother before.

She yelled up the ladder, "Nick, can you get it from there?"

"Yes, I can see the break in the roof. I think we're set. Go make us breakfast and check on Ronnie."

"Aye, Stephanie, piece n' jam for me," Ian chimed in, peeking his head down the opening of the ladder.

"You'll get what I'm serving, clothead," Steph said, annoyed at his bossy tone.

Chapter 31 - Ten Feet

Jeffrey's eyes glazed over as he stared at the computer screen. He knew he had time to let this adventure stew. The power levels were exceptional due to the storm being an amazing generator with no end in sight. Everything was going peachy, other than the strangeness of being in someone else's house, a cheap horrible one at that. It would be done soon enough and then he could sleep. No rest for the wicked, and damn it all to hell he felt wicked. *Wicked smaat* as they said back in New England. His graduate thesis at MIT had begun his exploration of time travel with just the kernel of the idea.

He checked the numbers again for the umpteenth time, but all was well. Until it wasn't. As he watched the screen a horrible message popped up: *Lost contact with subject.*

"Oh no! No, no, no! Not again!"

This is exactly what happened during Charley. Ronnie took off the damn watch and there was no way to pull her back. How the hell could she have gotten around the implant in her back? There was no way. Had he known he'd be a house away, he would have installed a microphone or video so he could hear what was going on. Although adding video to the bathroom was not ideal, he'd have to witness that asshat Earl take a shit or worse. Or was that Ian?

"What the hell, Ronnie? How are you doing this?" Jeffrey stood staring into the screen willing it to reconnect. He looked up to the ceiling and noticed a crack from the house settling. Rather like the crack that was forming in the experiment, yet again.

He sat down and stared numbly at the screen, contemplating what of a hundred variables could be the cause of the disconnect. It could be as easy as the time machine's battery winding down hours before it should have. Maybe damage to the roof and the tarp covering TOTO allowing water to seep in?

He typed madly checking all the avenues of betrayal. The biggest experiment of his career and the damn system fails him. After an extensive exploratory examination of the time travel device, all was well. TOTO was in good working order. Next was the time to check out Ronnie's connectivity.

Jeffrey typed frantically, working his fingers almost numb. Bing.

He did some further exploring but couldn't find the reason she was no longer connected. Jeffrey stood abruptly and knocked over the stool he was sitting on. He absently righted it.

"No! Don't make me come over there and ruin my cover. You will definitely pay for that if you do, Ronnie." He could feel his pulse beating in his head and he glanced outside. He'd have to give it some time, maybe it would reconnect on its own. Doubt nagged at his conscience. If something happened to the machine while he waited for it to fix itself Ronnie might be stuck in that time-space continuum. A stabbing pain knifed through his grey matter and he winced. This damn broad would be the death of him.

Jeffrey walked to the French doors and watched the trees flail about. The yard was littered with branches and leaves. The pool was a sea of green, with more debris in it than swimmers could possibly fit.

"Ronnie, come back to me. We need to get you back in one piece so I don't have to explain this." He glanced over at the computer hoping for a miracle.

"God damn it. Are you going to make me come over there?" He mumbled into his arm that was pressed to the French doors.

***

Jeffrey had emptied the jar of almonds. He pulled the lightweight windbreaker over his head. His running shoes were almost dry, but he hesitated. He did *not* want to go out in the storm. He'd watched the radar for the last hour hoping to see the eye of the storm come across but it was too far south. The current plan to pull this experiment out of his ass was to go examine the equipment and get a fix on Ronnie's location. If she'd moved out of range of TOTO she would not be able to return home and that would fuck everything up. He patted his shorts pocket that contained the tool kit wrapped in a kitchen trash bag just in case TOTO had sustained damage, or if he needed to pick a lock or something. He chuckled at that. Like he'd know how to pick a lock.

"Well fuck it." He pushed the French doors open and stood under the lanai, watching the storm rage around him. This was stupidity. Unfortunately, it was the risk he had to take to finish off this round of experiments and to save Ronnie's life. She would be trapped if he couldn't figure out how to reconnect. This was the risk of running an experiment remotely.

He stepped out into the rain and instantly his hood was blown off. Rain blasted into his eyes and he wiped them fighting to pull the hood back over his head. Finally giving up, Jeffrey fought the wind and rain. His foot caught on a branch and he tripped, falling on his hands and knees on the lawn. "Shit." He stood and wiped the small twigs that had jammed into the skin of his knees. He was now covered in mud adding to his agitation.

The rain was blowing sideways and he fought his way across the backyard carefully picking his footing so he didn't fall again. He pushed against the gate but the water was so high in the yard that the bottom of it caught in the mud. Kicking and leaning his shoulder into the gate, he managed to open it just enough to squeeze through. He ran across Ronnie's side yard and under the eaves.

"Well shit." Now what? He'd not thought about how to get into Ronnie's house without being seen. Tugging on the garage door handle he realized it wasn't barred as he had feared. Lifting the door, he held it open with his foot and crawled under, hoping no one noticed the loud noises. He stood and brushed off his arms that were now covered with wet leaves and debris from the garage floor. Voices echoed around. The attic ladder was down and fear choked him. Had they found TOTO?

Jeffrey squatted behind Ronnie's Thunderbird and listened intently. Stephanie's brother's voice was distinct with the Scottish brogue. Was it Evan or Ian?

"In Scotland, there are spiders the size of your head, man. They've been known to carry away a small child."

Nick's laugh echoed in the garage. "You don't say. Hand me that hammer, Ian, the small one."

Ian it was. They must be repairing the roof. They sounded like they were nearby, and therefore couldn't be close to the guest bathroom where TOTO was hiding.

"Are we nearly finished? I'm starving." Ian said.

Damn, how could he get to TOTO with these two imbeciles blocking the way?

"Dude, it won't be too much longer. Help me here, make yourself useful," Nick said with frustration, followed by a loud hammering.

As if called by the thought of her, Stephanie opened the door. "Boys breakfast, such as it is, is served."

"Yesssss," Ian said and instantly descended the ladder.

"I'll be down in just a minute, Steph," Nick said.

"Come on, come on," Jeffrey whispered impatiently waiting for Nick to go into the house. Finally, he heard footsteps on the ladder and the door to the house closed behind him.

Jeffrey quietly climbed the ladder and used the light from his small flashlight to find TOTO. The machine was still covered with the tarp and green lights blinked happily. Jeffrey checked the tarp making sure it had fully protected the time travel device. All was well on this end. It looked a little like R2-D2 in cold storage when it was covered like this.

He followed the voices below and stealthily made his way back toward the kitchen as he listened to the friends chatting over breakfast.

"What are we going to do about our lass?" Ian's brogue was obvious once again.

"Nick, what do you think?" Steph's milder brogue chimed in. Jeffrey sat down and leaned against the rafters. "I'm really tempted to take her to the hospital. She isn't responding at all and what if it's something life threatening? What if we don't act and she is really hurt or worse?"

"I don't know what to do," Nick responded. "If I knew she was back in time I'd say let it settle itself and she'll return liked she did before. I don't think it's smart to drive in the hurricane."

"True, but I feel like if she's in some kind of diabetic coma or low blood sugar event and if we don't do anything until the storm ends she may not survive," Steph said.

"She's nae diabetic, Stephanie, is she?" Ian's voice was muffled around the food in his mouth.

"No, she does have these weird spells without food, but I don't think she's diabetic. Who knows though, the stress of the storm, the time travelling or whatever could have put her over the edge."

Steph was right, it could mess her up. Maybe it wasn't something she could tolerate cumulatively. Jeffrey moved closer to where they were talking.

"I've got to go check on her, Stephanie. It's got me really worried." Ian's voice again.

He heard the scraping of a chair on the kitchen floor.

"You're choosing Ronnie over food little brother?" Steph's chair scraped too and then their voices moved toward the living room. Jeffrey followed above them with one hand wiping away cobwebs and the other holding the flashlight lighting the way.

Jeffrey imagined where they were in the house. It must have been the living room.

Ian said, "Aye, Stephanie, this whole thing is weirding me out. I can't wrap my head around what you said earlier about her going back in time. It's unholy, and I don't like how she bloody looks so lifeless."

"Unholy," Nick repeated. "Look guys, let's stay calm, I'm sure there is a perfectly logical explanation for what is happening to her."

Jeffrey walked to TOTO patting its head and paced to where the voices were twenty feet from TOTO. The range for the device was ten feet to the subject for the ideal connection. That was the issue. They'd moved her out of range. Shit! That was going to be a problem. This whole experimenting remotely with a houseful of enemies was not working out so well. The people who were supposed to be helping her were now risking her life.

"I don't know what to do," Steph sobbed. "Nick check her vitals again. I'm really tempted to take her to the hospital. It's not very far from here."

"Shit!" Jeffrey's heart raced. "Please don't take her out of the damn house into the storm!" He held his head in his hands. "Damnit!" He dashed toward TOTO. There might be time to bring her back. The computer was next door. He couldn't activate the device without it. He yanked the tarp off and lifted TOTO by the handle, moving as quietly as he could toward the living room. He checked the connections and covered it again, then rushed down the dark corridor toward the ladder. Jeffrey hovered near the attic opening listening intently for anyone nearby.

If they came out when he was heading down the stairs he'd be caught for sure. He listened again and heard his heart beating rapidly in his chest. Every second he waited was bringing the experiment closer to a screeching halt.

Jeffrey lowered down to the floor, skipping the folding stairs. If he could open the garage door and slide out quickly he'd be home free. He listened again and decided to make a break for it. In one deft motion, he pulled the handle to lift the door and rolled out into a puddle, heart slamming in his chest. The wind blew him off-balance as he ran across the lawn toward the neighbor's house. He would only have a few minutes to get her back if they were going to the hospital!

Chapter 32 - Lost

Dust kicked up behind Ronnie as she ran away from Morris's house. She glanced back to make sure he wasn't following. Male voices angrily volleying back and forth still met her ears to confirm he was still occupied with the other colonists. After a few minutes, her weakened host body begged for rest. Out of breath, she glanced back and could barely see the men through the trees.

Her bones ached but she continued into thicker brush and ran into a fence made up of young trees packed closely together reaching ten or twelve feet in height. The ends of the logs were sharpened to a point making an effective deterrent. She followed along the fence until it abutted a large boulder that made up a portion of the fence.

Ronnie sat down leaning against the relatively cool stone face and gathered her energy. The smell of the forest reminded her of happier days in Virginia Beach when she would hike with her father near the tidal creeks. Off in the distance, she heard voices heading her way. No rest for the wicked. She stood and walked away from the voices. How would Morris react when he returned to the house?

A rustling noise startled her and she stopped, her heart beating in her chest. Images of huge bears or hungry cougars flashed in her mind. *Don't run.* That is what her father had always told her while they traversed trails. Thank God she'd never been put to the test because she knew with every fiber of her being she'd want to run.

"The instant you run, you become prey," he had said. Instead, Ronnie held her breath and waited for the creature to appear. It was considerably smaller than a bear and she almost laughed in relief at the black and white back of a skunk and the acrid odor that clung to its fur. The critter waddled by not even glancing in her direction.

A skunk meant she was definitely in North America. Was she in North Carolina before it was born? Goosebumps formed on her arms. What a thrill to have a glimpse of early America. She wracked her brain for the dates of the settlements Plymouth Rock and the St. Augustine. It smelled so much like the part of the country where she'd grown up, it had to be Roanoke Island. It reminded her so much of the wooded area just north of here in Virginia.

She followed a small stream that showed signs of previous vigorousness but was now reduced to a mere trickle. Dry parched grass took up where the stream had left off. She walked in this flattened area devoid of any harsh brush or brambles and made her way to an unknown future. At least it wouldn't adversely affect Morris and his kind heart.

Ronnie slowly walked the streambed until her muscles screamed for rest again. A large rock close to the stream would be ideal. She imagined removing her shoes and dipping her bare feet into the cool water. Something hit her back and scared the bejesus out of her.

Ronnie spun around. She couldn't see anything through the thick brush behind her but she listened intently. A disturbing sixth sense of being watched, hunted even, overwhelmed her. Something whizzed past her head and she caught her breath. She turned around briskly.

Out of the corner of her eye, a brownish object moved in the thick brush. The something was small, which gave her hope. Ronnie stooped and picked up a few rocks from the ground and flung them where it had disappeared. Ronnie threw another and almost immediately a return fire landed near her feet, but it was thrown without menace. Was It Morris? Why didn't he just announce his presence?

"Who is there?" she called out, not sure if she should brace herself to run or face the unknown entity. A small face peeked from around a tree.

"Hello there," she said. It was a young child, maybe eight or nine years old with beautiful bright eyes, and brown skin, a Native American boy. He stepped in full view and spoke in an unfamiliar language. She took a step closer, with an overwhelming feeling of curiosity and awe. Was this a true native boy unaffected by the horrible things the settlers had done to them?

He spoke a bit louder but it didn't help her understand the foreign words. His skin was sun-kissed and his almond eyes were framed with dark lashes matching silky black hair that hung lose around his shoulders. On the top of his head feathers stood up in a circle forming a crown of sorts. He wore only a strip of animal skin covering his groin and beads around his neck.

The boy took a step toward her with a shy smile touching his hair and pointing at her. Ronnie remembered the pale blonde locks in the reflection and wondered if he had ever seen such a hair color before. He continued asking questions she couldn't answer.

Everything about the boy was beautiful. His presence conjured up all the romanticized thoughts she'd had as a girl about being an Indian, as she would have called it then, prowling around in the woods in moccasins and sleeping in a teepee.

He stepped closer and reached out to touch her hair. She leaned forward to let his fingers run through the ends. His beautiful eyes widened. Pure joy bubbled up in her heart connecting with him in such an honest and delightful way. It could be the first time he'd ever seen a white person, or at least up close.

Together surrounded by the beauty of the forest they were lost in each other's presence. An odd feeling spread through Ronnie like a wildfire and she was sure he was looking into her soul.

Her heart filled with wonder, bursting with joy to be able to see natives in their given lands, in a time and place where their glory was fulfilled. She shook off that thought and realized he was looking at her light eyes. It had been hard to tell what color they were in the reflection of the wash basin but they were a contrast to his dark brown that flicked back and forth between hers.

An angry male voice startled them out of the magical moment. A man pushed his way through the brush and spoke in low tones. He was similarly dressed but wore deerskin leggings and had the added adornment of black paint around his eyes, giving him a much more menacing appearance than the wide-eyed boy. He was powerful with broad shoulders and lean muscles that flexed as he prowled around them like a cat preparing to pounce. The right side of his head was shaved and hanging in his hair were bones and feathers. Were these trophies from his exploits?

He shoved the boy backward and stepped between them. Tension filled the clearing and pushed away the wonder and awe that floated so freely just moments before. Ronnie took a step backward but the man lunged forward and grabbed her upper arm.

"Get off me!" Ronnie tried to pull away but the man overpowered her and forced her to walk quickly to keep up. The boy said something quietly to her but the words were lost in the wind.

"Where are you taking me?" Ronnie asked but was met with angry silence. She tried to tamp down fear. Did it really matter what happened? Every time she went back she died, and for what? It was baffling, but maybe this time she could be an architect to her future and squeeze the life out of it. She would go boldly into the night taking what she wanted this time, creating a memory she could savor for the rest of her life, with no regrets. If only she'd taken that tact with Mathias. She had been far too cautious.

They walked for a few miles in rough terrain. Doing so used up every spare ounce of energy and was made worse by the heat of the day. The long heavy dress and linen shift were completely soaked with sweat. Miss Coleman's body was weak and dehydrated and had trouble keeping up with the quick pace of her captor.

Ahead on the trail, several dark heads picked their way through the underbrush until they found the path. Her heart beat faster and she was marginally rejuvenated with the prospect of witnessing more living history. She hoped it was peaceful living history and not the type that would outright murder her. A bird-like call echoed through the trees. She didn't realize it was man-made until the man next to her responded.

Scents of wood smoke, cedar, and fish filled the air making Ronnie's stomach growl. She had no idea how long it had been since she'd eaten. It could have been days. It felt like weeks. They reached a clearing and the hustle and bustle of a busy village took all her attention. Smoke rose from small fires as busy workers prepared meals. Houses intertwined between the trees and created a perimeter that circled the clearing currently being used for work. The women had more of a variety of skins in different forms from skirts to almost dresses, where the younger children played and roamed freely without anything covering their tanned bodies.

The men in the village wore a small loincloth draped over a string around the waist, where a few of the men had full leggings protecting their legs, like the man who marched her aggressively forward. She wanted to linger and soak it all in not be shoved through quickly. Ronnie jerked her arm free. He glared at her, with eyebrows nearly touching and his lips pressed together but he allowed her this tiny freedom.

A woman sitting on a log weaving a reed mat looked up with surprise, then nudged a young girl working nearby. Ronnie smiled, totally enraptured by this experience. They smiled back and Ronnie felt a wave of relief. There was some affection or at least not outright fear toward her. Another woman stood over a fire, tending to fish cooking on planks of wood, watching them pass, her face expressionless. Ronnie tried to gauge their thoughts but most kept their expressions neutral.

Ronnie soaked in every detail of the village. The houses were fascinating and so much more complicated than she had expected. Young trees were bent to form a half circle and were covered in woven reeds like the woman and girl were constructing. Some were hung with sections of bark but had the same frame.

Ronnie counted nine of these constructions as she passed and guessed there were twenty or more in the circle. It was astonishing to see how large they were, with some long as a modern house. Most of the huts had the sides rolled up, allowing a view inside. What an ingenious idea, to allow airflow but still offer the protection when needed.

Children gathered around the boy talking excitedly until the man turned and shooed them away with angry words. A growing uneasiness bubbled inside and was enhanced by the look on the boy's face. Would she regret leaving the relative safety of Morris's cabin?

They stopped just outside the largest hut, constructed entirely of tree bark with several panels rolled up along the side. It was five or six rooms long.

They entered an opening on the end of the structure into a dark room. She forced her eyes to adjust but before she could see more than shadowy forms she was pushed to the ground. Ronnie stifled a scream.

Chapter 33 - Coma, Coma, Coma, Chameleon

Nick held Ronnie's wrist, "I don't like the feel of her skin. She's cold Steph." His eyebrows knit together. "Could be going into shock."

"Cold?" Ian reached out and touched her ankle. "How can she be cold? It's hot as fuck in here."

"I don't like it, Nick. I just don't think we can wait any longer." Steph said.

"I'm heading to that conclusion, too. Sorry to say because getting anywhere in this damn storm is going to be crazy. Do we want to call nine-one-one?"

"Can't hurt. Maybe they'll give us some advice, too." Steph stood. "I'll get my cell, Ian can you find the home phone and see if we have signal?

"Oh aye, where is it?" Ian followed Steph down the hall to the master bedroom.

Steph pointed to the dining room. "Near the corner cabinet."

"Babe, we should probably take my Jeep. It'll do better on the roads." Nick dug in his pocket for the Wrangler keys. "I'll move it closer. Be right back."

Ian handed her the portable landline. "Stephanie, call the emergency number. An ambulance will come," Ian said.

"It's nine-one-one here, Ian," Steph said.

"I doubt they'll come, it's a State of Emergency out there. They've told everyone to stay inside and not expect help," Nick said. "They have to protect the first responders."

"Just wait a second while we try, Nick." Steph pulled the phone out of her purse and dialed 911. She had no signal. "Crap, nothing on here. Ian?"

"I've got it, Steph, but the battery is dead on the handset. We've not had power for ages." Ronnie only had the cordless kind.

"Crap," Steph said. "Okay Nick go get the Jeep and I'll pack a bag for Ronnie." She sat on the couch with her emotions churning knots in her stomach.

Ian followed Steph to the master bedroom. "Can we all fit in the Jeep?"

"No, Ian." Steph shook her head and pulled a bag from the closet and started gathering clothes for Ronnie. "I think you're going to have to stay with the house."

"Och, no, Stephanie. All alone here without you guys out in the middle of the storm? What if the roof leaks again? What if a tree falls? Just let me come with."

"There isna room in the Jeep. Nick has one of those sporty Wranglers and with Ronnie in the back seat with me, it'll not be comfy. Plus, having you here will make us all feel better about the house. At least someone is keeping an eye on it." Steph looked at her little brother's sad expression reminding her of when they were kids and she was going out with her friends leaving him behind.

"Uggghhh, really? So, I don't get to be by her side when she awakens and …" Ian shook his head, his voice was shaking.

"She doesn't want to see your ugly mug when she wakes up. She deserves better." Steph smiled, hoping his grim expression would lift. She grabbed clothes from her bag and Nick's and shoved it on top of Ronnie's gear.

"Oh, aye, Stephanie, if you think so," Ian said in a deflated tone. He didn't even retort with his usual bravado.

She hugged him. "At least you don't have to be out in the storm. That is not a good place to be with wicked Frances raging about."

"Steph, let's go!" Nick yelled from the kitchen as he walked in. "We seem to be in between the rain bands right now." He walked toward them soaked to the bone.

"Okay, just giving instructions to wee man here." Steph walked out of the bedroom handing the bag to Nick and then turned to Ian. "Ian do not under any circumstances, go through Ronnie's knickers drawer."

"Oh aye, I dinna think I'll be up for that," Ian said shaking his head, "but now that you mention it." A devious smile crossed his lips.

Nick shook his head. "Don't you even think about it, Ian. Steph really? Did you have to say that to him, to plant the seed?"

"I got him to smile," Steph said. "Ian come help us get Sleeping Beauty into the Jeep." Steph pulled off the blanket covering Ronnie. Sadness washed over her seeing her friend so helpless when she was usually so full of life.

"She's going to be all right, Steph," Nick said rubbing her back.

Steph wiped away the tears and stood. Nick scooped Ronnie up in his arms.

Ian grabbed Ronnie's hand and kissed it. "Bye lass." Tears shone in his eyes.

Nick headed out to the garage and Steph grabbed the overnight bag and her purse. "Oh wait, I'll need Ronnie's purse too. Her insurance card is probably in there."

Steph opened the door to the garage for Nick, who delicately passed through being careful with Ronnie.

"You'll have to get the door, the Jeep is just outside," Nick said, nodding his head toward the garage door.

Steph noticed water along the garage door and what looked like footprints. Must have been Nick's, but there seemed to be three sets of prints. She lifted the door, as heavy as it was she struggled to keep it open for Nick to pass under and let it drop. Then she opened the Jeep's rear door and the wind blew her off balance. She had to drop the overnight bag to keep from falling over. Nick gently placed Ronnie in the backseat and Steph crawled in beside her, pitching the bag on the floor and lifting Ronnie's feet to rest on her knees.

Nick got in the driver's seat and turned around, "You okay?"

She nodded. "Let's get her to the hospital."

Chapter 34 - Prince

Ronnie's eyes adjusted to the lower light and a moment of fear swallowed her reasoning as she fought the urge to run away. A square of sunshine brightened the dirt floor and she looked up to see a similar shape cut in the roof, likely to let the smoke out. No fire was burning today, but a charred dirt patch just under the opening in the roof bore evidence.

Ronnie stood and brushed the dirt off her dress and realized an older man was sitting nearby in the center of the room. The expression on his face conveyed anger and surprise, with his eyebrows drawn together. He sat on a wooden bench and was surrounded by five native men who turned around giving her the same look, striking fear in her heart.

She stepped backward landing squarely on her captor's foot. He yelped and shoved her forward. "I'm sorry." The death grip on her arm conveyed his feelings.

The men dispersed and she stood face-to-face with the angriest man in the room if she was decent at reading expressions, and unfortunately, the one most likely to decide her fate. He wore a small crown of feathers in his long black hair, a string around his waist, and an animal skin covered his groin. Tattoos blackened his eyes and continued along his cheeks and forehead enhancing the frightful stare.

This must be the chief. He spoke a few words in a manner that could only be described as disgust.

She tried to respond but the only sound she could make with such a dry throat was a croak. The man next to her spoke to the chief. They exchanged brisk sentences back and forth. Ronnie hazarded a glance around and found all eyes on her with a mixture of deadpan expressions or similar, yet less obvious scowls.

Her captor spoke in an introduction to the chief with solemn demeanor, "Wahunsonacock," and then a stream of rapid unfamiliar words, occasionally glancing at the other men in the room. Nothing made sense until he said mamanatowick and later Powhatan. Could this be Chief Powhatan, a man that had left his mark on the land hundreds of years later, the father of Pocahontas? Chills crawled up her arms and Ronnie tried to tamp down an excited giggle, scolding herself for acting anything but cordial and calm.

She bit her tongue and waited out the speech. Finally, the chief turned his attention to the man who brought her and they began a heated exchange. It took her awhile to notice that sitting directly next to the chief was the boy who had been her original contact. His face lit up. Ronnie smiled and he returned the gesture, almost squinting into the smile, showing the tenseness that she also felt. Was he the chief's son? They had similar feather treatment in their hair, giving the impression of a crown that the other men didn't have. The chief pointed to one of the men standing nearby and he left abruptly, probably following an order.

The hut was efficiently laid out with benches built along the walls, with reed mats and skins tucked underneath out of the way for use at night. Her attention wandered back to the boy. He smiled and she took a step toward him finding his presence comforting in direct contrast to the aggressive masculine vibe from the others. He sat with his elbows on his knees, hands clasped much like her niece would sit when comfortable and bored but in polite company. How could they share this posture despite the hundreds of years separating them?

Loud angry, unfamiliar words pulled her attention as the exchange grew more heated. The chief was not happy. The boy shook his head and stood up, his fists bunched in anger. He spoke in high-pitched words in contrast to the men's deep rumbles. He stomped and kicked up a mini dust cloud that floated through the sunny patch on the floor. The chief said nothing but pointed to the opening that served as a door, apparently banishing him from the hut. The boy stood his ground for a second but then stomped over to the rolled-up bark siding, glancing at her just before ducking under.

Ronnie's heart sank. The amount of energy the chief and her captor expended could have burned the whole village down. Finally, the chief grunted and crossed his arms, resulting in the onlookers raising their hands in victorious chants.

Her captor spoke quietly to the chief and then turned toward her and said. "Wahab." He touched his chest and nodded, his expression softening and the words were spoken with almost eager anticipation.

Relief flooded through her veins. "Wahab. Very nice to meet you." She wanted to hold her hand out in a proper American introduction, instead, she bowed slightly, unsure of the custom. She touched her chest, "I am Ronnie Andrews."

Wahab smiled and nodded. Her emotions were still on guard but with the genuineness of his smile, she relaxed a little bit more. This was such an incredible moment.

An older woman entered the hut and the chief stood and motioned for her to sit on the reed mats that laid in a circle at his feet. Wahab sat next to her and motioned for Ronnie to sit as well. It was strange to be the center of their attention not knowing if she were a friend or foe. Everything was so different about their mannerisms, their expressions, making it difficult to read.

The woman's long hair flowed over her shoulders like silk, and she wore only an animal skin skirt. Bead and shell necklaces draped over her bare chest. Her smile revealed a few missing teeth and an intricate pattern of tattoos scrawled across her forehead and along her cheekbones resembling the chief's. A band of tattoos circled her upper arms and the ink, while crudely done, was a beautiful work of art in pattern and effect on her. She touched her hand to her bosom and said, "Ogundah," repeating several times.

"Ronnie." The woman smiled and tried the name, with a few corrections she said it correctly. Wahab nodded and spoke rapidly to Ogundah who listened patiently, eying Ronnie as he spoke. When he paused, she reached out to touch the fabric at Ronnie's wrist and spoke quietly and waited for a response.

Ogundah's eyes were more like the child's, bereft of the malice she'd seen with the men. A feeling of anxiety tore through her. She knew they were asking something of her but she didn't understand. Ogundah tried again, asking a series of questions, pointing at Wahab.

Ronnie nodded her head, "Yes, this man found me in the woods. I left my village and met the boy along my escape route." It was a stab in the dark. She had no idea what this was about.

Kindness showed in her bright eyes, and she tried again, by touching Wahab's arm and then her sleeve again. Wahab, sat closer and leaned in and spoke, nodding and gesturing but it was all lost on Ronnie.

"I know you're asking me something important, but seriously I have no idea what you're saying." She looked back and forth between Wahab and Ogundah.

After a half hour of intense conversation, they stood. Ogundah spoke quietly to her and led her out of the hut. Wahab then walked next to them toward the other side of the village.

Wahab led them to a hut that looked like it had just been built, for the reeds were still green. Ogundah took her inside and they looked around. It was a single-room with benches built similarly to the chief's hut. Ogundah held a mortar and pestle up for her inspection. Ronnie nodded. She pointed to the benches along the far wall and urged Ronnie to sit on them. Were they giving her a hut to stay in?

Wahab pulled out a long blond fur blanket and handed it to her. It was incredibly lush, was it a cougar's pelt? She handed it back to him and he folded it and placed it carefully under the bench. He took her hand, leading her to another bench. He lifted the wooden slab and inside it was stocked with various bone tools, rocks, and other goods. She would have to learn what they were used for if she stuck around long enough.

Ogundah reached in and handed her one item out of the stash. It was a small knife fashioned out of bone, with the design of a face beautifully crafted and intricate carvings along the handle of woodland animals. Ronnie ran her thumb over the piece and smiled at Wahab. "It's beautiful."

He led her to the fire pit in the center of the room and spoke with passion and more animated than she'd seen him before, enhancing his handsome features. He motioned for her to sit down on the bench. She did and Ogundah sat next to her. The talks continued and Ogundah seemed to be negotiating. As confusing as it was, she was happy to have the tone change from angry looks to cordial smiles and attempts to impress her with the hut he seemed to be offering.

They both stopped speaking and turned to her. Ronnie stood, "Thank you so much, this place is lovely." She turned to Wahab, "I'm so grateful for your kindness, I would love to stay here and be part of your community for a while."

His face lit up and Ogundah stood and hugged her. Wahab bowed slightly to Ronnie and spoke briskly to Ogundah, apparently giving her instructions as she glanced at Ronnie and walked out of the hut. Ronnie sat back on the bench and looked around the rustic structure wondering if she'd be able to light a fire and find water and handle the other basics to spend the night. Most likely she would feel utterly useless, with only her modern skills to cope with this new world.

For the first time, they were alone and something in Wahab's look sent a wave of panic to her core. The affection and charm he'd displayed moments before were gone and in his dark eyes revealed lust, anger, and violence. A look crossed his face and he spoke to her in a way that could only be described as dangerous and on the verge of evil. He gripped the back of her neck and shoved her out of the hut.

Chapter 35 – Messages in the Sand

Wahab pushed Ronnie forward through the busy working center of the village toward a gathering of people. Without a way to communicate, vulnerability gripped Ronne. She was at their mercy for kindness or ill will. All romanticized thoughts of absorbing Native American culture were dashed for the moment and a small core of fear returned deep in her gut, enhanced by the glances of the men as she walked by. There was a distinctive downside to showing up back in time as a woman.

Her panicked thoughts were interrupted by the sight of Chief Powhatan, Ogundah, and the prince standing in front of a huge bonfire surrounded by the villagers. They milled around, finding seats in a large circle around the fire. Ronnie focused on the chief's lean, tanned body and noticed some of the dark marks on his forehead and cheeks weren't tattoos at all but piercings. He looked to be in his mid-forties but it was hard to tell.

A strong image of being burned at the stake flashed in her mind as the smell of wood smoke grew stronger. She swallowed and tried to hold herself together as if acting like a welcomed guest would keep that vibe going. Chief Powhatan sat on a small reed mat. Wahab sat to his left and shoved Ronnie into a seated position next to him.

Men dressed like warriors circled the fire laughing and talking. The excitement of the group transferred to her mixing with the sheer panic to make her stomach tighten in knots. Wahab joined the warriors who circled the bonfire. They all stomped their feet and a hush fell over the crowd.

Ronnie was lost in the performance of strength, power, and agility as the men moved in unison around the circle creating a percussive beat with foot stomps and slaps to the chest, thighs, and arms, accompanied by grunts. The crowd continued to grow as they performed and soon reached ten people deep around the circle.

The sheer passion and power they displayed was enthralling and Ronnie tapped her feet to the beat. It occurred to her, once she regained her whereabouts, that she had told everyone here that her name was Ronnie. Here she could be Ronnie Andrews and this simple fact flooded her with relief.

KJ Waters

The men performed several dances, pausing in between to drink from long animal skin containers and talk with the crowd. Wahab knelt in front of her and smiled during one of the breaks as sweat dripped down his face. She couldn't help but return the gesture and feel overwhelmed in the moment. He handed her an animal skin flask and encouraged her to sip. She lifted it to her lips, wanting to refuse but also aware of possibly offending him, and took a tentative taste. It was strong and sweet and thick in her mouth.

He stood and did something quite like a rebel yell from the backwoods of West Virginia and held up the flask. A lot of the crowd cheered too, looking between the two of them. Her cheeks pinkened at the attention and she wondered if she'd unknowingly accepted an offer for a more intimate audience. Ogundah spoke quickly to her and Ronnie imagined she was saying great things about Wahab.

When the men were finished, the crowd dispersed into the cooling evening. Ogundah took Ronnie's arm and used her as support as they walked across an open area to a reed hut. It was a similar size to the structure Wahab had shown her and inside the dirt floor was neat and tidy. Seven younger women filed in behind them and sat on smaller reed mats in the center. Ronnie looked at the eager faces, all with such perfect skin, and shinning brown eyes. Some had their hair loose about their shoulders, covering bare breasts, with the occasional one-sleeve outfit that covered one side.

A young woman, maybe fifteen or so, took Ronnie's hand and brought her over to a bench built into the side of the hut. She pulled out several animal skin coverings similar to what the women were wearing and offered her a choice. Ronnie had long sweated through her outfit, allowing her to smell the results of a day's worth of heat. Choosing a half sleeve dress that covered more than the other choices, the girl helped her removed the heavy black dress, shift, and stays that had bound her tight. Ronnie felt shy disrobing in front of the women, but she also let go of some of the more modern embarrassment about nakedness, especially since this was not her body. She shed long wool stockings, and underskirts, leaving her completely naked with her clothes in a pile on the floor.

It was such a freeing moment. As if by removing the clothing, she also shed the customs and beliefs of English settlers, coupled with the welcome reprieve from the hot clothes. Another girl brought a gourd filled with water and dipped in a small strip of suede. She squeezed the water out and to Ronnie's surprise placed it on her shoulders, and worked it across her back, scrubbing the sweat from her body. The girl continued washing down to her feet while another girl combed out Ronnie's hair with a crude tortoiseshell comb and then braided it into two smooth long plaits.

Ogundah spoke quietly to the six younger women who talked and laughed enjoying their time together. They were obviously a close-knit group. The cooling evening air felt amazing on her still damp skin. It was a unique experience having someone else bathe her and she tolerated it until the woman reached her groin area. It was awkward enough to be naked in a room of strangers but this was a bit too personal.

The braider held her arm up to Ronnie's and pointed at the difference in skin color. Ronnie's arm, or rather Miss Coleman's, was almost translucent in the low light of the room where the girl's was a beautiful goldish brown. The women who

156

were seated stood and surrounded her, giving Ronnie a rush of excitement as their energy merged with hers.

They reached out to touch her hair, her arms, and shoulders, her light pink nipples, gently, not in a sexual way but in a moment of wonder. The feeling was of oneness and acceptance, something she'd never completely felt in her modern life and certainly not in any of the places she had traveled. In an instant, the garment she had picked out was pulled over her head and many hands pulled it down over her back and hips. She glanced down to see the dress she had picked out that covered one breast and left the other exposed. They spun her around and draped beads and shells over her neck in her hair and around her waist.

In a matter of a half hour, Ronnie was transformed into a likeness of their culture, but her light coloring did not hide the differences between them. Despite the complete language barrier, Ronnie felt special, unique, and not at all uncomfortable in her new clothes, even with most of her body left bare. It was freeing to let them attend her, to make her feel so welcome in their group. Miss Coleman would likely have been utterly abashed at such nakedness but Ronnie had spent a good portion of her life in a bathing suit as a child and in her summer job as a lifeguard.

She was led to the circle of women and sat next to Ogundah. There was a certain sexuality about this experience, with her American views of nudity, and her body responded with arousal in mind and spirit at the excitement of the many layers of newness, from bare skin to sitting with a group of women who accepted her so readily despite their many differences.

Ogundah took Ronnie's hand and spread her fingers, then pressed her palm to her tattooed forehead. Ronnie felt the raised bumps on her skin and the sweat on the woman's brow. A hush came over the room. Ogundah let Ronnie's hand go and opened her eyes, looking surprised.

After a long-hushed silence, Ogundah spoke slowly, carefully, almost in a whisper with her eyes half closed. Ronnie did not understand but closely watched her lips form the foreign words as if she could lip read the meaning. Off in the distance, a few rowdy men called out in the fading daylight, breaking the silence of the room.

As the woman spoke, a young girl sat on the dirt floor between them and drew with a small stick. Ogundah's words blurred into the images in the sand. A bear stood on two legs and a cloud with lightning struck in front of the animal, complete with a shadow behind the bear at the moment of the flash. The girl's hand swiped across the sand and erased the image. Next, she drew a triangle of broad shoulders and small waist making it clear it was the figure of a man. Staccato words made the girl hesitate, stick in hand, and Ogundah reached out and erased the man leaving a print in the dirt and pointed at Ronnie. Wild thoughts swirled in Ronnie's mind. Was the man Morris? Jeffrey? Someone else?

Softer words again flowed from her mouth and the girl drew a mountain range with a stream in between. A jagged line midway up one mountain slowly caved in and slid down to block the stream in a massive mudslide. A bird flew above the top of the mountain while one man rode its back and another man lay under the water in the stream.

Ronnie struggled to understand. Was she describing something from her past or her future? She absorbed every nuance and accepted everything as the utter truth, memorizing the pictures before they were wiped clean. Ogundah leaned toward her, pressing her finger into Ronnie's sternum. She pointed to the man in the stream and took Ronnie's hand and pressed it into the dirt. Ogundah's hand covered hers, impressing upon her the importance of what she was saying, as their hands made an impression in the sand. Clearly, the message was important but it was so convoluted. Who were these men? Where were the mountains? This part of the country was flat nearly sea level. There were mountains to the west but that would days or weeks to walk there.

Ogundah tried to communicate again, touching Ronnie's sternum then her hand in the dirt covering the man. A young girl kissed the back of her hand and pointed to the man in the mountain stream. With her finger, she put an X over the man flying on the bird's back. Ronnie shook her head, still not sure of what was being said but carefully placing every detail of the story in her mind, repeating the pictures to help her remember every nuance of the story.

Was she telling her something that Miss Coleman lived through here in this time period? Or was it in her own life back in 2004? Something deep in her psyche told her it had to do with her own life but there were no mountains in Florida. Were the two men Morris and Mathias from her past? Or did the crude images represent Jeffrey and Mike from her present?

A chill ran up her spine and she thought of the lightning. Was she seeing the hurricane? Worry took over the wonder and she knew something was wrong in Florida. Was it Nick? Did he get hurt by the storm? Jeffrey? Would one of them drown in a stream?

The overwhelming fear of something going wrong with her friends dulled the magic of the moment.

Chapter 36 – Road Block

Steph gripped the door as the Jeep hydroplaned and skidded wildly. "Jesus, Mary, and Joseph! Nick!" She tried to keep Ronnie from rolling onto the floor.

"Sorry babe, the roads are slick." Nick glanced back. "You okay?"

"Yeah, Ronnie almost …" she couldn't say it. Talking about her friend as if she weren't there was too upsetting. "We're okay."

They made their way slowly to the hospital with the storm raging. The wiper blades flicked a rapid tempo matching Steph's heartbeat. Trees were down, houses were damaged, and stop signs were blown sideways.

"Nick, are we almost there?" Steph wanted this part to be over. It was too frightening to be in the middle of Hurricane Frances with no one available to help if they ran into trouble. They didn't even have working cell phones to call for help.

A downed tree blocked the road in front of them. Nick stopped and turned around. "Well, we're only a few miles away, but at this rate, I'm not sure if we can get there." He jammed the Jeep in reverse and turned the car around.

"There has to be a way. Try Maitland Avenue that might be clear." Steph took a deep breath and blew it out.

"Alrighty, we'll see if the weather Gods are willing." Nick laughed.

"Turn the radio on, maybe they'll have some info we can use." Steph welcomed the distraction.

Def Leppard blared out, "Pour some sugar on meeeee." Nick sang along while Steph tried to think happy thoughts.

"Turn here babe, this is a shortcut over to Maitland Avenue." Steph pointed, not that he could see her hand.

They drove through a neighborhood with a mixture of expensive larger homes and smaller nice houses. The wind was blasting directly at windshield making it nearly impossible for the wipers to keep up.

"This isn't going to work, Steph, I can't see anything!" Nick stopped in the middle of the street. A huge crash on the windshield shattered it, leaving a circular hole and cracked glass flowing outward from the center to take up the entire driver's side.

Nick yelled, "Shit!" And quickly turned the car around to make the next right turn. "The storm is just too strong to drive directly into it. We're going to have to make right angles and let the buildings protect us from the wind."

159

"Look at your windshield." Steph's heart was beating madly.

"It's okay, it was out in the storm either way. Who knows it may be better off than at Ronnie's curb." Nick said.

"Can you see enough to drive?" she asked, the tension ramping to near vomit levels.

"Yes, we'll get there, Steph, don't worry." He spoke with confidence he could not have felt.

They drove for another ten minutes dodging debris in the road until Nick turned down the radio, "Steph, this road is blocked."

"What? Is a tree down?" Steph leaned in to see but the cracked windshield didn't give her much of a view.

"Flooding. The lake has swallowed the road." He looked behind him and put it in reverse. "We could risk driving through but if the car stalls we're screwed." He turned off the radio.

"Don't risk it." Steph looked at Ronnie and brushed the hair off her face. Her stomach was in knots, just too many things to worry about all at once.

"We'll get there." He turned the Jeep around again and they drove in relative silence. The only noises were the wipers, the wind battering the Jeep, and the occasional debris hitting the side.

A bad feeling crept up her spine. This was how things went south. Piece by piece the world crumbled around you. She thought of Ian at home alone and what he would do when she didn't return.

"I'm turned around now. I'm not even sure where to go," Nick interrupted her morbid thoughts.

"I'll see if I can spot a street sign. We just need to get to Maitland Avenue." Steph clutched her stomach. "Turn right, Nick."

"Say a prayer that it's passable," he said.

Steph crossed her fingers and prayed silently. The wind shoved the side of the Jeep and nearly lifted it. Nick jerked the wheel and managed to keep it from careening off the narrow road. A downed tree blocked the way. Nick drove to the far right where the branches were thinner and drove over, madly jostling Steph and Ronnie for a minute.

"Wow babe that was intense," Steph said, doing her best to calm down.

"Yeah, tell me about it, I was praying electrical wires weren't part of the mess." The car stopped short and made a horrible noise. Wind buffeted them and Nick put the Jeep in a lower gear and tried to get it moving again. A grinding noise made Steph cover her ears.

"Oh shit," Nick said and hopped out of the Wrangler. Steph watched in disbelief as he passed her rear window, bending down near the tire. He tried to push the Jeep forward.

He banged on the window, "Steph, get in the driver's seat and drive forward slowly."

"What? Crap, how do I ...?" Steph quickly untangled from Ronnie and climbed to the driver's seat. She put it in gear and inched the Jeep forward stopping when Nick banged on the rear window.

A few minutes later Nick appeared at the driver's door and opened it. Water blew in soaking Steph's left side.

"Scoot over." A dripping wet Nick pointed to the passenger seat.

"Well that's gonna fuck us over," Nick said, cussing uncharacteristically.

"Oh no, what?" She bit her lip.

"Axel is broken. Driving over those trees got a branch caught and now ..."

"We can't stay here!" Steph glanced back at Ronnie again, picturing Nick carrying her in the rain somewhere safe.

"That's a fact, Jack," he said as he wiped water off his face. He sat back in the seat and gripped the steering wheel. "Any ideas?"

Steph looked around to see if she could figure out where they were. It was a neighborhood and a nice one. "Do you know where we are?"

"Sort of. Hand me a map." He pointed to the glove compartment. Steph reached in handed him a map of central Florida. He tried to dry his hands on his shorts but there was no point since they were soaked. Nick opened the map and found where they'd started at Ronnie's house and tried to retrace the steps of where they had driven. "I think we're about here." He pointed at the map and Steph leaned over to look.

"No, I think we're here." She pointed at the map about two inches above him and he looked closely.

"Maybe, maybe," Nick said.

Chapter 37 - Panic at the Disco

Jeffrey ran through the puddles in Ronnie's side yard up a small hill until the wind pushed him over and a branch smacked him in the back of the knee.

"Ouch." He swiped at the injury and came away with blood on his fingers. He ran through the muddy yard and pushed open the gate. He then ran to the lanai and entered though the French door. He stood dripping on the kitchen floor. The last thing he needed was blood in this house that left DNA evidence if they should ever look for such a thing. He slipped his shoes off and sloshed in wet socks to the paper towel roll. He did not have time for this, but leaving evidence wouldn't do either. He wiped up his footprints and dabbed at the bloody knee, then went to the computer. With TOTO in place, he should be able to connect with Ronnie easily. As long as they didn't move her again.

He started the return sequence, crossing his fingers, and waited as the laptop processed the commands. It read, "No connection to subject."

Jeffrey calmly checked another avenue, not wanting to believe it.

The machine mocked him this time, "No connection to subject, *you dumbass*."

"What the hell am I supposed to do now?" He slammed his palm down on the breakfast bar, making everything rattle. The boring family's portrait toppled. He righted it and sat down hard on the barstool. "Oh my God." All the blood left his face. "Oh … my … God, Ronnie." He held his head in his hands. The reality hit him hard. Could he get her back now?

"Fuck, fuck, fuck!" He wanted to throw something but it wouldn't do any good. Or did they just move her to another location? He remembered the tracking device implanted in her back. He could see if she was traveling to the hospital or still in the house. He quickly activated the signal and sure enough, it was moving toward Maitland Avenue. "Damn you Steph!" At least that clarified his next steps. He needed TOTO and a way to the hospital. He'd have to go back to the house to grab it. Was Ian still there? Could he drive the car up there and just grab it?

"Jesus fucking Christ! How can I make an informed decision with so many unknowns?" He gathered his things. If he left this house, he didn't want to have to come back in again. He wanted all loose ends wrapped up.

Jeffrey grabbed the coffee cup and plate he'd used and carried them to the kitchen. "Shit, I can't be careless now." He cleaned up the rest of the kitchen and living room he'd spent the last day in. Once again, his career was on the line. All because of Ronnie and her inability to do as she was told. "Why are you so difficult?"

Once the house was wiped for fingerprints, and all the evidence of his visit was erased Jeffrey packed everything in his bag and went out to the garage. There was the tricky issue of sneaking into Ronnie's attic and moving TOTO without Ian hearing him. He'd rather park his car in Ronnie's garage to move TOTO so it wouldn't get wet, but how would he keep Ian from walking in on him if he heard noises?

A devious plan hatched as he opened the trunk. How was he going to make it there without damage to his car, or even worse to TOTO? So many potential ways this could end horribly. Jeffrey pulled the hood over his head, picked up one of the bricks stacked in the corner of the garage, and closed the door. Running against the wind, he crossed Ronnie's front yard, hoping Ian wasn't looking out of the window. He pushed his way through the trees and bushes to the east side where the back bedrooms were. It wasn't hard to find a large branch on the ground and he picked it up and laid it down under the bedroom window.

He gripped the brick and examined the window. It had to be loud for this to work. Jeffrey took a deep breath and wiped the water from his eyes. Vandalizing houses was not really to his liking but it was necessary for this to work. He pulled his hand inside of the windbreaker and held the brick as best he could through the jacket. No need to damage himself in the name of science.

He hesitated. Was there anything in this room Ronnie valued that would be destroyed by this act? Then anger welled inside of him, this whole situation was her fault. If she'd just not invited her idiotic friends over. In one giant arc, he brought the brick dead center of the window and enjoyed the loud shattering of the glass. He threw the branch into the gaping window and ran back across the lawn to the front window, ducking down low. A figure ran through the living room and a muffled sound of cursing ensued. Bingo!

Jeffrey ran with the wind at his back toward the neighbor's house and jumped in his car. He parked in front of the garage and jumped out of the car. Pressing his ear against the wet metal of the garage door he heard nothing but storm sounds. Jeffrey opened the door and rolled inside. Quickly he opened the attic, pulled down the stairs, and ran toward TOTO. He pulled the tarp off, wadded it up and shoved it down the front of his jacket. In the house below he could hear the scraping of furniture and some loud cursing. Ian was enjoying the diversion as much as he deserved. The little shit.

Jeffrey lifted TOTO and carried it awkwardly toward the stairs. This was not going to be easy. He set it near the opening and stepped onto the top rung. A noise below startled him. A flashlight beam on the floor below made him jump. He quietly stepped back into the shadows.

"Fucking hell! Where did she say the tarps were? Why Stephanie did ye leave me behind?" What followed must have been a string of advanced Scottish cursing because he couldn't understand a word. Ian finally shone the flashlight on a shelf in the corner and snatched a tarp. Jeffrey didn't move until he heard the door to the house shut. He let out a sigh, not realizing he'd been holding his breath. A few minutes later he heard hammering and could feel the vibrations on the floor below his feet.

Would the Scot remember the attic ladder was down? Or would it be wiser to leave it closed the way Steph and Nick left it? Bets were on Steph would notice.

Jeffrey grabbed TOTO and carefully made his way down the ladder. A distinct odor of whisky hit him as he reached the bottom rung. That settled that, the Scot was drunk. He set the time travel device on the garage floor and closed-up the attic.

Ten minutes later he had the device safely in the back of his car and was heading toward the hospital. So many additional variables would come into play now. Would he be able to get it within range of Ronnie without Steph and Nick noticing? How could he explain why he was in the hospital in the middle of the storm if either one saw him? Goddamn, this was such a mess. Would all of this happen before the storm wound down? Would he even make it to the hospital?

His car swerved with a gust of wind and he ran over something solid. His wipers were on full blast but he still couldn't clear the water from his windshield fast enough.

Chapter 38 – Dude, Where's My Car?

"Now what?" Steph asked feeling sicker. "We can't stay out here. We'll be hit by a tree or something."

Nick held the flashlight up to the map in an effort to get a better look, "There's a fire station here." He pointed with a thick finger.

"Babe, that's like ten blocks away. How the hell do we get there?"

"I could run there, no probs," Nick said with vigor.

"Oh hell no. Leaving us here? What if something happens to you?" The fear and horror from Hurricane Charley washed over her. He had almost died in that storm.

"What choice do we have? We can't leave her here." He looked at Ronnie.

Steph grabbed the map out of his hands. "Nick!"

"What?" He mimicked her excited tone.

"Maitland Avenue is right here." She stabbed her finger into the map. "What house numbers would it be here? It's only a few blocks away!"

He wiped his eyes, "I'm not sure, let me see if the map shows that. Why?"

"Mike lives on Maitland Avenue." A click of hope ratcheted up her heart.

"Mike who?" Nick shook his head.

"Mike Walsh, Ronnie's boss. Remember him?"

"No." Nick stared back.

"Never mind. He lives near here. Maybe you could run to his house. He could take us to the hospital," Steph said.

"If he's close. If he's home. If his car will drive in this. If he'll risk life and limb for us." He rubbed the back of his neck. "That's a lot of if's."

"I've got nothing else." Steph shook her head. "At the very least he can give us a safer place to figure this out."

"You have his address?" Nick said.

"Well, I think I do. He sent her a note with his address a few weeks ago. Let me think." She'd not thought of it since the day after Charley. She could see the note written on in her mind's eye and rattled off the address.

"Are you sure?" Nick grabbed her hand.

"Crap I'm not sure," Steph said and spat out another combination of numbers. "Where are we now?"

"Not sure, I can jump out and run to the corner to see the sign," Nick said. "Did you bring Ronnie's purse? Maybe she has the note in there."

"I did." Steph knelt on the seat and reached the purse.

Steph opened it and dug around. Ronnie's wallet contained a business card for Mike Walsh, but it only had the company's address. It did have a cell number scrawled on the back, but that was useless right now. "Nope."

He turned toward her. "Visualize the note. What does it say?"

Steph closed her eyes and concentrated. She clearly saw 2405 Maitland Avenue in neat tidy handwriting. She said the numbers again. "It has to be that."

"How sure are you?"

"Eighty percent." She tried to smile.

"Okay let me see where we are and then we'll know if this is doable." Nick leaned in and kissed her. He opened the door and let Frances splash across the steering wheel.

"We're getting help, Ronnie. Hang in there." Steph said.

The door opened and Nick sat down. He shut the car door but not before a gust of wind blew tons of rain in. "We're on the corner of Horatio and Maitland Avenue." He reached for the map and located it quickly. "Woo-hoo! Steph! He's about two blocks away."

"Get out!" A wave of relief washed over her. "Now let's just hope he's home and can help us."

"Right. So, you'll be okay while I'm gone?" He looked worried.

"Me? I'm not the one to worry about. Remember the last time you were out in a hurricane?" She touched his cast.

"How could I forget? But this is different. I get to go for a leisurely jog down the street. What could go wrong?" His smile was perfect.

"Don't even get me started. Just go fetch Mike and come get us out of this storm baby." Steph tamped down the fear and worry about Nick's safety. "Go, on with ye."

He kissed her. "I'll be right back. Keep Ronnie safe and we'll be on our way to the hospital lickety-split." He squeezed her hand. "Recite Hail Mary's until I get back."

"Good idea, Nick." Steph prayed to Saint Medard and then recited, "Hail Mary full of grace. The Lord is with thee. Blessed art thou among women, and blessed is the fruit of thy womb, Jesus. Holy Mary mother of God, pray for us sinners, now and at the hour of our death, amen."

The storm seemed to intensify the second Nick left. She clicked the keys and turned on the radio to drown out some of the terrifying sounds. The weatherman sounded tired but he still managed to scare her with his words. "Frances is covering almost every county in Florida, battering nearly every home in the Sunshine State. Current wind speeds are one hundred and five miles per hour near the eye of the storm. Frances is still picking up energy from the warm Atlantic waters and is expected to make landfall sometime this evening. It has slowed dramatically leaving millions of Florida residents without power and incredible amounts of rainfall battering the already damaged state."

A branch landed heavily on the hood of the car and skidded across, startling her. "Nick come back!"

The radio announcer continued, "Hurricane Frances formed as a tropical wave on the same day Hurricane Andrew devastated Southern Florida. A disturbing date for Floridians and now nearly six million are without power. The path of the storm is expected to take it northwest across the state and possibly make a second landfall along the gulf coast."

Steph turned the station, hoping for music or something less upsetting. Hurricane Frances was raging for almost twenty-four hours and it hadn't even made landfall yet.

"Hey, shorty I know you wanna party," the radio commented.

"Um, no not exactly," Steph responded. The Black Eyed Peas were much more soothing than the tune sung by Hurricane Frances so she turned it up, closing her eyes and imagining will.i.am's braids bouncing as he danced to the rhythm. An eerie howling started to overpower the music and Steph turned the volume down. It had to be the wind through part of the car but it sounded like spirits crying. She looked at Ronnie and decided to crawl in the backseat to be closer to her.

Ever so slowly the Jeep skootched inch by inch off the road. The wind was brutally tearing up everything around and the windows fogged up. Ronnie's pulse was steady but her clammy skin continued to freak Steph out. If anyone could find Mike it was Nick.

The Jeep rocked in a gust of wind and a terrible crack sounded above. Steph tried to see out the shattered front window to no avail. A dark blur was visible in a hundred pieces through the broken glass. Steph cradled Ronnie's head and squeezed her eyes shut as all hell broke loose in the Jeep. They lifted up and slammed into the seat in front of her. Steph braced herself trying to keep in control of her body but the impact was too great.

Terrible metal scraping sounds assaulted her. When it stopped, Steph was still cradling Ronnie's head. The Jeep sat at a jaunty angle pitching forward making it hard to stay on the backseat.

A huge tree laid across the hood of the Jeep. A really close call. A few feet difference and she and Ronne would be pancakes. In any other circumstance, she would have evacuated the car.

Chapter 39 - Ceremonial Ties

Wahab entered the hut and interrupted Ronnie's intense moment with Ogundah. He spoke to the other young girls. Their eyes met and Ronnie felt his power, his need. She looked away biting her lips, trying to keep the panic inside.

His presence filled the room, changing the relaxed atmosphere to a chill of formality. He took a step toward her and everyone gave him space. The way he looked at her now returned the fear she'd felt earlier. In the low light, his eyes shone and a glimpse of his raw power reflected in the set of his shoulders down to his narrow waist.

His eyes lingered on her bare flesh and without thinking she crossed her arms. A flush crept up her neck and made her cheeks hot. He spoke to her in a husky voice and while the words were lost in translation his meaning was clear. Wahab reached out to touch her. Ronnie tensed her arm and took a step backward.

She looked at Ogundah. "Please, I want to stay here with you."

The friendly open smiles of the last hour were replaced by tight-lipped avoidance. The other women crowded around and pushed Ronnie toward Wahab. He took her hand and nearly crushed it as he led her out of the hut. It was clear now—the bathing, the dressing, and attention—they were preparing her for Wahab. The realization hit like a punch in the gut, leaving her breathless. To refuse him after all the setup would be embarrassing, but she did not want to be presented to him like a slab of meat. It was never her intention to promise intimacy.

Ronnie's mind raced as she tried to find a way out of this situation. If she left with him he wouldn't be embarrassed but what would he do when they were alone? Would he become angry at her refusal or force himself on her?

Her stomach lurched and she pulled away from his grip and turned toward Ogundah. Sympathetic dark eyes stared back. Staccato words from Wahab punctured the air and it was clear who carried the power. Ogundah bowed her head.

Wahab pushed her toward the exit. The sun had set and the air had cooled considerably to a more comfortable mid-eighties, still damp with humidity. A crowd was gathered and Chief Powhatan stood in the center. A flash of lightning off in the distance lit up the faces of the people nearby.

"No, I …" she shook her head and tried to walk out of the circle. Her status seemed to have shifted from welcomed guest to prisoner and she was reminded of her treatment in prison in London. She tried to sense the mood of the crowd as she glanced around, but their unfamiliar faces and customs masked what she was hoping to find. A trickle of sweat dripped down her back and she swallowed heavily. *Crap I'm in over my head.* A low rumble of thunder miles away plucked at the fear already growing inside.

Chief Powhatan, as Ronnie now thought of him, spoke and the crowd pulled in tighter, making a circle around Ronnie and Wahab. Ogundah stood by her side looking serious. Claustrophobia overcame her but she suppressed the urge to run away. She wouldn't get far.

The chief held out a string of beads up to Wahab's shoulder and let it drape down to his hand. Ogundah held up the knife she'd seen in the hut and cut the beads, deftly tying a knot in the string that held them together, and held it out to the chief. Wahab took Ronnie's hand and offered it to Powhatan, who quickly wrapped the beads around their hands, binding them together. Ronnie pulled away trying to get lose, but Wahab's grip held her fast, and as the beads bound them together there was no way to pull free.

Ogundah placed her hand on theirs and spoke to the group. When she was finished, the chief held their joined hands in the air and the crowd yelped and hollered. Ronnie held back tears, terrified of what the ceremony meant. Was she now married to Wahab? Ogundah unwound the beads and draped them over her neck. The crowd disbursed and several warriors approached congratulating Wahab and nodding to her.

Full panic overcame her and she looked around for some way to escape. A commotion twenty feet away caught Ronnie's attention. A group of natives approached with spears in hand. In the center of the melee was a man in old-fashioned clothes, the stark black standing out even in the low light against the mostly bare skin of the warriors.

There was only one man Ronnie wanted to see. She held her breath as they approached, bracing herself for an angry outburst from one of the unknown colonists when she had first arrived. It was too dark to make out any facial features but the man spoke with an English accent, confirming what his clothing said clearly enough.

A flash of lightning gave her the view she had wanted. "Morris." She stepped away from Wahab. "I don't think I've ever been happier to see anyone in my entire life."

"Mistress Coleman." He approached with eyes lit up. "I most humbly apologize for this intrusion, for this ..." He stopped short and looked at her long slender bare legs and turned away. "I ..." His expression fell, and a look of surprise replaced the polite humbleness.

Wahab stepped between them and pushed her backward. Morris surprised her by saying something in their native tongue and Wahab responded angrily.

Another man that Ronnie recognized from the bonfire stepped in and pulled Wahab aside. They spoke rapidly back and forth and repeated the same word over and over. The chief stepped out of the crowd and spoke sharply to Wahab, who bowed his head and turned to look at her.

Morris stepped closer and glanced her over, a deep blush rising from his neck to make his cheeks splotchy. "Relief overwhelms me, I do not wish to be rude, but your manner of dress has taken my breath away. Please, will you wear my doublet so I may speak without averting my eyes?" He removed a sleeveless vest and unbuttoned the doublet. He stood shirtless and Ronnie turned away to not embarrass him. His body was incredible with thick shoulders, chest, and arms tapered to abs of steel. He held the black doublet out and quickly put the jerkin back on. Now he looked like Conan the Barbarian wearing a black vest that revealed his strength.

Ronnie slid the doublet over her shoulders and buttoned it from mid chest to waist leaving the remaining buttons undone. A cooler wind was blowing now, another sign of the approaching storm and the remaining warmth from his body wrapped around her protectively.

Morris spoke softly, "It was necessary to portend an untruth, for I hath told them you are my betrothed. It is under discussion this very moment."

Ronnie laughed, "You told them we are married?" Relief washed over her. "Morris, that is brilliant. Will that help?"

Morris spoke rapidly, "I am not certain. Wahab, a favored warrior, has claimed you as a concubine wife, his third wife ... you will be his slave." Emotion overcame him. He cleared his throat, "It is foreseeable that hath I claimed you as my betrothed, the chief will not overrule in Wahab's favor, as you are already spoken for, and they shall give you leave in my care."

Ronnie felt weak in the knees. "Morris, thank you for risking your life like this. How did you find me?"

"It is my utmost pleasure to see you. I feared greatly for your life when I returned to my home and you were absent." He wiped a trickle of sweat off his forehead. "One of my many skills is tracking animals for the hunt. It was easy to follow your footsteps through the dry creek bed. I lost track of you midway and I was found by the gentlemen. Men? Indians? What does one call them? I hate to use the word savages for I see their homes are more solidly built than our own."

"Men, yes that will do." He smiled and his expression softened, making his eyes shine in the low light. "These men encountered me and brought me into the camp. That is when I found you." He lowered his gaze to her bare legs and back to her eyes. "In a marriage ceremony with ..." He nodded toward Wahab who appeared to be in a heated argument with the chief now.

Another flash of lightning showed the worry on Morris's face. "Please, Mistress Coleman, pray tell what came over you to leave with such haste and make your way into the woods. Do you not know the dangers that await a colonist away from the safety of our village?"

"Morris." She reached out to touch his hand, "Please understand, I did not want you to come after me. I wanted to you to not be persecuted because you helped me."

His eyes teared up. He blinked and looked away.

"You were so kind to take me in but I'd rather take my chances out here and let you live a happy life. You need your friends to help you survive out here. You don't need someone they will attack you over."

He shook his head. "That is my fight, not yours. I am man enough to handle their wrath. I prevented their attack and will provide a haven for you. They will bend to my will in time, as you say we all need each other to survive."

"Morris, they were about to burn your house down. If they didn't then they would find a way. I wanted you to be safe and not in danger on my account. My life is temporary." She wondered how to express that, for it really was. She could die here now and it would take her back to Florida, she hoped. He'd still have to survive the situation.

He took her hand. "Mistress Coleman." Thunder interrupted him.

The corresponding rumble in her bones piqued her adrenaline. "Please, call me Ronnie."

He squeezed her hand and brought it to his lips and kissed it. "Ronnie, I am honored to call you by your given name."

"It is an honor to have you call me this." He made her feel all fluttery inside.

"I want to convey my deepest gratitude for providing me with an explanation so considered and finely expressed. Your motive was to protect me." He shook his head. "Such a selfless act on my behalf brings me great happiness. It was an unwise thing to do though if you will permit me to say such impudent words. Your life is valuable and precious. The fact you were spared from the grave this very day must mean something of great importance."

Chief Powhatan spoke harshly to Wahab hushing the crowd. Something important was happening.

"What are they saying?" Ronnie whispered.

"They are discussing your fate. For our own safety, we must leave this village at once. If I can distract them from you, if that is at all possible, please leave with the utmost haste. If we should become separated, please, head east." He nodded to the left. "There is a large stone as a marker just beyond the camp here. If you are able, crawl under, there is a small gap on the east side. I will meet you there."

She squeezed his hand but before she could respond Wahab stepped in between them. He barked angry words and pushed Morris backward. Morris stood with his hands in front of him and responded in cool even tones in their tongue. They spoke back and forth for a few minutes with Wahab quadrupling Morris's words, but finally, Morris removed a knife from his belt and set in on the ground at his feet. Another burst of lightning caught the blade and blinded her for a second. This time thunder followed close behind. A rush of wind blew leaves across the ground in front of her but no one seemed fazed by the encroaching storm.

Chapter 40 - Knight in Shining Ford F-150

"Please Nick. Come soon!" Steph yelled. They should have stayed home and waited for the storm to end. "Ronnie, I'm so sorry." Tears fell down her face and terror overtook all emotions. "Hail Mary full of grace …"

Finally, after what seemed like days of waiting, headlights shone through the broken windshield. Two car doors slammed and Nick was at the driver's side door yelling, "Steph, oh God, Steph."

Another figure stood on the passenger side. Nick tried to open the door but it wouldn't budge. The men yelled back and forth to each other but Steph couldn't make out what they said.

The passenger door opened and Mike Walsh's handsome face poked in. "Steph, holy crap. Are you okay?"

"I am."

"How is Ronnie?" He reached out to touch Ronnie's foot.

"Same," Steph said as Mike pushed the passenger seat forward.

"Here let me grab Ronnie and then you can get your stuff. The sooner we're in my truck the better." Water dripped down his face and his white T-shirt clung to his chest to make him look like a muscly ghost.

Mike leaned in and awkwardly tried to get ahold of Ronnie. He reached under Ronnie's neck and managed to scoop her up. Carefully he pulled her from the Jeep and disappeared into the darkness.

Nick reached a hand out and helped her from the Jeep. He engulfed her in a wet hug and kissed her. "Baby, I'm so sorry I left you here. I saw the tree on my car and nearly died."

She held him tight and sobbed. Relief flowed over her. "You have no idea how happy I am to see you."

They separated and Nick reached into the backseat for the overnight bag. He opened the glove compartment and pulled out a few papers. As a last-minute thought, he pulled the keys from the ignition and took Steph's hand. They ran to Mike's truck and Nick opened the rear door and blocked the rain with his body as much as he could while she arranged Ronnie's head on her lap.

"How is she doing?" Mike turned around from the driver's seat.

"Mike, we're not sure what's going on with her. Thank you so much for helping us. I'm embarrassed that we got ourselves in such trouble." Steph pushed her wet bangs out of her eyes.

"I just hope we can get to the hospital." Mike put the truck in gear. "The roads aren't exactly ideal for an evening cruise. I'm really glad I could help out though."

The wipers flicked back and forth but the rain was pelting down so hard visibility was almost nil. They rode in silence for a while and Steph got lost in worry over her friend.

"Mike, thanks again for doing this. If you ever need anything ..." Nick trailed off.

"No, really, I'm glad to help. I just want Ronnie to be okay." Mike glanced at her in the rearview mirror. "Steph, how are you holding up? You really were lucky how that tree fell back there," Mike said as his blue eyes reflected the headlights in the rearview mirror.

"I know, it scared me nearly to death." Steph bit her lip trying not to cry. "What a day, huh?"

Nick turned around and blew her a kiss. Steph vaguely listened to the men talk about directions and road conditions before closing her eyes. In the quiet of the storm, she prayed for everyone's safe arrival and for Ronnie's health to return. She thought of Ian and prayed for his safety and hoped he would make wise decisions if something were to go wrong. He'd definitely have stories to tell his friends back in Glasgow. Most likely embellished stories, but anyone who knew him would take it as entertainment.

"Steph," Nick called out. "Steph, we're here."

"What?" She must have dozed off. The rain was no longer pelting the window and between rain droplets, the emergency room sign showed as a shattered image of bright red and white. "Oh, thank God. Mike, you're incredible." She then whispered to Ronnie while smoothing her hair down, "We're here at the hospital. You should get help soon."

"Couldn't have gotten here without Nick." Mike clapped him on the shoulder.

"We are so grateful for your help." Nick opened his car door and helped her out of the truck.

"Really, no need to thank me." Mike jumped from the truck and came around toward them. "I'm just glad you thought to come to me. I'll run in and get someone to help us." Mike waved and disappeared through the automatic doors.

A few minutes later a gurney burst through the doors followed by a man and a woman in scrubs. Mike trailed behind as they pushed the gurney near the truck.

"I'll move her," Mike said, pushing the gurney out of the way. He bent over and gently pushed Ronnie's wet hair out of her eyes. The gesture struck Steph as a bit too affectionate for a boss.

The two hospital workers strapped Ronnie in and lifted the safety rails. Steph followed them while Nick reached in the back of the truck and grabbed the overnight bag before catching up.

"Hey Mike, I'll come back to the lobby and tell you where we are." Nick waved. "Once they've worked her up. It may be a little while."

"Okay, no problem, I'll just get a coffee and wait. Really no rush." He waved back and climbed in the truck.

"He's such a good guy, isn't he?" Steph grabbed Nick's hand.

"He is. Thank God for Mike. He really saved our bacon." He stopped and turned toward her. "I'm so sorry about all of this. I never wanted you to be in danger. I ..." His mouth crumpled.

"Babe I insisted we go to the hospital. It's not your fault." She squeezed his hand. "We're here now. We did the best we could and I'm fine. Let's put our energy to getting Ronnie back."

"Okay, I'm just so sorry." He grabbed her hand and they walked into the lobby.

"Ma'am," a nurse behind the counter of the emergency department called out. "Please fill out the paperwork." She held out a clipboard. A few minutes later another nurse called them back to the bays where patients were seen.

"Your friend is non-responsive. Does she have any medical conditions we need to know about?" the nurse asked as they made their way down the curtained cubicles.

Steph looked at Nick for help with this one. "She ... ah."

"She has low blood sugar sometimes. She's been really stressed over the storms." Nick squeezed her hand.

When they walked into the cubicle Steph's heart sank at seeing three people working on Ronnie. She was already hooked up to a heart monitor with other machines nearby ready to be connected.

Chapter 41 - Primal Fear

"Ronnie, please, remember what we've spoken about," Morris said as Wahab shoved him backward.

Chief Powhatan bent to pick up Morris's knife and held it to the sky. He yelled for all to hear and made his way to the center of a clearing. Two men stayed close to Ronnie as she followed behind. Her stomach clenched with worry. Would they kill Morris on the spot? Why had he surrendered the knife? The others in the group gathered in a circle, leaving about fifteen feet in the middle where Morris and Wahab stood eying each other.

The chief stood between them speaking to the crowd, who responded by chanting one phrase repeatedly. Morris made eye contact with her and nodded his head toward the east. Deep male voices rang out in the night and vibrated into her soul, each shout driving panic deeper into her subconscious. Another man grabbed Ronnie's arm and brought her to the chief, who spoke to the group and nodded at her. A stray raindrop landed on her chest and tickled her as it ran down and soaked into the animal skin.

Morris unbuttoned his jerkin and removed it, handing it to her. "Their custom is to have a wrestling match to decide who owns you. Please, if you can find a way to depart this circle do so at once. I do not know if they will be honorable."

His eyes lit up with another flash from the storm burning his muscular form into her mind. They were deciding who owned her. The clap of thunder made her jump. The storm was close now.

Wahab pointed at Morris's feet, speaking angrily. Morris removed his shoes, set them at Ronnie's feet and pulled the hose off tossing them on the ground so he stood barefoot. Wahab stood to his full height and lifted his chin, feet in a wide stance, falling about five inches shorter than Morris, who mimicked his stance and stared back intently. Morris was powerfully built outweighed Wahab by at least forty pounds. He had the advantage of size, but Ronnie had watched enough of her brother's wrestling matches to know size was only a small factor in determining the winner.

She could feel the intensity of someone's eyes burning into her soul. She scanned the crowd. It was the prince, or whatever they called the chief's son. To her, he would always be the prince. His mouth crumpled and he looked away, crying. She had a sinking feeling. Could Morris win this battle? Would they honor his win if he succeeded?

Chief Powhatan raised his hand and barked out unfamiliar words. Wahab put one hand on the back of Morris's neck and gripped his elbow with the other hand in a wrestler's stance. Morris copied the posture, taut thick muscles flexed down his back and readied for the fight. His maroon breeches were tight against thick hamstrings. Another flash of lighting shone off the bare flesh of both men who were slick now with the scattered rain that fell from the night sky.

Tears welled in her eyes and the stress sickened her. She glanced around hoping to find an escape during the excitement of the match but two warriors flanked her side.

Morris and Wahab careened toward the crowd and forced Ronnie out of the way. Everyone was closely focused on the bodies in perpetual motion. The wiry native used leverage on Morris's arm to force him to release his legs, but in an instant, Morris pivoted and picked Wahab off his feet, spun around and slammed him down on the ground. The crowd yelled and several men encroached on the circle, but the chief held them back. Wahab stood slowly and rubbed his back where a gash had opened to release his life force.

The men were evenly matched despite the difference in size. Wahab was a skillful fighter and used Morris's inexperience and weight against him. In Morris' favor were quick reflexes and a powerful frame. The Englishman stood panting with his hands on his knees. Two warriors she recognized from the bonfire walked behind her. They shifted for a better view of the match and also blocked her way for escape for the time being.

Another flash of lightning lit up the eager faces watching the battle. This momentary distraction seemed to ignite Wahab who rushed forward to tackle Morris. The sound of air escaping large bodies permeated the cooling night air and the thunder cracked loud and close. Grunts and blows to sweaty flesh filled Ronnie's senses and she nearly felt each assault on Morris's body. The sky opened and rain ran in rivulets across the clearing. No one took cover as they were all too absorbed in the battle.

Wind lifted her hair and a chill crawled across her skin as she stepped backward to melt into the crowd, so focused on the battle they didn't see her slip off into the night. A loud cheer drowned out the sound of her running through the brush nearly blind from the darkness. She pulled Morris's doublet tight around her for protection from the thick branches. She'd never had much of a sense of direction and with the darkness engulfing her it was the moment she needed to master this skill. A flash of lightning lit the path ahead and the horrendous vibrating thunder pulled a scream from her throat. She veered toward the cleared path hoping she'd not run afoul of something in the way.

Ronnie stopped and wiped her eyes, willing them to see to no avail. A foul wet stench permeated the air and she recoiled, mind frantic with possibilities. Another flash from the heavens revealed a true nightmare—a huge form stretched above her with sharp glistening teeth. Ronnie screamed. The bear that stood on hind legs over her towered nearly nine feet in height.

Panic like she had never felt before caused her to burst forward as she dodged the bear and ran at full speed into the night in hopes she was running toward something that could save her from the beast. She knew running was her enemy with a bear on her heels, but there was too much adrenaline coursing through her veins to stop for even a second.

Guttural grunts behind her indicated the predator was up for the chase and Ronnie screamed again, releasing the pent-up fear gathered in her chest. The sonic-esque boom overwhelmed her and pushed out any logical thoughts, leaving only primal fear. The intensity of the rain bore down on her head and blurred her vision. The next flash was immediate and knocked her backward, her entire body tingled and she smelled the acrid scent of burning hair and all went black.

Ronnie woke from a dark and dangerous feeling deep in her gut. She inhaled and choked on water that had pooled in her mouth. The rain was relentless. She rolled to her hands and knees and crawled away from the spreading fire. A tall tree nearby was burning and despite the torrential rain, it spread to the forest nearby, lighting the way. Lightning must have struck the tree and knocked her out. Thank God it did, the bear was nowhere in sight.

Ronnie covered her mouth and nose with Morris's doublet to bar the smoke that billowed up into the night sky. On shaky legs, she stumbled away from the flames grateful for the light but doing her best to breathe. Which way was the rock? She had lost all sense of direction. Then it hit her. Ogundah had described this scene exactly with the lightning strike and the bear. She wiped the rain from her eyes and let the thought echo around. The hairs rose on her arms as she cleared her mind to focus on what was foretold. Was Morris the man in the stream caught in the mudslide?

A shadowy figure in the distance was crashing through the forest. She choked back the fear, how many times would she be terrified tonight? Stealthily she moved behind a thicket. Was it the bear? A large branch, likely broken from the storm rested on the ground. She bent down and gripped it in her hand, ready to use it on whatever approached.

Chapter 42 - Questions Outweigh Answers

The crew working on Ronnie asked endless medical history and lifestyle questions. Steph answered them numbly while caught in the whirlwind of activity around them.

"Has she had a fall or head injury of any kind?" a heavyset nurse asked.

"Not that I know of. I think she was just sleeping," Steph responded.

"Did she have issues with dizziness or blurred vision?" The nurse checked off her answers on a clipboard.

"No, she didn't say," Steph answered in a daze.

"Did she have any health issues before this happened?" The nurse impatiently blinked her long eyelashes. "A fever, headache, strange behavior?"

Nick shook his head. She answered "Uh ... no."

Steph interjected, "She may have had exposure to the bubonic plague."

The nurse stopped and gave her a puzzled look. "Bubonic plague, are you certain?"

"Yes," Steph said. Nick looked puzzled as well. Steph would have to update him about the watch and the blood that was on it when Ronnie returned from 1666.

"Did she display any signs of confusion, disorientation, or numbness before she went to bed?"

"No, I don't think so." Part of her wanted to tell the nurse about Ronnie's experience. Her life was at stake after all, but Nick's insistence kept her on track.

"What medications does she use? Is there a chance she used something new? Either prescription or ... street?"

Steph shook her head, fighting back tears.

"Is she pregnant?" The nurse pressed into Ronnie's stomach.

"I don't think so." Steph started to feel sick and it worsened by the thought of Jeffrey's child growing inside her friend.

"Her vitals look good." The nurse smiled and squeezed Steph's arm. "Don't worry we'll figure this out and take good care of her."

A tall Indian doctor rushed in the room and everyone seemed to stand a little straighter and work a little more efficiently.

"I am Dr. Patel, I am the chief resident on duty. Please allow me to examine your friend."

Nick shook his hand, "Thank you, Dr. Patel, great to meet you."

Steph shook his hand too. "Thank you."

The staff updated him with vitals, meds they'd administered, and a litany of things Steph didn't understand.

The doctor turned to Steph, "Please tell me what brings you here today."

Steph glanced at Nick and he spoke for her. "During the storm, she woke several times feeling strange and then we went to check on her and she was unresponsive."

"Strange?" Dr. Patel asked. "Please explain the behaviors she exhibited that were unusual."

Steph answered this time, "She woke up several times during the night with a …" Steph glanced at Nick, "nightmare and she seemed to be eating like crazy. She gets low blood sugar spells sometimes and maybe it's connected to that. I'm not sure."

"I see. How did she tell you that she was feeling poorly?" Dr. Patel motioned toward the two chairs near the bed. "Please sit as we talk."

Steph and Nick sat down. "She just told me she felt strange."

"I'm sorry I wasn't clear I meant to say, was her speech normal? Did you notice her slurring words, or a side of her mouth drooping? Maybe her hands were shaking."

Steph looked at Nick for help. He answered, "No she spoke fine. She was just hungry and upset because of her weird dreams." Nick took her hand and squeezed it.

Dr. Patel turned to the staff working on Ronnie. "Have you done a glucose test?"

The heavyset nurse answered, "We have CBC heading toward the lab now."

"Please, rapid glucose and let me know the status." He turned back to Steph and Nick. "Approximately at what time did she last ingest food?"

"I have no idea." Steph turned to Nick. "Do you?"

Nick looked at his watch. "Wow, I'm not sure. At least three hours ago."

"Did she manage to eat a meal?" Dr. Patel's demeanor was calm and reassuring.

"Not exactly a meal. Crackers and cheese." Nick shook his head. "I was rushing around helping with the roof. Do you know how much she ate?"

"No, I was doing the same and yelling at Ian." Steph cheeks burned. "I feel so bad, none of us spent much time with her." She held back tears.

"In emergencies, we do the best we can. Don't berate yourself. The problem was not of your doing. It was something inside of your friend. She is young and you couldn't know she was in such distress."

On the word distress Steph couldn't hold back any more. Great embarrassing sobs escaped from her mouth. Nick handed her a box of Kleenex from the side table next to him. He pulled her close.

"We will do everything we can for her," Dr. Patel said.

"Thanks," Nick said into Steph's hair.

The next hour went by in a blur. So many questions without answers. Steph sat in her wet clothes and watched as the doctors and nurses worked on her friend. Nick left briefly to update Mike, who was waiting patiently in the lobby. Finally, the nurses left. Ronnie looked peaceful despite all the tubes, wires, and machines that extended from her body.

Nick stood and stretched. "Well, this is fun."

"Not my first choice of ways to have fun," she responded.

A new nurse entered the room. "I wanted to let you know we are admitting her. They will be taking her up to her room shortly."

"Okay," Steph said. "Did they find anything out yet?"

"The blood results should be back soon. Dr. Patel is concerned she's still unresponsive and would like to do a CT scan. Once they're done with that they will admit her."

"Okay." Steph still felt numb. Why wouldn't Ronnie wake up?

"Are you a relative?" the nurse asked.

"No, she's my best friend."

"Visiting hours are almost over. If you're not related, you'll have to return at nine in the morning when visiting hours resume."

Nick stepped toward her. "We are her only family here. How will we know what's going on with her care?"

"Sir, please come back during visiting hours and we can discuss more then."

"We can't go back home in the storm. Is there somewhere we could …" Steph broke down again. Nick held her close.

"Ma'am, we have a nice waiting room. There is a cafeteria but it's closed. We are saving essential power for the patients. There are vending machines for coffee and snacks if you're hungry."

"But what about Ronnie? How will we…" Steph stepped close to the bed and took her hand. "Nick, I can't just leave her."

He stood behind her and put his hands on her shoulder. "She's not gonna miss you much, Steph. Let's get some rest and we can see her in the morning." He turned to the nurse. "Will you notify us if anything changes?"

"Yes, if you are in the waiting room we will have someone come find you. I don't think cell service is working right now." Her tone was all business. "We won't be able to reach you if you're not there."

"How will we know where she is?" Steph wiped her eyes.

"During visiting hours you can ask the front desk and they'll give you the room number."

"But that's not good enough. I need to be here for her," Steph yelled. "I need to know what's going on."

A male nurse walked into the cubical. "We're ready to take her to the CT scan. Please grab all your belongings. She won't be back in this room."

"Okay," Steph looked around and picked up her purse. "Nick."

He already had the overnight bag on his shoulder. "Let's get some rest. We'll rattle some cages if we need to. If she wakes up they'll get us, right?"

The male nurse shrugged his shoulders, "I'm not sure. The floor nurses are in charge of the patients."

The heavyset nurse escorted them to a family waiting room. A droopy older man was snoozing in the corner. "If we hear anything we'll let you know."

"Thank you," Nick nodded.

"Why did you thank her? She kicked us out." Steph clenched her fists.

"Babe, it's just the hospital rules. We'll have a great night in here and in the morning, we'll see what they've found out."

The drab room had lingering bad vibes of family members waiting on dead and dying relatives. She wanted to be by Ronnie's side and not in this claustrophobic sterile room. They sat on the puce pleather chairs and waited.

"I wish the TV was on anyway," she said.

"Me too. At least it would be distracting." Nick pulled her close and Steph rested her head on his shoulder.

Chapter 43 - TOTO We're Not in Kansas Anymore

Jeffrey was not one to work with a partner but today in these circumstances one would be pretty damn handy. He needed to unload TOTO under the overhang and then park his car. The likelihood of someone taking it in the minute it took him to return was small but the downside was horrendous. An ornamental tree in a large cement pot was the only dry place he could leave it without being obvious.

"God, what if they thought it was a bomb?" Other unlikely but dangerous scenarios rolled around in his mind as he pulled up. The rain was pelting him even under the large cement roof that covered the door to the staff entrance.

He lifted the tarp-covered time travel device and carried it to the potted plant. It barely fit between the wall and the planter. A second later he tucked the laptop in the case under the tarp away from the violent winds. He quickly parked the car and ran back through the driving rain to the secreted items near the planter. He left them in place and walked into the employee-only section. Thankfully the hallways were empty. Jeffrey wandered for a few minutes and found a staff changing room. He grabbed a large set of scrubs and quickly changed, leaving his clothes in an empty locker, but keeping his wallet tucked in the rear pocket of the scrubs. His work ID badge was in his wallet and he clipped it on the scrubs but turned the ID part backward and hoped it looked enough like a hospital badge so long as no one looked at him closely.

Fifteen minutes later and a lot of locked doors he followed the stairs to the basement and found the laundry area and a cart used by the custodians. He stacked a few towels and supplies on it and took the elevator up one flight and returned to the door where his gear was stashed. Quickly he grabbed TOTO and the laptop, placing the large device on the bottom rack of the cart and arranging the towels along one side and toilet paper and other supplies around the other. He threw the laptop case in the soiled linen basket in the rear of the cart and covered it with a few towels.

Jeffrey set the laptop on the top of the cart and fired it up. Damn. He'd left the extra battery in his car. There were about twenty minutes of power left. He would have to find Ronnie and find a plug to get this party started. The tracking software showed a blip moving on a floor above him. Making careful notations he then shut the laptop and placed it in the case in the soiled linen bin and pressed the button for the elevator.

He moved with head down past the nurse's station and followed his calculations to where Ronnie was, or had been when he'd last checked. Full blown panic hit him when he came to the imaging sign in the hallway. Would an MRI or CT Scan show the item he'd inserted in her back? It was made from titanium so it shouldn't be damaging to Ronnie during the MRI, but what would they do if they found it? Most likely they'd just check her head, not anything further down her spine, but there would be a lot of questions and it would draw suspicion if discovered.

They were most likely looking for an aneurysm or something wrong with her brain. What would her brain look like in this state? Would she have brain waves like in a dream state or would it be flat only using the brain stem for breathing and heartbeat? It fascinated him, he would have to get his hands on those MRI files.

In the meantime, he had to set up TOTO to get close enough to Ronnie. Doing so meant in an adjacent room or in a room above or below her. While he waited for Ronnie to emerge from the imaging room he moseyed along the hallway in search of a facility map to further his plan of attack.

Chapter 44 - Dare

A man ran past Ronnie and bounded over a fallen log. Relief washed over her until his state of undress was evident. Bare skin slick with rain and all the fears rushed upon her of Wahab's plans. She held her breath hoping the man wouldn't see her. Ragged breathing grew closer. The man had turned around to face her but still hadn't found her hiding place. To her utter surprise, he had light hair and a reddish beard.

"Morris!"

"Mistress Coleman!" he gasped still breathing hard. "Dear God, Ronnie." Morris's chest was crisscrossed with blood. A cut above his eye dripped down his cheek.

She stood and walked toward him. "Morris, oh my God. How did you find me?"

"Mistress, I assure you I have not found you. It must be divine intervention for I merely made my escape. The gathering of Indians watching the skirmish disbanded upon the appearance of a great beast galloping through the clearing." He indicated with his hand that the animal was eye level with him. "To my utter and complete astonishment, I might add. I had no idea such an animal could move so rapidly. It must have been startled by the storm for it made haste. I took the liberty to run to our meeting place hoping you'd be nearby." He folded her in his arms. "What a blessed relief to find you unharmed."

Her cheek pressed against his chest and his solidness calmed her taut nerves. He pulled away and took her hand. "With haste let us make our escape before they are upon us. My fists may have taken out a few of the warriors who blocked my path. A search party may be gathering now." He bent low and adjusted his black leather shoes. "Luck was with me as I was able to grab my footwear before I departed."

They ran in the waning light from the fire as they covered a decent amount of ground, dodging areas of thick brush, and moving away from the danger of the fire. The light was fading quickly and their pace slowed to a careful walk.

His hand was muscular and solid giving her more energy than twelve cups of coffee. "Morris, I was close enough to smell the bear's breath when the lightning struck. The storm saved my life."

He looked up at her with mouth agape. "Mistress, I do believe that strike saved my life as well, for it was the bear upon our camp that scattered the match. It is unclear if I could have won that contest." He blinked the rain away with long wet lashes.

The skies opened and the sounds of the rain crashing through the canopy halted their conversation. If anyone was following it would be impossible to hear them coming. Ronnie prayed with everything she had they were too busy with the beast and the storm to find them.

Soon they found the streambed that had been dry when she first left the colony. It was full now and running swiftly but provided open ground to walk on, giving them a reprieve from the thick underbrush.

Morris pulled her under the shelter of a thick pine tree for a moment of reprieve from the pelting rain. Ronnie was overwhelmed by a mixture of gratitude for his rescue attempt and passion for the strong, brave man standing next to her. She imagined kissing those firm lips. He must have felt her mood change because surprise showed on his face. He took her hand and brought it to his lips.

The gesture caught Ronnie off guard and tears welled up. Gratitude, lust, excitement, and fear all jumbled up in her chest and burst forth in a laugh she tried to stifle, but it wasn't doable. The situation was so far from anything she'd ever experienced. It struck her as completely absurd.

"Ronnie, I fail to see the humor in our situation."

Ronnie wrapped her arms around his torso, hugging him, holding him close. "Morris, it's not funny at all. I am just overwhelmed with relief you're here. You're okay and so am I."

He pushed the wet hair out of her eyes and looked down at her. "It is a blessing to be away safely. We shall be eternally grateful to a wretched bear. It is a completely unexpected turn of events."

He wiped his eyes. "The rain is a blessing. It has been a very difficult few years. We have endured hardships without the water and we have had to rely on the Indians to assist us with new seeds and crops. So many plants we are not familiar with have turned into our most valued harvests." His eyes shone with the flash of lightning.

"Then the thunderstorm has saved more than just the two of us." Ronnie found it ironic the storm had helped her now but the same phenomenon was the impetus for bringing her to 1588.

"It will not make up for the year of dry hot weather," Morris said. "We need a miracle to bring us more rain to end the drought. The success of our colony has been at risk for some time now. The drought is merely one way we have been weakened."

"I am eager to hear more, Morris."

"We were doomed from the very start of this journey. This was not our destination, rather we were to settle north of here. The wretched fleet commander, Simon Fernandez, barred our return to the ships, stranding us farther south than we had planned." The rain lightened up a bit and he took her hand to lead her out of the temporary shelter. "Let us continue toward the perimeter fence to return to the safety of our colony. We are still in grave danger."

He helped her over a fallen log and continued, "Captain Fernandez journeyed in search of the garrison that was left nigh a year prior. Upon finding no one he insisted we return to the ship. Governor White informed us afterwards that Fernandez found the remains of a soldier from the garrison and it spooked him. He felt letting us back on the fleet would bring ill will to the voyage."

Ronnie shook her head imagining the nightmare of being left with nothing but what they'd brought, no food, no additional supplies, or clothes. "Instead it brought ill will to your settlement. The colony is doing well now though?"

He looked away from the path to give her a curious look. "Pardon me, Ronnie, I do not take your meaning."

It was frustrating to speak the same language as Morris, but still fail to convey her thoughts. His English was so cumbersome. "Do you believe our colony will survive?"

He shook his head. "It is difficult to say. We have made terrible blunders." He held the long prickly branch of a bramble for her to pass without getting tangled. "In error, we attacked our closest ally, the Croatoan tribe over a silver challis. We had hoped to retaliate for the theft of this precious item, but failed by attacking the wrong group."

"Oh, that is really dangerous."

"Our man, Mr. Howe, do you remember him? His hair was black as midnight and he loved catching crustaceans along the shore."

Ronnie shook her head.

"It was a tragedy when the Croatoan's took his life, likely in response to our attack. In truth, we are lucky that is all the revenge they sought." He took her hand.

"It must have been a grave shock." Ronnie sensed the desperation in his voice. What could they do? They were a small group thousands of miles away from their homeland who were completely dependent upon the tribe's goodwill to tolerate their presence.

"Grave shock to us all."

"Is Wahab from the Croatoan tribe?" Ronnie asked.

"Wahab and the rest of the tribe we were with are in the territory of Tsenacommacah. The Croatoans are our closer allies, despite the troubles that have plagued us. We urged our governor to sail back to England a year ago to provide assistance and replenish our wares. Please, tell me if I prattle on like an old maid over things must you already know."

"No please, Morris, I am eager to hear about this." All of this sounded familiar. "Is Eleanor Dare in our colony?"

"Why yes, she is the daughter of our governor and the reason he did not want to part with us. She bore a female child upon our arrival here in the colony and named her Virginia. Governor White has been gone nearly a year having sailed to England to bring back supplies and more protection for our situation has become precarious."

Her mind spun with a mixture of excitement and terror. Her father had taught her about Eleanor Dare. She and Governor White were distant relatives and an area of fascination to him. How immensely poignant to bear witness to their struggles in one of America's first colonies, even more incredibly to live as one of them. To face their demons and mingle with their foes. It had been America's first mystery when Governor White returned the entire village had been wiped away, not a trace of their homes or civilization other than a carving on a tree to show their peaceable departure. She knew that Dare County in North Carolina was named for Virginia, the first child born in the colony. Ronnie tried to remember any other details but as it was the history was quite vague.

"Do you think Wahab will try to find us?" she asked.

Morris shook his head. "We all pray every day for the safe return of Governor White. I fear today's activities have again brought us closer to a dangerous precipice."

Ronnie contemplated her role in this latest blow for the colony. If she had not left Morris's cabin, he would not have had to put himself and the colony at risk. An enormous guilt weighed down on her.

"I am so sorry Morris. I never meant to put you in harm's way. I was trying to relieve the burden of my care, and look what I've done." She tried to keep her voice from shaking but the emotions were overwhelming.

"If you please, Ronnie, I do not want you to be concerned. It was noble of you to risk your life to alleviate this burden from my shoulders. You could not know I would give chase or what would find you in the wilderness." He stopped and smiled with his teeth glowing in the low light. "And may I add, if it is not too forward, the ways you have expressed yourself to me in the short time I have known you have captured my soul."

A flush crept up her neck. His words made her almost giddy with excitement. "I feel it too, there is a closeness I cannot explain, feelings that defy the fact I've just met you."

"We are nearly to safety, let us explore this when we can be comforted by four walls and a fire to warm us. All my attention must be given to the task of finding our way back to the colony. The feelings expressed will keep me grounded and give me a purpose of working with haste." He squeezed her hand and gave her such a tender look that it was enough to nearly make her float the remainder of the way back.

They walked quickly toward the perimeter fence fighting an intense gust of wind, blowing wet leaves and small branches in her face, reminding her of the drive to Jeffrey's lab last month. That was an eternity ago. Correction, that was an eternity from now. America did not exist yet. Her mind struggled with the simple fact that Jeffrey was four hundred years in the future.

Damn Jeffrey! The anger boiled inside of her from their last fight. No! She wouldn't let him affect what she was going through here. This was her time to learn what she could, to be open to the feelings and possibly deeper meaning of this situation. What she needed was to forget him, enjoy this magical, albeit strange, journey and make the most of it. In her mind, she crumpled the essence of Jeffrey and their fight like a piece of paper and mentally tossed it into a trash can. He would not occupy the space in her mind today in this time.

Chapter 45 – Candy Striper

Mike sipped his coffee and wished he'd brought a change of clothes. It was a bit embarrassing to be in a completely soaked white T-shirt. Every time he looked up the nurse at the front desk would look away and try to act like she'd not been staring. Finally, he stood and walked toward her.

"Miss, is there any update on my …" Mike asked.

The nurse stood, knocking over her chair and visibly blushed. "Yes, I …"

Mike smiled. "Oh, I'm so sorry I didn't mean to startle you."

"No, no. I'm just…" She righted the chair and her face was bright pink. "Oh my. I meant to tell you your friends were in the lounge upstairs. The man came down to find you when you were getting coffee."

"The lounge. Why aren't they with Ronnie? Is she in the emergency room still?" Panic struck. What if they had her in surgery?

"I'm not sure. Here let me look her up."

"Thank you. I'm so grateful for any information."

She smiled and typed. Then stood and held her hand out. "Candice McGovern. So pleased to meet you."

"Candice, it is a pleasure to meet you." He smiled and had to inwardly chuckle at her exuberance. "Mike Walsh."

She beamed. "So nice to meet you. If there is anything you need please just tell me what I can do for you."

"Sure, that's really nice of you," he said. "I want to see my friend. I'm really worried."

"Okay, right." She giggled. "I was looking her up for you." Her cheeks were pink giving her a healthy glow. She typed into the computer and read off the screen. "CAT scan before being admitted to room two-two-seven."

"Okay, so not surgery. Good, I was worried."

"Is she your girlfriend?" Candice asked.

"Oh, no, she's my employee. I just drove her here when her friends got into trouble in the storm." He leaned on the counter flexing his shoulders. "Candice, I'd like to go up there to her room but I'm soaking wet. Is there anything I can change into that would be more comfortable?" He smoothed the wet T-shirt over his chest and abs. "I'm getting kind of cold."

The smile left her face. "I could help." She stood and walked around the desk. "Just don't tell anyone I helped you. It's kind of dead out here so I don't suppose anyone would miss me for a few minutes."

"I've not seen anyone come in at all," he agreed.

"Please, Mike, follow me." Candice led him to the elevator. "What do you do for a living?"

"I work for MHS as head of the information systems department."

"Oh nice. A businessman. That's ..." She looked up at him. "Hot." Candice looked away quickly.

Mike laughed. She must be in her early twenties and was hitting on him. He took in her slim figure in the blue scrubs and shook his head. Definitely too young for his taste. She was pretty enough. "Thanks."

Twenty minutes later Mike sat in the room reserved for Ronnie in clean dry scrubs with his clothes in a plastic bag at his feet smiling at Candice who had promised to bring him food. He insisted she get back to work but she wouldn't be swayed. A custodian wheeled a cart past his room pausing briefly to eye him. The man looked vaguely familiar but Mike brushed it off. He picked up the hospital brochure and thumbed through the PR piece on how fantastic they were. Better be, Ronnie was in trouble and they needed to make her well again.

Candice returned with a tray of snacks from the cafeteria. "Oh, your eyes look so blue in those scrubs." She looked flustered. "I brought you some food."

"You are so nice. Thank you so much." He took the tray from her.

"You're so welcome." Candice lingered uncomfortably.

A commotion in the hallway startled him and a male nurse pushed a gurney into the room. Mike set the tray down and stood. It was Ronnie. His heart skipped a beat. Seeing her so still, so lifeless. It was heartbreaking.

"Any word on her condition?" he asked the male nurse.

"The doctor will be in soon. I'm just the transporter. Oh, hey Candy, what's going on?"

"Nothing much. Just helping Mike out here." She smiled.

"See you." The nurse left.

"I should go, the floor nurse will be in soon and I could get in trouble for being here."

"Okay, thank you so much for all of your help."

Candice shifted on her feet. "I left my number if you ... uh." She pointed to the tray. 'Bye, I'll see you later, okay?"

Mike glanced at the tray of food and under the milk carton, a small slip of paper stuck out. "Okay, bye Candy." She walked out and Mike went to Ronnie's side and watched her breathe. He ignored the food, too disturbed by the sight of Ronnie unconscious on the bed. His eyes roamed over her perfect jawline, her long black lashes resting on her cheeks. The sculpted cheekbones and her little nose. What could have brought this on? She seemed so alive, so healthy at work the other day. It put life into perspective, it really was so fragile. He thought of Kelly and how quickly her life had ended. It was senseless to snuff out such beauty so young.

Another nurse came and rapidly hooked Ronnie up to all the machines. She introduced herself as the floor nurse in charge and wrote her name on the whiteboard on the wall.

"Mr. Andrews, the Doctor will be in to give you the scan results. I'll be back to check on her soon."

Mike chuckled at the mistake but didn't correct her. "What do you think might be the cause of the ..." He wasn't sure what to call it.

"Coma. She's in a coma. I'm not sure. If I had to guess it would be some type of head injury or a brain tumor." Her lips pressed together.

"Brain tumor?" Mike felt weak in the knees. "Oh God, that doesn't sound good."

"Don't panic yet. We really have no definitive information to go on. Her vitals look good, but we just don't have any explanation for her state of consciousness."

It seemed strange that he was in the room alone with Ronnie, while her close friends weren't here.

Chapter 46 - Blow

Jeffrey ducked into an empty room and fired up the laptop. Ronnie would be out of the CT scan soon and he needed to bring her back before this got any more complicated. Sweat dripped down his back. This really was a nightmare. How could he have made contingencies for this outcome? It really spoke to the number one reason for keeping everything in a controlled environment. Goddamned Ronnie.

He opened the tracking program. It showed nothing. Ronnie had disappeared from the face of the Earth. "Shit, shit, shit. Where are you, Ronnie?" He closed the laptop and hid it back in the bin. Had they removed the tracking device during the CAT scan or MRI? If they'd found it they could have surgically removed it and she would have no way to return. Worse they'd be trying to find out who put it there and why. A bad feeling crept into his bones. This could turn out very detrimental for Ronnie and for the experiment.

It was time for some reconnaissance. Jeffrey left the cart in the room and shut the door, not wanting to move too far away. As he made his way down the hall a man followed him.

"Sir!" the man yelled.

Jeffrey turned around ready to run if he had to. "Yes."

"Sir, please. I went to the cafeteria and now I can't find my wife. She was in one of these rooms. Can you look it up for me?"

"Well, I …" Jeffrey stalled.

"Please, sir, I've been wandering around and can't seem to find any nurses."

"I'm not sure if I can find it. Let me try." He shuffled some papers on the desk and found a clipboard nearby. It had a map of the floor and in small neat letters last names were written inside the picture of the rooms.

"What is your wife's name?" Jeffrey asked flipping through the pages. The man told him and in a minute Jeffrey figured out where to send him. The man thanked him and walked away. Jeffrey stepped away from the desk and looked down the corridor in both directions. Everything was quiet. He sat back down and quickly found the room the staff had reserved for Ronnie.

The room to the left was occupied but the one on the right was empty. He drew a line through the chart that showed the empty room and scrawled REPAIR.

Within minutes he set up in the room next to Ronnie's and fired up the laptop awaiting Ronnie's arrival next door. To his great relief, the blip from the tracking device activated showing Ronnie coming down the hall toward him. Relief was fleeting because he wasn't ready. The coils weren't in position. What if they administered some detrimental treatment before he could bring her back? What if the machine didn't work and she was forever in a coma?

Jeffrey knelt next to the custodian cart and uncovered TOTO, opened the panel that held the coils, and gently removed them. He set the coils on the rolling table near the hospital bed on top of a wad of linens from the cart. He pushed the cart into the tiny en suite bathroom and pulled out a wet floor sign from the side of the cart to set in front of the closed bathroom door. Hopefully, this would keep anyone out of there until he could return.

He returned to his precious coils laid so neatly on the table. To an unsuspecting observer, they looked like a flattened lightbulb bordered by chrome made from artistry glass in purple with swirls of pastel blues and greens. They were the culmination of all the blood sweat and tears he put in on the power research in Norfolk, Virginia. Two stinking years to design the power capture devices to pull energy from the storm. It had been a crucial step in the time travel experimentation, although he impatiently toiled for those years yearning to be right here, at this juncture involving human testing. But he had reached an impasse with the need for more power with a larger human subject everything had been on hold until this problem was solved.

Jeffrey picked up the first coil and kissed it. It represented his genius neatly packaged in compact physical form. With the feds keeping an eye on his lab now he had removed everything from the lab pertaining to the experiment and needed a portable carrying case for the coils. Ironically the storm had slowed down delivery of the custom case he had ordered.

With great care, he wrapped each coil in a washcloth, gently placed it in a pillowcase and tied a knot. He tucked the three bundles in another pillowcase and tied a knot and tucked it under his arm. He left the room and walked briskly toward the stairwell.

As he climbed the stairs toward the roof his worries mounted. He was about to step outside into utter chaos on top of a three-story building. What the fuck was he doing? He didn't know if there would somewhere to affix the coils where they wouldn't be immersed in water. Would he be able to place it near enough to Ronnie's room to have them transfer the energy to his computer?

By moving the coils and TOTO from Ronnie's house he had lost the stored power it had collected. It would take time to recharge TOTO and boost the power needed to bring Ronnie home. Would the doctors move her again? Would she have more serious medical issues that would require her to be transferred to a different wing of the hospital for more tests? Did the coils create some type of electromagnetic pulse when they brought Ronnie back that could interact with the hospital equipment or stored nuclear material?

Dr. Vasu shook his head in his mind's eye. Would Homeland Security hone in on this place after the storm? He stopped mid-step at this thought. Wow, that would be a truly unforeseen outcome. Every last blessed thing had to fall into place before the storm wound down.

Jeffrey pushed the jumbled worries out of his head. In this moment, he couldn't be distracted by what could cause a catastrophic failure. He had to find the way to make it all work, to bring Ronnie back and hope she was okay.

"Shit!" In the corner of the ceiling, a video camera was mounted near the door to the roof. No lights were blinking. Likely with the emergency power on they had to shut down nonessential power uses. Under normal circumstances there would be an alarm, camera, or some other way to warn security there was a door open to the roof. No need to have patients up there to off themselves or terrorists entering the building from the rooftop.

Jeffrey sprinted up the steps two at a time and tried the door handle. It opened. But would it lock behind him? Quickly he decided he could do without the shirt. He set down the pillowcase and pulled off the scrubs shirt and wadded it in the doorframe, keeping the door from closing.

Jeffrey walked into the ravaging winds. A huge gust pried him off the wall and he fought to regain his balance. Splashing in the puddled water along the cement roof he saw a raised section of the air conditioning unit. He sprinted like a drunk man and ducked behind the metal structure where he found relief from the storm. Water soaked through his pants as he opened the pillowcase, pulling out one coil and retied the pillowcase at the top.

A gust of wind blew down from above and knocked the coil out of his hand. He scrambled after it and dropped the pillowcase.

"Damn it!" He snatched up the coil. Thankfully the casing was intact. As long as that was solid it wouldn't matter if it got wet. He reached down in the pillowcase for the tube of putty. The metal of the air conditioning unit should serve to enhance the signal. Quickly he opened the putty and liberally spread it on the back of the coil, and affixed it to the metal air conditioning casing. He scoped the roof for the other two locations. The coils needed to be positioned in a triangulation pattern ten to twenty feet apart. That would be a challenge.

The giant H of the helicopter pad was not far away, he could see the huge platform in the low light. He opened the pillowcase and pulled out another coil, retied the bag and took a deep breath. This would be a wicked ride. He stood and sprinted to the next location and the wind blew him backward, rain pelting his flesh, stinging madly with each raindrop delivered at maximum velocity.

Dropping to his knees he crawled the rest of the way taking advantage of the lip of the outer wall blocking some of the fray. He pulled out the putty and affixed the coil to the wall pressing it deeply into the rough brick, hoping it would have enough grip to keep it in place with the storm raging around it. He picked up the pillowcase and in an instant Frances grabbed it out of his hand and flung it over the side of the hospital and out of sight.

"No! Fuck! No!" He carefully looked over the side. Frances tried to pull a fast one and lift him over the edge to follow the pillowcase but he caught himself just in time and ran back to the door, pulling it open and throwing himself inside. He bent over gasping for air, not sure if the water streaming down his face were tears or merely rainwater.

"Now what?" Would it be able to bring Ronnie back without the third coil? He wadded up the scrubs shirt and wiped his face and hair, making it stand on end. He sat on the top step and put his head in his hands. It is going to have to work. It just fucking had to. He slipped on the shirt and calculated the force of the drop to the ground factoring the wind as he descended the stairs. It was possible that it would withstand the impact. Barely.

Chapter 47 - Doctor Who

Steph slowly fell apart. It was killing her to not be near Ronnie. What if she came back and no one was around to be there for her? What if she crashed and died? She shifted positions and buried her face against Nick's neck.

He hugged her tight and kissed her hair. "It's gonna be okay, you'll see."

A tall figure in navy scrubs walked toward them. Steph thought it was a doctor until recognition set in. "Mike, what …"

"What are you doing in scrubs?" Nick stood and walked toward him and shook his hand.

"Oh these old things?" Mike laughed. "Got soaked and a very nice nurse gave them to me."

Steph stood. "I'm glad you found us."

"Me too, they've brought her back from the scans. The doctor will be in soon."

"She's back? How do you know that?" Nick asked.

"Come on, let's go." Mike held the door open. "The doc will be in to share the scans with us."

"How … Mike how do you know …"

He motioned for her to go through the door and told them her room number. "Somehow they think I'm her husband. Anyway, come with me."

Nick laughed. "How did you pull that off?"

"I have no idea. It's just a misunderstanding but I thought you'd want to talk to the doctor."

"Hell yeah we do, thank you so much, Mike," Nick said, patting him on the back.

They walked into Ronnie's room and the first thing Steph noticed was how the steady beeping of her heart on the monitor was at once disturbing and comforting. Steph went straight to her side and picked up her hand. Why wouldn't she just wake up? It had been hours now.

A tall heavyset black man with a thick mustache burst through the door and greeted them. "Hello, good evening. I'm Doctor Smith." He was holding a large envelope and shifted it to his left hand to shake Mike and Nick's hands and nodded at Steph.

"We have the scan results on Ms. Andrews." He looked at Mike. "Sir, your wife is quite an unusual case." The doctor shook his head. "I'm sorry to say we still don't know what's causing this coma. I do have some results from the scan, but I'm afraid it isn't very good news."

Steph suddenly felt hot.

"Are you comfortable with me giving you an update with your friends here?" the doctor said quietly.

"Yes, of course." Mike shot Steph an uncomfortable look. "Absolutely."

"Your wife is in a coma. The causes can range from drugs and alcohol, seizures, toxins, an infection, diabetes, traumatic brain injury, stroke, or a brain tumor."

Mike ran his hand through his short hair. "And ..."

"We've taken blood and done the CT scan to see what is affecting her brain. The good news is we have ruled out a stroke and seizures. There is no swelling in the brain from an injury or disease. Her blood sugars look in the normal range, maybe a bit on the low side, but there is definitely no distinct cause for her coma that we have found."

"That's good then," Steph said.

Doctor Smith turned to Steph. "In a way it is, but we have no definitive answer as to why she's in a coma. We search for markers in her brain activity to give us clues." He looked at Mike and back to Steph. "The scans show very little brain activity. The brain stem is active, helping her breathe and keeping her heart beating, but normal brain activity isn't present."

Nick spoke up. "Not present? What do you mean?"

Mike sat on the couch in the corner and Steph felt like sitting too. Nick came to her side and took her hand. The doctor flipped a switch on the wall and a panel lit up. He pulled what looked like an x-ray out of the large envelope and inserted it under a clip on the panel. Light shone through a scan of Ronnie's brain.

"See this region here." He pointed with a fat finger at the lower-right quadrant. "It usually has a lot more activity, even in a coma state. The brain is not functioning properly." His dark brown eyes showed kindness and empathy. "There is a small lesion on her brain here. We aren't sure if this is a past injury or a recent one, but it may be responsible for the coma."

Dr. Smith paused to let his report sink in. Then he continued. "Her vitals look really good considering what is going on in her brain, or rather what is not going on. But the blood levels are very odd." He rubbed his mustache. "Was Ronnie a drinker?" He looked at Mike.

Mike showed surprise and Steph covered for him. "No, she hardly ever drinks."

"I only ask because she's showing a condition that alcoholics demonstrate after years of abuse."

Steph shook her head. "How can that be? I know she doesn't drink. She isn't an alcoholic."

"There are a few rare diseases that can cause the deficiency. It isn't compatible with her other symptoms or bloodwork, though."

Nick walked to the scan and looked closely. "I don't know her well but she's not a drinker. Definitely not for a number of years. You can tell that by looking at her."

"I'd like to do further blood tests and we may need to start some therapies to preserve brain function until we can figure this out. I'm very conservative and would like to have more information before we start messing around with her system."

"Doctor, what do you think her chances are for recovery?" Steph asked.

Doctor Smith shook his head. "I'm sorry. Her prognosis isn't particularly good. If she ever regains consciousness, there would likely be systemic brain damage. I don't know how that would affect her but …" He chewed on his lips and looked away. "Let's just stay positive for now. It's a very unusual case."

A nurse walked in and checked her vitals. The doctor gave her orders but Steph couldn't take in any more information. Nick folded her in his arms and she sobbed against his chest. She wanted to scream or curse. Ronnie was too young to die and too precious to be brain damaged if she lived.

Mike stood and shook the doctor's hand. "I appreciate all you're doing. Please keep us informed as you find out more information."

"I will do everything I can. I'm sorry to bring you such bad news. Keep the faith, pray for her, call in every favor you have. Miracles abound," Doctor Smith said. "I'll be back if I find anything else out or if there are any changes." He shook his head. "This damn storm has the internet down so I can't do much research on similar cases. I'm digging through my journals and textbooks though."

"Bye Doctor, thank you." Steph managed between sniffles. Mike handed her a small box of tissues from the table.

The nurse spent a few more minutes taking blood, writing down her vitals and then turned to Mike. "Do you have any questions, Mr. Andrews?"

"What do you think is wrong with her?" he asked, shooting a glance at Steph.

"If I had to guess I'd say some metabolic process that is attacking her brain. The lesion is small but I'd be willing to guess it gets larger as time goes on. It's just my guess, but given her other tests it's my current theory."

"Jesus, I hope that doesn't happen. I'm planning on creating a miracle right here in this room to get her back." Mike waved his thick arm along the horizon.

"Well, I hope you succeed. She's a beautiful girl, I just hope we can figure this out and bring her to a full recovery." The nurse nodded and walked out of the room.

"Amen," Nick said into Steph's hair.

"Guys, I'm so sorry. I feel like I've butted in to your private hell." Mike shook his head. "This isn't right. I shouldn't be in the room. I'm so sorry I've invaded your privacy."

"Don't be silly Mike," Nick said, "We sucked you into this whole mess. I'm just sorry it's so horrible."

Mike looked away. "Ronnie wouldn't want me here. It's too personal. I …" He ran his fingers through his hair again.

"Mike, it's okay." Steph stood and took his hand. "You've done us a huge favor for risking your life getting us here. You deserve to find out what is going on. I think Ronnie would be grateful for your help."

"Thanks for that Steph." Mike squeezed her hand. "I just don't know her that well and think it's a bit weird for me to be involved."

"Seriously Mike. We need you," Steph said.

He shook his head. "Okay, Steph for you I will. Please tell her when she's completely fine my feelings about this. I just want her to be well and I don't want to invade her privacy."

Steph pressed into her eyes to wipe away the tears. "Nick, I need to go to the chapel. Will you come with me?" Steph needed the comfort of prayer and feeling of being close to God.

"Of course." Nick took her hand.

"Mike, please stay with Ronnie. I can't bear the thought of her being alone here."

"Yeah, I'll stay." Mike pressed his lips together and shook his head. "This is so screwed up though. She's so full of life." He glanced at Ronnie.

Steph followed his gaze. "Hopefully she'll be full of life again soon."

Nick and Steph walked hand in hand to the chapel leaving Mike alone with Ronnie.

Chapter 48 - Soul Binding

An intense, almost electric charge traveled through Morris' meaty hand into Ronnie's own. She let it fill her heart with joy and passion. His palms were rough and she tried to not think about how his touch would feel on her skin. The wind continued to blast them. Rain now mixed in and pelted with the force of hail on her face. She held Morris's doublet over her mouth to block the worst of it as he guided her along the fence.

Morris let go of her hand and leaned up to the fence to a small gap near the boulder she'd rested on earlier. He cupped his hands and yelled, "Hark, brothers it is Morris Allen, returning."

A man called back and Morris grabbed her hand, "With haste, we shall be inside the safety of the colony." In stormy darkness, they slowly made their way over a rocky area and to a gap in the fence.

Fifteen minutes later Ronnie sat in front of Morris's hearth dripping onto the mud puddle forming under her feet. Morris built a fire as the candlelight played along his rain slick skin, accentuating the muscles in his back and shoulders as he moved. She marveled at how solidly he was built with thick shoulders tapered deliciously to a narrow waist. A loud gust of wind from the storm outside made the shuttered window covering clatter.

Would the house hold up to the wind roaring outside? Along the walls rain soaked into the dirt floor. Ronnie looked around to see if any furniture needed to be moved out of harm's way. A wooden chest along the edge near the wall could be at risk but when she touched the back of it was dry. A spray of water snuck through a gap in the wood to mist a stripe along her leg.

The table clock reflected the candle and drew Ronnie to it. The timepiece was Morris's connection to his past, his family, and everything he knew and loved. He'd said as much in their short conversation before she had bolted.

In a way he was like her, stranded in a strange time and place with memories of what used to be. He turned to look at her and she smiled, overcome with affection. They were now stranded together.

Ronnie picked it up, running a finger over the smooth cool metal. Mr. Allen must have been emotional saying goodbye to his son knowing they would never see each other again. A little corner of her heart saddened at that loss, and a sneaking element of guilt about her relationship with Jeffrey snuck in as well mixing with the sadness.

Tonight, Jeffrey had revealed a side that deeply disturbed her. During his outburst just before he left, a glimmer of the selfishness Steph had warned her about slipped through his usual armor. With it a crack in her loyalty formed and Ronnie knew it would never be completely put right again. Would tonight widen that crack to do irreparable harm? Was she willing to let that happen?

Despite her brain's logical entanglement, her heart was drawn to this man who stood before her. Their connection was so compelling, so deeply felt she knew it had significance.

The fire came to life at his touch. He stood and the golden hairs on his chest glowed in the firelight, the scrapes on his chest etched into his skin. The cut above his eye had scabbed over and the rain left a smear of blood down his cheek. He looked like he'd had better nights.

She wanted to bring the conversation back to that intimate place they'd briefly touched earlier, "I'm sorry about your doublet." She slid it off her shoulders and held it out to him. "My run through the woods has not done it much good." Her deerskin clothes were damp and clung to her curves, a pink nipple gave away her excitement and chill. His eyes lowered to her exposed flesh and she immediately crossed her arms to cover what she could.

"It matters not, I am glad it could give you some protection from the claws of Mother Nature." He pointed to her legs and Ronnie followed his gaze to the blood streaked scratches on her shins. At least his doublet had protected her arms and chest.

He filled the basin with water from a large pitcher and set it down near the fireplace to warm. She stepped close to the fire and let the heat caress her flesh.

Why did she have such a strong connection with a man from a different century? Had she ever felt this way about Jeffrey? She held her hands out to the fire. A shiver from deep within made her teeth chatter—too much adrenaline coursing through her veins coupled with the heat of the fire on wet chilled skin.

He opened a drawer in the simply built cupboard against the wall and pulled out a sliver of soap. "I would be honored to wash the difficult day from your skin, mistress." A smile overwhelmed his face.

"Oh, please do." Her body responded with a layer of goosebumps crawling across her skin.

He pulled the chair out for her and knelt in front of her, "Your foot, if you please." His light brown eyes showed excitement. It was such an unusual coloring with the blond hair.

Ronnie tried to slow her breathing down, but it was impossible. She sat on the chair and lifted her foot to rest on his muscular thigh. He slid off the moccasin and set it on the floor. Her feet looked so tiny in his large hand.

A wave of excitement burst from her chest and she laughed. "Thank you, kind sir." She watched as he rubbed his hands in the soap and gently caressed her skin, washing her feet and calves, gently cleaning her many scrapes and cuts from their trek through the woods.

"I feel there is something very spiritual about our connection, Ronnie. I do not have words to explain it but it is a deep satisfying feeling as if our souls are two halves meant to be united."

Ronne looked away, the intensity of his words mirrored what she had felt all day.

He continued, "Something that defies logic, defies any of my schooling in the scriptures or training for it is something my heart knows to be true. The books haven't been written that could explain this."

"Morris, I feel it too. I don't have the right words to explain, but my heart feels everything yours does."

He stood and grabbed the pitcher from the stones near the fire and set it on the table, picked up the basin of muddy water and emptied it in the corner. "May I continue?"

Ronnie smiled and melted just a little bit more. "Yes, please do."

"It pleases me that we are in agreement. It need not have an explanation, but rather can just be a fact we both know to be true like mathematics. We need not understand why, only that it is." He took her hand and lavished equal attention up to her shoulder and took her other hand repeating the sensual caress with the warmed water.

When he was finished, she took the cloth from him and dipped it in the basin, squeezing it out, and re-soaped it, "Let me clean your cuts, please." She stood and pointed to the chair and he obliged, his eyes never leaving hers.

She wiped the blood off his cheek and dabbed at the scab forming on his eyebrow. "I'm sorry you had to fight for me." She rinsed the blood into the basin and rubbed the soap into the cloth.

"More that naught, Wahab is the one who regrets the battle. He spilled blood and is not in your company as am I." He laughed.

"May I wash your other wounds?" Ronnie asked.

"If you please, madam." He smiled and she wondered what it would be like to kiss those firm lips.

Ronnie contemplated her next move as she washed the scrapes on his magnificent chest. Electricity flowed off his skin through her fingers, and the look of surrender in his eyes fueled her desire. She should be chaste and dampen the smoldering sparks, as her conscience begged. The nagging doubt about what could have been with Mathias spurred her on and Ronnie imagined the devil on one shoulder sticking her tongue out at the angel.

She knew in this time and place, without the consequences that usually held her back—the risk of getting hurt, diseases transferred, pregnancy—all were meaningless here. The ice was broken with the dangerous few hours they'd just lived through. Everything he had done for her, the risks he so freely took for her broke down any resistance.

Tonight, she would take what she wanted, live with no regrets, and enjoy the beautiful man before her. She dragged the cloth slowly across his thick neck and he lifted his chin elongate it for her.

"Your touch is magic." His voice was deep and rough.

"I crave your touch, Morris." Every nerve in her body was on fire now and she could feel the excitement growing in her belly. She leaned in to kiss his full lips and melted further when he held her face keeping their connection longer than she had intended.

It was so easy to kiss him. As her lips pressed into his, a thought raced around in her mind. This inexplicably strong connection was an extension of her desire for Mathias. Was that proof of anything but unrequited love? Or was she connected to both men, layered in time?

She slid her tongue along his lips. His lips parted and their tongues mingled while his arms tightened around her pulling her onto his lap.

Ronnie lessened her grip around his neck and explored his shoulders, chest, and arms. He was magnificent, and the feel of his strong body made her weaker. It was such a cliché, but she felt dizzy fueling her need for more.

Ronnie debated for a split second if she should be so bold as to straddle him but decided to go with her heart. She hiked up the dress and swung one leg over facing him. She picked up the soap vigorously rubbing it into the cloth and washed his chest, then moved to his shoulders, her arousal growing intensely over how completely exposed she was in this position.

He lowered the one sleeve down to her elbow and Ronnie wriggled free letting the dress fall to her waist. She took the soap and rubbed it directly on her chest and handed him the cloth. "Your turn."

He smiled and set the cloth down, but took the soap out of her hand, dipped it into the basin and proceeded to soap her breasts and stomach, his big hands so gentle on her flesh, making her nipples hard and her body ready for more.

He kissed her with intensified passion and his perfect chest pressed against hers. They devoured each other with tongues dancing together until he pulled away and held her arms out to the side and looked into her eyes.

"Mistress, this passion overwhelms me, I cannot be held to gentlemanly standards in this precarious position." He made his point clear with a glance down her body taking in her complete exposure.

"Morris, I do not need a gentleman right now."

He pushed her to a standing position while he remained in the chair and pulled the dress over her head, flinging it over the adjacent chair-back. He picked up the cloth, dipping it in the basin and rinsed her soapy chest. Rivulets of soapy water dripped down her stomach and made her desires grow as they trickled between her legs and down her thighs. He gently turned her around and when he groaned, she glanced back at him.

"I want to wash the rest of you." His voice choked with desire. "However, you have my full arousal and I cannot pursue this any further unless I may have all of you in the bedchamber when I am finished."

Ronnie nodded and stood provocatively legs apart, sticking her butt out a little. It was so freeing to let the usual modest woman sit outside while she allowed this one moment to be set free with Morris, to be her true self expressing her desires without the reserve she usually let dictate. With Jeffrey, she always let him take the lead.

He stood behind her and moved the hair off her neck, and placed a kiss on her newly exposed skin, moaning into her neck while he cupped her breasts. She arched her back and pressed into him feeling his desire against her.

His hand slid down her stomach and cupped between her legs. She moaned, unable to stifle her arousal as his lips nibbled her neck and earlobe sending shivers down her body. He gently massaged the flesh in his hands making her heart beat madly, her lungs begging for air.

"Ronnie, relax against my touch." His voice was deeper now and his hot breath tickled her ear adding to the building of release. He pulled her backward so she straddled one thick thigh and he eased into the chair. Momentarily his hand left her growing wetness to open her legs further and his fingers met with soft wet flesh as his erection pressed into her back.

He whispered into her hair, "I wish to enter you here," and accentuated the words with fingers probing deeper and she lost control, shaking and arching her back, opening to him, letting him do as he wanted with her body.

Her climax was powerful, accentuated by the eagerness of his touch. He kissed her shoulder tenderly and pulled on her nipple as she let go enjoying the intensity that he had brought to her so quickly. When she calmed down, she removed his fingers and turned around to sit facing him. He kissed her with such passion. Ronnie felt so safe, so protected by his embrace.

Morris pulled away and smiled at her. "I beg your pardon Ronnie, I have failed in my duties in bathing you, my lady." He pushed her to a standing position and a wicked smile crossed his full sensual lips.

Morris lifted her arms to the side and she held them there. He soaped both hands and started on her ribs, his big hands nearly encircling her. He soaped every inch of her body, every curve and crevice slowly, sensually stimulating every nerve in her body until she couldn't stand any longer. He used the cloth to rinse the soap away as if she were borne of new flesh and could conquer the world. He poured fresh water into a small cup and with utter abandon for himself and the floor he rinsed her body, then poured it down her stomach to rinse between her legs sending waves of pleasure through her core.

"Now that is a sponge bath I could use every day," she said, surprised at how raspy her voice had become.

"It would be my utmost pleasure to provide such a service to you," Morris said. "Now for my payment."

He bent low and grabbed her legs, picking her up, holding under her knees and around her back and carried her to the small bed. Ronnie slid her tongue over the thick muscle that ran down his neck meeting his shoulder.

Morris gently set her down on the edge of the bed and bent over to kiss her, his hands on either side of her hips. Ronnie grasped his muscular arms then found the front of his pants. She tried to unfasten them. It was unlike any modern closure and after a minute of trying she had to drop the pretense of seduction.

"Sorry, I ..." Ronnie laughed.

"I shall assist you." He removed a belt and unbuttoned two buttons opening a flap in the front of his breeches and let them fall to the floor. She looked away as he removed the remaining items deciding that some things were better left unseen. Under the mattress covering, the bed was stiff, perhaps filled with hay.

Morris slid into the bed next to her and pulled her close, his warm skin touching along the length of her body. His excitement pressed into her stomach and she reached down to caress it. His mouth was on hers and he moaned into the kiss. His skin was smooth and soft in contrast to the hard flesh underneath. Ronnie wondered what a man of this time would expect in this situation and decided it would be her duty as a modern woman to blow his mind. From what she knew, woman weren't supposed to enjoy sex and were mostly passive participants.

Ronnie pushed Morris onto his back and with a wicked smile she straddled him holding her hips above him. She kissed his lips and slowly, as his hands moved from waist to hip, she lowered down pressing her slick wetness against him, sliding across his most sensitive flesh, sending waves of pleasure through her body.

"Ronnie, oooh," he said his eyes half closed. "I beg of you please continue."

She took his hands and placed them on her breasts and moved her feet to either side of his hips to squat above him. "As you please, Morris." She accentuated the words while guiding him inside of her, slowly working him deeper.

"You astound me," Morris gasped.

He held her soft flesh in his big hands as waves of pleasure filled her senses. Ronnie used her legs to rise and lower on him until he was fully inside. She tilted her hips forward and leaned in to kiss him again now obsessed with the feel of his lips on hers, grinding in slow circles until she lost control.

He held her hips and took over the rhythm she had set as small moans escaped her lips. He sat up to hold her on his lap for a minute and let her spasms continue as he kissed her neck and face, his hips rocking in sensual mind-blowing movements. Ronnie gripped his meaty shoulders for support and came hard again, letting out a long, satisfied moan.

Morris then pushed her backward. He held her hands to the bed and fervently impaled her in the traditional missionary position. Her face buried in his muscular chest while her hands wanted to explore his body. He held them fast to the bed to enhance the pure bliss of their connection. She was his and he took her with animalistic abandon bringing her to climax yet again. Morris groaned and his bliss filled all of her senses as if his voice was a part of her pleasure.

He collapsed on top of her out of breath, letting her hands free. She clung to him with her body still spasming against his hard flesh. He kissed her tenderly.

After a minute of soul-binding closeness, he rolled to the side and laughed. "I was not aware that a woman could—"

Ronnie interrupted with a kiss. "Yes, women can, if they are so inspired."

"Is this a common thing? For a woman to sit upon a man as such?" His eyes were soft and dreamy.

"What we have is an uncommon thing, Morris. It inspires extraordinary moments." He kissed her slowly and held her close. Ronnie savored every second in the bubble of passion they had created.

"Why is it so, Ronnie? What is this magic that we have woven between us?"

"I don't know. All I can explain is that it's a deep connection. Possibly one woven through the fabric of time. Does that sound mad?"

"Woven through time? I must express my delight in the phraseology you speak. It is utterly concise and full of strange and wonderful words I do not always understand. Mistress, please do explain what 'woven through time' represents to you." He propped his head on his hand forcing his huge bicep to bunch against taut skin.

Before she could gather her thoughts, a loud knocking interrupted. He was up and pulling on his breeches before she could react.

"Ronnie, it is of the greatest importance that you stay hidden." He handed her a long white shirt and pointed to a small wardrobe along the wall. "It pains me greatly to have you in harm's way."

She slid the shirt on and stepped off the bed onto the dirt floor. She quickly climbed into the tall wardrobe, pulling the door closed behind her.

Brash male voices made her jump. Ronnie lowered down to a squatting position and moved a blanket to cover her in case someone opened the wardrobe, thinking of the last time she played hide and seek with her niece. Except this was likely to result in more than just having to be the seeker next.

Chapter 49 - Gains and Losses

Jeffrey sprinted down the stairs to the ground floor and burst into the lobby of the hospital. A nurse at the front desk called out as he ran out the doors. Wind blasted him from the right so he shielded his eyes to try to find the part of the roof he was just on. He ran against the wind toward the opposite corner of the building. Would the coil be in the grass or had it blown away? Was it broken? Everything was so fucked up. His mission was clear: bring Ronnie back. Nothing was going right. Not one fucking thing.

Anger buzzed through his mind and spurred him against the wind. A clump of leaves smashed into his chest and he flung it to the side. The low light of morning allowed him to see more clearly now. It had to be here somewhere. He was under the roof near the helipad. Searching madly, he didn't see anything on the grass where it had landed. Every minute that passed risked Ronnie's life. This all had to come together soon before the storm moved out of the area and his power supply diminished.

Jeffrey slowed his thinking down. He stood stock-still and focused on the trajectory of the wind, of where he thought the pillowcase had landed. The wind did its best to topple him but he stood firm, calmly visualizing where it should be. He was laser focused now and scanned the landscape. There in a bush was something white. He ran to it, plucked it off the leaves, and yelled, "Hell yeah!"

By some miracle, the coil felt intact. "Oh My God! I might just pull this off yet." He ran back to the main entrance, bursting through the door.

"Sir, sir." The nurse rose from her chair. "Stop."

"Oh, sorry." Jeffrey slowed enough to smile and held up the pillowcase. "My wife's face cream. She insisted I go out in the storm to get it for her. Women, eh?"

"Woah that is dedication. I hope she appreciates you!" the nurse said smiling.

"Me too." He smiled charmingly.

Jeffrey walked quickly and was irritated by the horrible squeak his Nikes made on the tile floor. He opened the door to the stairwell and sprinted up the steps two and three at a time until he reached the top. Cold wet fingers fumbled with the knot on the pillowcase and he pulled out the coil. The inspection in the low light revealed a fine crack starting at the bottom and running through the outer glass coating.

"Shattered?" He shook it and it was silent. Perhaps only the glass was cracked, maybe the rest was intact. It could only be confirmed by testing.

He pulled out the putty and covered the crack and used the pillowcase to smear the coating into the fractured section. Then he turned it over and covered the entire bottom of the coil. He stepped outside and held the door open with his foot so he could affix the coil to the metal door. He continued to hold it while the wind battered him. "One, two, three, four, five ... fuck it." He let go and the coil stayed.

A twinge of worry crept into his already stressed mind as opened the door, straightening the name badge and descended the stairs in record time to the basement. Quickly he found a clean pair of scrubs in the laundry area and shoved the wet dirty ones under a chair. He ran back up the stairs to the hospital room where he stashed his gear.

Jeffrey leaned over panting as he tried to catch his breath. This whole damned night was gonna age him about twenty years. No time to dawdle. He pushed the bathroom door open and the cart was gone. So was the wet floor sign. Instantly he stepped out of the room and rechecked the room number. It was room 226 but his laptop and time travel device were not here. He closed his eyes, tamping down the furious rage brewing inside. Next time you listen to me, Ronnie. Exhaling dramatically, he opened the door and calmly walked down the hall as he passed the nurses' station that now had two women chatting wildly about the storm.

"Hey ladies, I left my cart in two-twenty-six when I took a break. Do you know where it ended up?" Jeffrey asked as casually as he could muster.

Without pausing their conversation, the blonde nurse pointed to the left. His eyes followed her hand.

"Where?" He didn't want to push his luck and have them get a good look at him but time was running out.

"Hey, you can't just leave your cart in a patient's room, buddy," the brunette spat.

"I'm sorry. It's not a patient's room, that one needs a repair." Jeffrey looked away.

She scrunched up her face. "Since when? I'll call maintenance." She lifted the phone.

"No, I already did. I let them know before I took my break," Jeffrey said as he grew impatient with all the delays.

"The cart is in the janitor's closet down the hall," The blonde said peeking around her companion.

Jeffrey waved and briskly walked down the hall. Around the corner, the janitor's closet stood ajar. Two carts were in the closet and he had to sort through the dirty linen basket to be sure he had the right one. "Thank the Lord."

Within a few minutes, Jeffrey was settled back in the room. He pulled out the laptop to confirm Ronnie's location in the room next door. Then he fired up the coils and held his breath praying the shattered one would hold a pull in the power necessary to bring Ronnie back. It would take about fifteen minutes to accumulate energy from the storm. Two distinct male voices permeated through the wall. Nick and someone else. The voice was much deeper than Ian's. He pondered it as he set up the machinery for Ronnie's return.

Jeffrey checked and rechecked all the connections. TOTO was connected but would it function properly with all the battering in the car and possible water seeping in during the transfer? He tested the coils and a surge of adrenaline coursed through his veins. The green bar ticked upward indicating they were gathering and storing power. Would it be enough? Would they function properly? Worries gathered around him like electrons around an atom.

A beep startled him out of the wonderings and a window popped up on the computer screen. *Connected to subject.*

Jeffrey blew out some of the stress. Another beeping alerted him that TOTO had enough power to pull Ronnie back. He closed his eyes and looked at the ceiling. "Thank God!"

He began the sequence to initiate return and sat back while the code flew across the screen. He listened intently. Ronnie should cause quite a stir when she came back to life in the room next door.

The screen paused and showed a warning notice. "Oh no, now what."

Low battery. Only 10 percent remaining.

"Shit!" He rummaged around in the computer case for the power cord. The plug wasn't there. He looked around in the dirty linen bin. It wasn't there either.

"Shit!" Would it have enough power to pull Ronnie back? "Oh my God. I'm so stupid." He should have grabbed the battery out of his car when he had retrieved the coil. Should he run down now to get it? Would it shut down mid-process? He had no time to spare. He could cross his fingers and hope for the best or change the circumstances by getting the battery pack in his car. Did he leave the cord at the neighbor's house? "Shit, shit, shit!" He grabbed a spare trash bag from the cart.

Jeffrey watched the screen intently as it chewed on the code. Another message popped up. *Battery low 7 percent remaining.* What would happen if she was in transition when the laptop shut down? Once the process started it couldn't be paused. It had to continue. This thought spurred him out the door to the stairwell. He flew down the stairs and remembered his car keys were in the staff locker with his jeans.

He turned and walked quickly toward the employee lockers. A pretty nurse caught his eye and smiled. "This double shift is painful, eh?"

"I know, no way to leave with the storm outside though so might as well get paid for being here." He played along feigning a calm he did not feel.

"True, I guess that' the bright side." She turned and waved. "Bye, see you later."

"Bye." Jeffrey turned and walked as fast as he could without being too obvious.

He found the locker and pulled out the keys and slammed it closed. He rushed back to the front door and out into the raging storm splashing through the pooled water in the parking lot. It reached halfway up his shins. The image of Ronnie stuck between worlds tore through him violently. The culmination of fuckups mounted an attack on her life. Would she be retrievable?

Chapter 50 - Reckoning

Two angry voices volleyed back and forth just outside of the wardrobe, one obviously Morris's, but the other unfamiliar. Ronnie strained to make out what they were saying. Was it Wahab coming for her, seeking to finish the fight? It didn't sound like the odd language they had spoken before. Finally, a few familiar words confirmed it was the voice of an Englishman speaking rapidly, but the meaning escaped her. Morris's punctuated questions moved farther from the wardrobe and finally, he was silent. The door to the wardrobe burst open. Ronnie stifled a scream.

"Madam, it is urgent!" Morris reached for her hand and pulled her out.

Ronnie looked around for the owner of the other voice but no one was in sight.

"Who was that? What is going on?" she asked trying to tamp down a rising panic.

"Indian attack." Morris was a blur of activity.

"No!"

"With utmost urgency, I require you to prepare yourself to …" He ran his fingers through his hair, "We cannot remain here, it is not safe."

"What is happening?"

"They are looking for me, killing our men." He bent low to open the large chest at the foot of the bed.

Ronnie's pulse quickened. "Why would they do that?" she dug in the wardrobe and pulled out a pair of Morris's breeches. She slid them up and realized they were huge around her waist. He handed her a belt and she fastened it, tucking in the shirt.

Morris pulled out a musket and a small bag. Ronnie found the moccasins and slid them on her feet. They were stiff and cold with semi-dried mud.

"Ronnie," he called across the room. "It is me they seek. You will be in danger if you are here."

"No …" Her voice came out in a high-pitched squeak. "I know no one else. Why are they looking for you?"

"My knife was found deep in the chest of the chief's son. The young boy who found you in the woods. They are here for revenge."

It felt like she'd been punched in the stomach. Air escaped her lungs and would not return. She forced a breath to speak. "Your knife, Morris, how?"

He held the ramrod in his hand, priming the musket now as he spoke. "I last laid eyes on the weapon when I prepared to fight Wahab. Remember, it was placed at your feet?"

Ronnie took a few deep breaths. "Did you go anywhere before you came to me in the woods?"

"Mistress, what are you suggesting? That I murdered a child? That I ..." He turned away shaking his head.

"No, I just ..." Ronnie's head was spinning. A flash of the boy's bright eyes filled with curiosity blinked at her.

"There is an already delicate balance with all of the bad blood before we arrived on shore. To disturb it with such an act..." he turned toward her again face drawn in pain, "would be suicide. A despicable act upon a child would betray everything I hold dear, honor, and respect. It is against God's will."

"Morris, I wasn't accusing you, I'm trying to understand what's happening."

"What is happening? I find it utterly confusing your choice of words. I believe Wahab is behind this. It likely involves political maneuvers while setting up the scenario that implicates the colony. Perhaps the child is an obstacle to his succession to the chief."

"Morris, the boy was wandering in the woods when he found me. Is it possible Wahab was following him, looking for a chance to kill him? He was very angry when he found me."

He looked up from priming the musket. "Aye, I believe that would fit the acts of today but this being a more opportune choice as it implicates me."

The door burst open and Ronnie ran to Morris's side. A native entered. His head was shaved except for a high ponytail on the crown. His dark eyes glistened in the low light of the fire. Another man followed closely behind wearing animal skin leggings with his black hair pulled back tight against his skull with feathers randomly sticking out.

Without hesitation, Morris stepped in front of Ronnie and pushed her backward toward the corner of the house. Something poked her stomach and she looked down. Morris held out a leather-sheathed knife behind his back. She took it and pulled the blade free, throwing the leather on the floor.

He lifted the musket and pointed it at the men approaching. "Halt!"

Wahab entered the dwelling with his bare broad shoulders thrown back with confidence.

"Wahab." Morris lowered the weapon and held up one hand speaking in slow even words in their language.

As he spoke, Wahab slowly made his way to the left as another man moved right. The third one remained in the doorway. They stood no chance against the three men.

Morris pointed the musket at Wahab who angrily shook his fist and yelled in quick staccato words.

"Ronnie, he wants to take you with him. He demands I step aside. I have but one shot."

Ronnie looked down at her hand clutching the knife. She knew what she had to do. Her life here was expendable. Without her to worry about, Morris may be able to save himself. In the back of her mind, she knew the Roanoke Colony had been wiped out, that Morris had probably been killed along with the rest of the inhabitants. But she couldn't bear to think of his life ending. His beautiful vibrant loving spirit dying here and now. She had to give him a chance.

Wahab took another step closer in unison with the man on Morris's right.

Ronnie stepped away from Morris's protection and held the weapon high over her head with both hands.

Morris faced Wahab, with his back to hers. "I beg you to take me, leave Mistress Coleman. You may do what you please to me," Morris pleaded. He must have realized he said that in English because he then repeated it in their language.

Unaware of Ronnie's stance, Morris continued pleading for their lives. As he spoke all other eyes were on her.

Ronnie paused and looked deep into the souls of the natives. She finally rested her gaze on Wahab. His angry expression shifted quickly to surprise. She rapidly lowered her arms to plunge the blade into her stomach and wrenched it upwards. Pain seared through her gut as heat poured out of her body flowing down her legs and she collapsed to hands and knees on the floor. Wahab stepped towards her and Morris, unaware of her actions, took advantage of their attention shifting to her, fired the musket and blasted a hole in Wahab's chest.

Wahab leaned on the small table, knocking it over and fell to his knees, clutching the wound and then collapsed on the floor landing a few feet away from her, his breath forced from his lungs. The table clock lay shattered on the floor beside Morris's foot and Ronnie felt a pang of sadness for the loss of the precious memento from his parents.

Specks of black flitted around the edges of her vision but she locked eyes with the warrior as his life slipped away mingling with hers in the dirt until his blank stare held no spark. Ronnie couldn't turn away, mesmerized by the cold empty brown eyes. It chilled her to watch a man die, despite her hatred for the evil he had committed.

Morris was a blur, tangling with the other two men in combat. A bone-deep weariness engulfed her and she closed her eyes, unable to force them open. A warm comfort spread from her center and worked its way out to her limbs as her heart pumped more blood out of her body.

An urgent voice jolted her from the bliss. "Ronnie, no, no, no. What has befallen you?" He pushed the hair behind her ear and kissed her cheek, his breath warming her chilled flesh. "No, heavenly father, no. God's eye, I did not allow this to happen to you, by Christ." Morris knelt by her left side and held her hand. "Ronnie, please."

A hot tear landed on her cheek. Ronnie gathered every ounce of strength and forced through her lips, "You must go, Morris."

"I cannot leave you." He kissed her cheek.

"You must. Go now. Please, Morris." He sobbed and squeezed her hand. She tried to speak but a bolt of electricity shot through every fiber of her being. Bright lights surrounded her. White walls. She squeezed her eyes shut trying to make sense of it but her mind was too far gone to process its meaning.

The painful grip stopped and she focused once again on his face, memorizing eyes, lips, and voice before another blinding jolt of soul clenching pain engulfed every ounce of her being.

Chapter 51 - Shattering Time

Ronnie stretched her arm out to grasp at something but it was all fading. Reality fell away like a backdrop collapsing on a stage. The wind tore at her face and her hair flung behind her as she dropped at a million miles an hour. Stars like small pinpoints of light flew past her at such a great speed they blurred into small streaks in her peripheral vision.

She squeezed her eyes shut and screamed, terrified of the landing. In quick flashes the dry parched earth opened before her. Dust snaked into her lungs as pain possessed her.

"Aaaaagggggghhh" Her throat burned from the scream. A deep voice close by echoed in her ear, broken in pieces with the flashing of her previous surroundings.

"Ronnie, Ronnie." Someone squeezed her hand. "You're back. Oh my God."

She tried to place the voice but could not. It was not her father's even midwestern tones. It was not the English pattern of Morris. The splintering of her worlds at once made it hard to take in either reality. Hot dry air befouled with the stench of death and blinding pain, mixed with wet cool air and antiseptic smells were at opposite extremes. She opened her eyes and again, the dual reality terrified her. Two men merged into one strong figure before her, one eye blue and one brown with a gash splitting his eyebrow.

"No, make it stop!" She rolled over and pain tormented her hand. "Ouucchh!" Ronnie held her head willing it to stop. A deep bone wrenching vibration started in her feet and worked its way up her body. She screamed and the sound was continuous in both worlds. Her left arm was pulled in one world, her right in the other giving her the impression of being pulled apart. She fought but her strength was waning. She was overpowered.

"Ronnie, it's okay. It's Mike. I'm here for you. Hold my hand."

She heard him speak but at the same time another voice was in her ear, from another place and time. He spoke in the same pattern, the same tone of voice but with different words. Old-fashioned words.

The pain stopped and she was lost in the vibration. It shook her soul and shattered her world into a never-ending fracture of time and space.

***

Mike squeezed Ronnie's hand. A look of pure terror on her face shocked him to the core. "Ronnie, it's Mike, I'm here for you."

She looked into his soul and something deep within him broke, shattering his world into a million pieces. He was overcome with laughter mixed with great sadness as if he'd lost her more times than he could count. She was here before him but not able to see him, to feel his need for her.

Ronnie curled into a fetal position while bunching the IV in her hand. He pulled her hand out of harm's way and she reacted by letting out a bloodcurdling scream squeezing her eyes shut.

Mike pushed the nurse call button and summoned help. Something terrible was happening. He had no idea what it was but the frantic beeping of Ronnie's heart through the machine said it all. It had been steady and calm since they hooked her up.

A nurse rushed in. "What happened?"

Mike stepped away from the bed feeling weak in the knees. "She woke up and began screaming."

"Her heart rate is through the roof." The nurse pressed the call button.

A doctor and three more nurses rushed into the room. "Sir, please stand back."

Mike collapsed on the couch out of the way of the medical team, watching in horror as they tried to help Ronnie. Tears stung his eyes and Mike examined the gaping hole in his heart. He hardly knew her so how could he have such devastating feelings? He fought back tears and watched numbly as they injected the IV with sedatives and barked out orders.

A nurse approached and knelt next to him. "Sir, we need to do another scan. I think this will help us understand what is happening inside her brain."

"Yes, yes, please, whatever you need to do for her."

In seconds, they brought in a gurney and whisked Ronnie out of the room. Mike sat staring at the empty bed with tears streaming down his face. He reached for the box of Kleenex on the table and wiped madly hoping to understand what was happening in his heart. Upsetting as it was to see his employee carted off and possibly near death, it did not explain these feelings. Was it connected to Kelly's death? Was he reliving the moments before they told him she had passed away from her injuries?

His chest felt like it was going to explode and he stumbled to the small en suite bathroom and looked in the mirror. Dark-ringed eyes stared back at him. It would not take much to convince anyone he was a mass murderer with the stubble and the bloodshot eyes before him. Another wave of deep dark despair washed over him. Mike put the lid down on the toilet seat and sat down, cradling his head in his hands.

He went to the calm place, the one he had learned from his therapist after Kelly's death and explored his heart. Logic was not allowed here. He took a few deep breaths and used his mind's eye to examine his state of mind. Logic would not have done any good here, it had no purchase. What he was feeling had no basis in reality. He found desperate longing, fear, loss, and grief and mingled with it was an unbound love. Feelings that had been locked away for years, decades, maybe even lifetimes.

Tears stung his eyes as he released some of the pent-up emotions that had been there his entire life. He'd only just become aware of them and his is heart broke into a million pieces while he let himself fall apart, sobbing uncontrollably with tears splashing to the floor.

A light rapping on the door startled him. He stood, wiped his eyes. and wiped his nose.

"Mike, you in there?" It was Steph's voice.

"Yeah," his voice cracked. "Be right out."

"Where's Ronnie? What have they done with her?" Nick's voice was high and emotional.

Mike opened the door to the worried faces of his new friends. "She woke up. It was incredible."

"What?" Steph covered her mouth. "We were praying for a miracle, Nick!" Steph cried openly, her eyes bluer with the tears. Nick hugged her from behind.

Mike walked out and stared at the bed. "She woke and then screamed and wouldn't stop." The sound still echoed in his mind. "I called the nurse and they took her for another scan."

"Oh thank God. When I first saw the bed empty I thought something terrible had …" Steph sobbed and buried her face against Nick's chest.

Mike stood numbly. He looked at the empty bed and shook his head. "It was really spooky. She looked right at me but I could tell something was hurting her, causing her terrible pain." He wiped away tears, "That's when she started screaming."

Nick and Steph whispered back and forth. Finally, Nick asked. "What kind of scan did they say, Mike?"

"They didn't." He walked to the window. "How long did it take the last time?"

"No idea. We were in the waiting area. Usually, it's like a half hour or a bit longer," Nick said, still hugging Steph. "Probably another CT scan."

"It looks like the storm is winding down. That will be good." Mike ran his fingers through his hair. He needed some sleep and a few stiff shots of bourbon to make sure he didn't wake up for quite some time. But not yet. He had to see Ronnie and this time he wanted her to know he was by her side.

Chapter 52 – FUBAR

Jeffrey stood panting and dripping in front of the laptop. His face reflected at him in the black screen. A drop of water fell off his nose and nearly landed on the keyboard. He pressed the mouse to confirm the computer was off. The monumental question was whether or not Ronnie had made it back.

He grabbed a few towels from the cart he had hidden TOTO to dry his face, head, and arms. Tearing open the trash bag that held his extra battery he quickly removed the spent one and inserted the fresh so he could fire up the computer.

An excruciating minute ticked by as the laptop went through its startup sequence. Jeffrey held his breath and tried to tamp down the inner voice screaming at what a fucking dumbass he was for this mistake. Finally, he opened the program that had pulled Ronnie back and read all the messages on the screen: *Process aborted, low battery, lost contact with subject, incomplete sequence.* The bad news rolled in like a cloud of dust in a haboob blackening the sky.

He read them carefully again. *Lost contact with subject.* His heart skipped a beat. Did she move? Was it the battery dying that caused this? He flipped to the program that tracked Ronnie and again she was nowhere to be found. Gone. Off the face of the earth.

He pinched the bridge of his nose. There was no way to tell how long the computer had been off. It had taken him about ten minutes to retrieve the keys and then the battery. He sat on the hospital bed and ran through every scenario.

What he wanted to do the most was scream bloody murder but that wouldn't generate any positive results. Fury burned in his chest. Would anything go right with this experiment? It had all set up so well with Hannah Volpe steering another storm directly overhead. His tweaking of the system allowed a portable device and he had everything so perfectly setup in Ronnie's house. Damn Steph came in to ruin everything, and damn Ronnie let her. He grabbed his head and let out a silent scream, stomping his feet and clenching his fists.

He tried to connect with Ronnie again. It could still work. He needed to bring her back now. Maybe it just left her there and never began to pull her back. Maybe. If she had been in the middle of the process when the laptop died there was no telling how it would affect her.

Lost contact with subject. The message was clear. But why?

"Where are you, Ronnie?"

He listened intently to the voices next door. There was that deeper male voice again. Pressing his ear against the wall he tried to make out what they were saying. Muffled voices were indistinguishable. If he didn't find her soon the storm would end and she would be stuck forever. Then he clearly heard Nick's voice saying it was probably a CT Scan.

That would take far too long. There wouldn't be sufficient power to bring her back. "Fucked up beyond all recognition." Jeffrey exhaled loudly. That was why he couldn't see Ronnie on the tracking device. The CT scan had blocked the signal. It would likely mess up bringing her back as well. He'd have to wait or take matters into his own hands. He stood debating for a second. But then with determination stormed out of the room.

    ***

In the basement he rummaged around, looking for something, not sure what. But lady luck was there lurking in the shadows. There between two huge industrial washing machines, caught in years' worth of detergent, dust, and random gunk was a name badge. Jeffrey knelt and tugged on it. It was stuck under the machine. Working it back and forth he freed it. Bingo!

It was a lanyard, a set of keys and a name badge of Arthur Brown. "Thank you, Arthur Brown." Were they keys to the hospital? Or something personal. He wiped the brown goo off them. Carved in small letters across the top of the largest key was the word *Maintenance*.

A tiny smile crossed Jeffrey's lips and he scanned the room. On the far side of the laundry room was a dark hallway. He followed it along until the heavy metal door was evident. He pulled out the largest key and tried the lock, and went through the ring until it clicked and opened the door. An electrical hum emanated from the room. He clicked on the light and looked around. Large metal boxes lined the walls. This was the hub of the hospital's electrical supply. It must be running on a generator.

An unthinkable thought crossed his mind. If he crashed the entire hospital's electrical system many people would die. He just needed to pull the plug on the scanning equipment section. He perused the metal boxes hoping for labels and finally found a schematic map on the wall. The fourth box over would cover the part of the first floor that contained the scanning equipment and mostly the outpatient areas. Most the inpatients were on the second floor. He ran back to the laundry room and grabbed a bucket, filled it with water, and carried it back to the electrical room as water sloshed out and covered his already wet scrubs pants.

He took a deep breath, lifted the bucket, and tossed the water on the open panel for the first floor. Sparks flew out and steam rose off. He shut the light off, closed the door behind him, and ran with the bucket to the laundry area, then out to the stairwell and back toward room 226. As he walked down the hallway, he put the lanyard around his neck and slid his own badge into his chest pocket. Arthur Brown looked nothing like him but he was a white dude and that would likely be enough for anyone looking casually at him.

He paused briefly as he passed Ronnie's room. Sitting on the couch, one leg crossed over the other, was a dark-haired man in scrubs who paused to look up at him. A doctor wouldn't be sitting in a patient's room. For a split-second, their eyes met until the man looked away. Jeffrey quickly moved out of view and racked his brain. He looked familiar, but where had he seen him before?

Then it hit him. Sitting in Ronnie's room lounging casually just on the other side of this wall was Mike Walsh, Ronnie's boss. What the hell? Bile rose into his throat. What the goddamned hell would Mike be doing here? It made no sense. Jealousy reared its ugly head and Jeffrey imagined Mike there to help her when she woke up. He should be there to comfort her, not this idiot meatbag.

Chapter 53 - Dying to Return

Something about the way the man stared at him irked Mike. At first, it seemed like a simple glance in a room as he passed by, but the intensity of the look with its lingering stare didn't sit well. Nick and Steph hadn't seen him. They were standing next to the bed talking in whispers. Mike felt like an intruder, an unwanted lingerer.

"Hey, I'm going to roam the halls for a bit. This sitting around staring at walls is really wearing thin." Mike stood and stretched. "Do you all need anything? Food? Some coffee?"

"No, I'm good," Steph said.

Nick looked about as worn as Mike felt, "Yeah man, anything to eat would be great. I'm starving."

Steph smacked his arm. "You're always starving, babe."

"True, true."

"You're welcome to anything there if you want it." Mike nodded at the tray Candice had brought him. "I'll see what else I can scare up."

"Great. Bye," Steph said.

Mike took a deep breath still rattled by the depth of his feelings earlier. He hoped the mystery man would show himself. Maybe find out if he had some interest in Ronnie or Steph. Something nagged at his subconscious but he was too worked up to be able to access it. He walked slowly down the hall toward the elevator and glanced in each room, wondering if he was eliciting the same creeped out response he'd had at being gawked at.

Mike pressed the button for the elevator and remembered the limited power in the building. The elevator dinged as the doors opened and a gurney rushed past. Long blonde hair splashed on the pillow, but he hadn't seen the face. Was that Ronnie? He followed and they turned into her room confirming his suspicion. That was too fast for a CT scan. Torn between wanting to give them privacy and worry about Ronnie he paused in the hallway debating just long enough to see the floor was wet right next to her door. It struck him as being strange but that thought was pushed aside when he made his choice.

A flurry of activity surrounded Ronnie. Her head was raised but her eyes remained closed. Not in a peaceful sleep. She looked pained. A lump formed in his throat and a twinge of sadness tugged at his heart. Steph took a few steps closer.

"They had to stop the scan because of a blackout." Steph shook her head. "I guess the storm caused it. It's weird because we still have power up here."

"Yeah, I'd say so. I'm glad we do but that's really strange." Mike rubbed the stubble on his chin.

Nick held a bag of Fritos and was cramming them in his mouth. He nodded his head in acknowledgement. "You didn't get far did you?"

"No, I saw Ronnie and wanted to find out why they were back so soon." He combed his fingers through his hair. "Any change?"

"No, but her heart rate is still way higher than normal and they're taking blood now to see if they can get some information instead of the scan. They're worried about a brain bleed."

Mike's heart skipped a beat. "I hope not."

"Me too," Steph said. The flurry of activity slowed and the nurses left. Steph approached the bed and took Ronnie's hand. "Ron, it's Steph. I'm here."

Mike sat next to Nick on the couch and grabbed a bag of chips.

***

A familiar voice came to Ronnie and a comfortable feeling washed over her. It was Steph. She was here by her side. "Help me."

A blur of noises assaulted her and she couldn't distinguish between the worlds she was straddling. Steph's voice and comforting presence was shoved aside by the racket in her brain, a terrible reverberation and echo made her pull inward wishing to be in one or the other place. She was in no state of mind to contemplate what was happening. Instead every ounce of her being focused on making the vibrations end. The echoes faded and were replaced by a deep bone-wrenching buzzing.

A bolt of electricity jolted through her body and again she was falling, wind blowing in her hair. The vibrations sped up, making her ears ring as the pitch reached nearly too high to hear. It seemed to be endlessly going higher as she fell faster toward the blackness. And then inky darkness and blissful silence.

***

"Code blue, code blue," the nurse yelled.

The machine next to Ronnie was beeping madly. The heart rate was flat and Ronnie was turning a shade of blue.

"Miss, step back, please." The nurse stood close to Steph, waiting for her to get out of the way.

Within seconds five nurses and doctors crowded around Ronnie. Steph stood in the corner in shock. She had prayed for a miracle, not this. Not her best friend dying in front of her.

Frantic calls filled the room from the staff barking orders. They started CPR and one nurse straddled Ronnie to begin compressions. It seemed like an eternity passed as the horror unfolded in front of her eyes.

Tears flowed down Steph's face and Nick reached for her hand. This may be the last moments she would know her best friend. She soaked in everything not wanting to forget a second of this horrible and hauntingly intense moment. She took in the group of nurses and doctors working hard to save Ronnie's life, the firm warmth of Nick's hand, the crushing sadness in Mike's expression. Each image burned into her mind and created a beautiful tapestry of raw emotion and a higher sense of awareness, almost as if she were floating in the room looking down on all of it.

Sensing that her life would never be the same, from this moment on. Nick and Mike's lives would also be forever changed in this one instant.

The nurse stopped CPR and all eyes were on the heart monitor. A delicate blip crossed the screen followed by a steady heartbeat. The tension broke like a wave created by a stone piercing the surface of the water.

The CPR nurse climbed off the bed and stood nearby, out of breath from her effort. The only sound in the room was the beating of Ronnie's heart. For some unknown reason, Steph's mind played "Stand by Me" by Ben E. King to the tune of Ronnie's sinus rhythm.

She pushed her way through the crowd around Ronnie's bed and grabbed her hand. "Ronnie, I'm here with you." The doctor stepped back giving Steph some space. "Please come back to us."

In that moment, Steph felt powerful, as if her simple request would change everything. A peace washed over her and she knew in that instant that whatever happened to Ronnie was destined. The knots in her stomach unraveled just a little knowing this was out of her hands.

Chapter 54 - Beriberi Glad to See You

A disturbing electronic noise beat inside Ronnie's brain. Voices nearby made her pay closer attention. The vibration was no longer there tormenting her, incessantly. All she wanted to do was sleep. Uninterrupted sleep for months and months to be left alone in the quite darkness of her soul, curled in the fetal position blocking out everything horrible, everything that had tried to destroy her.

A familiar voice penetrated the dusky fog. Alertness sifted through to the surface and after what seemed like hours of trying to block out the splitting of her soul in two, she was able to unify her mind on one solid thing. Steph was here. A magical feeling engulfed her and a small hand reached inside the depths of her psyche and pulled her free.

In a monumental effort, Ronnie forced her eyes open. The beaming smile of her best friend was her reward.

"Hi Ron. Where you been?" Steph smiled and then glanced over her shoulder.

Ronnie tried to use her voice but only a crackle came out. Steph put her finger over her lips. "Save your breath. You can tell me when we're alone."

Ronnie's eyes shut again in an unwilling retreat to the dark corner that had been all she'd known for eons. A brief flash of the assault the moment she split in two and the image of two men in one visage danced before her. She examined one of them and was surprised to find her boss there. It must be a mistake of her memory in turmoil.

"Mike." Her mouth was dry as a bone and the words were like sandpaper in her throat.

Steph looked surprised and smiled. "She's asking for you." Her head turned toward another person in the room. Ronnie found it difficult to follow what was happening.

A deep voice was to her left and Steph was on her right. Slowly, carefully she turned her head and couldn't believe her eyes. The owner of that voice, Mike Walsh, was there smiling down at her. He took her hand and said, "I'm here Ronnie."

Terrified that he would split again and cause the deep rumbling she squeezed her eyes shut. "How?"

Mike bit his lip and shook his head. "I drove you here and ..." he wiped away tears and flashed a blue gaze at Steph. "I'm so glad you're back."

Ronnie felt her stomach expecting excruciating pain. It felt normal. Her fingers weren't coated in blood as they had been earlier. "I don't understand. What are you doing here?" she squeezed Steph's hand. "For that matter, what the hell am I doing here?"

Nick approached the bed and answered for them all, "Pretty much you've been scaring us to death."

Steph clasped her hand in both of hers now. "Ronnie, we left the house in the middle of the storm to bring you to the hospital. Our car broke down and Mike drove us here. He was a lifesaver, seriously, we may not have survived the night without him."

"Without him," Ronnie repeated and turned her eyes back to Mike.

"It was nothing really. I'm just glad you're awake and not screaming bloody murder. I was sure I completely freaked you out, Ronnie." His eye sparkled in the low light of the room.

"So, you were here ... I was here ..." the image of Mike just before she vibrated was true, it was real. What did it mean?

A doctor stood at the foot of the bed. "We really need to do a few tests on her. We still have no diagnosis or even explanation for what caused the coma."

"Coma?" Ronnie didn't like the sound of that. "I was in a coma?" She sat up a little and looked around realizing more fully now she was in a hospital.

"Yeah, little lady, you've had us worried sick," The doctor said.

Nick looked at her. "Steph, let's allow the doctor do what he needs."

Mike and Steph stepped to the back of the room and the doctor spoke quietly to her about what he was doing. He checked her pupils and asked her to do various odd things like follow his finger, touch her nose, and wiggle her toes.

"How do you feel, Miss Andrews?" he asked as he pressed into her abdomen.

"Exhausted. Hungry. Like I have low blood sugar again." She winced as he pressed hard, making her stomach revolt.

"Is that how you felt prior to this event?"

"Yes, I was crashing despite eating a lot of food. I don't know what that was about," Ronnie said, her eyes closing again from exhaustion.

"Is there anything unusual that took place prior to this feeling?" Dr. Smith asked.

Ronnie opened her eyes and sought out Steph. "Ahhh ..."

"It's really important that you share with me everything so we can figure this out." The doctor took a pen and pad out of his breast pocket and wrote a few notes as she spoke.

"So, well, just that I had a lot of stress before. The storm coming, a fight with my boyfriend." Her eyes met Mike's and smiled at her and she lost her train of thought.

"Don't forget the branch coming through the kitchen," Nick added.

"It does sound like a lot of stress." The doctor turned to the nurse. "What were the results of the last scan?"

"We had a blackout down there, probably storm related." The nurse handed him her chart. "Here are the first scan results."

He took a minute reading over the notes, flipping pages, and nodding. "Your CBC is showing you have a drastic deficiency in thiamine."

"I do?" Ronnie shook her head. "That's weird. What does that mean?"

"It's quite unusual for someone like you. Usually, alcoholics who are malnourished display some deficiency but yours is dramatic. It would explain your hunger. You can easily get enough thiamine through the eggs, beans, and bread in a normal diet."

"I was ravenous. And it happened one other time during the last storm. Just after I woke up." She nodded at Steph. "Remember the bread bag?"

"Och, yes. She ate an entire loaf afterwards." Steph gave her a tired smile.

"Did it rectify the feeling?" The doctor asked.

"It did. I felt fine a bit later."

"It's also called beriberi and is a result of a vitamin B1 deficiency. Your B1 is absorbed in the small intestines so it would take a bit of time to restore the levels, perhaps a half an hour or more to return to normal."

"That sounds about right," Ronnie remembered how she had recovered after Charley and went out to dinner with Mike and Steph.

The doctor continued. "The issue with thiamine deficiency is that it can cause hallucinations but is quite rare, especially in an otherwise healthy woman. Have you had any recent bouts of fever or diarrhea?"

Mike stood, "I'm going to grab some coffee, does anyone want some?" He was likely eager to escape the personal health details.

"I'll go with you," Nick said. "Steph hold down the fort, okay?"

"Sure," Steph said and took a few steps closer to Ronnie.

Ronne answered the doctor. "No, I've felt great except for during the storms and just after." The shaky, sweaty feeling was beginning to come on her hard now. The shaky, sweaty feeling. "Can I get some food, it's making me feel horrible now."

"Before you do let's get another CBC." He rattled off a few more tests. "Then we can see what your numbers are and can compare after you've eaten."

"The other thing that could result from a thiamine deficiency is Korsakoff's syndrome, but you don't have the signs of uncontrolled eye movements or swelling in your extremities."

"That sounds horrible," Steph said.

"The confusing thing here is that it takes a week or more of not ingesting thiamine for you to deplete the stores. If you just ate prior to the coma then it isn't a dietary issue. Perhaps a liver issue or," he glanced at the nurse before asking, "do you have the actual scans of her brain?"

The nurse put the film on the light board and flicked the light on. "Here."

The doctor examined it closely. "Do you see this region here?"

Steph and Ronnie looked. "Yes."

"There is a small lesion. That is classic Korsakoff's syndrome. It's starting to hemorrhage."

"Oh no, that isn't good." Ronnie was too tired to panic.

"Have you had any hallucinations or strange thoughts?" He looked between Ronnie and Steph.

"I have. Just before I wake." Ronnie felt sick and this news wasn't helping.

"Well, we need to figure out what's causing this." The doctor said.

Another nurse walked in. "Phlebotomy," she said to the doctor.

"Please, please, continue," The doctor said. "We need these results quickly. Please rest Miss Andrews. We'll find out what's causing this problem and do what we can." He put the pad of paper and pen in his pocket. "I'll return when we have blood results."

"Can I eat now?" Ronnie asked.

"Yes, as soon as she draws the blood, but let's keep it simple. Graham crackers or something for her," he said to the nurse.

"Thank you, doctor," Steph said and waited for him to leave. "Ronnie, do you think the time traveling was just the ... what did he call it?"

"Korsakoff's syndrome. I really don't know since to me it was all as real as you and I sitting here. It never once gave me disjointed dream feelings." Ronnie closed her eyes willing the sickness to calm.

"Did you go somewhere this time?" Steph held her hand.

"I did. I was ... it was horrible, I can't even talk about it now. Not with Mike and Nick about to return. But I have to say, the strangest thing happened when I came back and Mike was there."

"What?" Steph asked.

"It's like I was in two places. With Mike here, and with someone so much like him in the time I was in ... the place. They were merged into one body with each half in one time."

Steph shook her head. "Seriously? That's so weird."

Ronnie closed her eyes and relived that moment. "Then it was too much and a strange vibration took over that went on forever. I had to go deep inside to get away from it. It was horrible, devastating. It felt like nothing would ever be right again."

"I have to tell you something," Steph started but her voice cracked. Ronnie opened her eyes and noticed the tears flowing down her face. "They had to revive you ... you were dead for a few minutes."

Ronnie sat up. "What?"

"Yeah, it was horrible. I didn't think you were going to come back," Steph sniffed.

A terrible feeling crept over her. "Steph, I died back then too. I wonder if it almost killed me in this time too."

Steph wiped the tears away. "I don't know. I just want you to be well and for all of this to stop."

"Me too." Ronnie squeezed her friend's hand. "Why do you think Mike was part of that?"

"No idea. He has been great though, Ronnie. He's the reason we're in your room. They thought you were his wife, so he came and got us in the waiting room. It's probably why he stuck around. I know he feels a bit uncomfortable being part of all of this, not really knowing you."

"It is really awkward, Steph. Was he crying when I woke up? I swear I saw him wipe away tears."

Steph's eyes widened. "I don't know. I was watching you. But wow."

"There is so much I need to tell you. I'm seeing a pattern now. There is always a man. A good man helping me. A man like Mike."

"Mathias?" Steph said, shaking her head. "Unbelievable!"

"Yes, Morris this time." She inhaled the antiseptic smells of the hospital. "And there is always someone trying to do me harm."

"Jack," Steph said in unison with Ronnie.

"Right. I need to chew on this some more." Ronnie wiped away a tear. "I'm so tired. It's all so confusing. Now this whole monkey wrench that it may all just be some weird disease and my imagination."

"We'll figure it out. All I know about Mike is that he's gone out of his way to help us, to help you. If he is supposed to be in your life instead of ..."

"Don't say it." Ronnie pressed her lips together tired of the perpetual fight about Jeffrey.

"You-know-who." Steph gave her a smile. "Look you have to admit it's weird enough that Mike is here, of all places." She glanced toward the door, "And for you to have that strange vision, and feeling that someone like him is in all of the places you have traveled. It has to mean something."

"Maybe. But what?" Ronnie's mushy brain was spent.

"Who knows? Let's just keep an open mind and explore this more when you're recovered." Steph pulled the blankets to Ronnie's chin. "Rest. We have plenty of time to figure all of this out."

Ronnie sunk into the pillow and was asleep in minutes.

Chapter 55 - Code

Jeffrey watched the code scroll across the screen. Ronnie was returning. Power was flowing to the laptop and the coils had done their job. Now the only question was would she be permanently damaged? He had no prior issues experimenting with the cats other than the random one dying. He'd never had an interruption in the return module though.

A crackle on the loud speaker beckoned, "Code Blue. Code Blue." Annoyed by the interruption he didn't give it much thought until he could hear the commotion in Ronnie's room.

He bolted out the door and stood outside the room. Several nurses pushed past him, "What's going on?"

"Code blue, she's crashing," the pretty blonde nurse said as she brushed past.

"Oh my God." Jeffrey felt sick. All the effort to bring her back and she had the gall to die!

He lingered in the doorway, out of sight but listening intently to the commands, the commotion, the desperate sobs of Stephanie. This could *not* be happening. All the work he'd put in. All of this was Stephanie's fault. She should be crying. She would have to be punished for this, for risking Ronnie's life by moving her.

Never mind she didn't know the damage she'd caused her friend. But she'd brought Mike Walsh into the picture as well. How could that be? Did Ronnie invite him over to her house as well? The second he left she brought him over? Goddamn, he should have known something was up after the way they were all over each other her first day of work.

Anger boiled, mixing in with the fear of losing Ronnie and the stress of the night. The only saving grace was Stephanie could no longer blame him for the time travel. He was not, for all they knew, near her when all of this happened.

***

A half hour later Ronnie seemed to be out of the woods. The nurses left the room and Jeffrey went back to room 226. He quietly packed up his gear and checked the radar. The storm was winding down, only the last remaining bands were lingering along with the rain but he'd just made it with no time to spare. One more trip to the roof to retrieve the coils and he could stash everything back in his car and boot Mike out of Ronnie's room. As he worked on this last stage of the experiment he concocted the story of how he knew Ronnie was at the hospital.

He loaded everything on the cart and brought it down to the employee entrance, leaving it at the front door. He quickly ran to his car splashing though the newly formed lake in the parking lot and drove his car to the overhang. In a few minutes, he had all his gear loaded and then re-parked it in a drier location near the emergency room entrance. A quick trip to the employee changing room and he removed the wet scrubs and put on his own damp clothes.

In the elevator, he got into character of the worried boyfriend, forgetting everything he knew about this horrible night and steadied himself to confront Mike, Steph, and Nick. He walked down the hall and into Ronnie's room.

Steph was sitting by the bed and Ronnie was asleep. Steph turned around and saw him first.

"Jeffrey, what the hell are you doing here?"

"Hey, great to see you too, Stephanie." He tamped down the anger and hatred. "How is she doing?"

Steph stood and moved out of his way. Jeffrey took Ronnie's hand.

"How did you know she was here?" Steph asked.

He turned Nick was there too. "Ian."

"Ian?" Steph said. "You went to Ronnie's?" She shook her head. "In the middle of the storm?"

"I hated that I left in anger. As soon as the winds died down I …" Jeffrey turned. Mike Walsh walked into the room holding two coffees.

This distracted Jeffrey from his train of thought. "What the hell are you doing here?" He didn't have to fake the anger, just the surprise.

"I could ask you the same thing." Mike handed Steph and Nick the coffees. "Big storm out there and you're driving around?"

Jeffrey didn't like the tone. "She's my girlfriend. I should be the one here by her side, not you." He tried to quiet the rage growing inside. It gave away too much of his hand.

"Looks like you are the one by her side. No beef here, man," Mike said holding his hands up.

"You should show more respect, Jeffrey," Steph stepped between them and pointed at Mike. "He is the reason we made it here safely."

"He is?" Jeffrey had to bite his tongue. *She* was the reason Ronnie was in the hospital. "Stephanie, mind your own fucking business." He turned his back on all three of them and went to Ronnie. Her eyes were opened now. "Hey baby, how are you?"

"Jeffrey, how …" Ronnie's voice was weak, but her eyes were wide.

"Babe, I stopped by your house as soon as the winds died down. I wanted to apologize for being such a …" he turned around to glare at Steph and Mike. "Can we have some privacy please?"

Stephanie went to the other side of Ronnie, "Sweetie, do you want me here or shall we step out for a few minutes?"

Ronnie's eyes fluttered. She was exhausted. "Either way. It doesn't matter."

Nick took Steph by the elbow, "Come on, let's give them a minute."

"Thank you, Nick. That's very kind of you." Jeffrey held Ronnie's hand and watched them leave. Mike walked out with them too, but not without giving him an aggressive look.

"Babe, God what happened tonight?" He softened and got lost in her sleepy eyes.

"I don't know really. I was out. They say it was a coma. Then I guess I …" She wiped away a tear.

"What baby, tell me, please." Jeffrey pushed a stray hair behind her ear.

"Steph says I died for a little bit they had to do CPR on me." She sniffed.

"What? Oh my God. Ronnie, and I wasn't here for you. I'm so sorry." He shook his head. "Do they know what caused it?"

"Not sure. Beriberi? Something like that. I have a deficiency and it causes some brain issues."

"Beriberi? What the hell is that?" It sounded familiar and images of Caribbean natives in the 1800's came to mind.

"Vitamin B1 I think?" She yawned.

"You have plenty of that in your diet. What causes it?" Jeffrey wracked his memory for any information on beriberi.

"They don't know. Jeffrey, it happened again, several times."

"What happened?" He feigned ignorance.

"Time traveled. I went back several times during the storm." She sat up a little bit more in the bed.

"What? How? Do they think the deficiency caused those …" he looked away, "Dreams or whatever they were?" He noticed a film up on the light board. "What's this?"

"Don't know. That's my brain I guess." She yawned again.

He stood and examined the CT scan. He didn't like the look of it. A pang of guilt registered deep inside. The important work he had progressed rapidly with Ronnie's help but by causing her harm. He had been too aggressive, too careless with all the traveling in succession with no break for her to recover. The mistake with the battery pack may have nearly cost her life and that would have definitely given him reason to put the project on ice. At least for a while.

"Babe this looks serious. There's a weird spot on the CT scan. Did they say what that was?" He turned toward her.

"Korsakoff's syndrome? Something like that. A brain injury from the thiamine deficiency."

"Wow, so what do we do to prevent it?" All the blood left his face. They even had a name for it.

"I'm not sure yet, they're doing more tests." Her eyes closed.

"I'm not surprised, really. Something was causing those strange experiences and now we at least have a diagnosis for your break in reality. I'm so sorry it came to this though."

"Babe, I'm so tired. I just need to rest," Ronnie said, eyes still closed.

"Okay Ronnie, I'll sit here with you while you sleep. I'm here for you." He was relieved a legitimate medical reason had been found to explain her time travels. It might be time to retire Ronnie from this experiment. He could make improvements without her help. She had already sacrificed so much. There was no way to know what long-term effects it would have on her brain. He had learned so much this weekend and there were so many improvements to make and maybe someday he would bring another human into the fold, with vitamin supplements, that was certain.

He made a mental list of procedures and recommendations for future experiments and sat back in the chair, tuning out the *bleep bleep* of Ronnie's heart monitor

Chapter 56 - Choke

June 26, 1999, Rochester, NY
Kelly Ascobar stomped her foot and glared at Mike, her flesh bouncing nicely under the camisole, but Mike couldn't enjoy it.

"Why do you let them get to you?" Mike leaned in and tried not to raise his voice. He didn't fail at many things, but this was one area he had never been good at—controlling his temper.

"I don't know. I guess because they're my parents and I love them." Kelly wiped away a tear.

"Kel, they always wedge between us. We never get but two steps ahead and they poke their noses in our business and screw everything up." He sat down on the edge of an upholstered chair hoping he would seem less threatening looking up at her.

"I know," she said sitting down hard on the bed looking like she was either going to yell or cry. Maybe both?

"You have to tell them to butt out. They're ruining us. I'm just not sure if I can keep doing this. Can't we move away—to Florida or something?" Mike ran his hand through his hair. It was the same endless fight.

"But who would drive me when you're out of town?" The tears flowed freely down her face and she wiped them away with both hands. "I hate being so damn dependent on everyone else to drive me places. It really, really sucks!" She flashed angry brown eyes in the low light of the room.

A few minutes before they had been peeling each other's clothes off. How had it turned to flinging repeated complaints back and forth like a birdy in a badminton match?

"God damnit! It's a Catch-22 isn't it?" He stood and clenched his fists. "Damn!" Without thinking he turned and punched the wall. Pain screamed through the bones in his hand. Blood from a small cut on his knuckles distracted him. *That felt so good.*

"Mike, stop!" Kelly cowered in the far corner of the bed. Her camisole barely covering her breasts.

His anger was still fresh and acrid, he could almost taste it. There never seemed a way out of this situation and he was tired of her parents perpetually micromanaging their life. He walked to the bed, forcing his expression to soften, hoping to calm her down, but she scooted away and slipped out of the bed, landing on the floor. She was drunk and not very steady.

"Kelly, are you okay?" He reached to help her up.

She awkwardly stood and stepped backward with her hands up. "No, don't!" Her foot tangled on his shorts from the floor and she fell backward in slow motion. Mike reached out for her but as he had done all night he failed. Her head hit the corner of the bedside table making a horrible cracking sound. The impact knocked over a glass of bourbon and it rolled under the bed, the golden liquid soaking into the rug.

"Ouch!" She grabbed the back of her head.

"Oh my God, babe! Are you all right?" He reached to help her stand. "I'm so sorry."

"Crap that hurt!"

Mike looked around to find something to stop the bleeding and found at his feet the T-shirt he'd had on earlier.

Kelly pressed it against the back of her head, pulling it away to see the blood staining the white fabric. "Ohhhh."

He led her to the bed. "I'll get you some ice."

Oh God, oh God. He ran to the kitchen and grabbed a plastic bag out of the drawer near the fridge and filled it with ice. "Please be okay, please be okay."

He ran back to the bedroom and handed her the bag of ice. She was unbearably seductive sitting on the bed against the pillows with her camisole hiked up around her hips—her knees bent and apart exposing everything. Mike pulled the comforter to cover her up not being able to take much more of the sight of her nakedness.

"Kel." He handed her a Kleenex from the box on the night stand. "Are you okay?"

She nodded and took the tissue, much calmer now, and wiped her eyes and nose.

"I'm sorry I hit the wall." He looked at his knuckles and wiped at the blood. "Let me see your head."

She turned to the side to let him examine the injury. "It's just a small cut."

"Do you think I need stitches?"

"No, hun, it's already stopped bleeding. You've got a good bump though. Put the ice on it." Mike shifted his boxers to get more comfortable. "Let's not worry about your parents tonight, let's just watch a movie or something." He climbed on the bed next to her and grabbed her free hand.

"With that thing poking me in the side all night?" She nodded toward his crotch.

He looked away. "Hmm, what do you suggest?"

Kelly pulled the comforter aside and opened her legs just a bit. Her smile said it all. Thank God he'd not completely freaked her out with the wall punching and yelling. He found her thigh and felt soft, smooth skin. Mike leaned in to kiss her and felt her soft lips on his as his hand crept up her thigh. A gasp escaped just before he slid his tongue between her lips and his finger found moist warmth that he spread around her delicious flesh.

Her legs opened wider and her body relaxed more under his touch. She moaned into his mouth as her arousal increased.

Mike's breath mingled with Kelly's as they nearly panted together. A finger plunged into her flesh as his tongue did the same. He shifted his weight and laid next to her on the bed allowing both hands freedom to move. The camisole strap slid down her shoulder with his caress and his lips traced down to her newly exposed skin, pushing aside the silky material as his tongue and lips met hardening skin.

Kelly reached down and gripped the front of his boxers, finding a firm handful and more. It was his turn to moan, as she slid her hand down the front of his shorts and made contact with sensitive skin. He removed his boxers, tossing them on the floor, and reached for the hem of her camisole to pull it over her head, adding it to the pile on the floor.

Fleeting echoes of the anger he'd felt during their fight crept into his mind. A gentle caress of her long elegant neck as his eyes greedily took in her naked body. The lingering touch of her beautiful flesh quickly shifted into an overwhelming need to take her. His legs spread hers and he knelt between them while he caressed soft curves from breast to waist, and then hips. Her lust apparent, her eyes almost glowing in the low light from the TV.

A low moan escaped her perfect lips as he slid in, stretching her, forcing her to accommodate him. A small but growing part of him desperately needed to damage, to crush. Her neck was so delicate and small under his hand. He slid in further and pulled out, increasing in fervor, the warmth of her surrounding him, and the little noises she made as she approached climax drove his need, feeling the vibrations along her neck.

The crunching of something in her throat excited him to the point of orgasm as he thrust into her, deeper, urgently fulfilling his need for her wet tightness and destruction of her airway. So satisfying as his thumb pressed into her larynx. He knew it was wrong, it was horrible and undoable, but he couldn't stop himself. Such blissful feelings as he pumped every drop into her lifeless body as his hand still squeezed her neck. Her expression pinched and turned dusky in the dark room, the TV flashing shadows, the flickering mimicking movement on her face.

He imagined her bliss as he slid in feeling her walls around him, so warm and comforting. Then he pulled out and rolled off, letting go. His eyes closed enjoying the fulfillment of the release, the sensitivity of the caress still lingering on his body as he dozed off in a dreamy post-coital coma.

Mike woke with a start with the full realization of what he had done, guilt overwhelming him. The room was pitch-black and he felt the bed next to him, "Kelly! Kelly!"

Mike wiped at the tears, "I'm so sorry!" He found the bed as it should be— empty. Kelly was gone, dust in the wind. The desperate loneliness returned as fully as it had been the days following her death.

"Just a fucking nightmare," Mike rubbed his face, touching the stubble along his chin. He sat up disoriented and still feeling the horror of the dream, his heart beating fast and tension filling his body, erection fading quickly. *Why was it so miserably hot and dark?* Then he remembered the hurricane and resulting loss of power. Hand groping for the flashlight he left on the bedside table—the same table Kelly had hit her head on. Why had he kept it? It hadn't bothered him until now with the realization that her blood may still be soaked into the wood. He shook his head trying to let loose the horrible thought. A flash of the crunching under his fingers made him shudder and any lingering erection disappeared.

Mike hadn't dreamt that variation before. He always ended up killing her, but his guilty conscience found an endless array of methods for her destruction, but this was a new one. Sexual release while choking her—he was definitely morphing into a sick fuck, at least in his dreams. The one constant with the dream was the new variation in her death, a new way to torment his soul. What he needed was another drink. He grabbed the flashlight off the headboard and made his way toward the kitchen. Damn, power had been out several days, there would be no ice. His fridge had been off since Friday when Hurricane Frances hit. It was Monday morning now and still raining but the winds had died down to normal storm levels.

It was 3:10 am. His bourbon would have to be at room temperature. He poured a double into his favorite glass, a new purchase, and nice chunky highball glass, free of any memories.

When would this damn dream stop plaguing him? Would he be old and gray and still relive the nightmare? It had been five years, and thankfully it only happened a few times a year now, but it always set him back. He would have to try to convince himself he wasn't a horrible person for trying to move on, to forget it, to forget her. He couldn't bring himself to go back home to Rochester. Too many enemies, too many bad feelings. Thank God Billy had moved down to Florida with him. He could at least have a bit of his past making him feel less disconnected to that part of his life.

What had triggered the dream this time? It usually reared its ugly head at inopportune times, often brought on by stress. He cleared his mind and focused on what he felt was the cause, not allowing the usual logic to rule. It was a technique he had learned during the counseling sessions after Kelly's death, to help him recover. The booze burned its way down his throat and a comforting fire was lit in his belly.

A clear picture of Ronnie appeared in his mind, her long golden hair around her shoulders and that small blue necklace nearly the color of her sparkly eyes sitting neatly in the delicious little hollow just at the base of her throat. All the horrible events of yesterday rolled around in one tormenting stabbing pain in his gut. She nearly died and they were still not sure what had caused it. The deep release of emotions, as if he'd tapped into something much bigger than his life was so puzzling. Where had that come from? Why had this affected him so much?

Was she the reason for the dream? He took another sip and explored this interesting thought. He'd not really looked at a woman in years. The one's that forced their way into his view were usually pushy, desperate for his attention and always, without question, not of any interest to him.

He peeked out the plantation shutters to his backyard. It was pitch-black. He shined the flashlight out the window. The trees swayed and a giant branch that took up most of the length of the pool. It was going to be a bitch cleaning up the mess again. Charley had been bad enough but this beast has lasted for days. On his way home from the hospital, the news reported Hurricane Ivan was heading this way with 135 miles per hour winds. Would he have any trees left after the next storm?

His mind wandered back to the dream, and the horror. Why now? Why tonight? He sat down at the dining room table and mulled over the possibilities, swirling his drink. Ronnie's face appeared again with a shy smile.

At the interview, there had been a few sparks but he'd mostly made note of her full lips, her perfectly narrow jawline, and big gray-blue eyes without emotion or any stirring. Last night something deep inside him cracked, and a terrifying sense of loss overwhelmed him. His logical brain chimed in, *She's your employee, you dumbass. Don't even look at her.* But this was the time to explore how he felt and he closed the door to the logical reasoning that normally ruled his life. That could wait. Deep emotions were at play here. He had learned to listen when the dream appeared—it was usually important. If he didn't deal with the darkness, it would plague him for weeks, taking hold of his sleep and make him miserable until he took the time to delve into what it meant.

Another image of Ronnie appeared and he was sure she had stirred something in his soul. A deep sadness engulfed him, but he tamped it down, as he had for years. A loneliness swept through his heart, one that had haunted him since that day. Was he ready to open his heart again? Logic said no, never again, and besides, she had a boyfriend. But his heart wasn't satisfied with this life. There was something missing and he hoped that in time he would come to terms with it.

A flash of anger bubbled in his gut and thoughts of Jeffrey at her bedside. He should be there comforting her not that pencil neck. Something didn't jibe with Jeffrey. How had he ended up at the hospital just at that moment? Something tugged at his subconscious but it wouldn't surface. It would have to wait for a pot of coffee and some deep thought.

He swallowed his drink, placed the glass in the sink and headed back to his bedroom just past the living room. Mike paused at the foot of the bed and eyed the table. The heat in is gut was a steady fire now and he was ready for sleep again. Not in that bed though, the ghost was still lingering between the sheets. Mike made his way to the leather couch in his living room and grabbed the USMC pillow his sister had given him last Christmas. It was too hot for the bedroom anyway. The living room allowed for a cross breeze from the Florida room and the front porch.

He could hear the wind through the trees making a racket outside his window. It was almost soothing, with his tired boozy mind it made odd patterns that echoed around in his head. Waves of light brown and yellow floated around in his mind as he dozed off. The ends of the waves touched his chest as he sank into the couch. A woman's hair above him, sparkly blue eyes in the low light looked back at him a smile playing on her lips.

"No!" Fear gripped his chest. He wasn't ready for this. He couldn't risk his heart again. The body part in question was making an attempt to beat out of his chest. His sweat covered legs and back stuck to the leather of the couch and he debated joining the ghost in his bed, but that wasn't as frightening as the prospect of going through utter heartbreak again. He made his choice and crawled between the sheets and let sleep take him to oblivion.

Chapter 57 - Affectionately

Ronnie sat back in Steph's Jeep Liberty clutching the pillow her friend had brought to the hospital the day before. The doctors had given her the all clear after two days of tests and no real answers, not even a medical explanation for what had triggered her Korsakoff's syndrome. The doctors said the brain lesion would heal in time and was already shrinking. The medical team also recommended no preventive measures other than to lower her stress and allow for recovery. Rest and a few days off work would provide the cure. That would be totally doable as long as there were no more hurricanes,

She hadn't had the energy to delve into her own theories yet and was eager to be alone with Steph to share her experience and further explore its meaning. Was is just a jumble of neurons firing that caused her to think she'd been time traveling? Deep in her soul she knew this was false, but the physical evidence was unerring. A disease had caused damage to her brain and it just so happened she'd had a series of weird experiences.

"How are you feeling Ronnie?" Steph interrupted her thoughts.

"Exhausted, but happy to be going home."

"I have Ian there repairing windows. I didn't want to stress you out but a branch broke the guest bedroom window, too." She glanced at Ronnie, then back at traffic on the interstate.

Steph slammed on the breaks to avoid a rude driver cutting into her lane. A wave of nausea passed over Ronnie but subsided quickly. She'd not sat upright in two days, and her blood pressure wasn't quite up to the task. Spots floated in the edges of her vision and she shoved the pillow next to the window and rested her head on it as she closed her eyes.

"He may be a screw up but he's good at construction so don't worry about his skills in that area. He just needs a fire lit under him. You returning home is just that motivation, Ronnie."

Steph had brought Ian to the hospital the day before and he had been near tears when he saw her. Despite all his womanizing he had a big heart like his sister, and having seen Ronnie at her weakest his entire demeanor had changed. He was now more protective and brotherly and that suited Ronnie just fine. She hoped it would last, but suspected as she cleaned up a bit and got back to her usual healthy glow the horndog would return.

"Okay, I trust your judgement, Steph. How's the roof holding up?" Ronnie kept her eyes closed.

"Jeffrey came by and did some work on the attic side of things. He had a crew out yesterday to repair the roof. I think they replaced the entire thing, Ronnie," Steph said, the usual anger softening around Jeffrey over the last few days. He had turned conciliatory toward her in the hospital and Steph confessed she wasn't so sure he'd been behind the time traveling episodes now. Steph didn't say it outright, but Ronnie could tell she wasn't even sure if she believed she'd gone back in time. Ronnie didn't know either but the medical diagnosis provided a reason for the visions if that's what they were.

"That was nice of him." Ronnie knew he wouldn't ask her to pay for the roof. He had told her it was nothing, especially after all she'd been through. He just didn't want her to have anything to worry about while she recovered.

They pulled into her driveway and Steph got out and walked to her side of the car. Branches were strewn about the neighbors' yards but hers was manicured with every stray leaf and branch in place.

Ian burst through the door, his paint-splattered hair sparkling in the sunshine. "Surprise!" He nearly ran to her and took the pillow from her hands, before she could even attempt to exit the car.

"I've cleaned up your yard as well. No small feat, lass, but for you nothing is too much," he was beaming.

"Ya wee clothead, give her some space, Ian Brian McKay." Steph dampened the puppy-like greeting and shooed him away. "She is still feeling puny. Sorry, luv. He means well." Steph took her elbow and led her to the house.

"Ian, thank you so much it looks perfect." Ronnie stepped away from Steph and hugged him.

"Ooch, Ronnie, it is the least I could do for you. I only used the skills I have. I'm not much of a baker or the guy to pick out flowers."

"Steph was telling me about the windows too." She took his elbow and they walked toward the house with the humidity of the day curling around her ankles. "Thanks for everything. You're such a great friend." Ronnie was grateful for all his hard work. She knew the sacrifice he had made, not exactly being the most productive of humans, so it meant even more that he'd done so much.

"The wanker wanted to have his crew fix your windows too but I would have none of it," he jutted his chin out in defiance.

"The wanker?" Ronnie asked as he held the front door open for her and Steph.

"Jeffrey," Steph said. "That's his new nickname. Ian, you had no trouble with him paying for the windows and supplies, now did you?"

"Of course not, Stephanie," Ian said walking in behind them. "I'm no stupid, I'm Scottish. We pride ourselves on being thrifty."

"Right, and you knew the wanker would buy better materials than you could afford. No one is fooled, Ian," Steph mocked.

"I'll have ye know, Stephanie Diane McKay, his lads were going to install them into near-rotten beams. I'll take the time to do the job properly." His hands were on his hips.

Ronnie reached out to side hug him. "You are a wonderful man and I don't give a hoot about what your older sister says. It's a lovely gesture and I'm glad to have your hands on my glass." Ronnie knew where Ian would take this and he leapt in with both feet.

"My hands on your ass, you mean?" He laughed good naturedly.

Ronnie sat down on the couch completely drained from the minimal trek home from the hospital. A huge bouquet of fresh-cut flowers greeted her in a large glass vase. She reached out to take the small card from the plastic stick.

"They're from Mike Walsh, whoever the fuck that is," Ian said almost jokingly. "They delivered them just a bit ago."

Steph smacked his arm. "Ian, you nosy Neddy, why are you opening her cards?"

"Stephanie, I need to know who's after Ronnie. I feel protective of her now. Who is this guy?"

Steph answered for Ronnie, "Her boss. I told you about him. He's the one who pulled us from the clutches of the storm and delivered us to the hospital."

Ronnie opened the envelope and sat back on the couch. A warm happy glow washed away the tiredness as Ronnie read the note.

Ronnie,

Welcome home. I hope these flowers cheer you as you recover. Please don't worry about work. We're thinking about you as you heal and welcome you back when you feel ready.

With affection, Mike

Ronnie held the note to her lips. A twinge of excitement made her heart skip a beat. He had been the first person she'd seen upon returning from that horrible last moment with Morris. The man, as big and burly as he was, was crying at her bedside. She read the note again and savored how he'd ended it. *With affection.* Wholly different than the first note he'd written her that he'd signed formally with his full name, title, and company. The experience had definitely changed their relationship, although Ronnie had been out most of the time he was helping her. A pang of embarrassment mixed in with the excitement.

Her mind examined the details of that moment for the millionth time and still had no concrete explanation. Mike was somehow merged in her mind with Mathias and now Morris. How could she have made this up in the throes of some chemical imbalance? Was he somehow the key to this entire puzzle? Was he an unwilling participant in something larger than both of them? Or was it just a terrible hallucination with a Mike mixed in her jumbled brain?

Ian and Steph were bickering back and forth and Ronnie had tuned them out until Ian spoke.

"For fuck's sake, Stephanie. She's kissing the note. He's more than her fucking boss."

Steph smiled and plopped on the couch next to Ronnie. She leaned her head against her friend's shoulder and Steph handed over the note.

"Stuff it, Ian," Ronnie said.

Ian sat on the other side of Ronnie and took her hand. "As long as I'm still your favorite Scot."

Ronnie and Steph said in unison, "Nope."

Ian fake pouted and leaned gently against Ronnie creating a wholly satisfying Scottish sandwich.

Epilogue

September 11, 2004
Jeffrey Brennan parked his car in the garage under his condo and walked towards the stairwell with grocery bags in his hands. He gathered his mail in the lobby then jogged up the seven stories to his condo, slightly out of breath, and opened the apartment door. A wave of humid heat assaulted him. He'd forgotten to pull the blinds keeping the hot sun out of the condo. It was going to be another hot and sweaty night without power. He set the mail and the groceries down on the counter and opened the sliding glass door to the patio letting in fresh humid air.

He mulled over his limited options for evening entertainment as he prepared dinner -- salmon in olive oil, balsamic vinegar, and turmeric wrapped in foil on the grill. He left the fish to cook and rifled through the mail sitting out on the patio where the air was at least moving.

A FedEx envelope caught his eye and he tore it open with gusto. A small post-it note was attached to a newspaper article from *The Daily Record* from Rochester, New York. In the picture, the man's hair was longer, but it was definitely Ronnie's boss. The headline read: *Local Man Mike Walsh Suspected of Murder.*

Jeffrey sat up in his chair. "Holy shit!" He read more.

Michael Walsh has been arrested for allegedly murdering his fiancée. A battered and bloody corpse was found in the shower at the residence of the suspect. The neighbors, Cindy and Steve Johnson said they had heard the couple fighting when they were out walking their dog around 11:00 p.m. last night. The police have taken Mike Walsh, of Rochester Heights, in for questioning after he called 911. Kelly Ascobar was twenty-six years old and a graduate of RIT.

A picture of the smiling Kelly before he'd ended her life was on the right. She was gorgeous with perfect straight teeth and sparkly eyes.

"I knew something was wrong about this guy!" Why hadn't he thought to look him up before Ronnie took the job? Jeffrey paced across the small patio. Just this morning Ronnie caught a plane to Miami on her way to Puerto Rico with Mike. She had been adamant about going on the trip despite her recent hospital stay claiming it was because another massive storm, Hurricane Ivan, was blowing through the Caribbean towards Florida breaking records for intensity and damage.

His anger rose as he thought of the two of them in a first-class cabin with Mike pouring another glass of champagne as he had promised that first day at her new job. What worried him the most was the simple fact that the meat-bag had rescued Ronnie during the hurricane forever changing how she would see him. Now she would feel she owed him something and would have the freedom to pursue it while alone with him for a week in a tropical paradise.

Was this Mike's plan all along in taking her to Puerto Rico? To get her isolated to do her harm? He clenched his jaw and fumed with anger. "Damn you, Ronnie!" She was in jeopardy and once again because she had not listened to him.

An acrid smell assaulted his nostrils. The fish was burning. He rushed to the grill and rescued his dinner flopping it on a plate nearby. He leaned on the railing letting the fish cool down and dialed Ronnie's number. It rang to voicemail and he debated about leaving a message but hung up. This news was worthy of a live conversation.

Don't miss Book 3 – Killing Time out Summer 2018

Acknowledgements

What a wild and wicked journey to get this book out into the world. Again, I have so many people to thank for all their support and hard work in getting me to this dubious place of publishing my second book. First and foremost, my family has been by far my biggest support giving up a lot to let me write, so huge thanks are in order. My mom, sister, stepsister, husband, dad, and stepmom have been my first beta readers who always give so much of their time and talent. My father is an antique clock fixer-upper and provides great advice on clocks from various time periods. I'm ever grateful for everyone's gift of time and attention. My kids have sacrificed time they could have had my attention so I need to give them a shout-out as well. My son has been my storyline development assistant and has done a stellar job at giving me plenty to write about.

Perhaps my biggest supporter on all things bookish has been Suzanne Kelman, who has been my podcast (Blondie and the Brit) and social media partner in crime these last two years. Her guidance and weekly pep talks have been such a huge help in this lonely writer's journey. Thank you, Suzanne, for reminding me I'm human and have three kids that need my time and attention. You continually remind me I need to look back on all I've accomplished in a year, not just focus on what I wanted to accomplish. They are two wholly different animals.

Jeri Walker (www.jeriwb.com) is my magical editor who takes my writing to another level with her enchanted pen (or rather keyboard), Last summer I sent an early draft to Jeri for a stand-alone reader report and it was money well spent. Her crystal-clear suggestions gave me the focus to improve the draft immeasurably. She also did a follow-up copyedit on the manuscript.

It also took me longer than expected to get this book together but I think it's well worth the time spent building the plot to fill in all the spaces in order to give you a meatier story. This is by far my best work yet and I owe a lot of that to Jeri and Suzanne for their support and advice.

A huge thank you to Jody Smyers (jodysmyersphotography.com) for the excellent artwork on all my book covers. He's a master of photoshop and a superb photographer and a downright creative genius. The *Stealing Time* cover was our first joint effort that blossomed into our business, Blondie's Custom Book Covers (www.blondiebooks.com).

In addition to Jeri's edits, I also had specific editing advice from Paul H. Carlson and Tommi Dubois on the Native America sections of the book. Paul is a historian and author with eighteen books and over 200 articles published on various topics including Indian affairs. You can find his work on Amazon. Tommi Dubois provided me with a final proofread and gave me excellent advice on the Native American village life, marriage ceremony, and other important details. She is an Ottawa/Navajo/Chippewa Indian and has conducted extensive research in this time period with these tribes. She is also an editor.

I consulted Caitlin Barnett and Ben Coleman for the English sections of the book for language and time period quirks. Simon Dick was my Scottish editor who provided a few good laughs along the way. Those Scots are a friggin' hoot, which is why they keep appearing in my books. Ian's flair is reflected by Simon's distinct Glaswegian research and humor. Ian was a blast to write and I can assure you Simon and Ian will both continue to be involved in the next book in the series.

I really am lucky to have such a treasure trove of writer and non-writer buddies and other social media acquaintances who have given me excellent advice and support along the way. Just so you know all of us authors cringe at mentioning names because we are terrified of leaving out someone who was important in the process. I hope I've not made a huge gaff.

Thank you to my awesome Street Team: Anna B. Garza, Blair Wickstrand, Carlie Cullen, Christine Johnson Lachance, Cristie Poole, Dalton Anthony, DeWan Coffman, Dee Lobell Bratcher, Gary S. Pritchett, Gene Ostenkamp, Gregory Glines, H. Scott Johnson, Heather Mayhugh, Jody Smyers, Larry Johnson, Luis Tirado, Jr., Mak Makay, Maria Sussman, Mark Scantland, Marssaille M. Arrey, Melody Ferraro, Michael Blair, Naomi D. Nakashima, Paul Rygiel, Rick Stall, S.J. Hermann, Scott Makis, Suzanne Kelman, and Mindy Deeter.

In no particular order a huge thank you to some of my greatest supporters on the writing stage: Susan Wingate, Cynthia Davis, David Perlmutter, Mia Yeoman, Lori Anne, Ron Chapman, Brad Christy, Ben Coleman, Mark Combs, Martin Lastrapes, Catherine Shiver, Tom the Treeman, Paul Crome, Katie Rochet, and Munir Bello Abubakar.

Join My Street Team: If you'd like to be part of my writing journey and get exclusive access to early copies, book news, and cover reveals please join the KJ Waters Street Team. All I ask in return it to support me by buying my books, writing reviews for Amazon, Barnes & Noble, and Goodreads, and also by helping me promote my books and other projects.

You can join on my website by signing up for my newsletter (which will get you special access to my contests and other news) just type the words Street Team in the name section and I'll add you to the associated Facebook group.

Stay in Touch

I hope you take a minute to check out my website and social media sites. I also have a blog, **Blondie in the Water**, where I share water stories and updates on my writing.

Blog: kjwatersauthor.blogspot.com

Twitter: @kamajowa

Facebook: KJ Waters

Website: www.kjwaters.com, www.blondieandbrit.com

Pinterest: kamajowa

Instagram: @kamajowa

I am also CEO of **Blondie's Custom Book Covers** providing book cover service for authors and publishers.

Website: www.blondiebooks.com

Twitter: BlondiesBookCov

Facebook: Blondies Custom Book Covers

In October 2015, I started a **podcast called Blondie and the Brit** with Suzanne Kelman. It is an author podcast with interviews, social media tips, and more. Check it out here. www.blondieandbrit.com and on podbean at www.blondieandbrit/podbean.com and iTunes.

I've recently begun **author consulting** to help new authors master social media marketing, publishing independently with Amazon and other outlets, and converting their work from a vanity publisher to publishing independently. Please let me know if there is anything I can do for you in any of these arenas. You can find out more on my website www.kjwaters.com.

KJ Waters

Made in the USA
San Bernardino, CA
11 July 2017